The Players of the Fugue . . .

JOSHUA DAVIES—A mountain of a man, nicknamed "the Butcher" for his ruthless termination of the enemies of Her Majesty's government.

ANTON DRAKOV—Brilliant, unemotional, unmoving, unyielding . . . a man marked for destruction unless he can pull off the coup of his career.

GELI—A drug-wasted girl who hustles drinks in a Berlin bar . . . and who now could be the crucial link to Drakov's survival.

KROPTKOV—A KGB assassin with a taste for the sexually bizarre and a craving to kill like a brutal, uncontrolled animal.

SIDNEY RICKETTS—The key to Davies' investigation . . . a Cockney whose undying allegiance is to the Soviet juggernaut.

BERLIN FUGUE

J.C. WINTERS

AVON
PUBLISHERS OF BARD, CAMELOT, DISCUS AND FLARE BOOKS

BERLIN FUGUE is an original publication of Avon Books. This work has never before appeared in book form. This work is a novel. Any similarity to actual persons or events is purely coincidental.

AVON BOOKS
A division of
The Hearst Corporation
1790 Broadway
New York, New York 10019

Published by arrangement with the author
Library of Congress Catalog Card Number: 85-90853
ISBN: 0-380-89866-7

First Avon Printing, October 1985

AVON TRADEMARK REG. U. S. PAT. OFF. AND IN OTHER COUNTRIES, MARCA REGISTRADA, HECHO EN U. S. A.

Printed in the U. S. A.

WFH 10 9 8 7 6 5 4 3 2 1

For the Big Three
And JDV, *sine qua non*

Straws in the Wind

Pilate, at their request, delivered Jesus to them to be crucified. When, therefore, the Jews were dragging Jesus forth, and had reached the door, Cartaphilus, a porter of the hall in Pilate's service, impiously struck him on the back with his hand, and said in mockery, "Go quicker, Jesus, go quicker; why do you loiter?" And Jesus, looking back on him with a severe countenance, said to him, "I am going, and you shall wait till I return."

September 1970

Potsdam, East Germany

I Détente

It took the taxi driver a considerable time to find the address. Gary Letterville's German was fluent; that wasn't the problem. The difficulty lay with the driver, who had lived in Berlin all his life but was convinced the address on Arnulf Strasse had to be a mistake. He insisted no government office could possibly be located on such an insignificant street. Finally, having maneuvered around the street railroad yard twice, they did indeed come upon the home of the Bizone Economic Liaison Commission. The driver left Letterville there, shaking his head in disbelief as he pocketed his tip.

There was no elevator, so Letterville climbed the three flights of stairs, poorly lit and the paint badly peeling. The headache had disappeared, but he still found it hard to keep his officer's cap on above the bandage circling his head.

An unpainted door, offering no indication of what lay behind it, was the door he sought. Opening it, Gary found himself in a tiny outer office being regarded with acute suspicion by an intimidating Teutonic blond female.

"Letterville. I am expected," he said in German.

The secretary glanced pointedly at a squat clock on the mantelpiece, and Letterville was irritated to find himself explaining, "The cab got lost."

"Of course, *mein Herr.*" She sounded unconvinced. "I will tell Mr. O'Mallory you are here."

One minute later, he was sitting in a small inner office talking to his new boss. An entire wall was lined with battered government-green filing cabinets. On the wall behind O'Mallory's desk was a framed picture of President Kennedy. Of the current American Commander-in-Chief, there was no sign.

"Gary, welcome to the back of the beyond, as the Brits say." Paul O'Mallory seized the young man's hand and shook it vigorously. "Surprised you could find the place at all." He wore a broad smile.

"It wasn't easy."

"I bet. We don't get many visitors."

Letterville heard the sounds of trains in the yard behind the office. The noise was deafening.

"How do you get used to that noise?"

"What noise?"

They both laughed.

"I'll tell you this much," said O'Mallory. "We have to be the only government office, East or West, with a misaligned *e* on its typewriter. Can you imagine? A goddam *e*, the most popular letter in the English language. But listen to that Magda go, anyway. Talk about raw courage. Of course, I get paid an extra twenty-five a month to stay here and do nothing. Money always helps. You're not Catholic, are you?"

"No."

"Well, the Pope has a lot to answer for," continued O'Mallory with a sigh. "We got free education for everyone in the States, but I pay a hundred-fifty a month here instead. The only extra I know of is that the nuns hit my kids' knuckles with a steel ruler when they need it."

There was a brisk authoritative tap on the door. The secretary entered with a wooden tray bearing two large ceramic mugs, a sugar bowl, and a milk jug. She placed the cups on the desk carefully.

"Thank you, Magda," O'Mallory murmured as she withdrew. "Boy," he added, sotto voce, when the door was safely closed, "talk about *ordnung.* Even the sugar bowl matches, for chrissakes. We borrowed this 'elevensies' break idea from the British wing of the Bizone Comish. 'Bout the only good thing they've come up with."

Settling into his chair, a large stuffed-leather monstrosity capable of bending in a dozen different directions, he waved Gary to a seat and took four lumps of sugar with his fingers, pointedly ignoring the dainty little silver tongs.

"Did your wife pick Magda?" asked Letterville, taking his coffee black, army style.

"She probably did, by remote control. But you won't find anything as faithful as a German secretary. Hitler's asked permission to stay with him to the end."

O'Mallory blinked a few times, blew on his coffee to cool it, and shook his head, baffled by yet another example of the love that passeth understanding.

Letterville had been taking him in. O'Mallory's countenance supported Letterville's impression that he would be no pushover. His nose had been broken long ago and hadn't set correctly, but he didn't seem the kind to walk into doors. He was just above medium height with a shock of white hair clipped straight and close to his skull in a crew cut. His dark blue jacket was unbuttoned and his tie knotted loosely.

"We're shit-kickers with nothing to do," said O'Mallory after a pause filled with train whistles and banging sounds. "The Bizone Economic Liaison Commission sounds impressive, but we are essentially mundane." Reaching over, he took another lump of sugar, dropping it into his cup. "We came into existence in the years after partition to run the economic life of the British and American zones. Naturally, the French wouldn't cooperate, to say nothing of Uncle Joe's guys."

"What do we do?"

"Sweet Fanny Adam. We're phantom."

"Phantom?"

"We remain open in case needed; no matter what, we count for three warm bodies. Suppose there's an agreement to cut forces in East and West by ten percent. We add three legitimate bodies to our total. It means an important department someplace can keep one more person."

"Or half a person."

"Or an eighth. I play my part. I send in forms, I request things. I seem busy."

"Idle hands do the devil's work," muttered Letterville.

O'Mallory looked at him shrewdly across the top of his cup, then put it back on the tray. "You're going to do well here, Gary, I can feel it. We're a department of last resort. If there's nowhere left to send something, it will end up here in one of those filing cabinets. Hurry with your coffee."

Before Letterville had time for questions, there was a rap on the door and Magda marched in and took the tray, pausing in horror when she saw there was only one cup on it. Letterville quickly placed his next to O'Mallory's and was rewarded with an unsmiling "*Danke, mein Herr.*" The secretary swept the tray and herself from the room.

"See what I mean about *ordnung?* Mary, Mother of God, suppose they'd won the war? You see, the 'elevensies' are a British idea, the 'eleven-fifteensies' are the German riposte."

Letterville grinned.

"That must have been one hell of a fight you got into, Gary, to make them send you to Arnulf Street."

"It was."

He's just a kid, thought O'Mallory. An all-American boy, blue eyes, even features, the intense look of someone who thinks he can make a difference in a world determinedly going to hell in a handbasket. You could look at that muscled neck and just know Letterville had quarterbacked his high school football team to the state championship. Probably believed he could grow up to be President.

"You should have seen the other guys."

"Huh?"

"The other guys. In the fight."

"I'll bet," replied O'Mallory. Then his eyes narrowed below the white-tufted eyebrows. "It didn't go on your permanent record, did it?"

"They needed someone to come here. That was the deal."

O'Mallory nodded. He'd already heard that from one of his sources, and now Letterville was confirming it. He liked open, forthright men, though it was his duty to remind them that those qualities weren't likely to advance their careers.

"A couple of years ago, the American Ambassador asked me to find his dog," O'Mallory continued, leaning back, hands clasped behind his head. "An enormous goddam wolfhound called Grendel or some damn thing. Found it too." He dwelt on the memory. "Somewhere in the files—" he waved his hand toward them— "is the entire saga recorded for posterity."

There was a knock on the door and Magda brought in a letter, which she handed to O'Mallory, who took it while continuing his monologue. "Well, can you imagine what would happen if that SOB were elected President? I mean, where in hell—?" He broke off, dug in a drawer, found a spectacle case, and took out a pair of reading glasses. "Where in hell do you walk your dog at night when you live in the White House? You can't have dog shit on that lawn. And it was a big brute—Holy Mother of God!" O'Mallory took a long, deep breath. "Saints preserve us."

"What is it?"

"It's a first. This letter is actually addressed *to this office,* not forwarded from somewhere else." He took off his glasses, tucked them into their case, and pushed them to the back of the drawer. "Your first day too. Treasure it, boy, it's addressed to you."

Letterville read it quickly. "It's an invitation to a Big Four reception at the *Sans Souci* Palace. But not for me. It says 'Commissioner Bizone Commission.' "

"Oh yes," the older man assured him, "but I never attend receptions. Don't have the stamina." Failing to meet Letterville's forthright stare, he looked away. "You see, they want officers at those things. The Russkies will be out in force, loaded down with scrambled egg on their hats. We civilians would look totally out of place. And," he added piteously, "I *do* have a vision problem. Might bump into an East German *Frau* and slop imported caviar on her ample bosom. I might—"

"Okay, okay, I'll go."

O'Mallory beamed. "Knew you would; you're such a Christian."

"I'm only a second lieutenant."

O'Mallory laughed and waved his hand; Letterville noted that his shirt cuff was frayed. "What they want at those things is some young blood. A guy like you, especially if the head bandage can come off, would set the fat *Frau*s atwitter. They'd just love to pass their stubby fingers through your wavy brown hair." Overplaying, he added, "I wish I could go." He failed to sound sincere.

"What's it in honor of?"

Raising his voice above the trains and the remorseless tapping of Magda in the outer office, O'Mallory shouted, "Frau Baum—the Four Power map, please." Quietly, he added, "When I got here, I made a tremendous gaffe. I called her by her Christian name. In this country, any title counts. You get Herr-Doktor-Professors up the ass. You better start out right and call her *Frau.*"

The lady in question came in just then with a large rolled map. She handed it over, and there was the usual *"Danke schön,"* *"Bitte sehr."* O'Mallory unrolled it on his desk, covering everything on it, which added a false topography to Berlin.

"The Russkies have been trying to grab our sectors since the 1948 blockade. The Wall"—he traced its path with a pencil—"was their last gambit to stop East Berlin from running out of people completely. On September third, this year, we finally signed an agreement. It will ease tensions all around and maybe, just maybe, World War Three can be avoided. There's the *Sans Souci,*" he added, pointing. He waited until Gary had studied the area, then rolled up the map, tossing it on top of the filing cabinets. He finished by saying solemnly, "This shindig, my boy, is to celebrate the first two successful weeks of the agreement."

Two nights later, his bandage removed and uniform perfectly pressed, Gary Letterville crossed by limousine into East Berlin by way of the Glienicke Bridge.

O'Mallory had tut-tutted when he found the reception was to be held in the music room of the palace. "It means they're going all-out to impress. Don't be surprised if the food is edible."

Letterville saw what the Commissioner meant when he got out of his limousine at the foot of a giant floodlit staircase. The palace had been built by Frederick the Great. Guests were using the garden entrance, which was even more magnificent than the courtyard front. The single-story dream palace was built on the summit of a hill. In rococo style, it had thirty-five massive caryatids supporting the cornice. On the huge green central dome the words *Sans Souci* were inscribed in gold.

A footman in mid-eighteenth-century costume but looking more like a country boy drafted into the *Volksarmee* took his invitation, checked it against a list, and returned it to Letterville with a smile. Another liveried footman with a prominent overbite took his overcoat to the cloakroom.

Letterville passed by the coldly magnificent columns and cornices of the marble hall. Above was the great dome. Beyond lay the music room, splendidly decorated with murals and mirrors. All around were gilded carvings on musical themes. It was hard, looking around the room with its uniformed men and formally dressed women, to visualize the Emperor with his notorious tin ear, playing his flute with a group of chamber musicians.

Letterville had enough experience of receptions to know little happened until everyone was well past his third drink. Prior to that people were stiff and talked only to previous acquaintances. He resolved not to let himself be dragged into some corner by Americans to discuss the World Series.

A buffet had been laid out on three huge tables. Gary had discovered that there was a real German cuisine apart from the doughy, uninspired food he'd been eating in Berlin. He recognized *Hase im Topf,* an excellent rabbit *pâté; Rheinsalm,* pale pink salmon from the Rhine; and Schwetzingen asparagus. The wines looked particularly inviting, and he started with a glass of Monzinger.

"Going on a binge?" He looked up. A British colonel was addressing him.

"Sir?"

"Going on a binge, Lieutenant?" He pronounced it as though it had an *f* in it. "The wine comes from near the river Nahe, which flows through Bingen. It's a city with a reputation for hard drinking. So in England we say, 'Going on a binge' when someone gets drunk. What do you Yanks say? 'Getting pissed,' what?"

With a laugh he was gone, clutching two glasses of wine.

It began to look as if that exchange might be the high point of Letterville's evening. The Russians turned out to be the friendliest people present. The British spoke when spoken to but didn't volunteer much.

People came, people went. Toasts were drunk to everyone and everything. The Russians wouldn't toast with anything but vodka, which they tossed back in single throat-burning gulps.

"Cast-iron stomachs," muttered a Marine Corps general to Letterville. "More fun than the Brits, though. Those guys are still going on about some cricket game they lost in the summer. What do you think of the Pirates' chances in the Series?"

The alcohol-induced fog was soon thickened

by cigarette smoke, and Gary wondered if the smoke reached all the way up to the ceiling, forty feet above. He considered leaving but he kept drinking. Female shapes, looking more attractive than they would when he wasn't tipsy, passed to and fro. One or two hinted at intimacy.

He was drawn into a discussion on literature by a British general and his tall spindly daughter, who was tediously expounding a thesis that the American novel was descended from *Wuthering Heights* via Charles Brockden Brown. Letterville, who couldn't remember which of the Brontës had written *Wuthering Heights* and had never heard of Charles Brockden Brown, was gripped by an insane desire to hustle the girl outside and screw her brains out on the top terrace. He resisted, remembering O'Mallory's final warning, "Don't give a horse-fucking to anything but a horse."

More food was brought out. Someone knew his Bible; the best had been saved for last. It was a Russian smorgasbord of epic proportions: huge silver bowls of caviar, platters of roast beef, sturgeon, and pressed duck. There were at least a dozen chafing dishes filled with meat and cheese *piroshki*. He ate, watching the scene.

The Russians, who had been toasting the palace dome suddenly snapped to attention and Letterville expected to see some high-ranking officer. To his surprise, a beautiful young woman in a black strapless gown appeared. Russian glasses were raised and knocked back in an instant. The girl gave them a smile revealing neat white teeth. "Pigs," she muttered, not seeing Letterville until she'd almost walked into him.

"I'm sorry," she began in German, looking at him with fear in her eyes. The American uniform seemed to help. She switched to English. "Excuse me. I didn't mean you. I meant those Russians."

She was a looker. No question. Straight ash-blond hair reached down to soft ivory shoulders, and wispy bangs fell across her forehead, accentuating blue-green eyes in an almost perfect, heart-shaped face. Her lips were full and sensual, with just a kiss of red lipstick. Surely she was under twenty-five, wasn't she? There was no wedding or engagement ring on her finger, and there was no one with her.

Instantly she was surrounded by a host of admirers, bees to honey. One fat German, his eyes bulging like those of a startled prawn, was transfixed by the lovely, gentle mound of her breasts. Gary found himself quickly displaced toward the edge of the growing group of her courtiers, and was taken by surprise when she gracefully detached herself from them all and slid her arm through his, guiding him away from her disappointed admirers.

"I'm Leni," she murmured. "Just move slowly around the room. Did you see that Russian? Poof. He's a lecherous old goat. You look like the only bearable man here."

"Thanks." Like all handsome men, he vaguely resented women who were accustomed to admiration.

She flashed him a smile. "Let's get something to eat. What's your name?"

"Gary Letterville. Bizone Economic Commission."

"Sounds dreary."

"It is."

Leni seemed to have no fear of losing her figure. She sampled every one of the delicacies, giving a running commentary. "Too sweet . . . too fishy . . . delicious." When she wanted to try some champagne, Letterville signaled a waiter, who was only too delighted to bring her a glass.

"And you?" Gary asked.

"Me what?"

"What do you do?"

"East German Trade Bureau. We try to sell tractors to Russia."

"Oh."

"It's dull, dull, dull. All day I type, type, type."

"And your husband?" inquired Letterville, gazing inquiringly around the room in a childish attempt to make the question innocuous.

"Dead."

"I'm sorry."

"I'm not. He was a pig."

Leni was delicately licking the tip of her finger. She caught his look and said, "I came tonight with Herr Rosenberg, the head of the bureau. He likes to be seen with younger women."

Letterville admitted Herr Rosenberg had wonderful taste. Had Leni possessed the slightest blemish, the elegant black dress would have magnified it a hundred times. Although her legs were entirely covered, Letterville knew they would be long and slender. As for her breasts, he could visualize the pointed tips, nipples set in large rose areolae . . . In a panic, he realized she was looking at him quizzically; she had asked him something, and he groped desperately for an answer vague enough to cover any question.

"I'm not really sure," he said.

"Well, I am. I want a cigarette."

Letterville searched his jacket pocket and produced a pack of Marlboros. He couldn't find any matches, but Leni had a lighter in her black evening bag. He took it from her and lit first her cigarette, then his own.

"I like American cigarettes," she said contentedly, expelling smoke in a lazy exhalation. "Don't you?"

"Sure. It's just that . . . it's kind of stuffy in here."

He waited expectantly. Leni seemed to be thinking about it. Finally she said, "Perhaps we could walk outside on the terrace."

Letterville placed his arm around her shoulders, gently steering her through the great French doors. "What of the Herr Doktor Rosenberg?" he asked boldly.

Leni hesitated, and Letterville recognized this as the moment of decision.

"He will understand," she said firmly. "After all," she added with a soft musical laugh, "we are not lovers." She slid her arm through his. "I have a car," she said. "In the courtyard. Herr Rosenberg's. I have the key, too."

They had communicated. Something had begun.

January 22, 1979

Beirut, Lebanon

II Red Prince

Faris Ghantous, a Palestinian of markedly hangdog expression, was one of the bodyguards of Ali Hassan Salameh, architect of the Munich Massacre. He was, truth to tell, a nonentity. He was also singularly stupid. Unfortunately, Ghantous' lack of mental agility was counterpointed by an overly active libido that would not be denied. After six months in Paris guarding the Red Prince, who continually enjoyed the connubial comforts of his ravishing second wife, Ghantous was desperate. Frenchwomen of even the lowest kind despised Arabs, and money, even lots of it, seemed not to affect them at all.

Ghantous asked for a week's leave. He booked a ticket for Dublin, Ireland, for reasons so vague even he could hardly understand them. Faris picked Ireland because he had heard that that great Muslim, Muammar Muhammad al-Qaddafi, President of Libya, was supporting the freedom fighters of Ireland against American aggression.

In Dublin, sweating in a heavy wool suit and thick overcoat, he was disturbed to find none of the taxi drivers spoke Arabic or French. He was rescued from this dilemma, ill-fitting suit, heavy overcoat, and all, by two men, Neil Bushell and Trevor Ivorson. There was nothing in the mind of Ivorson, who had learned his Arabic in the Sultanate of Oman, other than an honest desire to help. The fact was, it was pure coincidence that Ghantous made friends with two undercover members of Britain's Strategic Air Services.

Indeed, all might have been well had Faris not allowed his new friends to steer him into the friendly Patrick Conway pub on Parnell Street. There, seated among the paneled walls and semi-partitions of that famous establishment, the devout Muslim hungrily ate the specialty of the house. Of course, he had no idea what its name meant, and his hosts discreetly refrained from telling him it was ham cooked in red wine. The Arab was hardly a sophisticate, but even he knew that toasts are always drunk in the liquor of the country, so he downed several glasses of a fiery native potion in the spirit of Irish-Arab friendship.

The cumulative effect of excitement, alcohol, and anticipation of blond Irish flesh caused the Palestinian to lose all of his usual restraint. As the two Irishmen were settling him into a taxi, Trevor Ivorson asked an innocent enough question. "Who do you work for, lad?" His Arabic was excellent, but the drunken Palestinian was fuddled.

"Work for?" Faris repeated.

"Aye, lad. What do you do for a living?"

"Bodyguard," drawled Ghantous. "Work for a great man," he said proudly.

"And who might that be?" asked Trevor cheerfully. He liked Faris. "King Farouk?"

"Farouk is dead," Ghantous said scornfully. "Bodyguard for Ali Hassan Salameh. He is a big man. He . . ." His head lolled back on Neil's shoulder.

Trevor leaned forward and tapped sharply on the glass partition. When the driver slid it back he whispered urgently, "Wellington Quay, and be quick about it."

Three hours later, Faris Ghantous was in Northern Ireland. Four days later, he had told his interrogator everything that most persistent gentleman wanted to know, and a great deal he didn't.

2

That interrogator's report reached a small, unassuming office in Whitehall at nine o'clock on a Tuesday morning, and by noon of that same day, two men were sharing a table at Bloom's Restaurant at 90 Whitechapel High Street. Neither man seemed in any way remarkable—that was the intention. They were gray men, passed unnoticed on the street, seen but never remembered.

The Englishman was attired in a slightly soiled three-piece suit, making him look like a shopkeeper who had seen better days. The Israeli looked thoroughly at home in Whitechapel, where many of his people had lived for centuries.

Solomon Cohen, who was not really named Solomon Cohen and did not even know anyone of that name, decided not to risk the miltz. Instead he dug into a large helping of chicken soup and dumplings and gamely sipped at a glass of Grenache rosé from the Rishon-le-Zion cellars.

Adrian Hill, who likewise had no legal claim to his *nom d'occasion,* was in his sixties but could remember his father, Radford, taking his wife and children to purchase salt beef from Morris Bloom in the twenties. He ordered roast lamb even though he knew it wouldn't be pink. It was served with tsimmas and kren in place of mint sauce.

For ten minutes Adrian lamented the falling of standards at Bloom's, and Solomon discoursed upon the Israeli wine industry after Baron de Rothschild sold out. At last, they came to the point.

"We found an interesting chap the other day," said Adrian.

"Oh yes?"

"Mmm." He paused as a waiter, looking patriarchal in a skullcap, his graying side curls neatly pinned up, stomped out of the kitchen in Wellington boots and cleared their dinner plates.

"Palestinian."

"Yes?"

"He had this theory that an Irishwoman would make an interesting bedmate." He paused while the waiter came back for their dessert order. Both ordered lockshen pudding. Solomon added lemon tea, Adrian a bottle of Avdat.

"And was she?"

"We had to put him on hold, but I think we feel an obligation to let him find out. It's being arranged. After all, we did ruin his holiday."

The waiter returned, uncapped the bottle of Avdat, and poured the wine into a glass.

"It doesn't pay to experiment," Adrian said. "Avdat is safe—robust red with character and depth."

The waiter put down the glass of tea and they began their desserts. "And how does this, this . . ."

"Mr. Ghantous."

"Mr. Ghantous interest our people?" asked Solomon.

"He got lost in Dublin. A couple of our chaps helped him on his way, but he got a little drunk . . ."

"And ended up in jail?"

"Well, something like that. He turned out to be a bodyguard."

Solomon Cohen wiped his mouth on his napkin and surveyed the huge mural of Petticoat Lane; it was the only decoration in the garishly lit room besides the gilt-framed portrait of Mr. Morris Bloom himself. It never failed to fool newcomers, who took it to be a portrait of Charlie Chaplin. "And?"

"We felt you should know. Collegiality and all that. We have his employer's address in Beirut."

His companion continued eating, then said lightly, "And you could supply this name and address—for a price."

"Oh, there's no talk of a fee," insisted Adrian with just a hint of disappointment. "This is all in the name of mutual cooperation and friendship. After all, Israel is a British idea, what?"

A waiter plodded by, a huge tray balanced precariously on his right hand. Solomon took a long drink of water.

"Of course," continued the Englishman, "should there be an occasion in the future . . ."

"Where we could aid you."

"In the name of Anglo-Israeli friendship."

"You would have money in the bank."

Adrian looked across the table at him. "Exactly."

"And the employer's name and address?"

"Salameh. Ali Hassan Salameh." The long sibilant intake of breath was what he'd expected. "Of eight-thirty rue Verdun, number two-two-seven."

Solomon Cohen took a second long drink of water before he could trust himself to reply. "The State of Israel is in your debt."

"My dear chap," replied Adrian Hill, "think nothing of it. What are friends for?"

3

A coded cable to Tel Aviv arrived on the desk of the Prime Minister within one hour after Solomon Cohen's lunch at Bloom's. The Prime Minister had it hand-delivered immediately to an unassuming office building near an airfield in the center of Israel.

Ali Hassan Salameh! The Red Prince himself.

The fiend behind the Munich Massacre. Salameh was one person on earth who could expect no mercy from the Israelis.

Brigadier "Fatti" Eytan sat at his desk, sipping sweet Arab coffee as he studied the report from London. It never ceased to amaze him that the British treated Israel so unpredictably. One day, they opposed some minor action; the next, they sent out a piece of priceless information. With one name and address, asking for nothing—the shrewdest move of all—they had put the State of Israel in their debt forever.

Apart from two or three Nazis, Salameh was the most wanted man in the world. Golda Meir had promised revenge for the Munich Massacre however long vengeance might take. Damn the British for being so unfathomable!

Absently he fingered the furrow in his forehead, a legacy of the Six-Day War when he had dropped behind Egyptian lines with the 101 Paratroopers. He sometimes had blinding headaches, but he'd refused the 10 percent disability pension awarded him.

Retired from active military service, he now commanded Sayaret Matkal, an organization so secret that it was virtually never mentioned by name. As with Yahweh, the ineffable name for God, it was known by all and uttered by none. It was "the Unit," its members "the Guys." The Arabs referred to it in official correspondence as the Israeli General Staff Reconnaissance Unit, and in conversation as the "Eye-for-an-Eye Brigade."

"It is laid down in the Talmud," Fatti Eytan

told his new recruits, "if someone comes to kill you, rise and kill him first." Fatti longed for nothing more than he longed for the opportunity to avenge the Munich killings. He had a flair for the dramatic as well as boundless courage. It was he who had led the paratrooper raid on Beirut airport that destroyed thirteen Arab aircraft without a single loss of life. During the operation, he drank coffee and paid for it with Israeli money. The money was still on display behind the counter.

In the cosmopolitan, if battle-scarred, atmosphere of Beirut, Ali Hassan Salameh, cousin of Yasser Arafat, no longer spent sleepless nights thinking about Israeli vengeance. After the tragic incident in Lillehammer, when the Israelis killed a Moroccan waiter by mistake and were caught by the Norwegian police, the Red Prince began making the mistake of believing his own propaganda. He still took precautions, and bodyguards accompanied him everywhere, but he lived as he wanted to. Many came to see him, for the Red Prince was a man of influence. He sat for hours, never raising his voice, offering thick, sweet Arab coffee and advice. Men were sentenced to death with a barely perceptible movement of his elegantly manicured fingers. It was a matter of regret to him that he had lost some muscle tone, and to conceal this, he had begun wearing a bulletproof vest, complaining that it made him look paunchy. To the last, Ali Hassan Salameh was a vain man.

Despite the guards and the caution, he still believed himself fireproof. "I'm a devout believer in a 'sense of place,'" he told his cousin Yasser. "The Israelis can never predict my movements accurately enough to get an assassination team together and catch me unprepared."

Salameh had even appointed himself a kind of roving ambassador-at-large in the war-torn streets of Beirut. The man who had delighted in calling himself "the ghost that haunts the Israelis" now took on flesh and blood.

His extended stay in Paris sealed his fate. He delighted in his new bride, a beautiful Lebanese girl who had been crowned Miss Universe in Miami Beach seven years before their marriage. It was his loud and extended periods of lovemaking that had roused the longings of Faris Ghantous and precipitated that man's fateful journey. Even so, Salameh thought very little of the telegram he received from his bodyguard explaining that he was in jail on charges of assaulting a woman. Salameh refused to send bail money and made no further inquiries, leaving his hapless employee to stew in Irish juice.

The Red Prince had bought an apartment for his divine Georgina on the fashionable rue Verdun, in Beirut, and he began spending more and more time there. A good father, he also kept in close touch with his first wife and his two sons. He developed a routine. That was a luxury he could not afford.

A middle-aged woman called Erika Chambers, traveling on a British passport, moved into an apartment opposite the second Mrs. Salameh. She became well known and insisted, in good French, on being called Penelope. Salameh's bodyguards kept an eye upon the Englishwoman, whom they soon came to regard as dotty. She collected stray cats and painted untrained but accurate cityscapes from her balcony opposite the Salamehs' apartment.

Within two weeks, she was waving across the rue Verdun at Mr. and Mrs. Salameh. Once she rescued a stray cat from underneath their Chevrolet station wagon.

Several weeks later Peter Scriver, British passport No. 260896, arrived at Beirut International Airport. He gave his profession as technical consultant and checked into the Mediterranée Hotel, where, unlike any visitor of record, he requested a room facing the city, not the sea.

A week after that, Hassan came home for a late lunch with his second wife and, at 3:20, kissed her good-bye and strode to his car. He met Penelope carrying a mangy cat which she'd been chasing around his Chevrolet. His bodyguards gently eased her away and made the customary check of the vehicle. Penelope left the parking lot and within five minutes was in a taxi bound for Beirut International Airport. She left on the same plane as Scriver, though she did not acknowledge his presence.

Salameh's bodyguards inspected their master's station wagon. The hubcaps were all taken off and the trunk opened very carefully while one of the men felt gingerly along the underedge for wires. The same process was repeated for the hood. Then came the ignition check, with Salameh shielded by a trash dumpster. All was well.

The guards looked under the seats, and one of them examined the underside of the vehicle with a large concave mirror on a long aluminum pole. Nothing.

"Can we go now?" demanded Salameh. It irritated him that one as talented and important as he should have to behave like a guilty man, afraid of reprisals for an act of courage carried out years ago.

Of course he was no fool. He knew the score: Mohammed Boudia, Wadal Adel Zwaiter. Like himself and his revered father Sheikh Salameh, they had sworn to drive the Jews into the sea. All three were dead, and it was his cousin Yasser who was almost driven to the sea.

The bodyguards were scarcely to blame for what happened. They did not suspect that the bomb was not in Salameh's Chevrolet, but a quarter of a mile away in a parked Volkswagen.

The short-range transmitter, built by Fatti Eytan in his office, emitted a specific short-range signal on a non-radio frequency. It had been slipped under the fender of the Chevrolet by Penelope. The magnet held it securely in place, and its black color made it virtually undetectable.

The Volkswagen parked a quarter of a mile down the rue Verdun had been brought from Israel and was driven to a back street in Beirut by a cut-out who had no idea why he was bringing the car to that location. He went back to Israel on the bus.

Peter Scriver had filled the space under the front seat with an explosive similar to the famous C-4 plastique, but manufactured in

Czechoslovakia. He then drove it to its location in front of a bombed-out store on the rue Verdun and left immediately afterward on the four o'clock flight to Cairo.

Sitting in a stolen Simca, Fatti Eytan waited. He was a good quarter-mile from the doomed Volkswagen but couldn't see Salameh. He had an anxious time of it; several people passed the Volkswagen, including a woman completely enshrouded in black holding a small boy by the hand. In stark contrast to her purdah, the little boy wore bib overalls emblazoned with the word *JAWS*.

Fatti Eytan threw his cigarette from the window and decided to station himself in such a way that no one could pass near the Volkswagen. But he could cover only one direction. What if someone came up rue Verdun toward the car?

And so it proved. A blond girl in jeans and a T-shirt left the goldsmith's shop carrying an item wrapped in tissue paper, which she was putting in her purse. Fatti Eytan started toward her. At precisely that moment, he saw the Chevrolet station wagon turning out of the courtyard behind Salameh's apartment. He raised his hand and shouted, "Mademoiselle!" but she couldn't hear him. For a moment he was caught between two courses of action. Then he ran back to the Simca.

In the Chevrolet, though Fatti Eytan could not see them, were four bodyguards and Salameh. Another four bodyguards followed in a second vehicle.

At a distance of precisely thirty feet from the

Volkswagen, the transmitter's signal caused an electric current to pass through the filament. The heat of the flash set off the detonator, a small steel tube two inches long, a quarter of an inch in diameter, containing 1 cc of fulminate of mercury.

Later, people said it was the loudest explosion they had ever heard. The noise was instantly followed by a huge orange ball of flame that eclipsed the sun. An instant later, the street was dark.

Fatti Eytan had been sprinting back to his car; the blast picked him up and tossed him to one side. A dozen awnings from the fronts of shops flew crazily around in the air currents. There was a continuous tinkling sound, like light rain falling, as the shock wave knocked glass out of windows.

The Volkswagen was shredded into a thousand deadly missiles. White-hot metal was hurtled through the air at supersonic speed. The woman with the child was killed instantly as part of the rear fender destroyed her upper torso, leaving nothing more of her than a heap of black bloodstained rags and pulp. The metal missed her son. He was picked up by the blast and propelled through the window of the jewelry store; his left leg fractured when he bounced off the counter.

Dazed pedestrians found themselves in the midst of a scene of carnage remarkable even for Beirut. The street and sidewalk were littered with a score of bodies, most of them alive. A girl, twelve years old and completely naked, stared curiously at the reddened stump that was all that remained of her left hand.

Fatti Eytan finally staggered to his feet and shook his head; powdered glass fell from his hair like oversize dandruff. A second explosion threw him against the door of the Simca. The gas tank of Salameh's station wagon lit up the sky and made a thunderous noise. Flames and black smoke shot upward.

Of the station wagon there was nothing left but a pile of melting steel; of Salameh and his four bodyguards nothing at all. The guards in the second car ran into the wreckage but had the good fortune to emerge with only burns.

Two buildings had collapsed. Fatti Eytan saw a dog crying piteously and hopping on three legs. A guard put it out of its misery with a burst from his Kalashnikov.

The noise of the explosion had passed but now other sounds filled the vacuum. Dogs howled, and a dozen fire alarms added to the cacophony.

Then it seemed that anyone left alive who had a weapon began firing indiscriminately. Bullets buzzed like enraged bees, scattering sparks as they glanced off the concrete. One man, foolish enough to run away from the scene, was taken for the perpetrator and shot by three different people. He almost reached the sanctuary of an apartment building doorway before he was cut down. Even so, some internal mechanism kept him upright. Reeling through the doorway, he staggered up six steps and died.

A crater thirty feet across had been blasted into the pavement. Fronds from palm trees were scattered everywhere; not one branch had remained on the trees after the blast. A broken water main gushed out of control, sweeping burning oil and gasoline along its dangerous path.

The stone facade of the six-story Château Bellevue hotel, directly opposite the Volkswagen, slowly buckled as the steel girders supporting the structure began to twist. As they bent, the front of the building slid to the ground in slow motion. A dozen rooms were revealed; three were occupied, and their inhabitants fell screaming through the air as the floor beneath them tilted, spilling them into the street where they were crushed by more falling masonry.

Twenty seconds had passed.

Fatti Eytan joined the gathering crowd clambering over the wreckage. Terrible cries rose from the dying and the injured. His hand slid down between two huge concrete slabs touching something soft and pulpy; looking down, he realized it was what was left of the blond woman's face. He looked away, but there was no escape. Clearly imprinted on the bleached stucco wall of the Beirut Bank was the bloody imprint of a body. Someone had been slammed against the building by the blast, and only a red silhouette remained to mark his passing.

Justice had been done, but it was a long time before the bitter taste left Fatti Eytan's mouth.

Part One

A Part We See

In human works, though labored on with pain,
A thousand movements scarce one purpose gain;
In God's, one single can its end produce;
Yet serves to second too some other use.
So Man, who here seems principal alone,
Perhaps acts second to some sphere unknown,
Touches some wheel, or verges to some goal:
'Tis but a part we see, and not a whole.

Alexander Pope, *An Essay on Man*

1 The Way of Life

Joshua Bolivar Davies, Director of Department D of the British Military Intelligence, weighed 280 pounds. His bulk saved his life. He was late for his appointment with the agent Hawk, scheduled for eleven that evening, because he got into an altercation with the manager of Brinkley's restaurant in Hollywood Road. The *crème brûlée* had been made with custard powder; brown sugar was granulated at the sides and burnt in the middle. Davies was not happy and said so.

As a consequence of the extended debate on the quality of the *crème brûlée* and some added cruel, though just, comments on the characterless nature of the Mouton Baron Philippe 1970, the large form of the Director was already fifteen minutes late as he hurried along a narrow dockside lane. To his left lay the icy black water of the Thames. What little light there was came from two widely spaced streetlamps.

Davies had left his taxi some distance away, a professional precaution he regretted as he began breathing heavily from exertion. Soon the landlord of the Ship and Whale would be uttering his mournful, "Last orders, gentlemen, please." The Director feared he would be too late for a pint of Red Barrel.

He was fifty yards from the pub when he was blinded by a sudden brilliant flash of light that illuminated the street from end to end. Then all went dark. A mighty roar followed as if some giant train had leapt its tracks and was bearing down on him. When he could see again, he found the Ship and Whale reduced to rubble. Flames shot out of two adjacent buildings. A hail of dust and debris struck him, and then he was hurled into the black river.

The icy grip revived him, though his ears would not stop ringing. He came up to the surface, bobbing like a buoy. A hundred yards away, flames still shot upward; millions of sparks filled the night sky. Shaken, sure he had lost Hawk, Davies paddled and waded to the rotting wharf and hauled himself up. Shaking water off him like a giant shaggy dog, he walked away just as sirens began to shrill.

It was not a time for questions.

2

The Piccadilly underground line heads north of London, carrying with it those suburban dwellers who resolutely refuse to live in neighborhoods bearing such nonbucolic names as Caledonian Road, Holloway Road, and Arsenal. Once clear of city smog and confusion, the train emerges into sunlight and makes its way through regions where the words *park* and *green* may be added with some justification. At the terminus, Cockfosters, there is the great green swath of Enfield Chase, with its farms, golf links, and woods.

The stigma of suburbia cannot be avoided in Cockfosters; its inhabitants struggle to give the impression of country living, but the houses tend to be uniform prewar buildings. Each house has its square patch fore and aft. Trees dot gardens, fertilized and sprayed on a regular basis. Privet hedges guard the sanctity of the dwellings. Everyone is polite; Christian names are rarely used, and conversations across hedges or from doorstep to doorstep are vaguely discouraged.

In back gardens, shielded for the most part from all but neighbors' eyes, there is a decaying of standards. Here and there can be seen goldfish ponds, some guarded by cement elves in pointed hats or crouching stone cats.

Safely north of the stone cats and well south of the M25 Motorway lay Duncan's Farm, ten acres of meadow and woodland surrounding a large rambling mansion, the joint property of Joshua Davies and his sister, Dolores Evita.

The house itself, though Victorian in scope and aspect, was in part Tudor. Occasional narrow wooden beams could be found in ceilings, walls, and the exterior. Tristram Davies, patriarch of the family, had purchased the property in one of his perennial attempts to protect his income from the depredations of the IRS. His wife, however, had quickly tired of it, of England, and ultimately, of Tristram Davies himself. She returned to her native Argentina and refused to leave that country even if it meant never seeing her children again.

Duncan's Farm reflected the eclectic taste of its previous owners. Small mullioned windows vied with Victorian bow; wooden floors gave way to carpets, then to parquet, then reverted to polished wooden planks. Central heating had been installed at enormous expense by Tristram, but the steam boiler was erratic at best. Water cooled in the pipes, then exploded as steam passed over it. The noise caused Dolores' sheltie to bark in response; at her brother's urging, Dolores shipped the dog off to a friend's in the Orkney Isles, where, no doubt, it felt almost at home.

The house itself was called Willow Dene, an extraordinary choice in light of the fact of there being no willows for miles around, none, in fact, east of Monken Hadley. Tristram Davies had remedied this oversight by importing a willow and planting it on the far side of the lawn tennis court. And he'd lived there until he died, filling the house with bric-a-brac.

When Joshua Davies became twenty-one, he inherited half his father's wealth and exactly one-half of Willow Dene. Tristram had spent his declining years tucked away in the library reading the books he had never had time for. Shakespeare's *King Lear* had made a great impression, and he resolved to give his children nothing in his lifetime and strictly equal shares at his death. He further stipulated that his children got nothing if they failed to graduate from a decent university or refused to learn the Spanish language.

Both Joshua and Dolores were far above average intelligence; they spoke Spanish fluently and spent a year touring the Iberian peninsula defiling their perfect grammar and intonation so they sounded like natives. They formed a warm bond of affection with Carmen Davies, their distant mother, who once paid them the supreme compliment of visiting England. It was during a particularly gloomy English June, and Carmen returned to Argentina convinced her children would be content to live even on the Malvinas.

No one knew that the crafty Tristram had put all his money in gold, which rose feverishly in price. He also bought and sold commodity futures with an uncanny skill suggesting inside information. When he died, he left, after absurd death duties, over two million pounds to his children.

Entering into the spirit of their father's will, Joshua and Dolores, having arranged a liberal income in U.S. dollars for Carmen, divided the house equally. Joshua took the top floor, his sister the one below his, and the ground floor was communal property.

The living room presented a problem. It was huge, running the entire width of the house and most of its length. Joshua painted a discreet mark at exactly the midpoint of the room. The great oak worktable (it had once seated twenty-four dinner guests) was positioned so that half lay on Dolores' side, the other on her brother's. In the center was a wooden lazy Susan on which were placed a number of snacks and cold cuts to fortify them during the evening and weekend hours. Dolores purchased the food, Joshua paid for it. Dolores agreed to cook, so Joshua took upon himself, with less dedication, the management of the outside of the house, including the land.

At each end of the table sat an Apple IIe word processor. Joshua used his for his hobby, the translation of the Voynich manuscript, the only known version of the most intractable of all codes. No one had ever succeeded in breaking it. Dolores employed her machine for her life's work, the writing of a romantic novel of inordinate length and great sexual delicacy. Each machine could send messages and text to the other.

The attic floor was given over to a small ballroom where the Davieses practiced their Latin American dances. Currently they were tango champions of the North London region. For two years, the judges had unanimously awarded them a large silver cup. One stood on the table on Joshua's side, the other on Dolores'. What Dolores felt about their "way of life," as her brother had named it, was hard to say. She gamely fixed meals for which Joshua paid and passed everything through a serving hatch onto a buffet that was four feet on her side of the room, four feet on Joshua's.

The writing room, as it became known, was full despite being vast. Joshua had a large pipe organ on which to practice; he was the organist at St. Paul's Methodist Church. Dolores led the choir. Except for this large item, almost everything had been duplicated. There were two sets of file cabinets, two televisions, two phones. Each had a small work station including desk and swivel chair; there were two couches for relaxing and thinking or even napping. Joshua's library on codes and ciphers filled one of his wall areas; Dolores' library of romantic novels and her archives of historical material took up one of her walls and encroached on a second. In four large cabinets was her father's collection of English silver. She had promised to cherish and expand it. Dolores knew almost as much about silver as she did of the history of romance.

She was already hard at work thrusting Sunday brunch through the serving hatch when Davies came down and entered through his door.

"Morning, Dol," he muttered, dressed in his silk pajamas and gold robe. Blue tattered bedroom slippers adorned his feet. On his sofa sat a large calico cat that opened one eye and followed his every movement.

Davies weighed in on his scales every Sunday. His weight never varied. Precisely twenty stone. Two hundred eighty pounds. That was his set point. Even if he missed one whole meal and had a snack instead, his body always adjusted his metabolism to compensate.

Giving a melancholy sigh, he crossed to his work station, took a can of cat food out of the desk drawer, and inserted it in the electric can opener. This joyful sound summoned Raison from his perch on the sofa. He purred vigorously, rubbing up against his provider's leg.

Raison had been found by Davies wandering aimlessly down the Ridgeway. He took the animal home with him, where Dolores named him.

"You've given him a *raison d'être,*" she said, "so call him Raison." The name stuck. An additional bonus, besides Raison's delight in killing a wide variety of rodents, was the fact that the cat disliked fish. The trophy room which was on Davies' floor was inundated with stuffed fish that had foolishly taken Davies' lures. Raison was never tempted by the trophies.

Joshua was fifty years old. He had married in his youth; the experience soured him for many years, and when the hurt passed he was too well established in "the way of life" to risk marriage again.

One of his friends had likened Davies' marriage to a frog wedding a princess. The young woman, Davina Somerville, was a delight to the eye, but she was cursed with the fatal ambition most women suffer from; she sought to turn her frog into a prince. Her husband was content to lead a quiet life. She knew he worked in the export business, but nothing else. How she would have reacted had she known Davies was a highly placed official in the British secret service will never be known. Joshua had been recruited at Oxford; Cambridge had produced so many spies and traitors that Cambridge products were still suspect.

"It's a solitary life," said Foulkes-Grey, Joshua's tutor, as they sipped sherry on the bank of the Thames nearly thirty years before. "No recognition, but vital work."

"What do I have to do?" asked Davies, watching a strapping blond punting vigorously on the river.

"Ah. Well, that depends."

Davies, without even turning to look at his companion, sipped his sherry. He looked at the tiny white daisies scattered in the grass around them. "So," he said. "It's a job you can't discuss. The pay will have to be negotiated. There will be a lot of travel. I won't be able to tell anyone what I do, and you suggest I remain a bachelor."

"Ah."

Foulkes-Grey had known his man, and waited until he was sure. There was some demurring in Whitehall, especially when it was revealed that the new recruit's mother was Argentinian and had assisted her parents as a trapeze artist in the Ringling Brothers' circus.

"Well," as one wag put it with veiled reference to one of their discreet offices in London, "he *is* going to be in the Circus, after all."

So Davies was welcomed aboard. He did little jobs at first, kept to himself, and moved up through the various departments of MI5. There were several years in B Branch, of course; everyone did a stint there, looking through everyone's dirty linen in Positive Vetting. Then came a transfer to D and five years in Soviet Satellites trying to fathom the Order of Battle. A second step up brought him to the Soviet Order of Battle department. By that time Davies could speak five languages, and with great bureaucratic wisdom, he was never called upon to use the one language he knew fluently—Spanish.

Meanwhile, a cover was being skillfully constructed. In partnership with another comer, Allardyce Greene, Davies began a machine tools business. Finally he became head of Agents and, when Greene's bubble popped, head of Department D.

During his slow climb toward directorship and the unflattering nickname "the Butcher," Davies led a remarkably bland public life, despite his wealth. He worked hard at anonymity. People that claimed to know him proffered invitations to social events that he never attended. When it was pointed out that he was becoming a man of mystery, and therefore a celebrity, Davies attended two functions in quick succession and was so dull and boring that all interest in him ceased. He joined one club where even a Trappist monk would have been suspect and had some of his mail sent there. Above all, he steered clear of White's and the Turf.

Joshua was a pear-shaped individual whose hindquarters marked his greatest extent. His face was doughy and seemed to have been kneaded together in a hurry with blue buttons added for eyes as an afterthought. He still had all his hair, though there was as much gray as white in it. When he remembered, which wasn't often, he used Brylcreme on it. Usually Davies wore his pince-nez spectacles carefully secured to a fine cord attached to—nothing. But his face did not rest passively on its jowls; its creases were those of a shrewd man. Above all, he had a talent for plain speaking; he didn't care who was offended.

Someone, oblivious to anachronism, had said that Sherlock Holmes' smarter brother Mycroft was the model for Joshua Davies. "After the first glance, one forgot the great body and remembered only the dominant mind." For those who failed to see that dominant mind, the results were often fatal. Joshua Davies could be ruthless. Not without reason, Department D was sometimes called Department Destruction.

Joshua helped himself to breakfast: scrambled eggs and toast, juice, coffee, two croissants, bacon, liver, and grilled tomatoes. He was eating when Dolores came in to serve herself.

Whether it was a family genetic defect or not, Dolores Davies, too, tended to be overweight. Though not as vast as her brother, she did put on flesh easily and had a hard time losing any. For several years the scales had read 178 pounds. Heroic dieting had once resulted in a loss of 12 pounds. The following month she weighed exactly 178 pounds.

"Set point," her brother had observed philosophically. "And the will of God."

"I'll have my stomach stapled and my colon or whatever trimmed by ten feet." But she didn't.

Unlike her brother, Dolores had dressed for breakfast. Joshua assumed she intended to spend the day on her novel, *Passionate Captive's Revenge,* set on a sugar plantation in eighteenth-century Jamaica.

Conversation did not rise that morning and neither cared. The empty plates were Davies' responsibility; placing them in the serving hatch, he went around and put them in the dishwasher. When he returned, Dolores was already glaring at her CRT through pebble lenses. Her sweater looked even more strained than usual as it encircled the great bust. Pursing her full lips, Dolores rocked her head from side to side while reading the text.

"It's not working, Josie," she muttered. "Can't get the right phrase. It's the end of the foreplay and start of contact. I'll send it over."

Davies turned on his machine; seconds later text was scrolling up his screen. He grunted. Leaning forward in his made-to-order swivel chair, he opened a drawer he had had constructed and drew from it a large cigar cutter. Studying the screen, he methodically sheared off the end of the cigar, a Hofnar, and lit a match, holding it a quarter of an inch away from the leaf and slowly twisting as he puffed. Next he sniffed the air through his bulldog nose, rolled the Hofnar to the corner of his mouth, and typed rapidly without any break in rhythm:

> Dirk's eyes raked boldly over her, his gaze dropping from her eyes to her shoulders to her satin breasts. Rowena's body was electric with pulsating desire; she almost swooned as the imperious questing hands roved freely over her melting limbs. Did they now bask in the Paphian grove? Would they, as Rowena's palpitations rose, penetrate even the sacred cave of Cupid itself?

He sent this to his sister's terminal, then looked in a box of floppy disks and slid one into the A drive.

"It's good," said Dolores thoughtfully, "damn good, but I said that in the last chapter. I'll think of something, though."

"Okay, Dol," replied Davies, placing his cigar in the smokeless ashtray. His mind was now fully concentrated on the contents of the disk filling his screen.

He had played it twenty times that weekend, each time with a growing conviction that it was true. *If* it was true, agents were being eliminated methodically by the other side, their deaths disguised as accidents or natural deaths. If . . . if . . . if it was true, he was sitting on the biggest bombshell to hit MI5 since its inception. The entire organization was compromised. Worse, everything that MI5 did in counterespionage was known in advance. The possibility stunned him. Any enemy agents Joshua's people had located had to have been either plants or redundants. Whenever MI5 congratulated itself on a triumph, the Russians were celebrating as well—and with better reason. It left a sick feeling in the pit of his stomach. He was afraid to believe it, but D Branch might well have spent the last ten years gathering useless information. Four main sections were operational: the Soviet, the Soviet Satellites, Research, and Agents. And, yes, he had lost a number of men.

Trouble was, there was no norm to compare the numbers with, so Joshua had no idea whether or not his losses were excessive. The names on the disk included all those who had been lost in action as well as those who had supposedly died ordinary deaths. Joshua's most recent death had been Hawk, at the explosion in Rotherhithe Street. That had been an IRA outrage—or so it seemed at the time. A splinter group claimed credit, as usual. The IRA denied responsibility, as usual.

But now the names of all agents and MI5 workers were on one list. Prior to this, each department dealt with its own. "The need to know" prevented anyone from learning what was going on elsewhere in the organization. Hell, that made sense; it was absolutely fundamental. And maybe, just maybe, some clever bastard had taken terrible advantage of this compartmentalization.

Looking away from his screen, he watched Dol for a while. When she turned to him and their eyes met, he asked, "How much?"

"Josie! Don't do that."

"Sorry. It's part of my makeup."

"I can't *stand* that Sherlock Holmes stuff."

Her brother grinned, waiting.

"All right, you win. How did you do it?"

"Oh, you don't really want to know. . . ."

"I'm not going to beg, Josie."

"Damn right. Anyway there's not much to it," he replied smugly. "You looked over to the British Heritage calendar where you observed that large cross marking tomorrow's date. This Sunday is, as we both know, the day of the monthly meeting of the Romantic Quills at the Church hall, in Vinegar Alley. As recording secretary, you must be present."

"Right so far," she admitted grudgingly.

"And your usual ride is in the hospital with a gallbladder op. All the other members would have to come quite a bit out of their way to pick you up. How is Peggy, by the way?"

"Better. Go on."

"And you didn't want to ask me to drive you because the last time I did, some neo-Nazi stole the spare tire from the Rolls." He glowered at the memory. "So you looked through the bus timetable, which you keep in the top drawer of your filing cabinet. That confirmed what you already knew—the number thirty-six bus arrives too late to make a connection with the number twenty-three-A."

"Not bad, Josie."

"At that moment, like any true child of London, you thought of the incomparable underground. A cloud, if that's not too fanciful a word, passed over your face because you remembered the interchange at Finsbury Park is closed this month for repairs. That means you would have to go all the way to Saint Pancras to make the Victoria Line connection, thus doubling the length of your journey to Walthamstow Central." He leaned back, looking exactly like a conceited Buddha.

"Not bad, Josie."

"You already said that. Now, an American would have thought of a taxi first, but we English are tighter. You looked into your handbag, took out your purse, and from your reaction, it was clear the cupboard was bare. The paperboy nabbed you this morning and collected for the last two months. He cleaned you out. The banks are closed, so finally you thought of me. Looking in my direction, you were about to tap me for the loan of a few quid when I said—"

" 'How much?' "

"Right."

"You should write detective fiction, O brother of mine, but in the meantime, lend me a fiver."

"There's no future in writing, Dol, not unless you write diet books or romances. You know that."

Grinning, he took a crisp five-pound note from his leather wallet. "Those books satisfy the same desperate urge for something unobtainable—pure love at the right weight."

Folding the money into a paper airplane, he skimmed it down the table to his sister, who said, "Thanks, Josie. And after that tedious lecture, don't expect to get this back." She grinned.

Davies turned back to his terminal, his lightheartedness disappearing. His main responsibility was "scalp-hunting," the polite term, or "butchering," the more common one. His agents fanned out across the globe to deal with jobs that were too risky or dirty for the local agents. They swept dirt under the rug. In and out, quick and clean, was the rule of all Special Projects work. The agents might be specialists or recruited from other offices. They weren't licensed to kill because no one in government wanted the licenses traced back to him. So there was a division within D Branch that was simply called Special Projects. No one wanted to know any more than that. What was "special" about it, they deduced easily.

From an office in Lower Marsh Street, Davies conducted and ran an import-export business as a cover. Dolores worked as his secretary.

The Director leaned forward; his chair groaned. He spent the next ten minutes gazing at a spot on the table. Then he got to his feet, wandered over to the sofa, and lay full length upon it.

Dolores looked up; she knew the signals.

"Trouble?"

"Could be."

She went on with her work; he would tell her if he wanted to.

Treachery was abroad. Davies knew it, felt it. He'd known when his wife had taken a lover; things that important couldn't be hidden. Nor, he thought, could they be overlooked. Other matters, his wife's inability to do anything domestic—all her meals were "ill-killed, ill-dressed, ill-cooked, and ill-served"—might be ignored. But treachery? No.

The day after Davina first betrayed him was signaled by a meal attempted with some modicum of success: a ragout of crab, mussels, and scallops in spinach sauce. It was not served hot enough but represented such a quantum leap that no one but an idiot could have failed to suspect something.

Finally, when the truth came out, there was no blazing row, no tearful confrontation, no packing of suitcases in bedrooms. One day she told him she had found someone else, and he called her a cab.

Davies didn't ask after her, didn't spy on her, didn't want to know what she was doing. Yet even now he could feel an involuntary pang at reminders of Davina.

One thing a wife did supply, at least in the beginning, was sex. Davies began to put on weight in his first year of marriage. The doctors muttered about sluggish metabolism, but exercise didn't help and starvation diets made him morose and no lighter. Davina made half-hearted attempts to melt frozen Weight Watchers' dinners, but nothing helped. Simply soaking food in tomato sauce and calling it Creole didn't make it edible. Finally it reached the point where whenever he passed through the house he could be sure of her calling out for him to carry out some trivial errand. She never did anything when he was available. In the end, he was tiptoeing around the house. At his weight, it was too much of an effort.

Three years before the end, Davies' sex was restricted to once a week, and Davina complained throughout that he could not lie on her. She seemed not to understand his hints that there were other ways. It wasn't long before he was trying to convince himself that the Earl of Chesterfield's description of sex was immortal truth. Soon all he could remember was that the pleasure, however momentary, was still the greatest pleasure there was.

Then, until two years ago, Davies had remained celibate until it dawned on him that he was not unique; from the beginning of time men had obtained sex one way or another. From that time on, he was free, free of it all. No more being manipulated, no more *nouvelle cuisine*—tiny strips of beef and brightly colored veggies in scooped-out tomatoes. He shuddered. Most of all he didn't have to be amiable every day to the same person. Dol, bless her heart, didn't count.

London, he learned, was full of obliging attractive women who supplied services for a fee.

There was no requirement to listen to their problems and no need to feel obligations. Lust was undeniable, it wouldn't go away; the churches had run brothels for their clergy in the old days. Nothing sacrificed; nothing lost.

Of late, Joshua had been visiting a delightful oriental girl. Soo Ling was charming and her repertoire beyond measure. She never whined or complained, and when he left her apartment, he could forget her until the next time. Davies lifted his glasses from his face and massaged the bridge of his nose. A loud rumble, his version of a laugh, startled his sister.

Feeling much better, Davies lumbered to his feet and crossed to the French doors. Drawing back the draperies, he looked out across the meadow. It was a beautiful day, better than anyone had a right to expect in April. A few clouds in the sky, big, and cream-puffy.

Nowadays, he knew, intuition was decried in espionage. But Davies possessed it, and he felt something was wrong. Very wrong.

"Want to go down to Bushy Park for a while?" he asked over his shoulder.

Dol looked up in surprise. "It's Sunday . . . Well, all right."

"I'll get dressed," said her brother.

"Don't forget to take the dishes out of the dishwasher first. That's your job."

"Uh-huh," replied Joshua Davies, wondering if, perhaps, "the way of life" could be tuned a tad finer.

3

Davies forged upstairs, his bulk pulling at the stair rail; in one or two places there was a little play, as if screws were beginning to concede defeat. In the bathroom he shed his silk pajamas and gold robe and slid back the glass door to his shower. The design was his own, a large glass-enclosed area where the occupant was at the mercy of powerful jets of water.

He liked his shower hot and fierce—perhaps it was a kind of penance, possibly a faint subconscious hope that some excess weight might be sweated away; the enclosure was filled with steam long before he slid back the glass partition and stepped onto the floor mat. He had heard that one of his operatives used only cold water; this, he felt, was downright fanaticism, but secretly he was in awe of the man.

Cleaning the steam from the bathroom mirror and propping open the door, he contrived to shave. The cord to his electric razor had become defective, and he was careful not to pull on the razor when it suddenly lost power. He meant to get another one; somehow there was never time.

Within half an hour he felt better. Davies, completely dressed, inspired little confidence in British tailoring; he wore the clothes of a slightly eccentric bank manager. The buttons of his shirts were under constant strain, and the bow ties he favored were lost under jowls that gave him the air of a worried bloodhound. His trousers bagged inevitably despite the heroic efforts of a thick leather belt especially imported for him from a Mexican supply house. The socks did match, but his shoes were unshined and one was scuffed beyond the point where polish would help. Yet Davies' mind was impeccable, his paperwork precise, his intelligence unrivaled.

The phone shrilled and he picked it up. There was a click, and he heard the scrambler cut in. He couldn't believe what he heard next. He grunted one word, "Alex." Then he replaced the receiver slowly and deliberately.

From a drawer in the bedroom he took his automatic, a Beretta 92S, and a magazine of thirteen 9-mm shells, which he slid firmly into position. He drew back the slide and heard the first round chambered. The double-column magazine made the weapon more bulky than usual, but Davies' giant hand fitted around it comfortably. Some of the younger, more stylish agents in the branch fancied weapons like the Walther PPK and the Browning Hi-Powers. One or two sported short-barreled revolvers, carried butt down in spring-clip holsters for fast drawing. Davies called them cowboys.

Snapping on the safety, he put the automatic in a leather shoulder holster.

He phoned the duty officer at Five, giving his itinerary and expected time of arrival, then joined Dolores in the front hall. From the umbrella stand he took his sword stick. It was a made-to-order model purchased from James Smith and Sons, New Oxford Street. Since time immemorial, the celebrated house had been the purveyor to the upper crust of umbrellas, parasols, and canes. Sword-concealing walking sticks, while not greatly in demand, remained a specialty.

Dolores, like her brother, was not built for haste. She had compressed her vast bosom into a corset and cinched in her waist. Her pantsuit was both expensive and ill-fitting, and she carried a Gucci bag. Completing the ensemble was a large hat of indeterminate shape and texture and a pair of imported waterproof beige canvas boots with rubber soles and high heels. Her feet did not leave the imprint of the lotus blossom when she passed.

The premature summer was in its second week; their neighbor had already lit a bonfire, and the smell of burning trash wafted over the high brick wall. The early bulbs were already out, the tulips in a dozen colors ranging from bright red to black; iris, narcissus, and jonquil in wide beds would soon flank the gravel road to the garage.

Inside the garage was Davies' pride, a vintage 1914 Rolls-Royce Silver Ghost with London-to-Edinburgh touring coachwork painted olive green. The sides were open and the top raised.

"First time this year, Josie," said Dolores as she mounted the running board and took the passenger seat.

"I'm not worried," replied her brother, climbing in after her. Once settled, he reached out and released the nickel hand brake and set the switch on the steering wheel hub.

"You know, Josie," said Dolores, taking a vast plaid scarf from her handbag, "if I'm ever pursued by a mad rapist and get as far as this car, I won't be able to start the damn thing."

"I hadn't thought of that," admitted her brother. "Nor did Charles Rolls or Frederick H. Royce." He turned the crank handle; the engine started on the second attempt. "Off we go," he muttered, climbing aboard and removing the stick holding down the clutch pedal.

Before they left the driveway, Davies had the Rolls in top gear. His driving left much to be desired; only Dolores never seemed to notice that her brother assumed that all other motorists would defer to the Silver Ghost on principle.

Davies gunned the vehicle along the unpaved surface of Hadley Road. Soon he abruptly, without anything more than a vague wave of his hand that might have meant anything, swept onto Cockfosters Road.

"Where are we going?" asked Dolores, quite familiar with her brother's sudden whims.

"Sir Gerald's. Twickenham," he grunted. "He goes to his retreat every weekend now. The birds are returning from South America or wherever they were."

"I thought he was senile," replied Dolores.

"Well, who isn't in this business?" A bus stopped suddenly in front of him, and he was forced to apply the brakes. The Rolls pulled up without sliding. Davies double-clutched and pulled out into the center of the road, blithely ignoring a taxi heading toward them. If he heard what the driver said as he squeaked by, he gave no sign of it.

The Director used his own car despite its high visibility because he was convinced that all MI5 registration numbers were known to the opposition anyway. Davies' theory was, therefore, that even a highly visible vehicle like the Rolls was safer than one of the motor pool vehicles. Back in 1968, the vehicles were all kept in a garage in Barnard Road, Battersea. Two Russians had been arrested for loitering in the area. After that the vehicles were widely dispersed. As long as Davies' cover was not fully penetrated, he felt safe enough in the Rolls.

"Get me a choc, will you, Dol?"

Dolores reached forward and lifted the lid of the trembler box. Inside was a silver box; inscribed on the lid in elegant script was *Charbonnel et Walker.*

"What flavor?"

"Cherry. The coffee is gone, of course."

"Right."

She selected one, reached over, and popped it into her brother's capacious mouth. "I like scented truffles, Josie. Why don't you get some from Prestat's when you're in Molton Street?"

"I will, Dol. They've done a good job with the whiskey flavor."

They were passing the underground station at Cockfosters, the last one on the Piccadilly route; a gaggle of travelers in their Sunday best spilled from the exit, on their way to visit friends who had escaped into the green belt. Davies condescended to wait while they crossed at the light opposite the post office. A young woman hauling a boy of six in a Little Lord

Fauntleroy suit waved at Dolores, who waved back.

"Amy Declor," she said.

Davies grunted and eased the Rolls forward. "Was that the kid who found Raison when he got the urge to wander?"

"The same."

"Nice kid. Pity about the Sunday suit."

Not much was said after that until they had traveled the length of Chase Side and Davies made a sharp left turn into the High Street at Southgate. Dolores waited, knowing her brother would tell her what was on his mind when he had mulled things over long enough. There was plenty of traffic out for a Sunday, and lots of people admired the Silver Ghost as it passed.

A clock opposite the green read eleven when Davies suddenly said, "Hawk's dead."

Dolores looked at her brother. "How?"

"Accident. They say."

"What . . . ?"

"That IRA bomb, at the Ship and Whale; it was his local."

Dolores knew that the young man, code-named Hawk, was one of Davies' bright new boys. Educated, dedicated, Hawk was a fresh wind; he really believed in the old virtues: loyalty, trust, friendship—unlike some of the old brigade. Dolores tugged on her scarf because she felt embarrassed to admit she was one of them—some of the old brigade were cynical. It was often hard to know how her brother felt. Hawk had no such questions—whatever its imperfections, the West was infinitely superior to the Communist world. Period.

"I didn't know. About Hawk, I mean. I'm sorry to hear it."

"Hmm. He went there a lot. So did a lot of navy lads." Davies was feeling in his inside pocket for his cigar case; Dolores steered the wheel with her right hand. "It looked IRA. I've got T looking at the bomb fragments. Special Branch was very understanding, so were the Metro boys. I just assumed it was pure coincidence. Wrong place. Wrong time." He reached into his jacket pocket, took out his cutter, and lopped off the end of the cigar but did not light it.

"If those bastards ever discover the royal family usually sits in row G of the stalls at Drury Lane, we'll be in real trouble." He was revolving the Hofnar in his mouth and had taken the wheel from his sister.

They joined the North Circular Road at Muswell Hill golf course. Traffic began to pick up. The Rolls passed several cars, and Davies cut in front of a large truck carrying pigs. Snouts stuck out of the sides of the truck and busy grunting noises could be heard above the noise of the engine. As they shot under the railroad bridge, Davies looked to his left at the golfers beyond the fence. "We should play more, Dol; you were getting round in par." He paused. "The exercise might do me some good."

Dol patted his trunk of a leg. "Now, Josie. Remember the last exercise kick you were on. You gained half a stone."

Davies shuddered at the memory. "I was

starving all the time. You're right. No more golf. Silly game anyway, though Badger was . . . That reminds me. Badger."

"What about him? And call him Neville; I know who he is."

The Rolls shot under the flyover by Colney Hatch Road. A bus went by full of Japanese tourists and a bevy of cameras focused on the Silver Ghost. Dolores managed a smile; Davies resisted the temptation to have an obscene gesture immortalized on film. He was also glumly aware that for miles the highway had been flanked by swimming pools, golf courses, sports fields, and the like. Everywhere, it seemed, the human body was being tortured.

"Before he left the service he'd been at work on a little project for me. . . ." He broke off. "Got a light?"

Dolores dug around in her purse and finally found a Bic lighter. Her brother leaned over, pulling on his cigar until the tip glowed red.

"Mmm," he muttered. "That's a help. Well, Badger sent me a floppy disk with the results of his investigation a couple of days ago. He had access to the raw data, but keep that under your hat or I'm sharkbait."

"What did he say?"

"I'm coming to that. Badger had intuition. Oh, he examined all the facts and avoided assumptions. He didn't make wild guesses on sketchy evidence, but he could *feel* things. Damn, he was a real loss to the service. Anyway," he continued, "he knew instinct was what put all the pieces together. Now, I don't know if Neville is right but . . ."

"But what?"

"We're losing agents far too fast. Something's wrong."

"And you're going to tell the D-G this?"

Davies grunted. Smoke expelled from his mouth was whipped over his shoulder and away. "Not likely. By the bye, Alex is tainted. I don't know how to tell C about it, but I'll have to, in a few minutes. Dear God, you think about it, all those guys think they're running the most wonderful secret service in the world. They're not ready to hear more about infiltration. Badger . . . Neville . . . once asked me what it would take to get us into the twentieth century."

"And you said?"

"Just get them past World War One, that would be a gigantic leap forward."

They were alongside a Ford van; the passenger, a burly fellow in bib overalls, looked out at Dolores, lowered his window, and gave a loud whistle. Davies was surprised to see his sister blush and look away. It dawned on him that "the way of life" made no allowances for Dolores' sexual needs. Suddenly, ridiculously, he felt guilty.

"Drive on, Josie," she whispered. "It's clear."

They were passing under Hendon Way and approaching the entrance of the M1 Motorway before he spoke again, raising his voice above the increased noise of traffic.

"You can't explain to that bunch about ELINT and computers. It's too complicated for men who studied the classics. They form committees at Five; they never actually *do* anything. As Badger said, 'It's a hotbed of cold feet.' "

Broadway flashed below them and Davies noticed a cricket match was in progress; he looked away.

"What Badger did was to modify a program his brother Tony brought back from the States. It was an actuarial thing, designed to forecast how many people would die or get injured in factories, so the insurance rates could be set."

"Sounds complicated."

"Damn right. Of course, Badger—Neville—knows that stuff cold. He then fed in all personnel records for the last ten years. I gave him a lot of help to get at the stuff, and we both lied like billyho."

"And?"

"It's too high, Dol. Far too high. We're losing agents at four times the predictable rate; there are just too many damn accidents and so-called natural deaths, including suicides. Our field losses are double. That wouldn't attract attention normally. But add in the accidents . . ."

"What did Badger say?"

Davies tossed his cigar away. "He thinks it's a mole, code name Ivan."

"Oh, Jesus."

"He suggests looking into any deaths that could be considered normal. Forget agents in the field. Half the time, there's no body. But every day thousands of people die from natural causes or accidents. If you wanted to hide a murder, where would you put it?"

"Someplace where the coroner wouldn't question a thing."

"Right. A mole digs deep, comes up, kills, and the coroner certifies pneumonia or suicide or whatever."

After a moment's reflection, Dol asked, "What is Neville doing now, Josie?"

"He and that Russian friend of his have what they call a 'discreet inquiries business.' It's a sort of detective agency."

"Called?"

"The Nevcon Agency. It's very successful, I gather."

The Grand Union Canal was carried above them on an aqueduct; a brightly colored narrow boat with passengers on board stared down at the Rolls as it shot underneath. Only the elderly skipper, his arm hooked around the tiller, corncob pipe in his mouth, showed no interest.

They had traveled the length of the North Circular. At the clinic, Davies bore left and followed Hanger Lane due south, asserting himself at the junction with the Great West Road reaching Kew Bridge. Dolores seemed temperamentally, perhaps even genetically, suited to her brother's driving. Where passengers usually turned white after a few hundred yards with Davies at the wheel, Dolores was enjoying the ride.

Joshua branched right into Kew Road. The Thames was packed with pleasure craft; a yacht race was taking place, and by the bridge a yachtsman was standing in his lifejacket on the bottom of his upturned boat clutching the knifeboard as the craft bobbed about in the wake of a steamer.

The road followed the botanical gardens for

half a mile. A large red double-decker bus blocked their passage. When it moved away from its stop, Davies followed closely behind. The conductor, a woman with her hat stuck on top of a mop of red hair, looked at the Rolls admiringly. She looked at Davies and his sister, did a double take, then grinned. She swung around and disappeared up the stairs, making sure Davies saw a flash of thigh.

"Saucy creature," snapped Dolores primly.

"Right," said her brother, without conviction.

He swung swiftly around the bus and added suddenly, "You know, Dol, there's more sports grounds in London than you can shake a stick at. Who the hell goes to all these places? I don't know anyone who goes to one."

"Must be a different social circle than ours, Josie."

Davies laughed; the rumble was distant and basso profundo. "Hell, one day I made a list of all my friends. Ended up with just you, Dol."

His sister leaned over and kissed him on the cheek. "You're exaggerating, as usual. Neville really liked you."

"Yes, he did, didn't he?" said Davies, feeling better.

Crossing a roundabout brought them into the Quadrant and the incredibly complex system of one-way streets designed to discourage tourists. Richmond still clung to shards of elegance and a certain conservative prosperity. Although appearing on maps as a suburb of London, the region was more like a nineteenth-century English spa.

Davies had a firm route in mind that just happened to coincide with the one-way signs. Had it not, he would have followed his instincts and not the signs.

"Neville's problem was his lack of a sense of smell," muttered Davies, more to himself than to Dolores, as they went by elegant Georgian houses. "He didn't lick, he barked; he possessed integrity. He wanted to get out, and we were dumb enough to let him get away."

They stopped at a light. "Our esteemed secret service colleagues would rather live in leaky houses than have someone like Badger pull the roof in around them. They speak of him, to keep the similes going, as the fool who burned his house down to get rid of the termites. They won't believe him on this little lot. But I tell you one thing, Dol. I'm going to get to the bottom of this."

Dol knew her brother meant it. All his intellectual powers would be focused on finding who had killed his agents. And find him he would. Davies felt deeply for his agents. He trained some of them, and he liked the ardor of those who, like Hawk, believed fervently in what they were doing. Joshua wasn't cynical, but he leaned toward pragmatism. He admired idealism in others.

Her own thoughts were more personal; Dol knew the young doctor who was engaged to Hawk. The woman couldn't be told the truth. The Davieses wouldn't be able to attend Hawk's funeral in case some alert member of the opposition put two and two together. Two young lives had been ruined by Hawk's death. Other agents had been married, some with children. Children never overcame the loss of a parent; the surviving parent might turn to chemical consolation. Dol regarded alcohol and drugs as the devil's agents. Worst of all, in Dol's mind, was that an agent's heroism was never recognized by the victim's own family.

"Get him, Josie," she said suddenly and vehemently. "Find the son of a bitch and hurt him."

Davies looked over at her, surprised by the sudden bitterness. "I'm going to, Dol. I'll find him, one way or another. And when I do, he'll take the walk."

She nodded. Everyone in the Service knew the saying: "Two men go on the walk, but only one returns."

"It's going to have to be subtle. I've got to finesse him into showing his hand. I'll be alone. None of those department heads will help, and even if they offered, I couldn't trust them."

"Be careful, Josie. Be very careful."

"Damn right I will."

Marble Hill Park was on their right, a vast Palladian mansion build by George II for his mistress. Davies doubted any woman, unless she was a totally uninhibited sexual contortionist, was worth that pile of bricks and stone. Minutes later they sighted the elaborate Gothic monstrosity Horace Walpole had fashioned and called Strawberry Hill. Davies tried, and failed, to imagine what a woman would have to do to earn *that* excrescence. A large sign reminded anyone interested that the building was now St. Mary's Training College.

"So you are to be the Keeper of Queen's Moles."

"Not bloody likely! Well, here's Park Road."

He made the awkward turn, jagging right into Broad Street, then left into Park, narrowly missing a fruit barrow stacked with apples and pears. The frantic owner waved his fist at the receding Rolls and shouted loudly, "Come the Revolution, the bleeding aristocrats will get theirs."

"The trouble is not moles," Davies said reflectively. "It's ferrets. All the means of tracking a mole must be known to Ivan. To do a thorough vetting requires the resources of all sorts of people. Any one of them could be a mole. Who spies on spies, Dol? That's baffled us since Walsingham's time."

"Is that how Philby got by?"

"Not only him but a few more he protected. We're probably riddled worse than Gruyère cheese. Philby was helped by Otto Clark, one of the Whitehall mandarins. Blunt was sanitized and given a deal. Unless you catch a mole being serviced or lure him out of his hill, he's impossible to trace."

The Silver Ghost turned right onto Sandy Lane. A herd of deer and cows was grazing contentedly near the triple avenue of chestnuts and limes. The chestnuts were still in bloom. Beyond was the Diana Fountain that Davies stoutly maintained was actually Venus. Two miles away was the stately palace Cardinal Wolsey had given to Henry VIII—discretion being the better part of valor.

Davies turned abruptly into a rhododendron-lined driveway leading to an ivy-covered thatched cottage. It had been the house of a gamekeeper when the lascivious Henry used the park as a hunting preserve. Now the current Director-General of MI5 used it to escape the weekly viciousness of Curzon Street.

As Davies followed his sister from the Silver Ghost, he thought that the D-G should be given credit for not retiring to Oxford. So many of the mandarins felt the pull of the stones and spires. They wore straw hats and blazers and walked down The High, one of the last remaining Renaissance streets in Europe, or strolled by the Cherwell, believing they deserved their knighthoods. Davies gave his disapproving grunt. Damn fools, posturing in a world that no longer existed.

A couple walking a dog passed the end of the drive. The animal, a collie, ran up to them and sniffed around Dol's shoes. She petted it, but it lost interest and ran away. Its master and mistress were debating loudly about letting strangers touch the dog.

The D-G's cottage had only one floor; diamond-pane windows caught the midday sun and reflected it in a hundred shifting patterns. Curtains were drawn so they could not see in. The front door was modern, one of those atrocious hollow types with very regular stained-glass windows. On the jamb was a pushbutton bell. As Davies pressed it, recollections of his last visit assailed him. Lunch had consisted of a piece of meat from some animal's hindmost part which had apparently been singed under an x-ray machine. The cheddar cheese had tasted like soap.

"Now remember, Dol," Davies cautioned his sister as they heard footsteps approaching the door. "If they invite us to lunch, refuse. I want to eat at the Richmond Rendezvous. I've set my heart on the filet of sole cooked with litchis."

4

Millicent Tavistock answered the door; she was County. She rode to hounds, was president of the Women's Guild, and captained the women's golf team at Fulwell. She had a stallion at stud at Kempton Park. Above all, she was excessively outgoing and infinitely optimistic. She was one of those rare women who saw none of her husband's faults and thought him an intellectual when he was, in fact, a lightweight.

"Well, *quelle surprise!*" she gushed at the sight of the Davieses standing one behind the other in the narrow passageway. "Come in, do come in!"

Millicent was a decade younger than her husband; her hair was cropped short and dyed a color Dolores said was called henna. It brought a picture of a dead hen to Davies' mind whenever he heard the word. Dead henna, he mused, looking at Millicent and submitting to the obligatory kiss on the cheek. He squeezed past her into a long, pleasant room that served as the sitting room.

"Well, well, well," Millicent chirped, her sharp hazel eyes darting from one to the other. "This *is* a surprise. Sit. Sit. Sit."

Davies shook his head. "You two chat. I have to see Sir Gerald."

Dolores plopped herself down on the rusty brown sofa.

"You can guess where he is," Millicent burbled. "Out there with his wretched birds. You know he was the first to spot a cuckoo this year? He had a letter in the *Times* a week before anyone else."

The Davieses made admiring sounds, Joshua thinking how wonderful a pheasant would taste, Dolores wondering how a grown man could spend his time spying on birds through binoculars.

"I'll find him," Davies said hastily, crossing the room and leaving through the French doors. Behind him he heard Millicent saying to Dolores, "He claims he saw a red-necked grebe the other day. Imagine. There can't be . . ."

The garden had begun its steady march toward summer glory. The shrubs were putting out buds, and the roses were beginning to flower. There was a heavy musky scent to several deep red climbers. Soon wisteria would cover the mellow red brick of the house and spread along the trellis by the stone path.

The garden ended with a profusion of mock orange shrubs, their delicate drooping white blossoms just beginning to fade. Beyond them lay Bushy Park. Sir Gerald had one of the very few houses inside the park. To the right, Davies could see the National Physical Laboratory which had taken over Bushy House.

Following Chestnut Avenue until he came to Cobbler's Walk, he looked left, then right, before deciding to go in the direction of the Warren Plantation. With a sigh of resignation he realized it was Chestnut Sunday. Thousands of visitors were swarming along the avenue. Children, understandably less than thrilled by lime and chestnut trees in bloom, were running hither and thither, each accompanied by yapping dogs. He turned off the path by Hawthorn Lodge and cut up toward Half Moon Plantation. A deer looked up at him, then resumed foraging. Davies had thoughts of venison.

He caught sight of Sir Gerald, binoculars in hand, eyes fixed on a clump of trees. As usual he wore a navy-blue blazer with silver buttons, a precise white triangle of handkerchief protruding from the pocket. Davies remembered what Alaister Strachan, from Department C, had said: "His parents registered him for Eton at birth but it didn't help." Eton, New College Oxford, a stint in the Guards, finally the Home Office. None of it had helped. The man was finished, had been for years.

Davies moved toward him and the D-G, who was also known as C, sensed his presence and turned to greet him.

"Joshua, good of you to come down." Sir Gerald carefully packed his binoculars into their leather case. "All these damn visitors have frightened the birds away. Spotted another cuckoo, though." Then without a break or change in rhythm, he said, "Why did I send for you?"

Davies took his arm gently and steered him across Cobbler's Walk.

"You didn't. I came to see you. Dol and I were just driving around. . . ."

"You'll stay to lunch? It's tuna casserole."

Davies rather clumsily threw up his hands as if the fates were against him. "Love to, but some other time, Sir Gerald. Dol has a pressing appointment."

"Dol?"

"My sister. Dolores."

"Yes. Yes. Of course. I'm not senile, Joshua."

There was a park bench facing Warren Plantation, and the two men sat, Davies gingerly, testing the bench. Joshua felt sorry for Sir Gerald Tavistock. There was no joy in being head of MI5. Everyone carped. The Prime Minister complained, the Permanent Under-Secretary griped, the Minister huffed, and Sir Gerald was between all of them and all of his Branch Directors. The Director-Generalship was a thankless task. One of his functions was to be a lightning rod for all the usual office hatreds and fears. The D-G was also the faceless administrator who could be blamed for everything from job assignments to a lack of toilet paper. Some problems had no solution. MI5 was full of minor figures who vastly overrated themselves. When, like sediment, they sank to the bottom, there was always the urgent need to find someone to blame, someone other than themselves. They picked the D-G.

Yet Davies had to admit that Sir Gerald's record wasn't good. Only two agents uncovered in ten years, and neither of them would have ripened without defections from the KGB. The plodding, uninspired leadership of Sir Gerald had raised opposition, and he had many enemies in MI5.

Early in his career, he'd been stationed in the Far East. There, it was rumored, he had been turned. Davies did not believe it for a second, and any suspicions he might have had vanished as he became aware that Sir Gerald's grasp on affairs was too infirm to constitute a threat.

"See any?" inquired Davies.

Sir Gerald started. "Any what?"

"Birds."

"Ah! Went up to the Heron Pond. Those damn boaters on the upper reach disturb them. They have the damndest time nesting. Kids steal their eggs and blow them. Can you imagine it. Ought to be flogged."

Davies nodded solemnly, remembering his own childhood collection of three hundred bird eggs.

"Well, Joshua?"

"Thought I'd drop by. A couple of things have come up."

A young nurse pushed a pram by. Davies realized they were probably in au pair country. Some lucky insurance moguls would be getting their jollies with Swedish students; their wives would be free to support starving artists in Bloomsbury. Both men watched the high heels and long slender legs recede into the distance.

"I'm chucking it, Joshua," said the D-G suddenly. "Haven't told anyone except Milly. Out in less than a month."

The news startled Davies. It convinced him immediately that Sir Gerald was not compromised. If the Russians had got to him, they'd make sure he died in office as all their people did.

"What . . . ?"

"Made me do it?" Sir Gerald straightened his legs and brushed imaginary dust from his trousers. "Sick of it, Joshua. Never a moment's peace. Not like the old days, eh? Damn, it was fun then. Trouble began with that bastard Philby. God, how I hate that son of a bitch."

He slumped down moodily on the bench, regarding his shoes with detached interest. "How could he do it, Joshua?"

"Because he—"

"His father was famous, went to all the right schools. . . . Loyalty is like air: the farther up you go, the thinner it becomes."

Davies was reminded of the Russian proverb "A fish decays from the head first" but was tactful enough not to mention it.

"They play games with me, Joshua, I know they do." Getting up, he started walking across the grass toward his house. Davies hurried to catch up.

"Games? What games?"

"Childish stuff. Important cables are brought up to my office by minor figures, dated, and timed. They drop them on my secretary's desk. Then three days later, the flap begins. Investigation. Case officer cleared, D-G blamed. The other day someone started a rumor that I was so security conscious I locked my Bible in the safe, and that I looked in the mirror to see who I was."

Davies permitted himself a wide grin, and the D-G shrugged.

"Who started that one?"

"Probably that ponce Rossiter; he wants the throne, Joshua, and a great revenge it would be if he got it, too. I can't stand the man. If he gets gas, his pimp, Gilbert, farts for him. God knows why anyone in his right mind would keep Freddy Gilbert in the business and let someone like Neville Conyers get away."

Davies nodded.

Sir Gerald was almost running now, the binocular case around his neck banging against his side. He wants to escape, thought Davies. It's as if he thinks he can outrun his problems.

"I saw Philby's performance in fifty-five, Joshua. The bastard stage-managed a press conference at his mother's flat. Marcus Lipton was forced to apologize. And he did."

Davies was walking briskly by the D-G's side. There was no question that the last thirty years had been filled with disasters for the service and its sister organization SIS. And as Sir Gerald moved up, disaster had followed him like a shadow.

In 1961 there was the Navy Spy Ring headed by a KGB officer calling himself Gordon Lonsdale. In September of that year, poor benighted homosexual William Vassall was arrested. In 1963, the year Sir Gerald took over, Philby's defection. Then Blunt a year later. Brossard in 1965. On and on it went. From 1967 to 1977 Geoffrey Prime had passed all data from the top-secret electronic-communication center at Cheltenham. And what was more damning was that MI5 had caught none of them. Every one had been nabbed by information gleaned from Soviet and Polish defectors.

"So I'm going, Joshua," said the D-G. "Even if I don't get the golden handshake. Let the Knights of the British Empire do without me. I've got an ulcer, Joshua."

Davies stopped. "I didn't know."

"The pain's never far away. When it's bad, it's far worse than a toothache, yet waiting for the pain to return is worse than the pain itself." They resumed walking. "Sort of like Keats' 'Ode on a Grecian Urn' in reverse. But I don't expect the knighthood, Joshua."

"Oh, I'm sure . . ." Davies began, then broke off. He wasn't sure. The KBE was routine for retiring D-Gs, but guarantees no longer existed, and Gerald was . . .

"You think there's a mole, don't you?" Sir Gerald stopped and faced Davies. "I do hear things, you know. And maybe you think it's me."

"No. I definitely don't think you are a mole."

"I'm relieved," said the D-G. "Got any of those Hofnars you smoke?"

Davies gave him a huge grin. Reaching into his pocket, he pulled two cigars out and slipped the cellophane wrappers from them. Sir Gerald borrowed his cigar cutter. Both of them paused as a huge red-and-blue hot air balloon flew overhead. " 'Guinness Is Good for You,' " read Davies. "Wouldn't get in one of those without more than a dozen Guinness in me."

The D-G produced a butane lighter and Davies carefully rotated his cigar in the flame.

"Shouldn't use a lighter on a decent cigar,"

murmured Sir Gerald, "but needs must when the devil drives." He was still watching the balloon in the blue cloudless sky. "Wish I could get above it all, where the air is pure."

"Do you think . . . ?"

"There's a mole? I don't know. Used to think it was the stuff of espionage novels. Silly things. Ours is a world of dull, obscure people. Who'd want to write about us?"

He resumed his walk, slowly, with a more measured tread, and Davies fell in alongside him. They walked step for step, Davies over a foot taller than Sir Gerald.

"Our fondest wish is to be gray men. We ride buses, we hang on a strap in a tube train, and no one notices us. Assimilation. Trouble is we're the chameleons of policy, too. We're timid because years of avoiding confrontation make us afraid to stand up when we should.

"Hell, Joshua. Face it. These stable-door operations all showed one thing. Five is riddled with traitors; find one and you don't make a dent. The checks and balances don't work. Vassall, queer as a dog's hind leg. No one bothered to check him except that fellow who was so impressed to discover he was a member of the Bath Club. Jesus Christ, Joshua, what kind of a shop are we running?"

Davies nodded. The D-G had the bit between his teeth. He needed to have his say, poor bastard. "We could try the acid test," Joshua ventured.

"Oh yes. Add up the profit, subtract the loss. You think I didn't try that?" the D-G said. A strangled cry came from his lips. For a moment he seemed ready to fall, but Davies, who had been about to take his arm, thought it wiser not to.

The D-G recovered his balance and quickened his pace. A soccer ball bounced in front of him and he kicked at it savagely. "If I had any guts . . ." He mumbled something Davies couldn't hear.

The man was on the edge. Only retirement could save him now, and if he fell prey to his growing resentment, he would die a shriveled, embittered man. Davies let him talk.

"They've carved, in stone mind you, 'And Ye Shall Know the Truth and the Truth Shall Make You Free.' What is the truth, Joshua? Do you know? We don't allow ourselves mistakes. Make one, and the rules are changed so they're not mistakes."

They came to the embankment in front of the mock orange. The D-G stopped. "Do you see yourself in my job, Joshua? Or Strachan, or Rees, or that Uriah Heep, Rossiter?"

Davies started. "Well, it won't be me," he said and laughed. "Don't think I fit the corporate image, do you?"

"Lose sixty pounds and buy a pinstripe, and you'd have as much chance as any, better than most. Surely you've considered it?"

They stood together finishing their cigars.

"Well, I gave you Alex," Sir Gerald said. "At least I grabbed one prime asset for us."

Davies eyed the ash on his cigar. He didn't answer.

"Well? Didn't I?"

"That's one of the reasons I came," said Davies, tossing away the end of his Hofnar. "Alex was tainted. The Yanks caught him out. I got word early this morning. It's confirmed."

"Jesus!" The D-G's head went down. "Oh Christ. Everything I've touched . . . what's the damage?"

"He fed us a lot of poison. We're exposed in a lot of places, especially the Far East."

Sir Gerald's face was ashen.

"Can you pull any of the chestnuts out of the fire, Joshua?"

"We'll try," he told the older man. Then he said grimly, "Alex won't bother us anymore."

"He went for the walk?"

"Another fatal attack of the measles."

"I hope you'll consider running for D-G, Joshua. It's brains we need, desperately."

Davies linked his arm through Sir Gerald's and they crossed the ditch together.

"You need support and a campaign to run for D-G."

"Well, I'd take you any time. How could anyone take Rossiter seriously? Or Braithwaite. Hadn't even heard of him until last year. All that 'team-player' stuff and cozying up to the mandarins. Came out of nowhere."

They were walking down the brick pathway. "Or our new Penthesilea. Diana in a pantsuit. What's her secret? Where did all her support come from?"

"I suppose," said Davies carefully, "she hasn't offended enough people so as not to get support."

"Yes," said the D-G, opening the French doors, "that's what passes for leadership these days."

Millicent Tavistock and Dol were sitting next to a small table. On the table were a sherry decanter and glasses.

"Ah, jolly good," said Millicent warmly. "Just in time for sherry. You'll like this, Joshua; it's Verdelho."

Davies nodded, lowering himself to the sofa. Underneath him a spring twanged. Dolores looked apprehensive. Her brother clearly was depressed by his encounter with the D-G.

"Cheers," said Millicent brightly, offering glasses to the men.

"Cheers," muttered Joshua Davies, sipping carefully. It was as he supposed. The so-called sherry was Madeira; the Verdelho style was medium-dry, golden color. He did not feel he should tell his hostess that Madeira, while blended like a sherry, had first to be heated in an *estufa* at 120 degrees and then have brandy added to it.

When Millicent announced that Dol had accepted her invitation to lunch, he simply nodded. Dol, who had fought hard for his filet of sole cooked with litchis, was alarmed by his response. Either Josie had had a far worse time with the D-G than she thought, or he was sickening for something.

"Tuna casserole," he murmured. "Delightful."

5

The following morning, Millicent Tavistock's tuna casserole but an awful memory, Joshua Davies made his way to the office of the LCC coroner. His step was far from light, for the pathologist Davies had asked to examine some autopsy reports was a skilled scientist but also an evangelist on the vexing subject of diet. Only Davies' profound respect for Dr. Raymond Carleton's abilities made the Director face him.

At nine-thirty Joshua Davies, a white autopsy gown barely encompassing him, walked down a narrow fluorescent-lit hallway to the autopsy room. When he opened the door, he was assailed by the strong odor of the formaldehyde used to preserve bodies and organs. In front of him, under the cold white lights, was a long, windowless room. Stainless-steel autopsy tables were arranged in rows of three. Davies walked across the tiled floor to the table at the far end of the room.

Dr. Carleton was just removing the brain from a cadaver and putting it in a suspended scale.

"Joshua," he exclaimed, looking up. "That fellow's brain was four pounds—do you know Anatole France's was only thirty-five-point-eight ounces? Oh, I got your message and I've looked over the files." He nodded to a stack of them on a nearby table.

Davies looked around for a chair but had to content himself with a metal stool; it was cold, and he overflowed on all sides. "Did you eyeball those folders I sent?"

"Well, this chap's not going anywhere," the coroner said cheerfully. "Fell, or was pushed, from a third-floor window."

"I just wondered if there was anything odd about any of these cases." Davies tried to focus the man's attention.

The doctor stripped off his gloves, opened a trash can with his foot, and dropped them in. As usual his white gown was coming untied.

"One day you'll be on one of those tables," he declared in the same cheery tone. "It's all a question of what we eat."

"Er," interrupted Davies, squirming uneasily on the stool, "I'm in a bit of a hurry."

"Dairy products are the chief culprits," Dr. Carleton went on. "They cause more allergies than anything I know of—with the possible exception of buckwheat, though I did know a chap who swelled up at the mere sight of Swiss chard. Now, what have we got here?" The coroner took the folders to a stainless-steel autopsy table and arranged them neatly in rows.

From the top pocket of his lab coat he fished out a pair of reading glasses, stuck them on his thin pointed nose, and thrust his long, angular face close to the autopsy reports. Davies could remember when Carleton had a round, fat face. Now he looked like Abe Lincoln. There were deep creases around his mouth and eyes and his neck was scrawny. The white coat hung on his bony shoulders like a draped sheet.

A series of grunts, tut-tuttings, and a hollow laugh marked the doctor's progress through the files. At one point he looked up at Davies and said, "There's some cans of mixed vegetable juice in the fridge. You like tomato juice, I expect."

Davies shuddered. "No, thanks."

"When you think how much we medical men know about medicine, it's surprising we've not had better luck as murderers," the coroner said thoughtfully. "Palmer the poisoner, Pritchard, Lamson, Cross, Cream, the delightful Crippen, Smethurst. And they got him for bigamy." He shook his head. "Can't help you much, Joshua. The trail's cold. Take this stabbing, for instance."

Davies approached and peered at the victim's photograph.

"You see, the wounds weren't examined properly. These bruises on the skin indicated the knife was plunged in so hard the handle bruised the flesh. Yet no one poured barium sulfate in the crevices to determine the size and shape of the blade by x-ray. Sloppy."

He glowered at the next folder. "Here's a woman of thirty-five who commits suicide by mixing pills and alcohol. Hmm. That proves she wasn't a pill addict. If she had been, the pills would have been dumped into the intestinal tract."

"Could someone have forced them down her throat and followed them with booze?"

Without answering, the pathologist crossed the tiled floor and opened the refrigerator door. Davies caught a glimpse of pharmaceuticals and several cans of vegetable juice. Dr. Carleton carefully stripped off the metal seal and poured red liquid into a beaker. "Your health," he said.

"Right," Davies replied, "but—?"

"Come over here." The pathologist lifted a plastic sheet away from one of the tables. A corpse, its eyes open, stared up at them. The doctor lifted one of the hands; it was enclosed in a plastic bag.

"See this bag? It wasn't done in your cases. So if the girl struggled and got some hair or skin under her nails, there was no attempt to preserve it. There is a mention of some hair being pulled from her scalp. . . ."

"Well?"

"If you want to hold someone down and not leave any marks, the hair is the obvious place to grab." He drank from the beaker and, to Davies' amazement, seemed to relish the concoction.

The Director thrust his hands deep into his pockets. His gown was hitched up like an ill-fitting nightshirt. The pathologist was eyeing him, and Davies felt uneasy.

"Have you ever considered a cytotoxic test, Joshua? You get a computer readout on over a hundred fifty-three items." He paused dramatically, then nodded toward Davies' belly significantly. "Any one of which might, at this very moment, be breaking down blood cells by the million!"

"I—"

"From funguses to psyllium seed."

"Yes, right."

The pathologist picked up a folder. "This one is interesting."

"Oh?"

"The death certificate says the man died of mycloid leukemia. When the body was discovered, three days had passed since the probable time of death. There was some suspicion of morphine poisoning since a trace of it was found in the stomach." He carefully replaced the folder, keeping them all in precise piles.

"Morphine poisoning was rejected because the telltale pinpoint contraction of the eyes was missing."

"A natural death then?"

The pathologist paused, and Davies waited expectantly.

"Perhaps. But the eyes will dilate if belladonna is squeezed into them. And when people don't suspect murder, they miss the obvious."

He tapped an open folder. "This man was a drug addict."

Davies grunted. "No doubt about that. I know the case."

The pathologist eyed him over his glasses. "Yes, but did he inject himself the final time?"

Joshua Davies sighed deeply and scooped up the folders. "The needle doesn't talk."

Dr. Carleton walked him to the door. "You're wrong there. Everyone's body is a little different, and all punctures have distinctive signatures. But no one even took a picture of the marks. We'll never know now. You've got some circumstantial evidence but nothing I'd swear to." He touched Davies' huge arm. "Why don't you stay to lunch? I've got some goat's cheese and a kale salad with bean sprouts."

"Er, thanks," replied the alarmed Director, "some other time. Very busy, you know."

He was safely out of the building seconds later.

2 Molehill

In an anonymous building in Curzon Street, centrally located in West 1 and conveniently adjacent to Park Lane and Hyde Park, are the hermetically sealed offices of MI5. MI5 hosts all DIC conferences. But because everyone knows this particular location, it is thought expedient to hold important gatherings elsewhere. The weekly meeting of the Defense Intelligence Committee is, therefore, held in another, more secure, location. The British secret service is not in the business of assisting the two bored Russians who sit night and day with a light amplifier and camera above the tobacconist's on the corner of Chesterfield Gardens.

The conferences varied in size depending upon the issues involved, but the big three under the DIC umbrella—MI5, SIS, and Special Branch—were always represented at DIC meetings. MI5 was still referred to as Five. Name changes had taken place over the years and the service was, strictly speaking, DI5, but no one bothered to keep up.

The official duty of DIC was to coordinate policy, but its role usually was to keep MI5 and SIS from open warfare. Few people relished attending the weekly gabfest since the Foreign Office types were determined to wrest control of any action from their equally determined rivals in the Home Office. SIS was Foreign Office, MI5 was Home Office.

Meetings were held in an elegant Regency House built by Beau Nash for his crony, the Prince Regent. However, entrance to the meeting room itself could be made only via an underground passageway leading from a building two hundred yards away on Elizabeth Street.

The three meeting rooms were completely sealed off from the rest of the building, and the house itself was ostensibly the dwelling of an eccentric recluse who never left it. A small office was available to the chair of the committee; a large anteroom served as a collecting point, and the meetings themselves were held in an elegantly papered room, its ceiling ornamented by moldings on mythological themes. Gentlemen in full court regalia looked down from gilt frames. The windows were concealed by heavy red velvet draperies, not for aesthetic reasons but because laser technology had made it possible to "read" speech vibrations from windowpanes. To prevent microwave penetration, each window was shielded on the inside by steel mesh shutters. In addition, white noise was transmitted whenever a meeting took place.

The committee members sat at a long baize table, in high-backed green velvet chairs. Those under Foreign Office control sat on one side, the Home Office sat on the other. They could argue better that way. Only Waterford crystal pitchers and glasses stood between them.

As an unprecedented mark of the changing times, the Man from the Ministry was now the Woman from the Ministry. She dressed very severely in black and smoked little black cigarettes. Around her neck on a gold chain was a small watch that she tried hard not to look at too frequently. The WM's patience was often strained, and unlike her predecessor, who had let meetings drift aimlessly, she attempted to apply the choke chain when things got out of hand. But she knew how important it was to give the appearance of a democratically run meeting, so she permitted people to have their say as long as they were brief about it. That was one of the main reasons for the committee's existence, after all.

Julian Monteith from SIS Security, white-haired, hangdog, with a gap between his front teeth, was explaining the advantages of color badge security. Like all his ideas, he'd gotten it from the Americans.

"So Security Defense means green badges for all those having access to most things. Yellow is for foreign reps, and red for those having less than a full clearance."

No one said anything.

"Anyone transporting documents must first get a courier's badge." His voice rose to a falsetto, the signal that he was stressing a point.

Scruffy Rees was patiently examining the sole of his shoe; almost everyone else looked glumly at the green baize tabletop. Wallace Rossiter, Deputy Director-General, fixed a smile on his face and tried to look encouraging. The WM regarded Julian with an expression that betrayed nothing of what she was really thinking.

"And to the dozen color badges, you could add further access control by means of tabs attached to the chain above the badge."

"I'd like to jerk his chain," muttered Scruffy in a stage whisper.

Julian sat down. There was the usual stirring, shuffling of papers. There was always the faint hope that something interesting might come along.

"Very significant," said Wallace Rossiter. Rossiter intended to take over when the current D-G retired. The WM decided he had a good chance. As Rossiter had never taken a firm stand on any important issue, he was popular with Whitehall. One thing was agreed upon. Rossiter had staying power—that was infinitely more important than anything else.

"Yes, quite," echoed Reginald Compton-Basset, who resembled the hound of his name. Reggie was the parliamentarian. He had a vast knowledge of the rules of order—none of which was ever needed. Some complained that Bassie was never in his office because he was a member of every committee; most were just as glad.

Rossiter, was absentmindedly twirling his black horn-rimmed glasses. He had recently begun sporting a pencil-thin mustache, Ronald Colman style. He took out a slim gold cigarette case and extracted a Dunhill, and Freddy Gilbert hurriedly produced his porcelain lighter. There wasn't anything else for Freddy to do except toady to Rossiter. He was junior to everyone in the room and twenty years younger.

Even his aviator glasses marked him as part of another generation.

Rossiter had produced only one *bon mot* in all the time the Woman from the Ministry had known him. At a discussion around the sherry decanter someone had once said, "Davies is his own worst enemy," and Rossiter wittily responded, "Not while I'm alive, he isn't." Joshua heard of it and remembered.

Reluctantly the WM looked down at the agenda. "There's more on the Bitov business," she said. "Alaister?"

Alaister Strachan, from Department C, showed no sign he had heard her, continuing his ritual of cleaning, packing, and relighting a pipe that seemed incapable of staying lit. He had heard, however. The heavy-lidded eyes opened a little, the eyes slate gray and intense.

"You will recall we bagged a defector named Bitov a couple of years ago. Low-level chap. Anyway, he went back to our Russian friends with a tale that we had hit him over the head and kidnapped him in Italy," he said slowly.

There were hollow laughs and some tut-tuts from around the table. Scruffy Rees blew a raspberry.

"He's dead."

There was an embarrassed silence. The WM realized that despite Strachan's Scots ancestry, barely a trace of his lowland accent came out in his conversation. A scholarship boy, she thought. Ashamed of his poor background, he'd tried to eliminate all reminders of it. But Strachans' conversation was dry and witty, and he liked to tell the odd off-color joke. Certainly he was good at briefings, concise and clear. Unless addressed directly, he said nothing. Unlike many of his less talented colleagues, he did not delight in stirring the pot. He had finished and was concentrating on the edge of the table, the bulldog pipe clenched between his teeth.

The WM went back to her agenda. "Courtleigh, I think it's your turn."

The man addressed was the fourth child of a bishop, with a law degree and a tremendous inferiority complex about the successes of his famous and more talented brothers. He had an irritating habit of talking out of the side of his mouth.

"We'll be having a seminar on flaps and seals over in Admin next Tuesday at ten if anyone has an interest."

No one expressed any, so he subsided.

The WM looked at Leonard Rogers and his yes-man, Hector Sweeney. Rogers wore his hair long to disguise ears that jutted straight out of his head at right angles. He had begun to lose his hair, and he sported a red carnation in his buttonhole in the fond belief it made him look like Pierre Trudeau. Sweeney's only distinguishing feature was a ginger mustache. Rogers shook his head, and Sweeney did the same.

Scruffy Rees stirred in his chair. "I'm pretty busy, so if . . ." Scruffy was looking as untidy as usual. His jacket, made, it was rumored, of vole skin, hung from the back of his chair. Around Scruffy's neck was a Guards tie, loosened. Naturally, Scruffy's hair was mussed.

"There is one thing," the WM announced

quickly. "To do with Anglo-American cooperation."

The less respectful members of the committee made a great show of preparing to pay attention. Monty Abrahams of Ciphers said loudly, "Oh, *well* then."

Rossiter looked at him disdainfully. Monty, besides being Jewish, was a big, heavy man radiating an atmosphere of working-class pleasures—beer and rugby on Saturdays. It was Abrahams who had, as Rossiter heard from Freddy Gilbert, used the phrase "creeping Jesus" to describe his opinion of Rossiter's climb to the D-Gship.

Rossiter suspected all Jews on the grounds that they were potential agents of Israel's Mossad. Once, when he had voiced this theory in Abraham's hearing, the Jew had solemnly agreed, adding, "Same thing's true of Catholics, don't you agree, Wallace?"

Rossiter, who had occasionally felt Catholic longings, was startled. For an awful moment he believed Monty Abrahams had divined his dreadful secret. There was, naturally, no chance of a Catholic's becoming D-G.

"Not the same thing at all," he added huffily. "I didn't mean you, Monty."

Monty stood up; his pinstripe suit looked ragged. He only wore it for DIC meetings and could never remember to get it dry cleaned and pressed. He was also the only person in the room with a tan. Every year he spent a month in Anguilla; he had just returned, and the English weather hadn't yet reduced his skin tone to London pallor.

"The UK-USA Agreement signed in 1947 gives us access to everything the Americans get." He paused and looked around the room. "And vice versa." Only Scruffy bit, with a barking laugh.

His voice rose. "It's because of this agreement that our documents carry words like 'Vipar,' 'Trine,' and 'Umbra,' instead of 'Top Secret,' which does at least make sense. Anyway, the Americans suspect there have been leaks; they blame us, of course."

The WM had her mouth firmly closed; her lips were just a thin line of disapproval. Other members of the committee registered scorn in varying degrees. Scruffy contented himself with a loud "Shit!"

"All I'm asking," said Monty, toying with a pencil in his hands, "is that you lock your desks at night. And maybe—"

The double doors burst open, one side banging into the wall. Ignoring the commotion, Joshua Davies, a briefcase in each hand, made his erratic way to the end of the table. Scruffy, who had been tilting back in his chair, one foot against the table leg, hurriedly moved to his right to make room.

Davies was surrounded by cigar smoke, for he had a Hofnar glowing in his mouth. Without preamble or greeting, he opened the slimmer of the two briefcases. It was upside down, as usual, and there was a muttered exclamation as he flipped it over and delved into its contents.

Rossiter eyed his colleague over the top of his glasses. It defied all common sense. This lumbering ox was a full Director, only a rung or two below himself, and some had suggested Davies might rise even higher. Rossiter admitted this to no one, but he was relieved when Davies let it be known he was content to remain head of D Branch. Trouble was, this fleshy giant had the tidiest and best-organized brain in MI5. His memory was legendary.

The WM sat down and allowed the Director to speak, for, clearly, Davies had taken charge.

Referring to a folder, he said, "It's possible, even probable, we've been infiltrated at the highest level. If I'm right . . ." He stopped and stared balefully around the room. "If I'm right, everything—and I do mean everything—we've done in the last ten years was engineered by the KGB."

The reaction was what Davies expected. The WM came to alarmed attention instantly. Her eyes narrowed; others must have shared her thoughts. Why was Davies tipping his hand? This put everyone on his guard. It was a dangerous technique; call out, "Fire!" and see who runs for the exits.

The Director, while apparently glancing vaguely around the room, quickly scanned the faces; it was a faint hope and, he realized, futile. Deep penetration agents prepared for this moment all their lives. They knew how to play all aspects of their roles, even during a crisis.

Rossiter, seeing the alarm on the WM's face, attempted to gain points with her by adopting his weary-of-the-world tone and asking if Davies was going into the mole-catching business.

At the word *mole* there was a great deal of restlessness. "What's missing?" asked Sweeney incautiously. It was an error in judgment, for Davies now had the opening he needed. Sweeney saw his error. Waving an arm helplessly, he began, "I don't mean . . ."

Joshua Davies assumed his professorial stance, feet firmly on the ground, and said, "Espionage is robbery." He dug inside his jacket for a new cigar. "But the trick is to notice what's been stolen. You don't call in the Metropolitan Police, because nothing may be missing." He purposely adopted a tone of saintly indulgence, his manner indicating that he should not have been asked so simple a question. While searching for his cigars, he found his pince-nez, looked somewhat baffled to find it, and hooked it over the top of his waistcoat.

"Now, Joshua, this is all pretty . . ." began Rossiter, but the Director ignored him, waving his cigar cutter for emphasis while continuing his lecture.

"In fact, if any documents are out of place, it usually means nothing. Even the most half-arsed spy doesn't take stuff long enough for it to be missed."

He paused. Soon great clouds of smoke were issuing from the Director's mouth as he played a match around the flat end of the cigar. The WM leapt in. "I think we can discuss this another . . ."

Davies smiled benignly at her; she felt like a little girl being sent to the headmistress's study. She sighed. Could she possibly have wanted this job? Really wanted it? It had seemed like a great coup at the time. Resting her elbows on the arms of her chair, she supported her chin on interlaced fingers and prepared to listen to a long dissertation.

"You don't say," continued Davies with extraordinary patience. "Come and look. Someone has broken in and stolen the plans to the latest nuclear missile."

"Well, what have you got then?" asked Rogers triumphantly. "Eh?"

"Right," said Sweeney.

"I've got a list here of thirty agents at various levels who've died in the last ten years." He leaned forward over the table. "For your info, all of them could have been sanctioned."

My God," exploded Rossiter, coming to his feet, "you've gone too far! How on earth can you claim that?"

"Does seem a bit much," drawled Strachan, favoring Davies with an appraising look. "Sure you haven't gone a bit overboard?"

Rossiter subsided into his chair.

Davies pulled on his Hofnar until the end glowed fierce red. "If it's true, this organization is suspect at the highest level."

The WM decided to assert her authority. Rising to her feet, she asked Davies point-blank, "If we've lost all these people, how is it only you know it? And another thing—we must expect casualities. We're on the firing line. Regrettable though any losses are, the average is only three a year."

"God Almighty!" snarled Davies. "We're not talking about three a year, or about thirty. We're talking about years of training and 'next of kin' losses—to say nothing of the individuals themselves."

"I realize—"

"What Joshua is saying," Monty interrupted, trying to soothe things, "is that any loss is a severe blow. It may take years to get someone in that empty slot. A great deal, a *very* great deal, depends on personal rapport. Lose one man and a whole cell goes mute. Happened in Cairo; ghastly affair. Awful!" The last word was almost a squeak.

"Damn right," agreed Davies. "Damn right."

"All this talk of moles gets my goat," complained Rogers. "It all began with these so-called novels. Damn pain in the arse if you ask me. Not a bit convincing, the product of literary hacks and unscrupulous publishers. What I'd like to know is, What happened to good novelists like A. J. Cronin?"

"They died," said Davies.

"As a matter of fact," began Reggie Compton-Basset, "the term did not originate with espionage novels at all. . . ."

"I don't think—" interrupted the WM in alarm.

"—Karl Marx in a speech in 1865, if memory serves, said, 'the old mole that can work in the earth so fast, that worthy pioneer of the Revolution.' Naturally, there are antecedents, like Shakespeare's *Hamlet,* and nothing can be said with absolute certainty." He looked around as if mystified to have their attention. He had done what no one else could—reduced the room to silence.

"Er, yes, thank you, Bassie," said the WM at last.

Reggie Compton-Basset looked pleased. "A mole is a deeply penetrated agent; the correct term is 'deep penetration agent,' but after all those spy novels, our own people started using the term. Most moles are nationals, not foreigners, though there are exceptions. Some of the most fanatical, surprisingly, are those who have most to lose under Socialism."

The WM looked at him over the top of her glasses in what she believed was her chilling look. "I don't think the subject of moles is on the agenda."

"It is now," said Davies, refusing to sit down or yield the floor.

"Where did this info come from?" demanded Julian Monteith. "It didn't cross my desk." He made it sound as if this were the only criterion. Davies produced a large white handkerchief from his pocket and blew his nose in a loud trumpet of defiance.

"The deadliest enemy of all is a penetrator, an agent of an enemy intelligence service who has successfully infiltrated ours. This list"—he held it up—"is the work of one of our more distinguished ex-colleagues, *nom de guerre* Badger."

Rossiter let out a snort; Davies ignored him.

"Badger is no longer with us, but before he left he noticed some damn funny coincidences, and a very high accident rate. He began to compile a report, but before he had much information he resigned."

"None too soon," Rossiter said in a stage whisper to Freddy Gilbert, who nodded vigorously.

"I asked him to continue his analysis," continued Davies. "Once outside the wood he began to see the trees. . . ."

"Trees, but no facts," objected Leonard Rogers, his short, spiky mustache twitching at his witty sally. Everyone ignored him and he lapsed back into obscurity.

"Before Badger left, he made a very detailed analysis of the necrology . . ." Davies paused, then repeated the word slowly, "necrology of this organization."

Davies had their full attention. He drew on his cigar, looked around, and balanced it carefully on the solid-glass ashtray. "Nothing came of it. Then, a couple of weeks ago, his brother returned from America with an actuarial program produced by some whiz kids for insurance companies."

"I don't see," Rossiter muttered, "how—"

"The point is," Davies went on, "with some modifications this program suggested our losses were way out of line."

"Well, of course," said Rossiter. "We're in a risky business." He looked around for support. "It's them or us." Sensing majority support, he continued in the lazy tone he often adopted to show these errant children the folly of their ways. "Badger did have some damn funny ideas."

"What funny ideas?" asked Monty Abrahams, doodling on the paper in front of him; jet planes with swept wings filled the page.

"Well," said Rossiter, leaning back in his chair and straightening his legs, "it was Badger's belief that Hugh Gaitskell, leader of the

Labour Party in 1962, was poisoned by the Russians."

"For what purpose, may I ask?" demanded Sweeney.

"Badger's theory," drawled Rossiter, "was that our Russian friends poisoned his coffee and biscuits to induce lupus so Harold Wilson, whose left-wing credentials were more reliable, would get the job.

"Badger," he went on, "also wanted to get a defector out of East Berlin by hijacking a subway train and crossing under the Wall. His theory on the Kennedy assassination was equally exotic, but I won't bore you with it." He stuck out his arms and made a great display of adjusting his shirt cuffs. "He had talent, but he will be no loss to Five's diadem. He did not exactly bear the service up on empyrean wings."

"Empyreal," interjected Bassie helpfully.

"What?"

"*Empyreal* is the adjective, *empyrean* is the noun."

"Thank you, Bassie," said the WM.

"We have had more than our fair share of moles," murmured Strachan to no one in particular. "Look at Philby. Hard to take us seriously after that."

"Philby was an illegal, not a mole," said Bassie, rubbing the symmetrical bags under his eyes. "It's a nice distinction but—"

"There's no goddam difference," interrupted Davies harshly. "The bastards, whatever you call them, are getting our people killed."

Strachan looked at Davies curiously. The man was usually expert at times like this. He was normally the soul of patience, leading his listeners to his point of view instead of bullying and hectoring. Was the fat man losing his grip?

"Whatever they are called," summed up the WM, "there's no proof beyond Badger's word."

"Couldn't we impose a closer watch on the Russians?" asked Rogers. "Watch them around the clock, as it were, and nail the most suspicious blighters? I mean, we all know moles have to be serviced."

"That's right," said Monty eagerly. "Find the Embassy contact and you get the mole."

"There isn't any mole," snapped Rossiter, afraid he was losing momentum. "It's a fantasy of an ex-agent who shouldn't have had the data in the first place. Besides"—he resumed his lecture voice—"it takes a minimum of thirty men to maintain a watch upon *one* suspect agent. I'm sure Bassie can list the number of Russians who might be suspects," he finished acidly.

"It would be difficult," Compton-Basset mused thoughtfully. "There are consular and embassy premises in Kensington Palace Gardens, diplomatic addresses in Edith Road and Ken's Earls Terrace." He gathered steam. "And there is the trade and diplomatic enclave in Highgate. The press johnnies are in Rosary Gardens, and Aeroflot has—"

"I believe Bassie's made his point," said Rossiter smoothly.

"Well, what do you think, Freddy?" asked the WM, turning to him. "We haven't heard from you."

Davies sat down. He had to admire their new leader; she knew Freddy Gilbert wouldn't dare contradict his boss. Real leaders always asked the lowest on the totem pole first. No one would be afraid to have his say then.

As expected, Freddy mumbled something about Badger's jumping to conclusions, and Rossiter smiled as if Freddy's opinion had been given without prejudice and agreed with his own on merit alone.

Davies got to his feet and produced a folder from his slim attaché case. "Badger's analysis was no mere half-arsed computer comparison," he said. "The lad had talent and also determination. I just got this pile of stuff"—he waved his hand over his briefcases—"today. When you see it all together, it makes it look as if someone's been knocking off our agents one by one like the ten little Indian boys." He smiled deprecatingly. "It's a heavy rate of expenditure for an organization like Five and for SIS, too." He produced a sheaf of computer printouts.

"Item one: Code name Cowslip." There was a brief titter of laughter, quickly suppressed. "Courier section. Thirty-five years old; she commits suicide by swallowing pills and gin. Yet she's a damn sight better Methodist than I am and never touched alcohol. Also, some hair may have been torn out of her head when she was being held down—no bruises.

"Item two: Code name Lucretia. Apparent rape-murder. No suspects, though someone was arrested for similar attacks in the same general area."

"Well then?" said Rogers.

Strachan stirred in his seat, tenting his fingers and resting his elbows on the arms of his chair. "I didn't know Badger well, but he may be on to something. If I may quote Goethe, our problem is 'We only see what we look for; we look for only what we know.' Thus we're not suspicious because we haven't analyzed the data objectively."

"Neither has Badger," said the WM testily. "He only saw what he was looking for, too."

"I don't see anything," insisted Rogers. "As I understand it, Badger felt we were losing agents at too fast a rate, that accidents weren't really accidents and suicides could be murders. Well, surely there were coroner's reports and autopsies?"

"Damn right," Davies agreed, pulling a green folder out and opening it. "Code name Cobra. White male, forty-five. Heart attack. Forty-five and a heart attack?"

"It happens," said Rossiter loftily. "My cousin Cuthbert—"

"It also happens," replied Davies, "that the KGB has a spray that can be disguised as a pen or cigarette lighter that can simulate the fatal symptoms of a heart attack."

"That's pushing it a bit, don't you think?" inquired Rogers. "A bit on the paranoid side, what?"

"Is it? How about this, then? Code name: Florence. Shot herself *in the shower.* Reason given: She was becoming deaf. Verdict: Suicide caused by acute depression." He glared around the table. "Badger's program kicked that case out, and I looked at the reports."

No one said anything. "Her apartment was a mess," continued Davies. "She was sloppy, was our Florence, but she carefully drew the shower curtains so the blood wouldn't mess up the bathroom. Oh, and no one in the apartment building heard the shot."

"What's your point?" asked the WM, seated sideways in her chair and drawing on a cigarette.

Davies gave a derisive hoot. "The whole bloody thing stinks. For one thing"—he glared angrily at Rossiter—"when untidy people stick guns under their chins and blow their goddam heads off, I'm suspicious of drawn shower curtains. The curtain protected the killer and his clothes. When I find the bullet scarcely penetrated the top of the skull, I figure it was a low-power shell, probably carefully prepared to make minimum noise and also not go through the wall and kill the neighbor's castrated ginger tomcat."

Scruffy Rees tried but failed to stifle a laugh.

"Finally," continued Davies, "I wouldn't expect even a secretary to *type* a suicide note, much less an untidy Russian translator from the Government Codes and Ciphers School who was, according to her supervisor, a lousy typist."

"One finds it an interesting theory," allowed Rogers, gnawing absentmindedly on his lower lip. "Could it be proved?"

Davies looked at him. "No," he admitted. "I don't even have the fresh cup of hot chocolate Florence put on the bedstand for her little nightcap. All the evidence was destroyed by our people as a routine precaution.

"There's a lot more here. A hit-and-run. Another suicide—oh, left instructions for a wake-up call at eight the next morning. And there was Hawk, killed in that IRA bombing at the Ship and Whale."

"Well that's just like the IRA," commented Rogers. "It was down in the docks, and they got several navy blokes."

Davies whirled on him. "That's the damn point. Hide your murders as something else. Well, I ran Hawk, and I owe him more than bloody small talk. I don't expect anything intelligent to come out of here. All the wisdom this committee has produced could be written on the head of a pin and still leave room for plenty of angels." With that, Joshua Davies subsided into his chair and began pounding out his cigar in the ashtray.

The WM tapped the table with her fingers. She rose. "I think we all feel for Joshua's loss." She paused, perhaps expecting a reaction from Davies, but he continued to stare at the table. "There seems to be some circumstantial evidence, but I must confess I cannot—"

"Ah, I've no time for this mole, double-mole, triple-cross stuff," snorted Rogers.

"Right," Sweeney echoed.

"It's all guesswork. None of the so-called evidence is left to be examined. We're at the point where no one can have an accident without someone crying KGB." Rogers sat back looking very pleased with himself.

Rossiter decided to take over. "Paranoia's all right in this business," he said in his conciliatory tone. "C always used to say, 'Practice paranoia before all else.' But I honestly feel Badger and Joshua have gone a bit too far on this one." He took the briefest possible pause, then picked up a paper in front of him. "I want to remind all of you that the Diplock Committee Report back in . . . in . . ."

"May 1982," prompted Freddy Gilbert.

"Right, May 1982—thank you, Freddy—declared the government free of hostile penetration."

"It also," growled Davies, leaning forward pugnaciously, "warned that hostile infiltration of SIS and the diplomatic services was still a danger."

"I am prepared to believe that Hawk was simply an innocent victim."

" 'Innocent victim'! That's a damned neat phrase." Davies growled.

"I am prepared to believe the IRA planted that bomb at that pub," continued Rossiter. "Let's face facts. There was a telephoned warning just before it went off, and there was definitely an Irish accent."

"Oh? Did the caller use words like *boyho* and *begorrah?*"

Scruffy failed again to stifle his laughter.

"And there was part of a body near the bomb. I must say," Rossiter continued brightly, "there is a certain satisfaction in the fact that a great many people planting bombs become victims of their own ineptitude."

"They have admitted that more of their people have been killed planting bombs than by our security services," agreed Strachan, nodding slowly.

"Well, let's take their word for it," Davies put in. "We know we can trust the IRA."

During the embarrassed silence that followed, Davies mentally reviewed the men around him. Was it possible one of them was a mole? Could Badger be so far off the mark? He hadn't thought there might be a traitor high up in MI5 or SIS until he'd seen the list. What worried him was the wide range of people included; they ranged from top-level agents to typists. Of course even the typists took six months to vet; that was a long time when one was needed. But ten years? And why one mole? Why not two? Three?

Rogers was talking now. "Joshua seems to forget we have improved the system of positive vetting."

"Positive vetting," said Davies wearily, "is a snare and a delusion. It checks public records and bank statements. We have a dozen cases of people with criminal pasts who got by positive vetting."

Rogers continued, "There is something to be said for the old 'I-knew-your-father' system."

"The fact is," Davies said, "positive vetting applies only to those who have regular and constant access to secret info. People slip by. We've had black magicians, gays who got themselves put into novels, God knows what else. Can any of you see a bloody Russian spy admitting he is a member of the Communist Party of Great Britain?"

"I think Joshua's got something here," agreed Scruffy. "After all, the 'I-knew-your-father' system came a real cropper with Philby."

"Philby was thirty years ago," snapped Rossiter. "I do wish people would stop digging that up all the time."

"Well," said Strachan, packing his pipe with his favorite Borkum Riff with whiskey flavor, "don't forget that *Encyclopaedia Britannica* salesman who got to the third floor of Curzon Street."

"Sold three sets, as I recall," added Monty smoothly.

There was laughter at this and even the WM smiled. "Perhaps," said Strachan, "we should follow our American friends and introduce lie-detector tests and a Father Confessor? It's reliably reported that there has never been a single case of a padded expense account in the CIA."

The WM seized the moment. The crisis had passed. Davies had been neutralized and appeared willing to accept his fate.

"I think we should bear in mind," pronounced the WM, "Prime Minister Thatcher's statement that the real danger is the KGB's ability to penetrate secrets stored or processed electronically. That"—she cast a glance around the table—"is not, I am happy to say, within our purview."

"What's a damn shame," said Rogers plaintively, "is how difficult it is to penetrate the Russkies. Every bloody person from the Ambassador to the dishwasher is an import. We send in someone to screw the cook, and next thing you know she's a major in the KGB and our agent's head is fished out of the Thames at Purfleet."

The WM tactfully steered the conversation back to the topic in hand and neatly nailed its epitaph to the tombstone. "Joshua is to be commended for his investigation. We need more initiative in Five."

Davies made a face, unclamped his jaw, then subsided with a grunt that might have meant anything.

"We have a tenuous enough liaison with the police as it is," the WM went on. "Arthur will bear me out on that." Scruffy managed a nod of assent. "So, although Joshua has something that might, just might, be suspicious, I don't feel I can go to the Home Secretary and tell him the police may have missed the boat in a couple of cases. Nothing seemed amiss to the eyes of trained detectives, and I'm afraid, Joshua, we must go with that, however much impressed you are with Badger's list." Trying to be fair, she waited in case he had anything to add, but Davies' pouchy, lined face betrayed no emotion. He sat, apparently uninterested in the proceedings.

"I'm sorry, Joshua, but there it is."

At that moment, the arrival of tea signaled the end of the meeting. Two guards entered wheeling a cart with a coffee urn, several teapots of tarnished silver, and a silver cow creamer.

Scruffy joined Davies, who was munching on one of the gingernut biscuits that accompanied tea breaks throughout Whitehall. It was believed that only Davies ever ate one.

"Tough luck, Josh. They didn't bite; can't expect them to. Far too imaginative for this lot. Maybe for me too."

Davies grunted. He always found himself alternately repulsed and attracted by Scruffy's face—a road map of patches of skin grafted to cover the damage done in a flaming car crash almost ten years before. Every graft seemed slightly different in texture and color.

"Waste of time. Knew it anyway."

Scruffy took one of the cups and opened the tap at the bottom of the coffee urn; a gray liquid sloshed out. "Nobody wants a new fluency committee," he said. "Remember the last one?" Shuddering, he added three lumps of sugar to his coffee. "Nothing got done for the best part of a year. Why did they call it a 'fluency committee,' by the way?"

"Why not?"

"I suppose."

"Well, I've had my say," Joshua told him. "Might as well have written it in sand for all the good it's done, but my conscience is clear." He moved away, leaving Scruffy in sole command of the unwanted gingernuts.

"Joshua."

Alaister Strachan, his saucer placed over the top of his cup to protect the carpet from spills, moved to his side. "Damn fine effort. Best I've seen in a long time."

"Hmm."

"Don't be downcast." He slid his saucer under the cup and took a drink. "God, that's awful stuff."

"What do you think?"

"I try not to, Joshua, old boy. But I must say, I wasn't totally convinced. Your theory calls for someone a sight smarter than this lot."

"It might be you," said Davies.

"Or you, Joshua. It wouldn't be the first time the villain attracted attention to himself, then saw the matter laid to rest." He smiled. "But I don't think it is you, Joshua."

"Thanks."

"My concerns are twofold." Strachan took another sip, grimaced, and put his cup on the table nearby. "If we make a stink without being sure, the Yanks may get nervous. The UK-USA Agreement is vital, Joshua, vital. Lose that and we won't get one-tenth of what we get now. D'ye see what I am saying?"

Davies nodded.

"Second, I'm not so sure this isn't a little disinformation at work. Our Russian friends have a lot to gain by carefully planting the idea there is a mole at work in SIS or MI5. It turns everything upside down and it distracts us." He looked around the room; the committee had broken into small groups. "I mean, let's face it, Joshua, you can't announce to a bunch of administrators that every damn thing they've done for the last decade was useless. We've all made sacrifices for the cause."

"You're probably right."

"Of course I am. Hell, man, they've paid their dues, and they want to reach pension heaven without someone stirring up the hive." He sucked on his teeth. "Och! They have faced marital battles, children gone wrong because fathers couldn't be there, homes uprooted for postings to some godforsaken foreign pesthole. If they had to face the fact that it was all for nothing, how could they stay this side of madness? It's why I never married. Years in the military, then twenty more in Five and SIS. It's too much to ask of anyone."

Davies grunted. "Wish you'd given me that advice years ago. A mistress would have suited me better than a wife."

The Scot's face clouded. "What real difference would it make? Once you have an emotional attachment you lay yourself open to attack."

Davies nodded. "Hostages to fortune, eh?"

"Exactly. It's better to pay for it, eh?"

The Director flashed him a look; Strachan was smiling. "Know what I mean? Nudge, nudge, wink, wink."

Praying he hadn't blushed, Davies replied, "Wouldn't know about that." Anxious to change the subject he said, "The WM has gone."

"Aye. But she'll not tell the Minister anything. The rule is, and this lassie has her eye on a higher throne, Don't worry the mandarins unnecessarily. We don't want a flue brush put up our arses by some parliamentary committee."

Davies gulped his tea and made a mental note to insist that sherry be put back on the tea wagon. It had recently been dropped as an economy measure. He'd present the bottles himself if it came to that.

"Well, Alaister, what do you think?"

"About what?"

"Moles."

"History is on your side, Joshua, but it's like shouting, 'Fire!' Somewhere you can be certain there is one, but unless you see the smoke, there's no way to tell which building is burning." He gazed pointedly around the room. "Rossiter, Bassie, Scruffy—not much smoke there. No fire for damn sure."

"You forgot yourself."

"Aye. I did." He added, "And his nibs, Sir G. And you too, Joshua. It would be easier for you than anyone else." He looked the Director up and down. "But there's nary a whiff of smoke about you. Give me your cup."

Sliding his hand into his suit pocket, Strachan took out a curved silver flask. "Genuine Scotch, my friend, and you won't find this on sale at Harrod's."

Davies sipped the fiery liquor.

"Good, eh?"

Davies nodded agreement.

"Have you heard this one? Man goes to his doctor. 'I want to be castrated,' he says. 'Well, I won't do it,' says the doc. So he goes to another doctor. 'I want to be castrated,' he says. Of course the doctor refuses. Finally he finds one who'll do it. The doc does the surgery, and the guy wakes up the next day, his thing swathed in bandages.— You haven't heard this have you?"

"No."

" 'Well, is it done, Doctor?' asks the man.

" 'It is,' replies the doc, 'but you're the first man who ever asked me to do that to him. I have the odd request for a circumcision . . .'

" 'Circumcision! That's what I meant,' says the man. 'Is there a difference?' "

Strachan looked at Davies. "Well?"

"I heard it last week," replied Joshua Davies.

3 The Unknown Prisoner

The cell was square, perfectly square. If the prisoner chose he could verify the fact; he could pace six feet along one wall and the same distance on the door side. But he did not permit himself to perform for them. The cell was high, the ceiling just out of the reach of a high leap. The prisoner did not leap; he seldom moved and then only with a purpose.

He was in his sixties, a little gray hair along the sides of his head, otherwise bald. The man had worn glasses at one time; a tuck in the bridge of his nose had been surgically removed recently. There was a suggestion of dark puffiness under his eyes, but the eyes themselves were hazel and sharp. They missed nothing; of that, all observers were certain.

The floor of the cell was concrete; at night it was bitterly cold, during the day heat radiated from it.

The walls were freshly painted—institutional dark green to a height of six feet, then a brown border stripe, and above a light green. The prisoner knew they did not paint walls to cheer prisoners. The walls were painted to obscure any message of hope or defiance that might have been scratched there by the cell's previous occupant. The strongest prisoner will crack when his sense of despair reaches beyond a certain point. Despair will break the stoutest heart; it would break him—eventually.

The cell was dry. The cells he was familiar with were always damp; in the summer huge bloated insects sprang from eggs washed into cells by seeping drain water. Huge flies, flies that buzzed like bees, then suddenly flopped down on a prisoner's face. It was forbidden to kill the flies, for the smell alone could cause retching.

The pain was gone, along with the translucent envelope enshrouding him. Figures in white no longer looked down on him, shaking their heads and speaking words he didn't understand. He no longer lived for the vision of the angel of mercy and her blessed needle. For a long time, his whole lower body felt as if it were immersed in boiling water. The morphine kept the agony at bay for a short time; then, and only then, he slept. After a while the pain would creep back, conquering his extremities first, then the whole of him.

He knew he must have been in an accident; there was the memory of being high above the clouds, and then of a deafening explosion, and then of pain, pain far more excruciating than anything he could have imagined, pain racking his body from end to end.

After the morphine and nurses had come prison. He remembered the ride to prison clearly. At first he was unable to see anything because a hood had been fastened to his head. If he reached up to try and unfasten it, he was hit hard across the face. The blow did not always come at once. Sometimes it was ten, twenty seconds—an eternity—before he was hit. It was terrifying to wait in the darkness, knowing nearby someone was waiting to slam his fist into your face.

When they left him alone, after removing the hood, he could do nothing but lie on his narrow bunk. He had been around prisons enough to know the feel of them. No sound ever penetrated his cell, but there was no way to keep out the prison taste. Even the uniforms of his guards smelled; the disinfectant permeated everything in the prison.

He had no meals for the first few days. One cup of water, slightly salty, was sometimes offered, but only after he had fallen asleep. He had to be awakened to drink it.

His every movement was filmed; he was sure of that. Most of the time he lay still. Sometimes he allowed himself to fall asleep; his jailers promptly woke him and served breakfast. After a week, they introduced the sounds of a busy street corner, then sounds of a restaurant, then airport sounds. He did not react except, of course, by waking up. It was the one thing he could not control.

The mind is the key to all, so he kept it active. Counting the number of cinder blocks in the walls, constructing complex computer programs in his head, always remembering—the mind goes first.

At night the single bulb was extinguished, and around the steel door there was only a faint glow of light. But he knew he was below the ground; he could sense that. The concrete floor, the cinder block, the naked light bulb well above his reach—no suicide that way—and the meager furniture were his entire world. The chair was wood and bolted to the floor; the small table and the narrow bed were likewise shackled.

Twice a day he made a visit to the bathroom. He showered the first time. The sound of the toilet flushing was welcome in a world almost devoid of noise. At night the silence was particulary noticeable, and he remembered the corridors were all carpeted.

He always slept whenever he could; the mental strain was the worst. Put a man in a cell and keep him awake for seventy-two hours and he would say anything, do anything. So he slept, letting the many fleas jump where they pleased.

The guards soon became more careless. They were paid workers with nothing to prove. Sometimes they smiled at him as if wishing to apologize. Sentry duty is soul destroying; jailers are as much imprisoned as those they watch. For eight hours a day they must follow regulations and be always on guard. It is too much to ask. Sometimes they crack.

The man in the cell was aware of this; he knew everything about prisons and their monotonous routine. Once the door was not locked carefully enough. It slowly swung open, giving the prisoner a view of the corridor and the doors of two cells. They were open. Was he the only prisoner in the cell block?

They understood what effect leaving the cell door open would have on a normal prisoner; the sensation of freedom would be overwhelming, irresistible. But the man did not even rise from his chair, did not walk to the door to enlarge his universe, did not attempt to walk the length of the corridor and round the corner where they lay in wait for him.

He had known similar tricks in his own country; the guards got bored so quickly they welcomed any change in routine. In the cells the man had known, there was always a peephole. It was strictly forbidden to leave the peephole unshuttered on the outside, but warders grew careless. Sometimes the man had found it necessary to teach the guards a lesson.

One of the guards often peered through the peephole to watch the prisoners. The guard allowed them to masturbate. Masturbation gave pleasure; therefore it was forbidden. Prisoners were not allowed to put their hands under their blankets. But when nothing happened to them, they took the risk.

The voyeurism ceased when the man stationed one of his own people in a cell. The plant carried a thin stiletto made of elk horn. When the guard peered through the peephole the stiletto was driven into his eye. No guard left the peephole open after that.

They tried to disorient him; that was axiomatic. At first it was simple: they added time at the end of the day, or took it off. The prisoner couldn't keep a calendar; they would see it. But each time he showered, he fixed his eye on one of the cement blocks in the bathroom and then moved his gaze one to the left. By this method he kept count of the days.

When he had been in the cell three rows and two blocks, thirty-two days, they began intensifying the noise and the other things. He tried to conceal his elation; they were becoming desperate. The sounds woke him, as he knew they were meant to. They were human but difficult to describe as moans or screams. Once they were the sounds of a couple copulating. He put the noises out of his mind, triumph sustaining him.

A doctor was sent in regularly—another mistake. Every seven cinder blocks, he arrived. The doctor was particularly anxious about the prisoner's teeth. The dental work was poor, something would have to be done soon. The gums go first, he said. But he was wrong, the mind goes first.

The guards became familiar—a silly mistake. The one who took him to the bathroom in the morning talked to him in Russian. The guard who talked to him in the evening spoke a form of German, possibly Yiddish. The prisoner never answered.

Cell inspection took place suddenly, without warning. Each side knew it was a ritual; the prisoner had nothing to hide and nowhere to hide it. A camera, hidden inside the single light bulb, had recorded everything, so the prisoner's every move was on tape.

A thick, sweet coffee was served occasionally; once when the guard was pouring him a cup, the liquid spilled to the floor and the guard had to wipe it up with a rag.

The prisoner allowed himself a wintry smile.

He remembered the biologist Timofeyev-Ressovsky, who had spent years in the Lubyanka Prison in Moscow. What had offended him most was not the inhuman conditions, not the torture, not even the manifest illogicality of the place. No. His scientific mind had rebelled at the lack of professional pride on the part of the guards. Each cell had a teapot, placed outside the cell and filled twice daily from a pail without a spout. Inevitably some was spilled on the highly polished floor. Timofeyev-Ressovsky had filed a complaint. He multiplied the 27 years of the Lubyanka's existence as a prison by 730 (twice for each day of the year) and then by 111 for the number of cells. "Is it sane," he demanded, "to spill boiling water on a polished floor 2,187,810 times and wipe it an equal number of times when a spout costing a few kopeks would have saved all that trouble?" Nothing, of course, was done.

After he'd been there for a little over a month, he was questioned for two hours. The prisoner soon realized that Mordecai Peer was an unskilled interrogator. Any man who could not sculpt an interrogation from silences was an amateur. The pause was a weapon as great as any words, and Mordecai Peer did not know that.

Peer addressed him in English, a mistake. The battle of "forcing the tongue" was a crucial opening struggle in any interrogation. Using the prisoner's own language gave the prisoner a sense of being among his own kind. If he heard a foreign language, it reminded him that he was among aliens; it encouraged him to be wary.

They could learn that he was a Russian merely by x-raying his teeth and examining the cheap amalgam used for fillings.

On the second day with Peer, the prisoner refused to talk at all. Within a week, the interrogator began to look as though he weren't sleeping well; in fact, the pain from his ulcer had become well-nigh unbearable. More than ever his mournful face resembled that of an El Greco Christ.

The prisoner remained impervious. He wasn't persuaded to talk by threats of death or a long prison sentence. Sudden reversals of tone were ineffective, and the man made the interrogator feel foolish when he switched from a friendly tone to a vindictive one. He wouldn't be humiliated either. When told to lie down on the floor, he refused. When the guards were summoned and forced him onto the floor, it seemed mere bullying. Intimidation didn't work, because what could the prisoner be threatened with? He was too sophisticated to believe he could be taken out and shot. And, anyway, the key to intimidation lay in convincing the prisoner he had something to lose. This man's clothes were all he had, and they were prison issue. He had *nothing.*

His hazel-tinted plastic contacts had been impounded, so the prisoner tended to peer nearsightedly, but there was a brightness about the eyes that indicated a mind that missed nothing. There was no fat on his body. His back still maintained its rigidity; there was no sign of the slight curvature of the spine afflicting many of advancing age. He appeared somewhat gaunt;

his face had a hollow look and the bones stood out clearly. There was a slight peeling away of the gums from the teeth, but the doctor assured the authorities that once a decent diet could be prescribed, the prisoner's health would be excellent.

While unconscious, the prisoner had been shaved so photographs could be taken. The beard had since grown back; he found it uncomfortable and was making efforts to avoid scratching it. Whenever he was conscious of this reflex action, he purposefully withdrew his hand and fixed his eyes on a point on the wall.

The jailers admired willpower. Normally isolation would break a man in days. By the fourth day, some were literally trying to climb the walls. They became disoriented or even mad. Had the prisoner shown any signs of wishing to cooperate, he would have been permitted books and a radio. It was common for prisoners to be caught reading the dullest things. They became fascinated by the instructions on vacuum sweepers or read cereal boxes over and over.

Usually silence and darkness became horrors. The blackness assumed a solidity and prisoners cried out, thrashed wildly, sweated profusely. Some of them had problems moving their limbs at night. Darkness became a force like gravity. It was solid, and they moved like swimmers.

Not this one. His posture was eloquent, unmoving as he sat for hours on his bunk or in the chair. So they took the chair; then the table. It didn't affect him. Most people became nervous after days of doing nothing. Not this man. Most of them longed to feel something. Limbs assumed a variety of positions, legs stretched out, legs folded under the chair, legs crossed. This man sat like a rock, unyielding.

Then, all at once, when it should have been day, it was night. And when he should have been fed, he was not fed. When they should have marched him to the lavatory, they did not come for him. The hum of the air conditioner died away. He was left suspended in a cocoon of thick, impenetrable darkness.

First his bladder was full, and they ignored his shouts for the guard. The prisoner felt his way along the wall to the far corner of the cell, as far away as he could go, and pissed there. Later he was forced to squat in the same place. Days passed.

Once, while he slept, they placed a water jug where he normally began his journey to his latrine. When his foot struck the wooden vessel, he reached down cautiously; and when he found it, he knew they would not let him die. The following day, there was a piece of bread next to the jug.

But there was no light; and the water contained a narcotic so he was always asleep when they came.

A small voice inside began urging him to surrender. He had visions of the scorpion. In the desert, bored soldiers surrounded scorpions with a circle of gasoline, then set it afire. The terrified insect withstood the heat as long as it was bearable, then curled its tail back over its body and stung itself. The scorpion was one of the few animals besides man to commit suicide.

He began talking to himself. The words made no sense.

One day, the prisoner was lying on his bunk when he became aware of a new smell mingling with the stench from his latrine. His nose had lost much of its sensitivity, but of this there could be no doubt. Smoke! In pure terror, he blundered across the cell to the door. The smell of smoke was much stronger there. Feeling for the edge of the door, he pressed his nose to the crack. He began coughing; a burning sensation seized his throat and lungs. His ear now pressed against the door, he could pick up the faint crackling of fire in the distance. He visualized the fire coursing along the passages. Soon the flames would reach the cell—or worse, they would suck up all the oxygen in the air, suffocating him. In the distance he heard the strident jangling of a fire alarm and sounds of voices raised in alarm. Sweat poured down his face. The alarm bells became much louder. Voices were raised, calling in a language he did not know. The voices were the only hope he had. He shouted at the top of his lungs. Then, pressing his ear to the door, he listened. Had he been heard?

It was the moment of breaking. Now he would promise them anything, anything. Whatever they wished to know he would tell them. He was beaten, broken. The mind was gone. He pressed his ear once more to the door and heard the voices drawing near. He was about to be rescued. He was . . . But no! With a sudden cry of joy, he realized what had taken place; his hands confirmed the evidence. The door was cold, *cold.* If there had been a fire, he would have felt the heat. Eagerly he ran his hands over the surface, like a lover at the long-delayed consummation of his passion. Cold! Cold at the top, cold at the bottom. A trick. All a trick designed to snap his iron control.

They had brought him to within an iota of breaking his will. Now they would never subjugate him. He had beaten them. His trial was over.

The light came on soon afterward; he lay on his bed, a faint smile on his lips, watching without speaking as the men hosed out his cell. He changed into fresh clothes. He had won.

There was a tense consultation in the conference room two floors above his cell. Drugs would break him; that was a given. Injections of "soap" would eventually reduce him to mindless babbling, or snap him like a dry twig. Both sides knew that; that would break him, certainly, but gain them what? The prisoner's talking must be coherent. Drugs muddled minds, and their results were unpredictable. Jailers wanted converts; if they didn't, they could simply kill all their prisoners. Within the most powerful tyrant there shudders the strong desire to be proved right. The prisoner knew that; in Russia trials were held with incredible frequency even though the verdict was already decided. The captor wants the prisoner to admit his wrongs and confirm his jailer's omniscience. Drugs muddy the pristine spring.

There was some talk of a more "intensive" interrogation, but nothing was done. Torture was a two-handed sword; it dehumanized the questioner as well as the victim.

Finally Mordecai "Mota" Peer recognized the inevitable. Taking one last look at the prisoner sitting on his bed, a bony Buddha, he shook his head. Later he said to his colleagues, "There is a stone so hard the Arabs call it *mizzi Yehudi*, the head of a Jew. Now I know how Jesus Christ must have seemed to the Sanhedrin."

Nobody laughed.

2

The prisoner permitted himself another feeling of triumph when he awoke from a drugged sleep; the new cell was a vast improvement. He would see Peer no more; he knew that just as surely as he'd known they would treat him with new respect. He had won. Mota Peer had fallen into the trap of projecting himself into his prisoner's persona. Once he found himself thinking "Is he married?" "Is he a Jew?" "Is he a spy?" Peer had lost. The pressure had been reversed; victim was now interrogator. The prisoner, without speaking, had begun asking the questions.

True to the rules of interrogation, Mota had asked the same questions over and over again. And since he could not know the answers, there was growing frustration which soon turned to anger for which there was no release. The interrogator who lost his temper was useless. The satisfaction in verbally or physically assaulting a prisoner soon passed. Rational men, and no other type, were useful in interrogations; others grew sick with themselves and rapidly degenerated.

The prisoner dressed; he had a lightweight three-piece suit instead of the prison issue. The jacket of the suit bore a tailor's label in Hebrew, which he could not read. In the distance he could hear the hum of air conditioners; his cell was pleasantly cool.

He knew they would continue watching. There would still be a camera somewhere. In twenty minutes, he eliminated all possibilities except the air conditioner vent, high up on the wall.

The prisoner walked around his new quarters. There was a carafe of water on the sideboard; his lips and throat were dry from the previous night's drug. The water was deliciously refreshing.

A knock on the door made him turn.

"Come in," the prisoner said in Russian.

The door opened; a man entered, pushing a food cart laden with breakfast dishes, plates, and cutlery.

"There now. I knew you could talk," the man called out cheerfully, also in Russian. "I'm Abraham."

"Moiseyev. Yuri Semyonovich."

Abraham extended his hand; Yuri Moiseyev shook it.

"I've come to breakfast. We can talk while we eat."

While Abraham spread a tablecloth with a flourish and set the table, the prisoner studied him.

Abraham was strikingly handsome; blond hair and healthy suntanned skin. There was the aquiline nose of his race and blue eyes. A firm jaw ended in a cleft chin. In him the prisoner sensed the resolution that Mota Peer had lacked. There was more in the face; brooding eyes hinted at tragedy.

Abraham removed the lids from some of the dishes. "Breakfast is my favorite meal," he said over his shoulder. "Coffee?"

The prisoner took his chair. "The last cup I had was drugged," he said, accepting a cup nevertheless.

The Israeli smiled. "You interest us a great deal. We wanted to move you with the least fuss and bother."

The prisoner noticed a small gold Star of David around the man's neck.

"No ill feelings, I trust?"

"I would have done the same thing."

"We didn't want any slipups. That's why you're going to have to wear those shoes without laces. They're okay. Come from Hobbs in London."

"The label was Italian."

"You don't miss much. They import them."

"Does anyone in Israel wear a tie?" asked the prisoner.

Abraham laughed. "Some of the old guys, none of the sabra—that is, those born here."

"And you. You were not born here."

Abraham looked startled; his prisoner was not sure whether he was acting or not.

"Ah. My Russian. Too good."

"No. The opposite." A wintry smile. "Foreigners, those few who attempt to learn Russian, always speak it too well. They don't make the right mistakes."

"I see what you mean. Let's eat. You know," continued Abraham, "about fifty years ago, a Russian could emigrate and open up a restaurant and survive. Not anymore." He poured coffee for them from a tall stainless-steel pot. "Communism killed the good restaurants. Don't you agree?"

"I have no interest in such things. My work was my only interest. Food was of little consequence. Now perhaps I will begin . . ."

"Well, let me tell you, Yuri Semyonovich, the main contribution Israel has made to international cuisine is the kibbutz breakfast." Waving his hand over the table, he went on, "Breads and rolls, raw salad vegetables, smoked and pickled fish, fresh fruit and juice, soft cream cheese from Tnuva Dairy in Tel Aviv."

"A glass of orange juice would suffice."

Abraham poured him one from a large pitcher. "There," he said. "Now. I think I'll have a little of that *challoth,* it comes from Mea Shearim, the ultra-Orthodox quarter of Jerusalem. Even the buses don't run there on the Sabbath. Not boring you, am I?"

"I find it very interesting. I also realize you are using a voice analyzer stress test."

"Ah. You're an old hand at this game. You wouldn't talk to poor old Mota. He's very upset. Linguists are also analyzing your Russian to see if you might be a plant. Chopped liver is superb on challah." He handed Moiseyev a piece. "Try it."

The prisoner found it delicious and said so.

"Tricky place to eat, Israel," continued Abraham cheerfully. "Moses said no shellfish, no pig products, no carrion—that's okay—no birds of prey, and nothing that crawls on its belly." He wiped his mouth precisely, like a woman, and took a sip of coffee. "And so much of it, like those blintzes, is fattening. I swim ten miles a day in the pool."

The prisoner had noted the developed chest and forearms; another clue fitted into place.

"You might try the *garinim.* They are roasted sunflower seeds. No? Well, it is something of an acquired taste."

While the prisoner contented himself with an apparently undrugged cup of coffee, the interrogator kept up his amiable patter. It was a clever approach. The prisoner knew what he was doing. The same little questions were slipped in here and there between bites and asides, as if they had not been asked before. The object was to verify how many changes the interrogated party introduced in his replies, then to point them out and keep insisting until the sought-after reply was forthcoming.

The subtlety was that by avoiding any contradictions, Moiseyev had to reveal that he was skilled in the ways of interrogators. If he attempted to make just the right number of mistakes, the proportion an innocent man might be expected to make, he would have to remember these for several weeks. It was, as all interrogators knew, impossible to recall errors over a ten-day period—especially if the victim was deprived of sleep.

One of the things Abraham might do would be to raise the anxiety quotient in Moiseyev. He would continue his breakfast while the prisoner was prey to rising anxiety about what would happen next. There had been glorious cases in which the interrogator had been scolded by his victim and told to get on with the job.

Yuri S. Moiseyev did not crack; he merely drank his coffee and watched Abraham eating. Had the interrogator not been so skilled, he might have become uneasy. The Russian's eyes were still dull from the previous night's sedative, but soon they would regain their brightness. Abraham was reminded of the look in a ferret's eyes when it has a rabbit immobilized in terror.

After that they met often and talked like old friends. For several days, Abraham asked questions and Yuri S. Moiseyev answered them. Both knew it was a ritual. The interrogator questioned; the prisoner lied. The time passed pleasantly.

On the eighth day of their meetings, Abraham returned to some details of Yuri S. Moiseyev's childhood. "You liked living in Maklakovo, did you?"

"It was all right."

"I can imagine. I suppose the river froze in winter, and you went skating."

"I did."

"The Angara River is much too swift-flowing to freeze, surely. I mean, that far north it is."

"I told you it was the Jeniseh River."

"Ah! So you did. Why don't you pour me some coffee? Your father died . . . when?"

"In 1943 during the Great Patriotic War."

"And your grandmother was Jewish?"

"Yes."

"Hmm." Abraham picked up several pieces of fruit and stacked them neatly on his plate. "We noticed you had not been circumcised. Even if you had, it wouldn't prove anything."

"Quite."

"Your father was a sergeant. You yourself did not fight, though you were twenty-five when the war ended?"

"I was a political commissar, not a military figure."

"Your father helped retake Kursk on February 6, 1943, under the command of General Vatutin?"

"Kursk was retaken February 8; the commander was General Filipp Ivanovich Golikov."

Abraham looked up apologetically from his fruit. "These military details are so easy to muddle." Smiling, he took the sugar and ladled two spoons of it into his coffee.

"You moved to Moscow with your mother and brothers and sisters two years after his death in 1945."

"Yes."

"I thought you told me you lived at Arkhangelskoye—are you sure you won't try a little cereal? We have corn flakes imported from England."

"Thank you, no. We lived in Arkhangelskoye from 1947 to 1950. I had only one brother, Demetri."

"Three sisters?"

"I said so."

"Your father was decorated at Kursk?"

"Yes."

"After General Zhukov took over."

"General Zhukov took N. F. Vatutin's command."

"I'm sorry." He gave a broad smile. "I meant that."

He was buttering toast. "A lot of my time recently has been spent in England. Have you been to England?"

"Never. I am a poor man."

"Yet you have an exit visa."

The prisoner gave an expressive shrug of the shoulders. "Men can be bribed. For a price."

"And you had that price?"

"I expect to work. The borrowed money can be returned."

"I see."

"It's a common thing. Since it produces hard currency, it is unofficially winked at."

"Hmm. How old did you say you were?"

"Sixty-six."

"And you can work at what?"

"Translations, any kind of computer . . ." A moment of carelessness. The brain goes first. Had Abraham noticed? "Computer repair work, engineering, that kind of thing."

"You were a mechanic?"

"Yes."

"You repaired electrical machinery?"

"Yes."

"Men are dangerous when they tell only half the truth, Yuri Semyonovich. You are not telling me everything, and that worries me."

No answer. Those monitoring the cameras and sound equipment looked meaningfully at each other.

"Your fingers had microscopic particles of plastic in them. This plastic is identical with that used on the keyboards of the Minsk thirty-four computer, whose design is strikingly similar to that of an IBM model."

The prisoner said nothing.

"Similar particles of the coating used on computer tapes were also found, but nothing that might have been expected from someone who probed around inside the guts of a computer." He produced a gold pencil from his inside pocket, walked over to the sideboard, and took out a pad of paper. "We must find out the truth, Yuri Semyonovich. Why are you here?"

The breakfast grew cold as Abraham took Moiseyev through it all again. He scribbled, erased, rewrote. He made a studious effort to give his prisoner every opportunity to get things right.

The details that Abraham felt were true came first: names, dates, family matters. If Semyonovich were a plant, he would simply have taken someone else's identity or grafted their names to his own family; this latter course Abraham was sure was the one Yuri S. Moiseyev had taken. Then, when the facts were detailed, there came sudden unexpected shifts in time and place.

It was a battle, a seesawing back and forth. First a series of factual questions requiring a simple yes or no answer. A rhythm was established. Obedience was inculcated. Then came the true questions. How did you get to Vienna? Who processed you at the reception center? Where did you get the money for the trip?

Abraham divided the day into four two-hour segments, never stayed longer, and kept all his materials in the sideboard, where they remained untouched by his prisoner.

Then, one day, it was over. Abraham came in at ten instead of nine, and lay full length on Moiseyev's bed. "We are grown men, Yuri Semyonovich, but we play games." He gazed up at the ceiling. "The first requirement in secret service work is not shooting, chasing around in cars, or making love to beautiful women. Leave that to books and films. The first priority is intellectual work demanding great patience. The winner succeeds by methodically overcoming his opponent. He does this by anticipating his intentions."

Yuri S. Moiseyev watched him from the far side of the room. He was seated at the table where he had been studying a chessboard.

"You are a mystery. An enigma. A conudrum. No one believes you are who you say you are, but what is your purpose? You aren't a terrorist, because they don't arrive on airplanes that get blown up by terrorists. Besides, there is no trace of explosive material on your hands."

"Perhaps I am a computer repairman?"

"We do not think so."

"So my fate is decided."

"This is not Russia. My father was in the Lubyanka even before I was. He was told interrogation and trial are merely judicial corroboration; they cannot alter your fate, for that has already been decided. We have not decided your fate. At the moment, you are guilty of entering the country on a false passport—it happens all the time." He sat up effortlessly.

It was a trick of the light, Abraham decided later, but the prisoner suddenly seemed much older and frailer. He spoke in his usual dry voice. "If I tell you who I am, others will find out. I shall be hunted down throughout the world."

"No one's that important," Abraham said.

"I am," replied Anton Mikhailovich Drakov without a hint of arrogance.

3

"Before I became Yuri Semyonovich Moiseyev I was Drakov," said the prisoner. "I am now a nonperson, believed dead. I have come to Israel to live out my last years in peace."

Abraham swung his feet over the side of the bed and walked agitatedly around the room. "Can you prove it? Can you prove it?" he muttered. "If you can, we've got the highest-ranking defector ever to leave Russia. God, I can't believe it. They say one of the neatest tricks in Russia is to reach old age without either missing the special ruble allowance, getting a one-way ticket to Siberia, or treating one's wife to a premature pension. But"—he stared at Drakov—"there's never been anything like this."

He stood there staring as if Drakov were some rare exotic creature. Later he admitted to a sneaking fear that it was a dream and he would wake up and find his prize gone.

"Anton Drakov, Director of Department A of the First Directorate. You were killed in Berlin."

The prisoner seemed surer of himself now; the strain of keeping his secret all these weeks had lifted. "I was very nearly killed at Lod Airport," he said softly. "I must admit that was unexpected."

"You broke four ribs and had second-degree burns on your legs. The smoke inhalation did not damage your lungs, but you ruptured your spleen."

"I saw the scar."

"But you didn't ask."

"No."

"Do you want to know?"

Drakov waved an arm expansively. "I—"

"The plane you flew on was targeted by a splinter group of the PFLP." He could not resist adding, "They are all splinter groups; the Palestinians are the only people ever to fight a civil war without a country to fight it in. They're born losers too. Did you know that when they announced El Al would be a priority target, bookings actually rose? El Al has the highest load factor of any airline on the North American route."

"You were saying . . ."

"A young man, about twenty, purchased four tickets, for Lod, Ben Gurion Airport. He fit the profile—nervous, hesitant, foreign, young, multiple tickets, etc. On the day of the flight only two of the tickets were used. Two very attractive girls from Hayward's Heath in England flew off with you."

Drakov didn't stir. Abraham admired the man's uncanny self-possession.

"The man was watched. Mossad, the organization for which I have the honor of working, made a mistake for once."

"Indeed."

"We waited outside the man's apartment, and he was soon joined by a friend. We broke in at midnight, found them in bed together, and seized a very modern Soviet antitank weapon familiar to you—the RPG-seven."

Drakov nodded. "I have heard of it."

"We took pictures for later use, if needed, grabbed the bazooka and left. Oh"—he paused—, "we also cut off the little fingers of each man. The next day, two business letters, fingers enclosed, went to the boys' parents warning them not to allow their children to meddle in politics."

"I do not see what this—"

"The kids were smarter than we thought. The night before they got in the sack together, they picked up these two secretaries in some German bar. A little sticky finger led to bigger things. The boys suggested a trip, on them, to Israel. At the last minute they canceled, told the girls to go ahead, and . . ."

"And the girls had a little present to carry with them."

"A tape recorder, actually. You wouldn't be here if they had stowed it under the seat."

"Was this a time bomb or a pressure bomb?" Drakov asked.

Suddenly Abraham felt a surge of anger course through him. "How the shit can you sit there so calmly analyzing this? We're talking about a bomb that nearly blew a whole damn jumbo jet with four hundred people out of the goddam sky."

"I never get excited about the past; it is pointless. Nothing can change what has happened."

"It was," said the exasperated Abraham, "a barometric pressure bomb with a timer to prevent it from going off before the plane reached cruising height. That way it had to go off when the plane was coming down."

"Ingenious," said Drakov. "And did it perform as expected?"

"It went off at precisely five hundred feet as the plane was landing. However, all the baggage compartments on El Al planes are reinforced with steel plate. The blast tore a hole twelve feet long and blew off the left landing wheels. The plane dropped two hundred feet vertically." *Damn him*, not even an eyeblink. "The pilot kept it airborne just long enough to reach the end of the runway. The left wing hit the concrete and was shorn off. The cabin tore open like a ripped can."

"And you claimed it was a rocket attack,"

said Drakov, "not a bomb. That way, you gained points from a sympathetic world."

Abraham was reaching for his cigarettes. Drakov saw they were Gauloises. The tobacco was strong and the Israeli inhaled deeply, as if demonstrating to himself that his anger was under control. "The bomb was not the primary concern," said Drakov in the matter-of-fact tone his companion found so infuriating. "It provided important information. All the major powers monitor radio traffic, most of it is in code. If there was an attack at Tel Aviv, coded messages would have to contain groups for 'El Al,' 'rocket,' 'Tel Aviv,' and so forth. That's how we learn one another's codes." He spread his fingers. "But Israeli codes were never too complex."

Abraham turned away from the prisoner and walked to the window. He hoped it looked like a normal move. He didn't want Drakov to see his face until his emotions were under better control. The temptation to smash his fist in the Russian's face was starting to overwhelm him, and he was furious with himself.

Drakov had his back to the window and was rubbing an eye as if it were causing trouble. "You're right," Abraham said. "We sent several messages, but if anyone tries to crack them he will be at it for a lifetime."

"You put in random factors?"

"Of course. But then, that's your line, isn't it? Betrayal, lies, deceit, murder." He thrust his face near Drakov's. "Disinformation." He spat the word. "Giving the enemy 'misinformation for political and operational purposes,' as your

Statute of the Committee of State Security puts it."

Drakov looked at him; Abraham noted with pleasure that the Russian's right eye was watering. "That hardly does it justice," replied Drakov without emotion. "A man doesn't devote his life to something—"

"A man?" Abraham shook his head violently. "A man? You're no man. A killer—nothing more."

Drakov appeared to consider this carefully. "I don't think so. You are the emotional type; you fight to keep it under control. You care about things of little interest to me. My nature is intellectual. I harbor no grudges, resent no personal slights, value nothing you consider important. For me, the only thing in life that matters at all is exploiting the theme or flow of a contest. *Dezinformatsiya* was, for me, the supreme intellectual exercise. It is chess, and the world goes to the victor."

Abraham stubbed out his cigarette with more violence than was necessary. He was irritated to find Drakov watching him with a slight smile. Damn him, he had gotten under Abraham's skin.

"And is that all you did, disinformation?"

"I had one other task. I completed a computer data base of all the people in the Soviet Union who might become targets for disinformation."

"How many names?"

"Five million, less a few hundred."

Abraham realized immediately what such a data base would mean to the rulers of Russia. Complete, utter control. He studied Drakov through the thin spiral of smoke curling up from his cigarette. "And what happened to these *alleged* five million names?"

Drakov ignored the challenge. "I encoded them. If anyone can read the list before everyone on it is dead, I shall be disappointed. You should thank me; a lot of them were Jews. Over half a million."

Abraham sat at the table. "There aren't that many Jews left in Russia."

"There are half-Jews, quarter-Jews, and so on. My mother was the daughter of a Jew. I was to be eliminated as part of a new pogrom—that's the word, isn't it? Pogrom. So I left with a microfiche of several hundred thousand names."

"No such microfiche was found on you."

"I shall never know whether that's true. You may have it. Possibly it burned in the crash. It was my price of admission to Israel."

Abraham toyed with his folder. "You claim to be Anton Drakov of Department A of the First Directorate. You claim to be an expert in disinformation. Are you familiar with this quote by Lenin? 'Deception is an arrangement of light and dark . . . *chiaroscuro* . . . The people must be made to see white where there is black when this is necessary to the progress of the Revolution.' "

"It was not Lenin, it was his German escort, Willi Munzenberg, who gave him that when they crossed Germany in 1917."

Abraham slapped the folder down onto the table; the sound was like a shot. Drakov drew back as if he'd been struck. Abraham leaned across the table. "I want an example. Let us say, for the sake of argument, I wish to cast doubt on the divinity of Jesus Christ. How would I do it?"

"We are playing games now?"

"There is plenty of time; you're not going anywhere." Sitting back, he fixed Drakov with a challenging stare.

The Russian shrugged; Abraham found this particularly infuriating. "I thought Jews had already decided that issue. But if you insist . . ."

"I insist."

"First it would be necessary to undermine his credibility; there are books, I believe, that give a different picture of him. Everything people praise in him I would undermine. I would demythologize him. Show he was ordinary—married, had a family—was, in short, like other people. Next I would attack his alleged miracles. Explain them wherever possible, deny them when not. Demonstrate that all of his feats and the story of his birth have been attributed to leaders of the past, such as Buddha, Lao Tzu, et cetera. Show all the similarities, and parallels, make it seem they are part of the props of religious hokum. Build up a rival. Take someone from his day—say, the man who betrayed him . . ."

"Judas Iscariot."

"Make Judas appear as wronged. Quote sources. Make up sources for the grand lie, quote lost sources for the lesser lies. Claim they said something significant. The fact that the sources did really once exist—mentioned by writers still available—is the issue you focus on, not the truth or falsehood of the statement being propagated."

"And this would work?"

"Not immediately. People believe what they want to believe. It would be necessary to hint that the divinity of Christ is a plot maintained by those who have a vested interest in it—the established churches. They are an easy target—dwell on the history of Roman popes and their double-talk. People always suspect those in power of duplicity. When fact is mixed with fiction, you have begun to establish your 'truth.' "

Abraham stood and reached into his inside pocket. He tossed a pair of sunglasses onto the table. "Come with me. Put those on; you will need them." He banged twice on the door with the palm of his hand and the door was opened.

"Follow me and remember, you are under constant surveillance."

Drakov followed him up a short flight of steps and along a corridor. There were cells on each side. Each door had a small hole in it about a foot square neatly divided by a single steel bar. An occasional forearm stuck through the windows. Prisoners always did that, thought Drakov. Presumably they nursed the hope that if part of them was outside the cell, the rest of them would soon follow. Naturally there were no windows in the cells of Moscow's Lubyanka Prison.

"This was a hospital many years ago; the Jordanians captured it for a while, so a new one had to be constructed to the southwest."

Abraham paused at the end of the corridor and

signed a book; the guard looked curiously at the prisoner, his sunglasses fitting loosely around the stretched skin. He wondered what the little bald-headed guy could have done to merit the kind of cell he was in. He didn't look like much.

Abraham handed a badge to Drakov. "It says 'Visitor,' " he told him.

A minute later they stood outside the building in blinding light and ovenlike heat. "You'll adjust," said Abraham. "We may be one of the few countries with air-conditioned cells." He walked toward a circular iron stairway leading to the gardens below. Drakov followed closely behind. "For all your disinformation, you haven't undermined Christianity in Poland, have you?"

Drakov looked out over the city of Jerusalem spread beneath them. "It will happen in time. At the moment Christianity in Poland is a political matter. Once the Poles accept Russian domination as a fact, the religion will wither away. All the time, the most outspoken priests are being removed by the KGB. There are processions, even trials, but no real resistance. Eventually the Catholic Church will become ineffectual."

The ground fell away steeply at their feet; to the left was a conservatory filled with lush green plants and flowers, only one of which Drakov knew and that only because its name was so absurd—bird of paradise. Below, the road in front of the city was paved and crowded with buses and donkey carts and an occasional camel looking above it all. Honks from the struggling taxis reached them distinctly; it almost seemed possible to hear the speech of those gathered in clusters near the huge gate.

"To the north is Mount Scopus," Abraham informed him, "and the main road to Jericho. South is the Mount of Olives. And that"—he pointed west—"is the most fought-over city in the history of man."

Drakov was at last able to lift his eyes to the city of Jerusalem itself and not be blinded by the intensity of light from the almost copper sky. On the horizon were skyscrapers; it looked like any modern city in the distance. But closer to him lay the Old City. A hundred domes, small and large, reflected the sun. By a freak of the light, each seemed to have a golden cross on it.

"In the Old City," said Abraham, "is the Golden Gate, just right of center. The huge golden dome is the Dome of the Rock built over the Moriah rock on which Muhammad ascended into the Seven Heavens before returning to Mecca. Over there is the Garden of Gethsemane. Among those pine trees you can see some chalky yellow stones. Christ may have trodden there on his way to his crucifixion."

"Those very stones?"

Abraham wasn't sure what Drakov's tone meant. Glancing quickly at the Russian's face, he saw no answer.

"Beyond the Dome is the Wailing Wall, part of Herod's Temple. All in all, that area is the most holy spot in the world. The temple was where Jesus argued with the scribes and where he cast out the money changers. If you hope to eradicate religion, you have a lot of work to do." He stopped by a bench and sat; Drakov joined him.

"You don't destroy religions, you replace them," replied Drakov. "After all"—he toyed with his sunglasses—"Judaism replaced the Graeco-Roman faith, and Christianity almost replaced your religion."

Abraham felt another surge of hatred, and wondered if his anger stemmed from fear that Drakov could be right.

"Yet the Jew survives." There was no way Abraham could keep a note of triumph from his voice. "And you are the one threatened with extinction. For all your 'victories', you have nothing."

"And that pleases you?"

"It gives me hope, yes."

"Don't let it," replied Drakov grimly. "I'm hunted because I am one-quarter Jew, not for anything I did."

There were several seconds of utter silence. Then Abraham said, "I cannot feel pity for you, Anton Drakov. What if our positions were reversed?"

The Russian's expression did not change; Abraham knew that behind the dark glasses, the eyes would be as cold as ever.

"Pity is an emotion. What I feel, I feel intellectually." He turned to Abraham. "I agree with the KGB. Jews alone have the strength and organization to destroy the Soviet Union." He paused as a helicopter whirled by overhead, its rotors flashing in the bright sun. "Jews are always a fifth column; they alone place religion and a foreign country above the nation of their birth. Russian Jews are always Jews, not Russians, and their loyalty lies with Israel."

"And who drove them to feeling that way?"

"It doesn't matter who did it; the situation simply exists." Looking out over the city, he continued in the same reasonable tone, as if Abraham were someone he had to humor. "So the Jew survives only in Israel and New York."

"Not in Russia."

"As you know." Again the Drakov shrug. "I worked for Communism all my life, received the Order of Lenin, became a Hero of the Soviet Union, made no mistakes politically. My grandfather made the error; he married a Jew. And in Russia, as you know"—he offered his cold wintry smile—"Jews are being systematically eliminated. They are an easy target." He smiled deprecatingly. "Those of us in disinformation know how difficult it is to get the young Muscovite or Uzbek boy to hate the Americans. The average Russian may know nothing about America except blue jeans, but that is enough for him. Now, you take your bearded shekel-laden Jew, he's an easy target."

"And you are proud of what you have done?" Abraham fought to keep his voice level.

"I cannot change history—though on occasion I have altered it a bit." He stretched his legs; the muscles ached. "You see, to a Russian, a Jew is always a Jew. Unlike any other enemy, he is deemed unconvertible. I have seen it happen. The interrogator goes hard at the political issues; then comes the moment of realization, followed by the transition to despair. Then all he has to harp on is the Jewish thing. A lifelong opinion about Jews cannot be modified. It wasn't so long ago that Russians drank toasts, 'Health to the Tsar and death to the Jews.' "

Abraham got to his feet, hoping Drakov saw it as a natural, unprovoked movement. "We are very near Gethsemane."

Drakov stood. "The names mean little to me. I was never a practicing Jew."

"And yet," Abraham said as he opened a wicket gate, "you come to us and ask for sanctuary?"

Drakov drew back, startled. "I had brought a gift; I read that Israel must by law accept all Jews."

"The Law of Return does not apply to criminals."

"I am not a criminal."

"You are, by your own explanation, an executioner."

"But that was in another country. And I condemned no Jews *because* they *were* Jews."

Suddenly it came to Abraham that he and Drakov would never be able to communicate; they operated from two entirely different levels of conscience, Russian though they both were. Further, none of the Jewish part of Drakov's nature had grown. Indeed, it had atrophied, for it was never used. They would never agree on anything of value. If this were true of the two of them, man to man, then it would be true of Drakov and Israel.

He must not be allowed to stay. It remained only to find a reason for the refusal. Once Abraham had made the decision, his mood became lighter. All the rising hatred inside him faded, pointless now. This vicious criminal would never harm Israel or Jews again. What remained of his pitiful life would be spent wandering the earth, looking for someone to take him in.

And then, astonishingly, Abraham felt pity. The man was no longer a threat.

They followed the path gently sloping down to the east wall of the Old City. The lush greenery, the giant cypresses, the carefully spaced shrubs and flowers would soon give way to dust and Arab shepherds.

"What are the current jokes in Russia?" asked Abraham.

Drakov looked up at him in surprise. "Jokes?"

"You have not heard this one? In Russia a wise man stays away from intellectuals, beautiful women, and Jews. Or to put it simply, Jews."

"No."

"Or that there is a new cause of anti-Semitism. Russians are increasingly resentful of Jews because they alone are allowed to leave the country."

"No."

"It is as I thought. Hitler and Stalin became gods in Germany and Russia; in England or Israel they would have been laughed at. You may recall the joke about Stalin. He lost his pipe and called the KGB. An hour later he found it in one of his boots. When he called the KGB back to explain, he discovered six people had already confessed."

Abraham looked at Drakov expectantly. The Russian looked puzzled so the interrogator quickly changed the subject. "Do you feel strong enough to walk up again? I could call for a car."

"I can walk."

They waited while a boy dressed in rags ran by, chasing a young goat. The path was bordered by olive and fig trees, a rough carpet of cùmin plants in pink and white, with green plantains growing beneath.

"Israel is a difficult place to live in," began Abraham as they started a slow climb upward. "Our enemies are terrible, inflation rampant. We should be studying the Talmud, but our children learn about M-16s and Uzis. We teach some math, but fiction is saved for our income tax returns. We are also, with good reason, paranoid, perpetually convinced that the end is near."

"I have suffered a little of that paranoia myself," said Drakov dryly.

Abraham smiled. "The committee will meet tomorrow to begin your debriefing."

Drakov stopped and bent down. A small stone had become lodged in his sandal. He took Abraham's arm, stood on one leg, and shook his foot; the stone fell to the path. Still leaning on the Israeli, he said, "Debriefing?"

"Yes." The two of them resumed the slow climb. The sun was merciless, and Drakov began to long for the air-conditioned comfort of his cell. "They will want to know all about your work, the inner workings of the directorates and so on. Invaluable stuff, all of it, I'm sure."

The Russian stopped walking. "What is it?" asked Abraham. "Are you tired?"

"No. There has been a mistake."

Abraham frowned. "Mistake?"

"You must understand, I am not a traitor."

Abraham studied the Russian's face. "No one says you are."

"I will not consent to any debriefing. I ask for sanctuary."

Abraham felt the joy rising in him. "But you must have known there would be a price."

"Do all these people"—Drakov waved his arm at the city below—"pay a price?"

"They give, each according to his means. You are very rich," Abraham said dryly.

"I will not tell you or anyone else anything about my duties or the internal workings of the KGB."

"But they planned your elimination! Wasn't your predecessor thrown alive into a furnace before an audience of KGB colleagues?"

Drakov would say nothing more. At a signal from Abraham, four men materialized from nowhere and took the prisoner back to his cell.

That night they tried everything—threats, promises, cajolery. Nothing made the slightest impression on the monklike figure sitting on his cot.

"Just some names will do. I need some names."

The air conditioning was laboring to clear the cigarette smoke from the cell. The four-man team had departed in disgust, leaving stuffed ashtrays and a half-dozen coffee cups. Abraham was feeling very tired. He waved his hand at the wall. "I want to give you the whole city beyond that concrete wall," he said. "All I need is some evidence of goodwill on your part."

"I am not a traitor."

"No one has said you are."

Yet Abraham knew this was his triumph. Drakov could never stay in Israel now.

And the Israeli understood something else. "I realize now why you wouldn't identify yourself earlier, why you went through that interrogation without admitting anything. It was a demonstration, wasn't it?"

There was an almost imperceptible nod from the prisoner.

"You were telling us that whatever we did or promised, you have the willpower to resist us."

Years afterward, Abraham would wonder why he said what he said in the next moment. Perhaps it was pity, pity for a man without a home. Possibly it was scientific curiosity.

"We have many facilities here," began Abraham diffidently.

The prisoner's eyes shifted to the interrogator's face.

"Some people who spend a long time here are rewarded . . . or encouraged."

"And?"

Abraham was embarrassed to feel himself blushing. "We owe you something."

"You are offering me a woman."

Abraham made an affirmative gesture, not trusting himself to speak.

"This woman . . ."

"Yes?"

"Would she be a Jew or an Arab?"

"Either," said Abraham, now feeling utterly ridiculous.

There was a long pause. Finally Drakov rose to his feet and straightened the blanket on his bed. "I can have either?"

"I said you could."

"It's been a very long time," said the prisoner, "but I believe I would prefer . . ."

"Yes?" said Abraham.

"One of those cigarettes."

4

They met the following morning. For a moment, Abraham stood at the door; Drakov's dangerous eyes followed him.

Taking the chair, the Israeli spun it around and sat facing over the back.

"Have you eaten?"

"Yes."

"A cigarette?"

"Thank you."

Abraham reached into his shirt pocket and took out a crumpled pack.

"Is this about the debriefing?" asked Drakov.

"No. You've made your position clear, and the committee respects it."

"So." It was a statement.

"I'm sorry. You cannot stay in Israel."

Drakov gave no sign of having heard.

"I said you cannot stay."

"I heard."

"There is some suspicion that your defection might not be real."

"I skillfully designed it, you mean, *and* persuaded terrorists to blow up the plane for authenticity?"

"The crash was unplanned; we agree on that. It doesn't alter the possibility that you are a plant. After all, you have given us nothing."

"I see."

"Now, in other countries—Russia comes to mind—you cooperate, and if you're very lucky you get a pension and a flat near the Ring Road. If the authorities don't feel you've done your bit, there's the accident route."

"I'm familiar with the procedures."

They sat in silence.

"Look," said Abraham a bit later, "you could give us *something,* just enough to let you in."

"You don't want me in. You decided a long time ago that there was no place in your Israel for me." Drakov inhaled hard on his cigarette; naturally, the man would suspect he was a plant, but there was more to it than that. Abraham was afraid of him. "Someday you will need a friend, and you will understand why a man looks for sanctuary without betraying his past. I have no hatred for the people of Russia. Communism is like an old whore; for the desperate, it's all the hope there is. The *leaders* are my enemies."

"But it's those people we have to get along with, unfortunately."

Drakov carefully crushed out his cigarette. "And you don't want to offend . . ."

"We don't want to offend anyone. Russia has not exactly endeared itself to us, but we don't want trouble."

"And what happens to me? A slow ambulance, death en route to a life-saving operation?"

Abraham stood up and swung the chair back

under the table. "We want to help. Is there any other country where you . . . ?"

Drakov stared at him. "Won't they ask the same of me? Betrayal?"

Abraham spread his hands helplessly. "I don't know. I wish I did. What about America? Sweden?"

"There is one country. I know them by their secret service. England."

"England!"

"They consider themselves gentlemen and behave that way, but once they take the gloves off, the British are the toughest people on earth." Then he added, "And they respect integrity."

Abraham felt the barb. "In a thousand years I would never—"

"That is because you are blind; you have eyes but you do not see. Are you not familiar with your own history? It was the British who suggested Israel be born; finally, they alone were fighting you to protect Arabs."

Looking up at Abraham, he added, "And so, ultimately, instead of gaining the respect they deserved from both parties, they were heartily despised. Contact the British. Contact Joshua Davies of Davies, Greene and Company, Lower Marsh Street. Contact the fat man."

Climbing onto his bed, he lay full length, facing the wall. "And one more thing," he said.

"Yes?"

"Let me have a chess set?"

4 Contact

The few regular inhabitants of Lower Marsh Street, most of whom spent their evenings at the Spanish Patriot, were unaware that almost exactly opposite the pub was the headquarters of Section D of MI5.

Number 275 was not meant to attract attention; a piece of stained cardboard attached to the door announced the building's inhabitants:

Dr. Marswell Tinn—Trade Books
Miss I. French—Language Lessons
Davies, Greene & Co.—Exporters

The HQ of Special Projects was concealed within a legitimate export business occasionally showing a profit. The third floor was suspended from steel and concrete dividing walls and encased in metal mesh to prevent microwaves from penetrating the building. On the roof, invisible to anyone below and surrounded by a fake brick facade, was an eight-foot-diameter concrete dish for relaying and intercepting radio and television transmissions.

The roomy office of Joshua Davies, on the top floor, was reached by a long flight of steps from the second-floor office, the province of his sister Dolores, or via a small rickety elevator.

At eight o'clock, Davies entered his office. The evening sky provided little light since the windowsills were stacked high with newspapers, an ingenious protection against directional microphones. Newspapers absorbed sound well, and they cost little. Taking off his raincoat, he draped it over the coatrack, eschewing any particular hook. Davies was wearing a red-and-black-checked waistcoat with a bow tie that repeated the pattern. He tossed his battered hat onto the bust of John Wesley.

It was just warm enough for the Director not to have to light the gas fire that had replaced the white marble fireplace unbricked during the great Arab oil embargo. Tapping his large new barometer, he was surprised to learn the world was "steady."

He sighed as he took his chair, recollecting that it had once had two arms. One day the first chair arm was removed to accommodate his increasing girth; nine months later, the second had to be amputated.

For a few minutes, he sat and thought. By announcing his suspicions to the whole DIC, he was hoping one person might cut and run; only the mole would move now. The rest probably wouldn't believe him anyway. They would mutter about paranoia and the imminent crack-up of Joshua Bolivar Davies. The mole would know better, but it was only in plays that people could be surprised into looking guilty. Trained spies were always prepared. It *was* one of the men sitting around the table at DIC meetings. He was sure of that. But which one?

By announcing his suspicions, Davies had, of course, put his life in jeopardy. The mole knew who the catcher was; it didn't work the other way around.

A much-used Apple IIe computer specially hardwired to the main SIS Honeywell system in Whitehall sat on its trolley next to Davies' chair. His desk, solid oak, was tidy. The in-tray was empty. Three glass cases with trophies of stuffed fish reminded Davies of happier times. There were two phones on his right—red for scrambled calls, black for unclassified conversations.

Joshua had a few guilty qualms about having sent Dol home on the pretext he had to work late. The truth of the matter was it was the evening of his weekly meeting with the delightful Soo Ling. It was the one part of "the way of life" he had never confided to Dolores.

For over an hour, Davies summoned up biographies of senior members of SIS and MI5, seeking to establish some connection between them and the names on Badger's list. He found none. At last he groaned, took off his pince-nez, and lit a Hofnar.

Badger had been smart, too smart for the SIS and MI5. Small wonder he got out when he did. Davies sighed. He wanted to believe Badger, but if the ex-agent was right, then SIS and MI5 had been so horribly compromised, and for so long, that Badger's being right was unthinkable.

It was so simple, but he wasn't surprised no

one had spotted the possibility before. MI5 and SIS were purposely divided into self-contained cells; no one got the whole picture except the men of DIC. If a cell lost somebody, they didn't tell, so no one could put the picture together. All the mole did was pass on a name and a time to his tool; the victim was terminated but in a way that never suggested any overall design. Accidents occurred in the best-regulated organizations; secret organizations were bound to have high casualty rates; death in the line of duty was expected. If Badger's theory was correct, the Russians had come up with the smartest piece of espionage on record.

From his drink cabinet Davies took a bottle of J. & B. and carefully poured himself a half-glass. He rummaged in the tiny refrigerator and dropped in a cube of ice. A splash of soda followed. The first sip brought back happy memories of a recent visit to the solidly Victorian King's Arms in Fulham Road. Every Irish whiskey ever made could be found there, some even Davies had never heard of.

Sighing, he crossed the office and sat in his chair. He adjusted his terminal screen and pressed some keys. Several biographies began to scroll upward.

The first group contained names of possible suspects. Their behavior was thought to be symptomatic of their being double agents. Some of the names he'd forgotten. Simon Levers had taken to drink, married a divorcée, then had that marriage annulled on the grounds of nonconsummation. But the man was now in some minor official capacity at the War Office;

he had no access to any important files, though he had once been connected with computer records.

The big names included Rossiter. He would soon, perhaps, be in the catbird seat. As the next Director-General, he would know everything about everybody. Wallace Rossiter, now Deputy Director-General, was the eldest son of a prosperous wine merchant. He'd attended Oxford and received double firsts in classics.

Davies cast his eye down Rossiter's foreign service. Three years in Hong Kong, two in the embassy in Egypt in a minor cover role in the fifties. In 1960 he contracted malaria—mild case—returned home, and rose steadily to the top.

Alaister Strachan's career was a little more interesting. Second son of a Presbyterian minister living in Glasgow. Local grammar school, then Edinburgh University. After graduating with honors he joined the army and subsequently the SAS. Wounded and seconded to the Home Office, then put in charge of Positive Vetting.

Both men had been guilty of the usual minor fault. New recruits to MI5 were obliged to spend time in F Branch reading case histories. They were required to declare knowledge of any left-wing acquaintances considered potentially subversive by Five; these names were entered into their personal files. It was a long time ago, and everyone did it, but both men had fudged a bit. Like all new arrivals, they were reluctant to jeopardize their futures by naming unsavory characters as friends. The rule was often ignored. Rossiter had certainly known two men who later defected. An investigation had cleared him but delayed his elevation to the top spot.

Even Reginald Compton-Basset was a possible suspect, though Davies found that hard to swallow. But what a stroke of genius to adopt the bumbling vague nature of the parliamentarian while concealing a razor-sharp mind beneath the surface.

Davies leaned back in his chair scowling at the screen. Suddenly he came forward with a crash. He had forgotten the time. Logging off, he locked his terminal with a key and got to his feet, crushing the cigar stub and brushing his waistcoat in case any ash had collected there. He went into the little bathroom and vigorously brushed his teeth and gargled with Detol.

The Director rang several cab ranks before finding one that would deign to reply. He did not normally bring his Rolls into town on weekdays; the parking garages were always full. Davies was lucky, the radio cab service was 286, one of the few really efficient ones; he waited in the doorway of the Spanish Patriot, wrapped in his light Burberry overcoat and carrying a walking stick.

The address he gave was a street north of the river. Once there he would walk the last quarter of a mile from Fenchurch Street.

It was a relief to discover the driver was a Sikh; West Indian drivers were incessant chatterers and unfailingly cheerful and they always wanted to talk about cricket. Sikhs spoke when spoken to and seldom initiated conversation.

The first test match would begin soon, and every West Indian in the country would be speculating endlessly about it. In Davies' opinion there hadn't been a decent English cricketeer since Cyril Washbrook.

He looked forward eagerly to seeing Soo Ling. In his opinion, sex was now too casual a thing. When younger he had consumed a great deal of time and energy in finding a continuous supply of it. Before his sudden and dramatic weight gain, Joshua Davies had been quite a ladies' man.

The taxi passed the Old Vic; a few hopefuls stood outside convinced there would be some returned tickets even though the play had already begun. An Aston Martin Lagonda passed them without dipping its headlights. Davies decided if he paid fifty thousand pounds for a car, he wouldn't dip his headlights either.

He thought how good a cigar would taste, but he never smoked before sex; it took away some of the pleasure, he'd decided. His married friends were no better off than he. They became bored with their wives, started affairs, and finished with divorces. Davies permitted himself a superior smile. It hadn't dawned on them, as it had on him, that sex wasn't so much a physical thing as it was drama. No amount of fresh women or gadgets could help. There was nothing so pathetic as those who engaged in the endless pursuit of something that could never satisfy them. He knew one old goat in his seventies who still hadn't learned that sex was ultimately a ritual, not a physical release.

The driver knew his London; Davies was determined not to ask the man where he was from. You expected an answer like Amritsar and were told, instead, Manchester or Islington.

Soo Ling had been born in Shanghai. Four thousand years of non-Christian philosophy had taught the Chinese what sex was all about, he decided. The psychic satisfaction was what counted. In providing makeup, costume, and scenery at her apartment, Soo Ling provided the essential ingredients of a healthy sexual drama.

The traffic light at Bridge Road was green; Davies interpreted that as a good omen. They passed the great stone cathedral and were on the bridge in one easy movement. Beneath, the Thames looked somber and threatening. A few larger vessels were carefully following the deep channel marked out with red buoys.

"It is only," Davies had confided to one of his friends on the eve of the man's divorce, "when you realize that spiritual satisfaction outweighs physical that you'll see there is no future for anyone who asks questions like 'Do you want to watch the TV news or screw?' "

"Fenchurch Street," said the driver, disturbing Davies' reverie. The Director heaved himself out of the taxi, dug into his pockets, and sifted through change for the dull, elusive one-pound coins. His tip was respectable without being extravagant.

Soo Ling's flat was only a few minutes' walk from where the taxi had let him off.

2

The man watching from the cellar area in the mews opposite Soo Ling's apartment whispered urgently into his walkie-talkie as Davies arrived. Then the man settled down for a long, cheerless wait. It was a simple duty. There had been times when he'd been huddled in freezing alleys with legs numb from the cold and fingers that would have developed frostbite if he hadn't exercised them carefully in strict rotation.

May evenings in England were a snap for a pro, but there was no way to get rid of the boredom. He could always tell which trainees would make it and which wouldn't. Some of them tried to suspend their minds by clearing them of all thoughts; others took the opposite tack and focused on some mental pursuit. He knew one man who had tried to recite the time in French in five-minutes increments. None of these recruits made it. "When you watch, you watch," he told them. "You can't be thinking of nothing, or worse, something else." You had to feel the target through the walls, imagine what he was doing, and never forget that you were the watcher and he was the target.

So he sat, out of sight of any passerby, on a concrete step just below street level. A piece of corrugated cardboard beneath him kept out the cold, and an iron railing in front helped conceal him. He wore an old ragged coat, a nondescript muffler, and baggy trousers. In his torn jacket pocket was just enough money to prevent the Metropolitan Police from arresting him for vagrancy.

And so he waited, with the uncomplaining resignation of a true pro. Saw the curtains drawn, the lights dimmed. Poor bitch, he thought, servicing that mountain must be no joke.

An hour passed. There was little movement on the street; that, after all, was the principal attraction of a London mews. The watcher had no philosophical bent, and it was nothing to him if places that had once housed falcons, then become stables, were currently valuable real estate properties.

The couple who lived above the basement returned; he withdrew a little deeper into the shadows. He heard the sound of a key fumbling for a lock, then a curse followed by muffled laughter. The door opened, there was a brief flood of hall light into the street, the bang of a closing door, silence.

His orders had come as he was leaving for Covent Garden to see *Madame Butterfly.* It was a rush job, just decoded. By the time he reached Lower Marsh Street, the quarry was heading north in a taxi. He was a little piqued; the time did pass quicker when spiced up with dialogue. He hadn't had time to get his equipment, especially the new laser gismo which could translate the vibrations of speech on a windowpane into intelligible words, though something was always lost in the translation. And the portable battery was too damn heavy. It was only eight by six inches, but it weighed a ton.

He waited two hours, occasionally glancing up and down the street for anything unusual. He was able to smell trouble; that was why he was still alive. The fat man wouldn't give him any problems, though. A sudden gust of wind sent spirals of dust into the air; a piece of grit lodged in his left eye. He looked up at the window opposite and wished his quarry would leave.

The object of his attentions was, at that precise moment, preparing to depart.

Soo Ling, her high cheekbones framed by long straight black hair, was wearing a silk nightdress under her robe. Davies, fully dressed, was handing her a glass of champagne. The Director always finished with champagne; he was an incurable romantic.

Soo Ling eyed him under long eyelashes. She smothered a sigh. He wasn't the most imaginative of lovers—a solid missionary-position man—but he always paid and never caused any trouble. And, thank God, a true gent, he always rested on his elbows.

Davies poured the last of the champagne into his glass and put the empty bottle on the small cherrywood bar under the window. He and Soo Ling sat down on the sofa together, and the movement caused her to fall against him. Smiling, he placed a huge hand on her thigh.

"Nice place you have here."

She giggled. He often said that and evidently thought it funny; her job was to please him, so she giggled. Most of the men who visited her called her a China doll and wanted her to act like a teenager. So she did.

Davies looked around the room; he liked it. There were pleasant memories there and even more pleasurable ones in the bedroom beyond. The furniture was expensive and exquisitely matched, from the delicate prints to the cherrywood chairs. Even the stereo system was hidden in an antique corner cupboard.

"I've got to go," he sighed, giving her a last pat and clambering to his feet. He took a final swallow, placed his glass on the end table, kissed Soo Ling on the cheek, and moved reluctantly to the door.

"Same time . . ." she began.

"Next week," he finished, carefully leaving a book of matches in a porcelain ashtray. If anyone inquired too closely, they would be able to trace Davies to the Spanish Patriot, whose sign decorated the front of the matches. They could find his office, but anything pointing to the import company cover story was a plus.

She helped him into his overcoat, handed him his cane, and held the door for him. A minute later he was outside the building, where he grasped his stick firmly in his right hand, setting his bowler precariously on his head, and marched down the street, passing Middlesex Hospital, where Soo Ling was less gainfully employed as a scrub technician.

The watcher quickened his pace, looking for an opportunity to cross the street and approach his target. He was about to cross the street when a taxi almost ran him down. Damn! He told himself he had to remember to look to the right first in this crazy country. His view had been blocked for only a second, but when he looked again, there was no sign of Davies.

Quickening his pace, the watcher turned into a small side street. A single shop with the sign "Pollock's Toy Museum" was surrounded by run-down buildings. Black smog stains had not been sandblasted from walls; there were fewer streetlights, and they were farther apart. Only the lighted toy-shop window cast any real glow.

"Damn," hissed the watcher. He was in a quandary, unable to decide whether he had been given the slip or simply lost his target.

He listened. The dull noise of the city around him was on a different wavelength; he eliminated the sounds he didn't want to hear. But there was no sound of shoes on pavement.

A darkened cul de sac lay to his left. To enter it would be dangerous; anyone hiding there would see his shape framed against the light of the toy museum behind him. Opposite was one of the entrances to Goodge Street underground station. It was poorly lit. Deciding his quarry had entered the station, the watcher crossed the street and made his way along a white-tiled corridor. A thin, haggard youth was slumped against the wall under a sign that said "No Busking." His reedy voice was doing no service to a folksong as he abused his guitar. An empty corduroy cap lay in front of him, for contributions.

"Did you see a fat man?"

The singer shook his head, continuing his song without a break.

"Stoned," muttered the watcher in disgust.

An elephant could have gone by and he wouldn't remember.

The doors of one elevator began to close, and a disembodied female voice intoned for the millionth time, "Mind the doors." He hurried forward and held the doors with his hand. The cage was empty. The doors rolled back; there was another warning from the voice, and this time he allowed them to close.

The stairs beckoned; he began to descend, making good progress until the wide, lighted corridor abruptly ended. Ahead was an iron spiral staircase that disappeared into the darkness below. Tiny forty-watt bulbs, widely spaced, were all that showed the way. Many of the bulbs had been stolen, so great stretches of his descent would be made in darkness. Suddenly he thought he heard footsteps. Pausing, he turned his head from side to side. Yes, definitely footsteps, and well below him. He hurried, for all the man needed to do was catch a train, and he would have shaken his tracker.

He rounded a turn. There was a loud screeching animal sound and something forced its way between his legs. A mountain seemed to rise up and fall on him, and before he could gather his wits, the watcher found a steel blade pressing against his Adam's apple.

"Cats sometimes sleep down here," said Joshua Davies, retrieving his bowler hat with his left hand while keeping the sword stick on the watcher's throat with his right. "Do you want something? I'm not a rich man and seldom carry much cash."

The watcher cautiously pulled himself into a sitting position. "I was sent to get you."

"May I inquire by whom?"

"I was to tell you Red Prince and say someone will be waiting for you at London Bridge Station."

Davies stared at him. "Show me your wallet."

The man laughed softly. "You don't think I carry ID, do you?"

Davies leaned forward and the sword stick pricked the watcher's throat. "Wallet."

The man shook his head. Davies felt for an inside pocket. It was empty. That was true of all watchers' pockets.

"Who with?"

No answer.

"Why should I go?"

"I don't know anything more," the watcher said.

Davies' sword-stick blade slid back in its handle soundlessly. "London Bridge Station."

The watcher nodded.

"Well, get lost," said Davies, sure now that all he had caught was a cut-out. He sighed as he watched the man scurry away up the stairs. One of the problems of secret organizations was that they believed what they read about themselves. Why in God's name didn't they just call him on the damned phone?

3

Davies clumped all the way down the iron circular staircase. The stairs were endless and the dank air smelled like a sewer, so it was a sweating and vastly displeased Joshua Davies who finally rolled out on the platform ten minutes later. He had heard the trains with encouraging frequency during his long descent, but once in the infernal regions, it was fifteen minutes before a train limped into the station pushing a great damp wall of hot air ahead of it.

The rest of the Director's journey to London Bridge was not much better. His great perspiring face needed the continuous attention of his great white linen handkerchief. The compartment was filled with a variety of strange creatures and tiny old bag ladies. As he so often did, Davies gave thanks for the British restraint that proscribed conversation.

"I am Abraham," said the tall blond man standing by the closed news agent's stall.

Davies sized him up at once. Strong build, suntan, broad jaw, arrogant nose. The blond hair was too long for most military services. The man looked a positive Adonis. The Director wanted to dislike him on principle, but Abraham had a disarming smile. Davies took the proffered hand and engulfed it with his own. "It better be important. I like to get in a snack around this time of evening."

"I'm from . . ."

"Mossad, probably."

"How did you guess?"

"It wasn't difficult. The clown following me looked the wrong way when crossing the street."

"Nine-tenths of the world drive on the right; he could have been Mongolian."

"He *looked* Jewish."

Abraham nodded.

"He also muttered to himself in Hebrew when he was looking for me in a singularly damp, stinking subway station."

"I see. I am Abraham."

They were walking along London Bridge Street toward Railway Approach. Davies eyed the Israeli with his blond hair and blue eyes. So this was Abraham. He knew the man's reputation.

"Shall we ride," asked Abraham, as a car drew up along side them, "or do you enjoy walking?"

"Not so's you'd notice," said Davies, reaching for a door and piling into the backseat. With a smile Abraham slid in beside him.

Joshua Davies held no particularly high opinion of the Israeli secret service. He recalled Allen Dulles' remark that Mossad was one of the finest in the world, but he didn't believe it for a moment. Still, the Israelis were good, and they had the enormous advantage of having a potential fifth column in any country in the civilized world. A French Jew, an English Jew, would find it difficult to resist an appeal by Mossad or, worse still, the Guys. Yet, they had been caught napping before the Yom Kippur

War. They had killed the wrong man on several occasions.

Turning into Borough High Street, they passed in front of the post office. The Director thought he remembered reading of a small Arab restaurant's opening nearby recently. One good thing about the Arabs, they didn't subscribe to British fanaticism regarding early closing times.

"We owe you a favor," Abraham began, turning to face Davies.

"Really? I didn't know we had any cash in the bank."

"A drink?" Abraham offered, and Davies brightened immediately. The Israeli opened the back of the seat in front of him and a miniature bar lit up before their eyes.

"Absinthe?"

Davies nodded, studying the green liqueur as it was poured into a glass. He took a sip. Its high alcoholic content and bitter licorice taste suited his palate.

"Ah, wormwood, wormwood," he muttered. "I'll bet this came from some private stock."

"It was a gift to the people of Israel."

"No one gives anything like this to me," muttered the Director, looking gloomy. "I suppose your driver knows which way to go round St. George's Circle."

"He does."

It began to drizzle, and the driver switched on the wipers. Davies wasn't surprised when one of them scratched the windshield. The noise set his teeth on edge. "You said you owed us one."

"You will recall the massacre of Israeli athletes at Munich?"

The Director nodded. "Bad show that. The Germans botched it. Should have called on the SAS."

Abraham reached forward and slid a small wooden lid sideways. "I think you will like these cigars."

Davies took the cigar and slid off the case. "Romeo and Juliettes, eh?"

"The significance is, perhaps, more important than the taste."

"You got them from Lewis' in Saint James."

"Of course."

"All right," said Davies, mollified at last. "You bring me here, give me an absinthe and one of Churchill's favorite cigars, so—?"

"The architect of the Munich Massacre was Ali Hassan Salameh, known as the Red Prince. We wanted the man. It is laid down in the Talmud, 'If someone comes to kill you, rise and kill him first.' But we didn't get him first."

"You killed a Moroccan waiter in Norway as I recall."

"Salameh was in Norway, but by an incredible piece of bad luck, we got the wrong address."

"It happens," said Davies generously, wreathed in a fog of cigar smoke.

Abraham had no idea whether the Englishman was being ironic or not. "A Palestinian, Faris Ghantous by name, was a bodyguard to Salameh. It seems he took it into his head to go to Ireland for a vacation."

Joshua Davies was so shocked he swallowed a lungful of smoke and struggled with a coughing fit. Abraham looked anxious, but his passenger soon recovered. A huge white handkerchief appeared from nowhere and Davies covered his bright red face and blew lustily into it. "Hell, no one goes to Ireland, especially for a holiday." He found it significant that they were passing just to the north of the Imperial War Museum.

Abraham permitted himself a smile. "His knowledge of world history was profoundly Islamic. He'd heard that the Irish were involved in a holy war, so naturally he felt assured of a warm welcome."

"And did he get one?" asked the Director, intrigued.

"Unfortunately he fell in with a couple of SAS toughs on special assignment. He spilled his guts to his newfound friends. So we had Salameh's address."

"Alas, poor Faris. But what a nice bit of luck for you."

"We didn't kill him. As a matter of fact, he got laid."

"He what?"

"Another of his Islamic ideas was that women were more impure in the West. He was babbling about paying for an Irishwoman even when he was jailed. The interrogator took pity on him, and he did eventually have a woman."

"For thirty pieces of silver."

"He was too stupid to know what he'd done." He grinned and said in a singsong voice, "We won't tell if you won't tell."

They were on Lambeth Bridge crossing the Thames. To the north were the Houses of Parliament; there was a light in the clocktower indicating the House was still sitting. Joshua Davies was glad; he hadn't forgiven the Chancellor of the Exchequer for raising the tax on imported wine in the last budget. Besides, the government was always Conservative these days, and he and Dol always voted Liberal.

"When our WOG team . . ."

"*Wog* team?"

"A coincidence. The letters stand for 'Wrath of God.' Just coincidence. Well, when the team terminated Salameh, an Englishwoman was crushed by falling concrete. Another coincidence."

"So you owe us two favors."

"In a manner of speaking."

Both of them stopped talking as the driver guided the Rover past a double-decker bus and followed Millback along the river toward the Tate. Even the exacting Davies had to admit the man was a first-rate driver, constantly using his side and rearview mirrors and weaving in between vehicles expertly.

"An excellent driver," he said.

"Kaspar? Yes. I always hire him when I need a discreet ride around London. He knows what he's doing." Without changing his conversational tone, he said, "We have a high-ranking Russian defector. Very high."

Davies pulled on his cigar. "Oh?" The cigar ash glowed red. He looked down and found an ashtray hidden in the upholstery. "Who?"

"Anton Mikhailovich Drakov, of the KGB."

Abraham had been looking forward to an explosive reaction. He got none. The fat man didn't even turn to look at him. "Then you've got a corpse," he muttered, looking with greater interest at his cigar. He took a long, last pull on it, gazing moodily at the stub.

"He seemed very much alive when I spoke to him."

"Let me assure you." Davies wound down the window and pitched the remnant of his cigar in the direction of the Thames. "One of my men shot him in the heart. Unless he's a vampire or has two hearts, he's dead. Maggot bait, we used to call it when I was a child."

Abraham felt a guilty glow of pleasure at being able to undermine Davies' self-assurance. "You were *meant* to think he was dead. The man arranged his own death and fled to Israel."

"My dear chap," said Davies, "I got the whole story from the agent who was there. Drakov had a Russian called Novetsky programmed to kill one of my people. At the last minute the Russian fought off the conditioning and drilled Drakov." He sat back and stretched out his legs. Amazing what leg room there was in these smaller luxury cars.

"It wasn't like that. Novetsky was conditioned to shoot Drakov. The programming was to ensure he didn't go for Drakov's head," Abraham explained. "Drakov wore a vest of Kevlar, which, as you know, will stop an elephant gun."

Davies' confidence was beginning to ooze away. The victory he had celebrated with Badger and Novetsky might have been premature. He rearranged himself so he could look into Abraham's eyes; he saw that there wasn't doubt. It was extraordinary. It was ju Drakov. He'd used SIS to make certai sians believed him dead. His assassin, Colonel Novetsky, would assure them, and if they didn't believe Colonel Novetsky, the British secret service would confirm it.

"A body was found. . . ." He took a breath. It could have been any body, burned beyond recognition. And if there were any dental records of Anton Drakov anywhere, Davies would personally eat them. "So Drakov came to you."

"The devil did not look after his own. Some PFLP hotshots planted a bomb on his plane. It was supposed to be carried into the cabin, but the tape recorder in which it was hidden went into the baggage hold."

"An El Al plane?"

"Of course."

"So the reinforced steel luggage compartment absorbed most of the blast?"

"It came down with a bang."

"I read about it. I suppose you inflated the figures and made it seem a lot worse than it was."

"Isn't that Buckingham Palace on the right?"

"You're not going to answer, eh?"

"Would you?"

"Suppose not. Yes, and beyond the lake, if you could see the rear of the palace, you'd see the Queen's Gallery, domain of Sir Anthony Blunt—spy. Why don't you keep Drakov? Why come to you? Is he a Jew?"

Abraham shrugged. "No one can define a Jew nowadays. Descent was always traced matrilineally in the case of mixed marriage. His grandmother was Jewish, his mother didn't claim to be. Of course, the 1950 law allows us to keep out those who would endanger public security."

"Huh!" said Davies. "I suppose that means you're trying to cozy up to the Russkies again."

Abraham looked out of the window, avoiding Davies' eye. After suitable reflection, he replied, "We *are* trying to get the Russians out of Syria, as you know, and nothing must be allowed to rock the boat. Will you come and see him?"

"If my superiors agree."

"Naturally, naturally. Ah, here we are at Hyde Park Corner. Piccadilly Line direct to Cockfosters."

The Rover drew alongside the curb and Kaspar held the door open for Davies. The Director scrambled out, said his good-byes, and prepared once more to descend into the bowels of the earth. There was a certain lightness to his step now. Drakov in his power. It was unbelievable. That man knew more about Russia than anyone living, but would he talk? If he'd said anything worth knowing, the Israelis would have given him the world.

He was thinking about this when he nearly fell over a hand-lettered sign reading "Escalator Out of Order. Please Use the Stairs."

Joshua Bolivar Davies looked around; there wasn't a soul in sight. He drew back his foot and kicked the sign halfway across the concourse before limping off down the stairs.

5 The Prisoner

It had long been Joshua Davies' contention that national security would be better served by his flying on RAF planes in the dead of night. He was, he freely admitted, no wraith who would pass unnoticed through Heathrow Airport. When Davies surged through crowded lounges, people looked.

"Nonsense," he was assured. "It's like Poe's 'The Purloined Letter'; hide things in plain sight." So Davies suffered the ignominy of traveling by British Airways; of course, he held a first-class ticket which segregated him from the peasants and, closer to the point, entitled him to a wider seat.

Joshua Davies, easily recognized by the neatly uniformed stewardesses of BA, was not welcomed with quite the same smiles of neatly bonded teeth that other travelers received. On this flight to Israel, Davies resolved not to cause trouble. He resolved not to send back his lunch with a rude note, determined not to consume more than one drink while complaining it was watered down, corked, served without ice, and so on. He mentally promised to behave himself.

Alas, the best of intentions are often feeble straws.

The security measures at Heathrow were especially strict on flights to Israel. Bags were searched, electronic gates and hoops screened all passengers. Davies' cover required him to pass through the checks although a tiny top-secret device in his pocket prevented the metal detectors from sounding when they discovered the Beretta 92S in its shoulder holster.

The one comfort in a line of the sort Davies found himself in is the assurance, however faint, that one is getting *somewhere*. But there were so many Hasidim with broad hats, sidelocks, and beards, jumping about and gesticulating wildly, that Davies was never sure whether he was advancing or remaining in place.

The flight was a nightmare; a thousand children played in the aisle of the first-class compartment. He tried to listen to music, but all he could find was Montovani. He had three drinks to dull the pain in his forehead, sending two of them back because they were watered down. Protests that he had witnessed the opening of the minuscule bottles were airily dismissed. Lunch was supposed to be a Reuben sandwich; Davies claimed the meat was smaller than a ten-pence piece even though the head steward had secretly cannibalized two sandwiches to form Davies'. His very dry martini wasn't. The cherry cobbler contained enough parts to make perhaps one whole cherry; Davies demonstrated this to the entire cabin staff.

The crossword puzzle in the *Times* was too

easy; the only difficult clue was "formerly not lighted in Botswana"; this he took to be "Dark Continent," which gave him ten down, "intaglio."

He drank a second martini; it was no drier but contained three olives. After that he dozed, to everyone's relief. A couple of blue blankets and two pillows were liberated from the overhead storage bins, and, twisted like an enormous pretzel; Joshua Davies suspended his animation until the plane began its approach to Ben Gurion Airport at Lod.

He had slipped out of his shoes, handmade by Tricker's of Jermyn Street, when he took his nap. On awakening, he could find only one shoe, and it did nothing for his temper when a stewardess finally located it in coach. "Some of the Jewish boys were playing soccer with it," she said in a voice that did not imply they should be flogged. Davies struggled to drag the shoe on and, incapable of bending far enough, allowed the woman to slip it on for him. Then he permitted her to fasten his seat belt. He was the only passenger forced to use an extender.

Davies' face was near the woman's; she had big blue eyes and a delightfully ample bosom. He sighed. It would be nice once in a while to be able to proposition with some hope of success. But success depended on a strenuous diet for months. No woman was worth that.

The surcharge on a first-class ticket theoretically granted Joshua Davies the right to disembark first, but his Jewish traveling companions ignored his privilege and crowded the aisle long before the plane had taxied to a halt.

Repeated appeals in Yiddish, English, and Hebrew availed nothing.

Glowering, the Director was obliged to remain in his seat until the Hasidim had swept out, broad hats, beards, sidelocks, and all. It occurred to him that never in his life had he heard so great a proportion of a crowd talking at once to no one in particular. Likewise he was convinced that BA Flight 37 held the record for the greatest gross weight of carry-on luggage in the history.

A bus was waiting to carry them to the terminal; Davies refused to board it, as all the seats were taken, and there was no place for his large piece of hand luggage.

The sight of the florid Englishman standing resolutely on the tarmac dressed in a lightweight suit hinting of the great white hunter caused a good deal of merriment among his traveling companions.

Those employed by BA were not amused; the gentleman was constant trouble, but he was a regular traveler *and* he went first class. Moreover, he was British! A second bus was summoned, and in solitary splendor Joshua Davies reached customs.

Forewarned is forearmed; the Director was whisked through customs in a trice, leaving behind a trilingual babel. As he made his way through the waiting crowd; a thousand odors from sandalwood to garlic assailed his nostrils. The doors leading from the airport to the outside hesitated, gave a wheezy gasp, and finally opened, allowing the furnace outside to suck him into its embrace.

Life swirled around him. He received not a

few curious gazes from Orthodox Jews in white shirts and hand-knitted *kippah,* and girl kibbutzniks in khaki shorts and blouses. An Arab shoe-shine boy banged a brush on his box to attract Davies' attention, but the Director was too hot to bother.

Casting his eye over the waiting vehicles, the Director felt suddenly heartened as a large, certainly air-conditioned, Cadillac with darkened windows approached. Unhappily, it swept past him and was gone. He looked around. The limousines were filling rapidly. The heat was overwhelming. A young woman dressed in an army uniform was leaning against the side of an old World War II jeep, a pair of sunglasses hanging from her head. A 9-mm Beretta M1951 pistol, ancestor of his own 92S, was holstered by her side. Long, dark hair fell off her shoulders. Davies couldn't remember meeting anyone like her in the British army. She looked him over, chewing her gum. She had a dark Semitic beauty with high cheekbones glistening slightly in the heat. Davies was perspiring freely as the girl strolled over, eyeing him with a touch of amusement mingled with scorn.

Davies was struck by her dark honey-colored eyes. Her movements were feline and provocative.

"Mr. Davies?" she asked.

"Er . . . right," he confessed, feeling somewhat foolish as she looked him up and down.

"Put on a little weight, haven't we?" Her English betrayed a hint of an American accent.

"There's nothing *little* about my weight," huffed Davies, wanting to be severe but falling victim to the frank gaze and fine long eyelashes. She had the thin nose and full lips of a fashion model.

"You look English," she said.

Somehow the Director thought that was an unintentional dig. He may well have stood out in a crowd, but how could she see he was English? The airport was full of the weirdest-looking . . .

"It's the suit, you see. They don't make them like that anymore. This your only luggage?"

"Yes, I—"

She picked up his bag as if it were made of feathers, moved over to the jeep, and flung it in the back. Then she swung into the driver's seat while Davies scrambled quickly to the passenger side. There was scarcely time to grasp the top of the windshield and haul himself over the side before the sudden jerk of the vehicle flung him firmly into his seat.

"Raquela," she said.

"Joshua."

"I know." She looked at him. The army blouse was taut over her breasts and the trousers were cut to a small waist. A beret was perched rakishly on the back of her long hair. Davies assumed it was fastened securely, for the jeep had no roof. She put on her sunglasses. There was an animal sensuality to her face that was not lost on the Director of Department D. Davies fumbled for his own sunglasses before remembering he had left them on the hall table at home.

"You want some gum?"

"Er. No thanks, I—"

"Okay." Raquela reached into a pocket over her left breast and drew out a stick. Without batting an eyelid, she let go of the steering wheel, slit the paper wrapper with a fingernail, and took the pink stick from its silver case. Instead of putting it straight in her mouth, she pushed it against her tongue so it curled up first. Then it was in her mouth. There was something naively sensual about the act. She grasped the steering wheel again. "I was in the States for a year. Picked up the gum habit there. You been to America?"

"Many—"

"It stinks."

"It does? I rather like—"

"They talk a good scene, but they're still male chauvinist pigs at heart."

Davies sat back. His fondness for America, especially New York with its excellent restaurants—Cafe des Artists in particular, but also Gallagher's—was heartfelt. It did not seem to him, however, that Raquela would want to hear about them.

The girl drove with little regard for anyone else. The city traffic was a swirling mass of incandescence, gasoline fumes, and short tempers. Davies' suit had been made by Dolores to her brother's specifications. It was cotton and Dacron, which allowed the body to breathe. People perspired a lot in Israel, and because of the lack of humidity, they didn't always realize it. Nylon fabrics didn't wrinkle, it was true, but they were nonbreathing. Davies would look rumpled, but he would be less hot and ill-tempered. He had a jacket for the evening hours; once the sun set, it would be quite chilly.

Lod was chiefly a Jewish town, though he saw a few Arab headdresses mingling with the T-shirts and jeans. Shop windows were piled high with merchandise. Davies saw piles of Persian carpets, hand-embroidered silks, and an encouraging number of delicatessens whose windows were stocked with wine, dairy products, and sparkling boxes of Elite chocolates. A large number of flower shops offered tall gladioli. He decided not to inquire of his driver why this was so. He also knew she would not be interested to hear that Lod was the birthplace of England's patron saint, St. George.

With a start, he realized she was talking to him.

"In this country it's called the Golda syndrome," shouted Raquela.

"Golda Meir?"

"Right." Raquela's blue eyes fastened on his face. "We've created a myth out of Golda Meir. To rise to the top she sacrificed her femininity. . . ."

She looked away from him to scream an obscenity at an Arab who was beating a tired donkey with a stick. He shouted back. She gave him a raised finger and laughed. Changing gears, she hurtled around a stalled Dodge taxi. Everyone, as usual, was leaning on his car horn. "So people say, 'Golda made it, so can you.' And then they give you the shaft."

"Shaft?" he echoed, trying to be heard over the wind.

"Shaft. It's tokenism. Liberalism here is only skin deep."

"Ah." Davies settled back; he found it hard to concentrate on conversation in an open jeep, shouting to a person only two feet away.

"Women can't fight in the army; did you know that?"

"Yes, I—"

"I'd show them if I did. . . ." She grinned wolfishly. "How many women do you see in a general's uniform with an eye patch?"

Davies sat silent as his driver negotiated a traffic island.

"You go to the Wailing Wall, and there's a chain-link fence separating men from women. Separate but equal. Well, I don't go anyway. A few years ago I ate a piece of pork." The jeep swerved around a bus, narrowly missing a wandering goat. "On Yom Kippur, no less. Know what happened?"

"No," Davies shouted.

"I threw up."

"A punishment," said the Director, "from Divine Providence."

"Hell no. I'd bought it from some Armenian, and it had gone bad. Religion's just a way to keep women servile."

Joshua Davies, honorary organist at St. Paul's Methodist Church, felt he should show outrage at this remark.

"Religions should not—"

"Anyway, none of us believes that shit anyway. Do you think there's a god?"

"I hope so. I'm a Methodist."

"What's that about?"

"An evangelical faith begun by John Wesley. It is the most simple and honest version of Christ's teaching."

"Is it like the Catholic . . . ?"

"It is not!"

She gave him a puzzled look. "How can there be a god? If there was, why were six million Jews turned into soap and lampshades?"

"If I could answer that" said Joshua, "I'd be a rabbi, not a Methodist."

Raquela looked at Davies for a reflective moment. Suddenly she slapped him on a giant thigh. "Right. I've heard about the English sense of humor. It's very Jewish. You're okay. In fact, you're the type of guy I like to screw."

It occurred to Joshua Davies that if he had no duties and no pressing engagements he would like to spend his life driving briskly in a jeep with such a woman. And when Raquela delivered him to Abraham forty-five minutes later, he was still wearing a smirk of smug self-satisfaction.

"Raquela is a sabra," said Abraham as they left his office and began walking down the long white-tiled corridor. The old hospital signs had not been taken down. "Born here. They drive us mad and fill us with joy. The word comes from the Hebrew *sābhār*, meaning 'prickly pear.' "

"She holds strong opinions," agreed Joshua Davies.

"The only thing that kept me going in Lubyanka Prison was my belief that God had a purpose beyond my understanding. I was in solitary, hard regimen, for one year and one hundred days. In all that time, I heard only the sound of the guard once a day. Bread and water and toilet, once a day."

Davies grunted. "It's a wonder you kept your sanity."

"I felt better coming out than going in. It was as if I'd been"—he hunted for the word— "purified. I survived and I thank God for it every day. Yet my own kids won't even go to the synagogue. Who'll say Kaddish for me?"

Davies said nothing. Abraham led them to the left. The sign said "Triage Unit."

"The other day Dafna, aged ten mind you, asked me not to come to the school play. Do you know why?"

It was a rhetorical question. He answered it himself. "She was embarrassed because of my Hebrew pronunciation. My own kid blushes at my Hebrew and winces at my accent."

A sentry holding a 9-mm Uzi submachine gun and trying unsuccessfully to hide a cigarette behind his back checked Abraham's ID. He and Davies went on down the hall to a steel gate guarded by another man in uniform. "I talked to her teacher. Not much comfort there. She said, and I quote, 'We teachers are either pals or emissaries from the Gestapo.' What do you think of that?"

"It's hard," said Davies. "But I gather they don't smirk or giggle about sex."

"You can say that again," replied Abraham. "I could tell you stories would make your hair curl. Mind your head when we go down the steps there. And they know nothing about the world." Leading the way down a short flight of stairs, he turned at right angles and descended a second, longer flight. Their shoes clanged on the ironwork. "Julius Caesar gets an hour in history class and Theodor Herzl gets two months. And if you asked them to find Yotvata on a map, they could do it, but not Jamaica or New Zealand. My God!"

Before them was a massive steel door; Abraham placed his hand into the cipher-box, and a red light went on above them. From around his neck he took his plastic ID and moved the card down the edge of the door to about the midpoint. The light turned green, the door lock clicked. "Very cloak-and-dagger," said Abraham, "but you can't be too careful. We had Eichmann here for a while before moving him to Haifa."

A long table facing a dark window and two chairs behind it were the only furniture. "If you want anything else, you have to bring it with you," said Abraham, flicking on a switch. Immediately the window lit up. It was a television, the picture transmitted from the cell, twenty yards away. Davies leaned forward toward the screen as if by doing so he might see more of the legendary man who had once held more real power in Russia than everyone but the Premier and the head of the KGB.

There wasn't anything spectacular about the prisoner. Wearing prison khaki shirt and trousers and open sandals, Drakov looked rather like an aging librarian. *This* was the gravest threat in all Russia? The Director gave an involuntary shudder. How many thousands had made the mistake of thinking Drakov looked like nothing.

He was small, thin, and had lost much of his hair except along the sides of his head, where it was gray. His face was depressingly ordinary, and his chin was almost swallowed up by his neck.

"He has glasses on," Davies said in surprise.

"They were taken away from him at first, naturally. Later he was allowed plastic lenses during interrogation. Now he has them all the time. You see"—he spread his hands in a mixture of bewilderment and resignation—"he's committed no crimes against Jews."

Davies sounded irritated. "He's sent a few into the Gulag, hasn't he?"

"We don't have any *proof.* And whatever he's done might not necessarily be criminal acts we could try him for. Worst of all, he's a Jew."

"I see your point; trying a Jew wouldn't look good in Israel. Why don't you just kill him? You want us to?"

"Our law is specific. No Jew can kill another Jew."

Davies' laugh rumbled up from his great belly. "We've got laws too. The only one I *don't* break is the law of gravity."

Abraham sighed, his eyes fixed on the prisoner. "God knows I'd like to. Even so, I can't account totally for my hatred of the man. It's not so much what he says as . . . the subtext. I feel I must hate the man—but he is a Jew, and our religion is all I had when I was in the Lubyanka. You said it's a wonder I kept my sanity. Well, one thing kept me sane—my faith. Sane, yes, but not really alive. I wouldn't have cared if I'd died. That would have been easy."

He fumbled for his cigarettes. "I was afraid of going mad. I said *going* mad, not *being* mad. The process was what terrified me. It was like being balanced on the edge of a dark gulf. I knew on a gut level exactly what King Lear meant when he cried out, 'Let me not be mad, sweet Heavens.' How Shakespeare knew, God knows, but he did."

"But you survived, with your sanity."

"One day they put me on a cattle train. For the first three days there was no food or water. Finally I reached Vienna with only the clothes on my back and an unshakable belief in the God of my fathers. That's what held me up through all that eternal hell."

There was a silence; Davies waited.

"He's a Jew," Abraham pronounced simply. And that's that.

Davies looked back at the screen. The cell was a large one as such places go, about fifteen feet square, and the simple furniture was adequate if not comfortable. There was a chess set. Drakov would play a white piece, then go to the opposite side, study the position, and play black.

"He does that for hours. One of my men who's a chess nut says they are all famous games. The man's memory is beyond belief."

"We couldn't terminate him except for cause," Davies said thoughtfully. "He must be a proven danger to the realm. He's no danger here."

"He's got to go," said Abraham a shade too quickly. "He's too dangerous."

"Why not leak to the Russkies that he's

alive? They'll do the job for you. You can count on it."

Abraham cleared his throat; Davies was surprised to realize that the Israeli was on the defensive. "As I said, he is, technically, a Jew. At least there's enough Jewish blood in him to make it damn difficult to railroad him. And we don't want the Russians upset; they're hard enough to live with as it is. If we can get them out of Syria permanently, our lives will be a lot more comfortable. If word gets out we have this creature . . ."

Davies nodded. "I see." Studying Drakov for several minutes, he kept his thoughts to himself. "There are guidelines," he admitted finally. "This man is too dangerous to live; he has too much . . . power of detachment."

Abraham nodded. "He's shown no signs of remorse."

Davies shook his head. "That's not what I mean. At the moment his fate is in the balance, but all his attention is focused on that chessboard. His life hangs by a thread, yet he's concentrating on a game of chess played years ago. Detachment."

Abraham knew he was right.

"You have him under twenty-four-hour watch?"

"Absolutely. And in all the time he's never once shown any emotion. He performs every act methodically and deliberately; we've never caught him off guard."

"You won't," said Davies.

Drakov left his game and sat on his bed. He looked briefly at the light bulb. For a moment,

Davies was looking directly into the face of his nemesis. "Funny how disappointing people are when you really get a chance to see them up close."

"Had the same experience when I saw Eichmann," agreed Abraham. "I'd heard so much about him, I thought he'd be one of the movie Nazis, blond, tall, piercing blue eyes."

"And?"

"Terrifyingly ordinary. Nearsighted. Obsequious."

"Most mass murderers are bureaucrats at heart; that's what makes the world so scary," muttered Davies. "But you can't put this one on trial. Couldn't the Guys handle him?"

"This comes from the very top: no sanctioning of a Jew by any Israeli." He studied Drakov, who had stretched out on his bed, legs crossed, a cigarette in his right hand. "Sending him back would be the same as killing him."

"Worse. The Russkies are experts in wet affairs, torture or murder. They'd have a long talk with him in the Lubyanka before they killed him."

"Tragic irony?"

"Screw irony. What do you want from us?"

"Let's go, shall we?" He led Davies from the room, and they retraced their steps to the main level. An enclosed veranda gave them a panoramic view of Jerusalem. Each took a white wicker chair on opposite sides of a small wrought-iron table.

"This used to be the solarium," Abraham said, laying his pack of cigarettes on the table and carefully centering his lighter on top. "You know, I finally asked him why he refused a woman. I couldn't stand not knowing. It's one of the things that make me so damn angry with him. He makes me want to ask him things, when I'm the one in charge."

"What did he say?" said Davies, coloring slightly. "About a woman, I mean."

"Something about sex making people act irrationally. He felt whoever holds out longest has the upper hand in the end."

"That's a hell of a Freudian response," growled Davies. "Maybe he should have been a monk."

Abraham laughed. "If he had, I guarantee you he'd be the Pope. What about a drink?"

Davies brightened. The Israeli beckoned; a waiter with the thinnest pencil mustache Davies had ever seen detached himself from the shadows.

"I'd like arak," said Davies.

"Two araks," his host told the waiter.

"He's an Arab spy," Abraham confided. "Damn useful for feeding the odd bit of disinformation. Right now he's picking up hints of a captured Nazi being interrogated below. Later he'll find out the Nazi was murdered and buried in cement in the Dead Sea Canal."

"Won't you need to supply a name?"

"That won't be difficult; every year or so we bag a couple. You get the picture?"

The waiter reappeared; Davis sipped the arak. "Whew," he murmured, "the Arab doesn't skimp on alcoholic content."

"Arak isn't Diet Pepsi."

The sky over Jerusalem was an almost metallic blue, not a cloud to be seen. Davies appeared to be studying the Old City, spread out below him; in fact, he was puzzled. Things hadn't gone the way he'd expected. He was frankly surprised at Abraham's reaction; it was more personal than it should have been. The man was a professional, yet he'd let Drakov get to him.

"We can't take him unless he offers something," Davies told the Israeli finally. "We've long since abandoned our role as welfare state to the world's homeless."

"But you'll consider it?" There was a touch of overeagerness.

"That's why I've traveled two and a half thousand miles."

"Good. Good." Abraham finished his drink and Davies followed suit. "Let's go to the interrogation room."

When Drakov was brought before them he'd been blindfolded so that he could not get an overall view of the internment camp during his brief journey. A guard removed the blindfold at Davies' request and the prisoner blinked in the neon lighting, still standing. Abraham went to a wall safe and took out a folder, a large dictionary, and a pair of glasses, which he handed to Drakov.

"This gentleman"—he indicated Davies—"will question you."

Drakov carefully adjusted his glasses. Turning, he looked at Davies, who returned his gaze without faltering.

"Ah yes. Joshua Davies of Department D of the British Military Intelligence Service. In the parlance of our trade you have the nickname 'the Butcher.' " Drakov's English was excellent.

"Think of me as the rat catcher."

"Ah." Drakov took the chair in front of the desk; Davies took the one opposite and picked up the folder Abraham had given him.

"You are Anton Mikhailovich Drakov, late Director of Department A of the First Directorate?"

"We were elevated to service status."

"I congratulate you."

Drakov waved his hand deprecatingly. "It was more the result of reorganization than anything else."

"If you admit who you are, there is no need to examine your curriculum vita in detail."

"I'm relieved."

"Because it is so condemning?"

"Because I've heard it so many times here."

"Yet it is an interesting life, isn't it?" Davies persisted. "You rise to the top in a society whose intolerance of Jews is legendary. You receive the Order of Lenin. You are responsible for success after success. Your office is in the same building as the head of the KGB himself."

"I suspect my office is now in the hands of that suckling pig, Popovich."

"It was your plan that allowed Russian forces to occupy all Berlin briefly."

"Berlin would have been ours if the leaders had kept their nerve."

"The American President was willing to fight."

"Words. Words. Words."

"So you became the scapegoat."

A cold smile flickered briefly. "That's the way the game is played."

"Not in all countries, or so I hope. I'm looking forward to a pension one day."

"So was I."

Davies realized he had met his match. He stopped dueling. He sat back, his hands lightly clasped over his belly. It was time for facts. He picked up the folder.

"You left Russia disguised as . . ."

"Yuri Semyonovich Moiseyev. He had already gone to his reward, and Russia believed I was dead, too. Unfortunately my plane was singled out for destruction."

"You were extraordinarily lucky. A piece of steel no bigger than a bullet broke off and entered your face just to the right of the nose. Your jawbone slowed the momentum of the fragment until it became embedded a quarter of an inch away from vital blood vessels leading to the brain." He paused. "I imagine you've heard all this, too."

"No. I knew I had lost a tooth."

"If the fragment had been less irregular in shape, it would have severed those vessels and killed you. Any higher and it would have penetrated very thin bone to enter the brain." He put down the folder. "Lower and it would have smashed through the mouth to the spinal cord."

Drakov said nothing.

"Even so. Had you not been thrown on your stomach you might well have choked on your own blood." He paused, expecting a response. There was none, so he went on. "The rest of your injuries are attributable to the violence of the landing."

"And so here we all are."

A long silence followed. "There is a problem," said Davies at last. "I understand you are unwilling to pay for your keep."

"I am not a traitor," replied Drakov. "If Mikhail Gorbachev offered me a pardon, and if I could trust him, I would return to Moscow tomorrow."

Davies shuffled uncomfortably, his huge rear overflowing the chair. "I will have to have something."

"I am not a traitor," Drakov repeated.

"I'm not asking for the plans of your latest spy satellite. What I need is enough to go to my superiors with and say you've shown a desire to repent."

Drakov got up from his chair and Davies stood as well. "And if I give you something, what guarantee do I have that you will live up to your end of the bargain?"

"You're not in any position to wheel and deal."

"Oh, I think I am. Neither of you will kill me—too soft, both of you." He looked first at Davies, then at Abraham. "There are rules . . ."

"Which can be bent," growled Davies. He thrust his face close to the prisoner's. "And accidents happen."

Drakov walked slowly around the perimeter of the room. "Nothing happened to Adolf Eichmann, who had six million Jews killed."

"The world knew we had Eichmann," said

Abraham. "Everyone believes you are dead; we could put history right."

"Funny, I said something just like that once to a creature of mine called Lunts." Drakov's tone was almost conversational. "I don't think cold-blooded murder is in your line, however. *Mokrie dela,* wet affairs, are for the less squeamish." He sighed. "But I cannot stay in Israel. You don't want me. So I must give up the orange groves for smog and damp."

"Life is full of hardship," said Davies sarcastically.

"Which means," continued Drakov, "that I must give you something."

Davies was mildly disturbed; Drakov was leading the discussion.

"Very well," the Russian said. "I will work my passage. This information should prove valuable." He sat down again, made himself comfortable, and began.

"In 1970, I put into effect an operation designed to entrap an American solider. It was a routine operation and involved a young woman employed by the KGB—a swallow, as they are known. What happened was quite extraordinary. Remember"—he kept his eyes on Davies—"this was seventeen years ago in East Berlin. But it may change the course of history."

6 Flashback

They fled south into the dense forest, Leni driving Herr Rosenberg's car, Gary beside her. Within half an hour, they discovered a little *Gasthäuser* nestled in a tiny village. It had the low ceiling and oak panels of fairy tales, and round tables in the dining room that had darkened with age. There were two alcoves where discreet encounters could take place. The owner, red-faced and burly, with astonishingly profuse side whiskers, summed them up at once and escorted them to a table in one of the alcoves, occasionally flapping a small white towel against his thigh.

It was impossible that Leni should be hungry, yet she ordered with great enthusiasm, casting laughing glances at Gary when she wasn't talking to the owner.

Gary ordered *Saiten,* a juicy sausage, served with a wine, Elfinger, recommended by the owner.

"It is called 'eleven fingers' because the abbot of the monastery considered it too good for the monks to drink," the amiable proprietor explained, "but he let them dip their fingers in and lick them, so every monk wished for eleven fingers. Good, eh?" He gave a great roar of laughter, and the three men eating solemnly at a nearby table looked up in surprise.

Letterville grinned, but not at Herr Krause's joke. He got a kick out of watching Germans. Even in an out-of-the-way place like this, the atmosphere was almost reverent. The inn was like a church where homage had to be paid to Bacchus and the God of Good Eating. Germans mostly had fun when told to. On their calendars they marked the first week in October as a time of gaiety, went to the Oktoberfest, and let themselves go, sitting on long benches, singing and shrieking in unison. While consuming beer from incredibly large jugs and eating a whole roasted ox, they roared with laugher at the sight of fat people attempting to dance, or huge bandsmen with silly little hats fastened to their heads with bright ribbons. At the end of that week, with a certain sense of relief, they looked at the calendar and realized they didn't have to be amused anymore.

The young people ate, sitting opposite each other, knees almost touching under the tiny table. Once Leni reached under the table and caressed him; when he looked up, as much startled as aroused, she laughed.

"Are we going to get a room?" she asked in a loud whisper.

"Shhh!" Letterville said, embarrassed, afraid the men at the round table could hear.

"Well, are we?" She had slipped out of her shoes and was lightly running the instep of her foot up and down his leg.

"Does he . . . I mean, is there . . . ?"

She leaned toward him. "There's always one—for times like this."

Leni was right; the room was cozy. They could thank the East German regime for the lack of electric lighting; a feeble sixty-watt bulb hanging from a bent iron bracket supplied the only illumination. The one piece of furniture with any character was a large mirror on the wall by the head of the bed. Most of it was mere glass, all its silvering having long since flaked off. Parting the heavy window curtains, Letterville could see the small courtyard with an old tractor and Herr Rosenberg's car tucked out of the sight of passersby. Besides the mirror, there was little furniture, only a sturdy chest of drawers and an oak wardrobe touching the ceiling, and the large bed.

"Do you approve, Gary?" she asked, sitting on the edge of the bed and sinking into the great down mattress.

He pretended to consider it.

"Cute, not tacky," he said.

" 'Cute' I know; what is 'tacky'?"

"An American word only an American can use."

"I see."

"Well, it looks authentic, like something out of the Grimm brothers. I shall change into a wolf and eat you up."

Realizing what he had said, he flashed her a quick look and was glad the double meaning had escaped her. He was relieved but couldn't explain to himself why.

Leni suddenly threw herself backward onto the bed. Raising her arms to him, without saying a word, Leni made it clear she wanted him to join her. Letterville needed no other encouragement. He took her in his arms and they lay across the bed, devouring each other eagerly with their lips.

She moved in lubricious ripples; he was hard instantly. Looking into his eyes, she murmured, "I love you, American officer. I love you. Tonight I will prove it."

Leni's lips reclaimed his; her tongue explored the recesses of his mouth; Gary rejoiced in her hunger. He ran his hands along the contour of her thighs and legs. A low sound, deep in her throat, reminded him of the purring of a cat.

As her long fingers stroked his shoulders and back, he eased the shoulder of her dress down and licked the mound of her breast, easing the lacy cup of her bra aside. "Stop, stop," Leni said, pushing him gently to one side and rising to her feet. "The light." She crossed the tiny room looking for the switch. "I can't find—"

"Well, we can crawl under this enormous quilt," said Letterville.

"It is all right," said Leni. "I am not a virgin." And she stepped out of her evening gown, letting it fall in a heap on the floor. Reaching in back of her, she unsnapped her bra and dropped it on the dresser.

Leni almost dived back into the bed, but not before Letterville saw the large, firm breasts and pointed nipples. He'd heard small-breasted women could be exciting, but he confessed to a certain prejudice in the matter. He stripped off his clothes in an instant, hanging them carelessly from a bedpost. Taking her in his arms again, he pressed hard against her; an involuntary shudder seized Leni as his hands searched for pleasure points. The woman, immersed in sensation, was no less interested in the man. The musculature of his chest, the fine hair of his legs and rougher fur of his chest; all these were wondrous to her.

Gary gently sucked her nipples and drew his tongue slowly along the furrow of her belly. Then his tongue was flicking in and out of the silky hair; he went lower. And lower. For an instant, Leni felt a welling up of panic. This she had never permitted. Yet she knew, somehow, it was *right*.

Letterville parted her with his fingers, his tongue seeking the most secret and vital place in her creation. When his mouth closed on it, the needle-sharp sensation was beyond imagining. Leni gasped, arching her body sharply toward him.

At first his mouth was gentle, but as she built to her climax, he became more forceful, almost insolent. In the midst of her pleasure, Leni feared only one thing—that he would withdraw before the exquisite moment of release. She cared not if she was humiliating herself; at this moment he could demand anything of her. Her hands clasped his head firmly against her thighs, and she rubbed her slippery flesh and silky hair fiercely against his insistent mouth—building.

Building, to the point of pain.

Leni opened her mouth without being aware of it; her breath came in ragged spurts. And when the climax began, she moaned with joy and release, massaging her nipples between finger and thumb to increase what was already beyond bearing.

In ever-widening ripples the electric sensation expanded from its tiny, hard beginning until it absorbed her whole body, and great racking sobs were forced from her.

She was so utterly drained, she felt she could sleep forever.

But there was to be no sleep; again their mouths joined, and she could feel the smooth hardness of him as he entered her in one swift movement.

At first she was there to be used, unable to function, but the rhythmic thrusting imbued her with energy. She lifted her legs high, using her thighs to grip his hips.

Gary Letterville's breath was being driven from him; there was sweat on his brow, and salty drops were shaken loose to fall on her face. She felt him stiffen and was afraid. "Wait, wait," she urged, "a few seconds more."

She opened her eyes to gaze into his; they were one, nipples touching, her breasts crushed against his chest. He was enclosed in her and she in him.

Leni was on the edge; the preliminary warnings were radiating from her. A few seconds more. Only a few seconds. But in his face there was a look of pain, and she knew he could not wait.

Desperately she thrust up to meet him, knowing that by doing so she would precipitate his release. With a great groan, he reared up and thrust hard into her. At that same instant, Leni dug her nails into his back.

"Come, come now," she tried to say, but all she managed was a gasp.

Their orgasm was almost simultaneous. As he groaned, arching his back for the last time, her head was lifted from the pillow, then snapped back. Letterville fell across her, face forward on the great mattress.

The French call it "the little death." She knew why.

Herr Rosenberg wasn't pleased with Leni's explanation about why she had run off with his car. His Prussian heart was troubled by a suspicion that Leni had used it for some need of her own, and not, as she'd said, to rush a pregnant woman to the hospital.

One day, Leni did not appear at the office; he waited for a telephone call. At 11:45, he was informed by his superior, Herr Hoft, that he would be receiving a new secretary the following morning.

Fräulein Krumholz was an extremely ugly woman with pimples; she wore stockings with holes in them and refused to adhere to Herr Rosenberg's insistence on the need for one-inch margins on correspondence. She couldn't spell.

Summoning up a courage he had not thought he possessed, Herr Rosenberg complained to a higher authority and was told to mind his own business.

Gary Letterville's reaction was more dramatic. A day after their meeting he dialed Leni's apartment and was told the number had been disconnected. That did not disturb him unduly. In 1970 the East Berlin telephone service was erratic. He went around to her apartment and found it locked.

He knew nothing of Leni's family, and it was soon clear the East Germans were never going to tell him anything of her whereabouts. They added, after a month of stonewalling, that if he did not cease pestering them, they would declare him persona non grata, and demand his removal.

He persisted, and the East Germans carried out their threat. Paul O'Mallory drove him to Templehof.

"It's typical of these Commies, Gary," he said at the bottom of the airplane steps. "You can't have romatic love in a totalitarian state. George Orwell said as much." He shook his head. "Only Big Brother is entitled to that kind of devotion. Love between two people is subversive." He wanted to embrace the younger man, to help or comfort him, but he knew there was nothing he or anyone else would be able to do.

"Someday I'll find her," said Letterville fiercely. "Someday."

The two men stared at Drakov as he finished his tale and shook a cigarette from the pack in front of him. Automatically Abraham reached for his book of matches, struck one, and offered it to the Russian.

"I presume you would not have told us this story," said Davies, "unless it was the same man."

"Of course it is the same man. I do not go in

for romantic tales. This Gary Letterville is now the Vice President of the United States. A heartbeat away from the Presidency, I believe they are fond of saying."

"The girl Leni worked for you?"

"One of my subordinates. I was kept informed; doubtless you are aware the KGB still believes in the efficacy of blackmail. I myself . . ." He shook his head sorrowfully. "I myself am less confident of its power these days."

"Morality's falling apart," said Davies, with heavy irony, and Drakov nodded.

"So the girl was a setup, one of your swallows."

"Who took him to a country inn we have specially wired for such occasions. If you knew how many men visited that swallows' nest. Men seem to get in heat—"

"Get on with it," growled Davies.

Drakov stood up, stretched his back, and rubbed it. "It cannot be lumbago," he muttered in Russian. "It's too hot around here."

He sat on the edge of his bunk, straightened his legs, and crossed them. "The KGB is patient—unimaginative now that I am gone—but patient. Ten years may pass before an agent is activated, twenty before some old photos are allowed to surface."

"You expected Letterville to become Vice President of the United States," Davies said dryly.

"Ah," replied Drakov, "we are not that . . . that . . . *Delphic*." He looked pleased with himself. "And Mr. Letterville was only one of a hundred army officers targeted. There are some who resist, you know." Drakov paused. "But very few. These women are good. Then there are those who prefer young men. It always—"

"Get on with it," growled Davies again.

"The KGB waits for things to evolve. Eventually one of the targets may justify the expense and effort." A cold smile appeared on the Russian's countenance, and Davies longed to slam his fist into that face.

"If one of these men reached high office, we could apply a little subtle pressure."

"One favor leads to another, and another, until the victim is on the brink of treason," said Abraham. "It's the oldest method in the world."

"And at that point, the man has done so much he cannot refuse," finished Drakov. "It's a perfect method." Then, frowning, he added, "Unless you get someone like Sukarno, who demanded copies of the film to show his friends. Very funny."

"A disappointment," commented Davies ironically.

"Well, Letterville was filmed. In those days we had to use film cameras. They were noisy. But a couple in that situation makes its own noise. As for microphones, every piece of carved wood was a perfect hiding place. You understand, this was small beer. No one expected such a coup. To entrap the Vice President of the United States!"

"You have the films?" asked Davies.

"Alas, no. They were all destroyed in a fire."

Davies looked at him in astonishment. "So what do you have to deal with? You can't blackmail a man with a memory. You don't think you're going to sneak into England on this pigshit and get an old-age pension, do you?"

Spreading his hands expressively, Drakov replied, "The affair was long forgotten by all except me. The girl was pulled off Letterville because she was needed immediately on another job—the French Ambassador to West Berlin."

"Where is she now?"

"Wherever the people in charge of such things buried her."

There was a long silence. The Russian finally slapped his hands together, stood, and gazed off into the distance. "So now we come to the point."

"You don't have a point," snarled Davies. "No records, no woman. You don't have a damn thing." Turning to Abraham, he said, "He's all yours; let's go."

Davies reached the door.

"There was a child."

The Englishman's fist, raised to bang on the door, dropped slowly. "A child," he echoed, turning to face Drakov.

"A girl. The Vice President of the United States had a child. Do you realize what that could mean?" Drakov was speaking with an intensity he had not shown up to that point. "Think," he continued, "what pressure could be brought against a man whose daughter you hold. His only child, you understand."

"If he believes the story," muttered Davies.

"He will believe it. There are records. I made sure of that. All that is needed is the name the girl Leni used and the name of the village where the child was born. These I have."

Abraham, showing signs of agitation, suddenly raised his hand. "Stop. I don't want to hear any more."

"Why the hell not?" Davies asked.

Abraham looked embarrassed. "I represent the State of Israel. If something is said I can't overlook, I must act upon it. Whatever this man tells you must be in private. I cannot listen to anything that might compromise Israel's relationship with the United States."

Davies nodded. Without the financial support of the United States, Israel would collapse in a sea of international debts. Wondering if the same might not be said of Britain, he addressed Abraham. "Well, you've recorded all this so far."

Abraham cleared his throat. "No."

"All this is off the record?" asked Davies, clearly stunned.

A nod.

"Well," said Davies, "in that case take us somewhere safe but unofficial."

Abraham appeared relieved. "It's not a minor matter. Remember, the problem is, he may *technically* be Jewish."

The Englishman caught the subtext: "Please get rid of this man any way you can and, above all, don't let us know anything official."

They moved Drakov at night, in a sealed car, curtains drawn. Drakov was dressed in an Arab headdress and long cloak. The car followed the southwest wall as far as the Jaffa Gate connecting the old town with the Jewish new town.

In the shadow of the Citadel, they crossed Omar ben Qattab Square, reaching David Street and its continuation, Chain Street. To the north, in uneasy harmony, lay the Christian and Muslim quarters. To the south were the Armenian and Jewish regions.

Abraham was in the front passenger seat. In the backseat, Davies and Drakov saw and heard nothing. The night sounds were completely eliminated by the heavy soundproofing of the automobile. In addition, music was played through speakers. They might have been anywhere.

The car halted at an apartment building and Drakov was hurried into one of the apartments before inquisitive eyes could focus upon him.

"It's fully soundproofed," said Abraham. "You'll be safe here. When you need me, just lift the phone; it's a direct, secure line."

Drakov had rid himself of the Arab headdress and robe. He looked around the apartment. It wasn't elaborate—one bedroom, with mass produced modern furniture, a combination living room and kitchen. Everything was cheap, anonymous, ideal for a safe house. "I suspect we are in Jerusalem," said Drakov. "The driver avoided a direct route, of course, but—"

Davies put his hat on the coffee table. "Wherever we are is of no concern to you. This is not a Cook's tour."

"Religion is an astonishing thing," continued Drakov smoothly, as if he hadn't heard. "It is—"

"The opiate of the masses?" Davies finished.

The Russian fumbled for his glasses, found

some toilet paper, and polished the lenses. "Are you a Roman Catholic?" he asked curiously.

"No. A Methodist."

"Ah."

Davies had no idea what that meant. "You were about to say, back there, before you frightened the State of Israel?"

"I'll give you the details if you take me in," Drakov said.

Davies shook his head violently; rolls of pink flesh wagged in sympathy. "Not enough. I want that girl. Find her. Fetch her to me."

Drakov looked incredulous. "How can I find her? It was seventeen years ago. I don't know where she is. She'd have been born in 1971, so she'd be sixteen years old. Surely your agents . . ." For the first time, Davies thought he sensed agitation in Drakov. "Why me? If you have the names, your men could easily—"

"You find her; bring her to me in London. That way, if anything goes wrong, it's a Russian scheme, not British."

Drakov was gazing at the wall but seeing nothing.

"And if . . . if I can find the girl, what then?"

Davies relaxed but didn't show it. "One: Immunity from prosecution. Two: A new identity. Three: A government pension—scale. Four: Total silence from us on who you are to any other power, including both Russia and America. But look, Anton Mikhailovich, don't try to welsh on this. Once you're committed, it's all the way. No weaseling out, or I'll show my fangs."

"That sounds like a threat," said Drakov.

"Believe it."

"When do I report?"

"I'll give you a number to call when you're both in London."

Drakov walked slowly around Davies' chair; Davies wanted to turn his head and follow his progress but was afraid that would show fear. Suddenly Drakov's cheek was next to his.

"I could kill you now; one blow and you're dead."

"But you won't," replied Davies. "I'm your only hope."

"It might be worth it, fat man," the voice hissed, "because I'm going to die anyhow one day, by accident or design."

Davies remained immobile, looking neither left nor right. "Accident is best. Then you don't have time to worry," he said casually.

Drakov stood and faced the Englishman. "And now, my terms . . ."

"You don't have—"

"My name is prominently listed in your KGB necrology files. I want everyone absolutely certain Anton Drakov is dead. Check your KGB Wanted List to make sure my name has been removed."

Davies dug into his inside jacket pocket for a cigar. "Do you want us to ask the KGB to check and make sure you aren't on their List of Wanted Criminals?"

"I doubt even you could do that."

When the cigar was lit, Davies studied the glowing tip. "All right."

"I'll need two passports, a South African and

a British birth certificate, a marriage certificate . . ."

"Abraham will handle all that," growled Davies. "You just deliver."

"It will not be easy," Drakov cautioned. "There was a routine surveillance procedure, so I followed the girl's progress for a few years. She was brought up by an aunt."

"Her name?"

Drakov gave a chuckle without any warmth in it. "Frau X. She moved from the country to West Berlin, where the social programs are generous. That was ten years ago. Then Letterville was defeated in his run for the Senate, so surveillance was dropped."

Joshua Davies was increasingly uncomfortable in the apartment. Not only were the windows nailed shut, they were curtained. Was there any oxygen at all? He picked up his hat and fanned himself. Drakov appeared unaffected, of course.

"You find that girl, and we have a deal. Otherwise you get forty-eight hours in the cold, then the KGB gets a postcard." Davies got to his feet. "I'm leaving," he said, lifting the phone. "We're done," he said into the instrument, replacing it before there was a chance of a reply.

Abraham unlocked the door two minutes later. Looking around quickly, he hurried to the far side of the room. The hum of an air conditioner followed immediately. "God, how could you stand it?" he asked.

"I didn't notice anything," said Drakov. "I often find myself in uncomfortable settings."

His irony, though probably unintentional, did little for Joshua Davies' simmering temper. "I'm off," he announced again. "Let him go. Buy him a ticket to Tegel Airport and give him some German money." Reaching gracelessly into his pocket, he peeled off several large-denomination bills. "And don't put it through the books."

"There is, of course, the question of a weapon," said Drakov in a silky tone.

"The hell there is," retorted Davies, carefully snapping a rubber band around the remaining money. "You don't get any popgun out of me."

"There is a Czech pistol known as the M-52," said Drakov. "I usually have a nine-millimeter Makarov."

"The M-52 is a piece of shit," Abraham put in.

"Oh, I agree," replied Drakov, "but with Czech ammunition, it has a high muzzle velocity of four hundred twenty meters a second. It passes through a lot of things before losing its impetus."

"You damn Russians are all the same," said Davies. "The pistol is a close-quarters offensive weapon. You don't need an elephant gun, double-handed grips, and all that rubbish." Davies looked at Abraham. "You've got some Beretta semiautomatics, haven't you?"

"The 22s."

"Right. Fit them with a West German shell. They're deadly at close range, and they don't make much noise. If you've got any the sky marshals don't want, give him one of those." He marched to the door. "Now I'm going to find something to eat along Ben Yehuda. My heart is set on either thick chocolate cake or sugar-coated apple strudel." He paused. "Or both. And then I'm going home."

"That might be a bit difficult," said Abraham. "It's now the Sabbath."

"Then I shall eat Muslim," retorted Davies.

"There's a strike among the Arabs. Something to do with—"

Davies left the apartment at full speed, slamming the door. He stopped only once to ask a startled donkey driver, in sign language, for directions to the Armenian quarter.

7 Habeas Corpus

Joshua Davies slept late the day after his return from Israel. His last hours in Jerusalem had been somewhat ameliorated by his discovery on the way to the airport of an excellent restaurant tucked away down a dirt track by a gas station. It had been recommended very late the previous night by an understanding Armenian who had kept his restaurant open past midnight solely to accommodate the still-steaming Englishman.

At the Mei Naftoah, Davies encountered the culinary cognoscenti of Jerusalem and chatted pleasantly with its London-born owner, Mira Kedar, among cool rustic stone, Turkish brass, and filtered sunlight. The house special and chef Sima's tour de force was *tajine*, pot roast with prunes and nuts. Washed down with Mizrachi wine and topped off with a distinctly Israeli version of *crème Bavaria*, the meal restored Joshua Davies' faith in human dignity. He gave thanks that this bougainvillea-surrounded paradise was outside the city proper and thus remained open on Saturday—if only until lunchtime.

The flight home subjected him to a variety of impositions that would normally have brought him to the boil, but the happy memory of his early lunch at Mei Naftoah soothed some of his choler. There was a brief discussion of bumping him and seven others to accommodate a group of American nuns. His roar of refusal scattered the sisters like a flock of windswept penguins. The dinner on the flight was so atrocious that he managed only half of it and one dessert.

But the journey had not been wasted; fate had dealt him an excellent card. Drakov would become his stalking horse. The mole would rise to the bait when he discovered what Davies had learned. While everyone was focusing on the hunt for the girl, Davies could go mole-hunting relatively undisturbed.

The jumbo jet had to circle Heathrow for an hour because of a work stoppage by ground staff crews, and it was a weary Joshua Davies who entered Duncan's Farm, suitcase in hand, looking like a fat Willy Loman.

Fortunately, his sister Dolores had experience in these matters and was ready with a large steak-and-kidney pie and a plum cake.

"Don't know what I'd do without you, Dol," Davies said, consuming his way back to good humor. "Thank God a man can have a sister," he intoned, to her astonishment.

After breakfast the next morning he donned a huge set of overalls, called by some his Churchillian siren suit, and crawled in the pit below the Rolls. Davies knew everything about the vehicle; most of it he'd taught himself after he received a ten-pound bill for a new radiator cap.

Joshua Davies didn't mind getting himself dirty, though he did wear a porkpie hat squashed over his head. He was not normally fastidious, and the feel of metal, oil, and grease relaxed him. After an hour in the pit, he expected to be dirty, and no one could complain. He took his time checking nuts and bolts for wear and metal fatigue. Yet all the while, he was thinking of Badger's list and the grim truth it represented if the ex-agent was correct.

The oil slurped comfortingly into an empty bucket. He changed it more often than necessary; Silver Ghost engines didn't grow on trees. Inevitably his mind drifted to the question of Anton Drakov. It galled him to think the Russian had put one over on them all. Even Badger and Colonel Konstantin Novetsky of the Russian GRU had been taken in by the master of disinformation.

Hauling himself out of the pit, Davies carefully selected the high-grade oil used by Rolls aficionados. While it was flowing from its can into the engine, Davies wiped his hands on a rag. He knew he wasn't going to tell anyone in DIC who Drakov was; already he was getting the glimmering of an idea how the Russian might be dealt with. If Drakov felt trading knowledge for sanctuary and a pension would be easy, he had another thought coming.

Gently wiping the traces of oil from around the spout, Davies began to feel a lot better. The Russian had gotten beneath his skin. He knew how Zeus felt when Prometheus was being punished. Like the ancient Titan, Drakov had secrets; he was safe until he coughed them up.

Davies found a slow hatred building for the Russian prisoner. Knowing that he was permitting personal feelings to enter where they might become dangerous, he tried to banish them, but he couldn't. Drakov was evil. Because he looked tired and old, the man got sympathy. Before long, like many ex-Nazis, he would be living a fairly normal life, as if nothing had happened.

Angrily Davies rearranged his locking wrenches; as usual he couldn't find the quarter-inch one. The worst of it was, Drakov had already shown that he wouldn't talk. The Israelis had discovered that.

He glanced at his wristwatch, realizing it was almost time for lunch. With the DIC bunch waiting for him, he'd have to fortify himself. The thought of food cheered him. As he walked from the garage to the house, he breathed deeply. A fine day, warm, clear. Soon it would be summer. Truth to tell, he didn't care much for the English climate. Too damp, too unpredictable. Of course it was hard to find *the* perfect climate. Israel was way too hot. Another few days and he might have melted down to a hundred pounds. This Christmas, he and Dol were off to Jamaica. His sister would be researching the setting of her romance, *Passionate Captive's Revenge,* while he sampled the restaurants. Already he could taste salt fish and ackee and the local tipple, Pimento Dram.

His thoughts full of luncheon, Davies stripped off his siren suit in the scullery, then trudged upstairs via his staircase to his floor.

He would lunch at Rules, he decided. Everything there, except the Dover sole, was safe. Sighing, he thought perhaps it was time to retire. He had seen it all: sanctions and murders by gun, knife, bludgeon, poison, stomping, strangling, garroting, and everything in between. There wasn't a single example of sick behavior he'd been spared: fingers chopped off to steal diamond rings, teeth pulled for the gold fillings, once even a glass eye stolen. When the Russians had caught an SIS casual swimming around one of their boats, they had cut off his head and kept the rest of the body. The bastards no doubt enjoyed the sight of SIS trying to explain the affair as an accidental death caused by a navy frogman swimming into a propeller.

And Drakov was part of the KGB. And now he expected to waltz into England and draw an old-age pension.

There were agents who shunned public places and hated to be recognized by maître d's. None of this applied to Davies, who knew the secret of good service was to establish a presence. However, as a simple precaution, he never ate too often at the same restaurant, limiting himself to a maximum of once a week.

Enthroned in state, surrounded by egg-colored walls hung with engravings, political caricatures, and fading programs from the Queen's Theatre, Joshua Davies relaxed.

It was indeed fortunate that the restaurant was in top form. The waiters, Spaniards and Italians with unusually good command of English, recognized him instantly. Still hanging in the kitchen was his communication to the ex-chef. "Dover sole criminally overcooked, pastry inedible and covered with dark rubber cement, grouse *not English!*"

Many an anxious eye watched Joshua Davies' progress through his lunch. In a bold gamble, the management substituted for one of the tired English waiters on the brink of retirement a young Spaniard with excellent English. Soon, Joshua and the youth were conversing in the waiter's native language.

Sitting under the curved beams and being served from massive silver serving trolleys, Davies looked more like an eighteenth-century aristocrat, which, perhaps, was what he should have been.

Knowing his restaurants as he did, the Director was careful in ordering. At Rules it paid to stick to the simpler standbys—roast Aylesbury duck, steak-and-kidney pie, mixed grill, grilled kidneys and bacon. The roast beef and Yorkshire pudding had, of late, become a gamble.

"I think the grouse and kidney pie, mashed potatoes, gravy, carrots," said Davies in Spanish, pleased he knew the Spanish words for *kidney* and *grouse.* "Then the sherry trifle." He had already ordered a Cabernet Franc with some trepidation.

The waiter relayed Davies' words to the anxious kitchen staff. The grouse with kidney pie was "good." The wine was "tolerable." The dessert, a giant square of sherry trifle, received the accolade "perfect," though the wine waiter was horrified at the proximity of the Cabernet Franc to a sherry base. Even the cheese board, where Davies and Rules had quarreled before, was "excellent," and the Cricket Malherbie "out of this world"; Davies made a note to purchase a pound or two of this cheddar when he was next at Paxton and Whitfield's.

There was a collective sigh of relief at Davies' passing; the waiter received a ten-pound tip—not munificent, but 1000 percent more than the waiter on Davies' last visit had received.

Feeling that momentum favored him, Davies decided to make a quick visit to Fox's and replenish his stock of Partagas cigars. All might have been well had he not fallen in love with a humidor made of thuya. This "brief" visit took the best part of an hour, and almost three hundred pounds from Davies' checking account at Lloyds Bank.

When he hurried through the doors of the DIC Committee Room some twenty minutes late, his ID badge upside down, everyone turned and eyed him with varying degrees of balefulness. The Woman from the Ministry had on her basilisk stare.

"Well," she said, "now we are all present, perhaps we can begin without any more time wasted."

Joshua Davies took his place at the end of the table, having intended to apologize for his lateness but deciding against it. As he looked around the table, he saw the same dreary bunch in their usual attitudes of despair. Only Monty Abrahams and Julian Monteith were missing.

"There's been a development of some interest," he began, rising to his feet and carefully uncapping a cigar tube.

"That'll make a change," muttered Scruffy Rees.

"Damn right," agreed Davies, not a whit put out. The entire assembly had to wait while he clipped off the end of his cigar, lit it with a match while carefully rotating it to see it was burning evenly. When the glow appealed to his critical eye, he looked up.

"Our Israeli friends"—he paused while there were a few grunts of disapproval and a snicker—"found a Russian defector."

"Name?" asked Strachan, his stubby pipe clenched between his teeth.

"Judas," replied Davies. Strachan smiled and eased forward in his chair, watching the Director through narrowed eyes under hooded lids. He knew Davies had something really big this time; he was being very cagey.

Rossiter, his arms on the table with white cuffs and monogrammed cuff links showing, said, "Joshua has a secret, Alaister; you shouldn't pry." His sycophant, Freddy Gilbert, laughed. No one else did. Davies continued. "The asset was too hot for the Israelis."

"Too hot? What does that mean?" demanded the WM, pursing her lips. "What's too hot for the Guys to handle?"

"It was a jurisdictional problem," lied Davies. "They preferred us to handle it."

Reggie Compton-Basset's face lit up. Jurisdictional fights were his bailiwick. Reggie alone understood the complex issues involved in the

Russian-Japanese dispute over the Kuril Islands. "Jurisdictional—"

"Case of *habeas corpus,*" added Davies, delighted with the taste of his Partagas cigar. "They had the body but didn't want it."

Reggie deflated.

"And so," continued Davies brightly, "I made a deal."

The WM looked at him icily. "What kind of a *deal?* Your authority doesn't extend to deals."

The look of innocent hurt in Davies' eyes would have demolished any lesser player. "I did what I thought was best." He drew out his handkerchief and blew his nose.

The WM was determined not to let Davies' histrionics get the better of her. "What did you offer? And what did you get?"

Joshua Davies, still on his feet, carefully laid his cigar in the heavy glass ashtray. "The Russian, code name Judas, was very high up. Some time ago, he learned of an entrapment."

Stirring in his seat, Rogers muttered, "Sounds like some popsie's going to be involved, eh, Sweeney?"

"Right," echoed Sweeney, doodling something on his sketch pad; it looked like a horse but had horns.

Smiling benignly, Davies assured them, "There was a popsie, a delectable little swallow run by the Russians in Berlin. This was lo these many years ago."

Looking around the table, he was pleased to find he had their attention. "Our little sparrow went and got herself pregnant. She had a girl, then died."

The WM smoothed her blue pinstripe skirt. "And how is this girl important?"

Davies picked up his cigar, pulled gently on it, then put it down again. "She is the daughter of the Vice President of the United States."

There was a shocked silence. Then Scruffy Rees let out a long whistle; the others were plainly shaken. The WM took out a little black cigarette from her purse, lit it, and dropped the match into an ashtray. Davies gave her credit for immediately realizing the value of his information.

Rossiter was not so bright; he had to hear himself speak before he could appreciate Davies' news. "You mean Vice President Letterville has a daughter he doesn't know about?"

Beaming at Rossiter, the Director nodded in assent. "And whoever gets to her first is in a very powerful position. If we can—"

"If we can get to her, the Americans will be very grateful," said Rogers excitedly. "Jolly grateful, as I see it."

"Right," said Davies, "but if our Russian colleagues get wind of this . . ."

"They always do," interposed Strachan.

"Don't they?" agreed Davies, looking him directly in the eyes. The heavy lids came down.

"The question is," said Reggie, "if this is really an SIS op, then Joshua is *not* within his rights. But if"—he studied the table carefully—"if it might be called counterespionage, then it would be in Five's bailiwick."

"Thank you, Bassie," said the WM, and meant it.

Strachan spoke. "What Joshua is saying is that it wouldn't be in anyone's interest to know too much." He looked around the table, his gaze not lighting on anyone more than a second. "There may have been leaks before; I'm not, please excuse me, Joshua, entirely convinced, however, we are harboring a mole in our midst."

"Pure supposition," said Rogers.

"Exactly," added Sweeney, adding wings to his horse; they were not in proportion.

"But Joshua must take precautions. However, you haven't told us what steps . . ."

"I'll tell you exactly what I decided on," said Davies, regretfully stubbing out the cigar. A final forlorn wisp of smoke curled up from the ashes. "I told Judas to find the girl and bring her to me, and we'd welcome him with open arms. Old-age pension, National Health, everything this country has to offer."

"And if he doesn't produce?" asked the WM.

"There'll be a most regrettable accident," said Davies grimly. "We're not Oxfam."

"I do wish I knew more," said Rossiter, "so I could form an opinion, as it were." He looked around hopefully; no one returned his look; he lapsed into silence.

They came up with a code name for the operation after the usual discussion. Joshua Davies was as eager as the rest to ransack the ancient mythologies and classics for something to sum it all up.

"What we need is some story about the search of a father for a lost daughter," mused Davies.

"Pity it's not a son," said Rossiter. "Then we could call it Prodigal."

"Yes. Pity," agreed Freddy Gilbert.

Finally the Woman from the Ministry suggested Demeter, and everyone applauded it with relief. At the very least it meant the tea trolley could be summoned somewhat before its usual time.

Rossiter took it upon himself to bang on the double doors, the signal for the two guards to wheel in the cart.

Joshua Davies was nibbling on a gingernut, dipping it into his coffee to make it palatable, when Strachan approached him.

"You did well, Joshua, very well."

"Thanks."

"Did you know that in a group of any ten men and women the average person would have only one testicle?"

Davies pondered it. "Hadn't thought of that."

"You should, Joshua, you should. Now, about this captive asset." He drew close so that no one could overhear. "You're going to deal with him once he's delivered, aren't you?"

The Director took a sip of his coffee. "How do you mean—deal?"

"Why, man, you can't let him live. He could be a plant, and if word gets out he's here, the Russians will be forced to grab one of our agents."

Davies nodded. "And then we'll have to go into the trading business."

The Scotsman favored Davies with a shrewd look. "Exactly. It's best if the man's dead."

"Hmm. I'll have him shot in some bathroom."

"Bathroom?"

"It's standard operating procedure. The tiles make it much easier to clean up the mess. Ah! I must have a word with Rossiter."

He moved away, leaving Strachan uncertain whether Davies was just having him on. One thing was sure. The fat man was up to something, and he, Alaister Strachan, would give a great deal to know what it was. A *great* deal.

Part Two

Ingrid

A damsel with a dulcimer
In a vision once I saw:
It was an Abyssinian maid,
And on her dulcimer she played,
Singing of Mount Abora.
Could I revive within me
Her symphony and song,
To such a deep delight 'twould win me,
That with music loud and long,
I would build that dome in air,
That sunny dome! those caves of ice!
And all who heard should see them there,
And all should cry, Beware! Beware!
His flashing eyes, his floating hair!
Weave a circle round him thrice,
And close your eyes with holy dread,
For he on honey-dew hath fed,
And drunk the milk of Paradise.

Coleridge, *Kubla Khan*

8 Gropius City

Anton Mikhailovich Drakov arrived at Tegel Airport at 7:38 on a dreary day, the last of April. In his pocket he carried a British diplomatic passport in the name of Alfred Lewis identifying him as acting head of security in the Hong Kong Embassy. In his plastic grip was a second passport, a German one bearing the name of Hermann Kreugar, a South African dealing with West German electronics companies. The documents, except for the photographs, were genuine. Within forty-eight hours, their owners would be instructed to report them missing. Discreet inquiries would begin, leaving faint but discernible trails. Thus, in the none-too-delicate words of Joshua Davies, "If it gets out, we have our arses covered." A *sub rosa* agreement with the West German government allowed Drakov to carry his weapon into Germany. His simple luggage would be put on the plane for him by a cut-out. It was all South African made.

It was possible to enter the city by land, but air presented an infinitely easier way. Drakov had no alternative but to cross East German territory, but the planes could not be searched. The Russian took a Pan Am flight, where he was treated so well he couldn't help making comparisons with Aeroflot, the Soviet airline. The Russian crews behaved as if they were doing the passengers a great service just by being there. As a high official of the KGB, Drakov had seen the accident record of the Soviet fleet; it wasn't encouraging, and it wasn't published.

He was in no hurry and did not join the herd charging along the wide corridors. Why they bothered he never understood, for they would be standing impatiently at the baggage claim when he reached it five minutes later. He walked leisurely along the brightly lit halls; most secret service operators hated planes and airports; it was obvious why. Once on a plane, they were surrounded; there was no way to duck out. On the ground it was no better. With few exceptions the journey was prescribed. A phone call from the takeoff point meant somebody would be waiting for the traveler as he left the last brightly lit tunnel and emerged into . . . what? The same might be in store for Drakov; relying on Jews and fat Englishmen was a dangerous business. On the other hand, he trusted his instinct. Davies wouldn't be setting him up this way, for with a nod to Abraham, Drakov would be dead, an unfortunate suicide or another "shot while escaping." But Davies wasn't to be trusted at all. Drakov's fake death had galled the English Director, and he would be looking for a way to even the score. A man wasn't nicknamed "the Butcher" without reason.

Taking a cheap suitcase from the baggage

claim area, he joined the "Nothing to Declare" line. For the first and last time, he presented himself as Alfred Lewis. He had brought in only one carton of American cigarettes, ostensibly purchased at Lod Airport, half the legal limit, and nothing else of interest to the customs officer.

The Russian stood quietly, ignoring the scowling woman behind him who vented her spleen by rocking her luggage cart back and forth, occasionally hitting him in the small of the back and muttering in German with a heavy Bavarian accent.

Taking a quick look at Drakov's documents, the officer rapidly scrawled his initials on the suitcase. Then he turned to the Bavarian woman and ordered her to open all her baggage. When she protested he took infinite pleasure in explaining that those standing in the "Nothing to Declare" line were not immune to searches. Drakov passed through the double set of hissing pneumatic doors long before the officer had finished rummaging through the first of her suitcases.

Of course Drakov was no stranger to West Berlin, but it had been some years since his last visit. Still, nothing much seemed to have changed. He threw the cigarettes away. He didn't like that brand, and they had served their purpose as cover.

As Drakov secured a taxi, carefully avoiding the first that appeared, there was little trace of the famous bracing Berliner *luft* in the dark, foggy night. The taxi was driven with the reckless abandon of all Berlin vehicles; Drakov knew there was a strictly enforced speed limit of 100 kilometers per hour, but he could see they were traveling at 120. He ordered the driver to take him to the Cafe Kranzler on the Kurfurstendamm. After that there was nothing to do but sit back. Visually, West Berlin had little to offer; a minimum of memorable vistas or landmarks from past or present graced the old Prussian capital. The real opulence and high style of prewar Berlin began beyond the Brandenburg Gate along the stately, tree-lined avenue of Unter den Linden.

Anton Drakov sat quietly, his grip on his knees, left hand occasionally tapping lightly on the plastic fabric, reviewing his strategy. The first thing he needed to do was find a base of operations. That meant lodgings. But above all, he knew he must avoid a high profile. So it was a mistake to go to the Kranzler.

They were approaching the Kaiser Wilhelm Memorial church, a tall modern honeycomb of a building perched uneasily next to the ruined tower of the old church. As they reached it, Drakov tapped on the partition. "Pull over," he said.

"By the Hallelujah Gasometer?"

"The what?"

The driver pointed to the church. "That thing."

"Yes."

The driver pulled up without glancing in either mirror; his passenger dismounted and felt for his money, tipping exactly 10 percent, neither too little nor too much. The man wouldn't remember him.

The Russian found a cafe less ostentatious than the Kranzler but commanding a view through its glassed-in terrace of the most important street in West Berlin. A light drizzle was beginning to fall, and the sidewalk artists were packing their tools and scurrying for cover. Drakov sat inside, near the window, at a minuscule table.

He ordered coffee and a large piece of torte. While sipping his coffee, he studied a newspaper. On the sidewalk outside there was a constantly passing show of capitalist decadence: American soldiers in uniform topped with great cowboy hats, young girls in shiny aluminum one-piece suits, young toughs with hair standing straight up and dyed a variety of clashing colors. Strangest of all were the Hare Krishna devotees, dressed in saffron robes, weaving in and out of the crowds on roller skates, trying to sell perfumed magazines.

It dawned on Drakov that he might well be facing one of the great challenges of his life; he was in alien territory, without a guide, knowing little of the terrain, and fighting for his life. A tall woman with an ample bosom who had sat down at the next table asked for his sugar. Absently he passed it before he realized the woman was, in fact, a transvestite. Incredible, but Drakov felt embarrassed—a feeling he could not recall experiencing in the last thirty years, at least. Pulling up the collar of his cheap fawn-colored overcoat, he turned away from her. Or him.

Outside the traffic moved with apparent purpose and direction, and department store windows were brightly lit. It was business as usual; on top of one building he could read "Marie—Die Grosse Stripper," on another, "Camping Equipment."

Finding the "Lodgings to Let" section of the paper, Drakov scanned the addresses, knowing exactly where he wanted to stay. He found a residence in exactly the right area; using a stub of pencil, he ringed the entry, then turned to finish his meal.

A second cab, which Drakov hailed while standing in front of the huge Europa Center, took him away from the high-rent district. His last memory of it was a huge, half-naked statue of a woman on Breitscheidplatz, which bore the legend "Angela Bubbles Bares All at the Red Rose."

Drakov had selected a residence in close proximity to Templehof Airport just inside the smallest ward in the city, Kreuzberg. A quiet street leading off Mehringdamm with a view of Viktoria Park would suit him perfectly. As the taxi drew to a halt, he knew he had chosen wisely. The region took its name from the two-hundred-foot-high Hill of the Cross. Once there had been a monument with an iron cross, now there was an artificial waterfall modeled on the Zackenfall in the Riesengebirge. Far more important, for one who wanted no one asking awkward questions, the ward was the home of the majority of foreign guest workers. An article in the *Berliner Morgenpost* had contained a long attack on the neighborhood. It called Kreuzberg a seedy but charming neighborhood but attacked the standoffishness of the Turks in Little Istanbul and bemoaned the official policy of paying *kindergeld* to families for each child. The article berated the groups of young people who simply moved into the empty apartments in the area while maintaining a tone of high moral rectitude.

Drakov dismissed his cab and entered a used-clothing store to select a suitable wardrobe; he emerged with his own clothes in a brown paper bag, which he dumped in a nearby trash can. Even his wallet was replaced by a German model. He did not let the shop's owner see that he was carrying several thousand marks in it. The suit was a black business three-piece, slightly shabby, yet clearly indicative of some official status. The shirt was white, his tie navy blue. Drakov had spent some time finding the right pair of shoes—they were one size too small and changed his way of walking. An overcoat and dark green felt hat completed the outfit. From a neighboring shop, he purchased three shirts, two pairs of socks, and several changes of underwear. A battered suitcase from the same store completed his preparations. Speaking with an atrocious accent, Drakov informed the uninterested proprietor that he was returning to Turkey for a vacation.

Although the Israelis had returned his contact lenses, he located a pair of dark horn-rimmed glasses with minimal correction. These altered his appearance considerably; he found himself holding his head slightly to one side so he could use his right eye to compensate for a slight blurriness in the left.

Trudging down the street, suitcase in hand,

Drakov was soon soaked by a fine but persistent rain. His shoes leaked and the cheap suitcase was streaked with water stains. He sought shelter in an apartment doorway, but the owner, a burly Turk, pushed him in the back and told him not to loiter around his property.

"I'm going," Drakov told him, not wanting to make an issue of it. He made his slow way up the hill, occasionally having to skirt a pothole full of water.

Finally he located a small printing shop, where he dried out somewhat in front of a coal fire while the wizened proprictor made him a selection of business cards printed with a variety of names and titles "to impress my relatives in Ankara," he confided in fair German. The man nodded and overcharged him 20 percent; his real business was pornographic books.

Frau Grafenberg had seen better days; she was immediately taken with the South African gentleman on her doorstep who made the pleasant mistake of calling her Frau von Grafenberg. She did not correct him. It was obvious that the new lodger—terms were decided in a moment—was a man of considerable influence. She knew how to behave; the Herr would not want to answer questions. Frau Grafenberg asked nothing. Certainly no documents changed hands. The West Berlin government would receive no occupancy tax.

Herr Kreugar presented her with his business card and the first week's rent. Two decades of hardship and scarcity had made realists of most landladies in Berlin. If the lodger did look a little down at heels, if he had only one suitcase, a shabby one at that, it was none of her business. The Deutschemarks had spoken more loudly than the rest of it. At least he wasn't a wog, smelling up the place with abominable cooking and living off the *kindergeld.* She would have mentioned her no-cooking rule, but decided not to.

As far as the ex-Director of Department A of the First Directorate was concerned, the apartment was perfect—an ugly brick building with small windows, part of a block that overlooked the park. The hallway was dark, covered with decaying linoleum in a blue-and-white-square pattern. Above each room was a dingy skylight. The bulbs in the hall were encased in yellowing plastic shades encrusted with roasted flies. There was an odor of cabbage and sounds of radios behind the ill-fitting doors.

Beyond the communal hallway, however, his room was comfortable, with ornate furniture, a double bed with bolsters, a solid mahogany chest of drawers, and a wardrobe. There was an elaborate chandelier, but it had been disconnected, so the only light source was two sixty-watt bulbs on each side of the bedstead. The bathroom was a long, thin room with a large porcelain toilet standing upon a plinth at the far end. All the fittings were elaborate and prewar.

"Do you have an electric razor, Herr Kreugar?" she asked. "I have adaptors for the current."

"I prefer a straight razor," the Russian replied. "It is so much less trouble."

Frau Grafenberg showed her new guest the room's best feature, a tall, narrow window opening on to a tiny balcony. "You can see the waterfall, almost," she informed him.

Anton Drakov looked out over her shoulder. Through the nighttime gloom he could see a tall hill with a light shining on its summit. To the west, the hill blocked out the city, but on two sides he could see the streetlamps and car headlights on Kreuzberg and Dudenstrasse.

"It will be a better day tomorrow, Herr Kreugar, I feel it in my bones," she said.

"I know it will," murmured Anton Drakov. "I know it will."

Something in his tone made her glance at him sharply, but his face betrayed nothing.

2

There was, Drakov knew, as much danger in being obsessive as in being careless. He did not propose to spend nights sitting in an armchair, automatic in hand, waiting for intruders. The gun had been risky enough; there were customs officers who ignored official documents just to make the point that each country was a sovereign power and had the right to search anyone's luggage. The Syrians were absolute bastards about this.

Yet there were precautions and precautions. Drakov's options were limited. One word to the KGB, and his fake death would become permanent—if he was lucky. More than likely he would spend a long, extremely painful time in the lowest level of the Lubyanka cells. Men shuddered at the mere thought of Subbasement C; death was a merciful release there.

Drakov took the black fountain pen from his top pocket. It had been made in England; the KGB technicians liked the superior workmanship. Unscrewing the cap and aiming the gold nib at the wainscot, he paced the room. At the two old-fashioned electrical sockets, he paused. There was no telltale buzz from the pen. Next he checked the cobwebbed chandelier with the same results.

Satisfied the room was clean, the Russian reassembled the pen. He could have set up a short-range jamming field by removing the nib, but to do so would have revealed too much about him. Besides, the West Berlin secret service was under so many legal restraints, he felt sure they wouldn't keep a close watch on all foreigners.

His few things were quickly arranged; the shirts, underclothes, and pants were hung up in the wardrobe, the toilet articles set neatly in the narrow bathroom. In those two rooms was everything Drakov possessed after almost forty years with the KGB.

He left the room, locking it behind him. In the hall was a pay phone; he had no coins and was obliged to go to the landlady's rooms and ask for change. She invited him in. While she rummaged in her purse, Drakov's eyes took in the whole room. It was better furnished than the guest quarters but, like the widow, gave evidence of declining fortunes.

Frau Grafenberg wanted him to take tea; he declined with regret. "The pressure of business," he muttered, taking elaborate care not to count his change.

"What business are you in, *mein Herr?*"

"The moving business," he said, trying to smile.

"Ah, travel."

"Yes."

The widow was reluctant to let him go. There was an air of authority about him, and attractive older men were rare in West Berlin. The city, once the proud capital of Prussian-dominated Germany, was dying. The only men who came to Berlin anymore were young punks avoiding the draft.

"Perhaps another time, Herr Kreugar?"

"Delighted," replied Drakov, catching her drift and not liking it. "Perhaps I could use your phone directory?"

As he expected, the girl's aunt was listed. He jotted down the address on a piece of paper provided by the helpful Frau Grafenberg. Perhaps she touched his hand a shade longer than necessary; he wasn't sure.

At a public phone, he called the number, introducing himself as a social worker. The aunt seemed nonplussed.

"But Herr Doktor Leibermann, surely you know, my niece Ingrid ran away two years ago. I reported it to the authorities."

"Exactly, Frau Thummel," replied Drakov, thinking quickly. "There are some questions about that. I trust they will not inconvenience you?"

The aunt agreed to see him that morning, giving him directions. Listening patiently, he asked when she'd finished, "Isn't it near the Johannisthaler Station?"

"Oh no, Herr Doktor. I am close to Wutzkyallee."

"Of course, of course. I know it well. In an hour then."

Drakov replaced the phone in its cradle. The girl had run away. He ought to have thought of that. It would complicate matters a great deal. If the aunt had no idea where the girl was, he might spend weeks chasing all over Germany looking for her. Without any resources to call upon, even Drakov would be hard pressed to locate one teenage runaway among thousands.

Frau Thummel's directions were useless; she assumed, and Drakov had not corrected her, that he had an automobile. Thinking he would not need one, the Russian had not asked Davies or Abraham for a driver's license. So he took the U-bahn; Line 7 ran directly from Mehringdamm to Wutzkyallee. He spent the time reading the *Berliner Morgenpost*, finding it more convincing than the East Berlin *Neues Deutschland* to which he had, during his years with the KGB, often contributed subtle pieces of disinformation.

The view changed as the Russian drew away from the city center. In the suburbs there were very German-looking villas with gardens just springing into life. Already the neat, square lawns were being manicured and rolled. *Ordnung* was still the rule. On the platforms, people looked well fed and scrubbed clean. The children were the Aryan blonds of Hitler's insane mythology. They were polite and well mannered. Visible, but seldom needed, were the blue-gray–uniformed police looking very smart in their white caps. Looks can be deceptive, Drakov thought, sitting in the comfortable brown plastic seat with an entire car almost to himself. These policemen were the descendants of the soldiers who killed twenty million of his people. Or was it six million? Was he now a Jew and not a Russian? He had questioned many Russian Jews who wanted to emigrate and some who had returned to Russia. One thing they all had in common, a passionate love of Mother Russia. However hated the Russian government was, the land exerted an almost irresistible force. But Drakov would never return, not even if the current government was replaced. Anton Mikhailovich Drakov would never be welcome.

The girl's aunt lived in a vast, sprawling residential development, a planned community designed by Walter Gropius. Gropiusstadt, as it was named after Gropius' death, was a concrete jungle divided up by a few trees and some tired, threadbare lawns. There were signs everywhere. "No Roller Skating," "No Transistor Radios," no this, no that. On each bit of green was a sign saying it was forbidden to walk on the grass. A tatty flowerbed some six feet square carried a sign "Protected Public Park" and under it was an extract from the rules about fines for picking the flowers.

When he reached the skyscraper, there was no sign of the elevator. No indicator light went on when he pressed the button, so there was no way of knowing if he was waiting in vain. Since Ingrid's aunt lived on the twelfth floor, he decided to wait before making the climb. There was a stench from the region where the stairs joined the lobby. The Russian knew what it was; the same problem existed in the towers dotting the Moscow skyline. Parents sent their children out to play. When the children wanted to visit the toilet, there was an interminable wait for the elevator, or the slow climb. Since the towers overlooked all the outside locations, the children squatted by the stairs.

When the elevator arrived, Drakov was joined by a little girl clutching a long wooden spoon. Before he could ask her what floor she wanted, the child used the spoon to press the button for the fifth floor. Drakov murmured, "Twelve," and the child used the handle to press that button. Then she watched him curiously. Undoubtedly her parents had warned her about strange men. Drakov managed a smile; its effect he could not evaluate.

The child gone, the elevator lurched to the seventh floor. Two teenage boys dressed in American jeans and identical T-shirts with Cyrillic lettering on them got on. Their hair was dyed green.

"Seen enough?" demanded one as Drakov looked them over.

The Russian nodded. Perhaps they did not know their shirts read "Property of the KGB." He permitted himself a cold smile. Nor did they realize they were in an elevator with the ex-Director of Department A of the First Directorate, KGB.

"Whatcha grinnin' at?" said the second punk.

Drakov shook his head.

The first boy leaned past Drakov and pushed the red stop button. The car jerked to a halt.

"I'm working this elevator, so I ought to be paid."

"That's right, Kurt," agreed the other.

Both looked at the Russian. "I'd say about twenty marks," added Kurt. "That's fair, isn't it, Rolf?"

"It is."

Drakov edged backward until he could feel his back square against the side of the car. The two punks edged to his left and his right.

"Well?" demanded Rolf. "You gonna pay?"

Drakov's eyes narrowed.

"Maybe he doesn't understand German," said Kurt, reaching forward and flicking Drakov's tie with his hand. "We'll just have to help ourselves."

"I understand what you want," Drakov said. His voice was low, almost apologetic. If the two toughs had ever had experience with truly dangerous men, they would have recognized his tone for what it was—*not* a sign of weakness. But their grandparents had beaten up old men, Jews, and this was no different. They were little more than children, ugly children at that. "I am considering my options," Drakov added mildly.

"Oh shit! 'Considering my options,' " parroted Rolf. "I like fancy talk."

"If I kill you," continued Drakov in the same calm tone, "there will be explanations and delays. I am a busy man."

For the first time Rolf looked closely at the

easy mark. There was a look in the old man's eyes he didn't like. There was a sudden click as his switchblade fell from its wrist holder into his hand. A touch of the little button, and the razor-sharp stainless-steel blade locked into position.

"On the other hand," Drakov persisted, "I considered inviting you to walk off the building on the third floor. That wouldn't kill you."

"Listen, old man," hissed Rolf, crouching and holding the knife almost at Drakov's throat, "you ain't doing any inviting."

The Russian hadn't moved, didn't instinctively draw his head back from the blade. "The fall wouldn't kill you, not unless you were unlucky. Then I could go about my business."

"Let's carve him," hissed Rolf. "Now!"

Drakov moved swiftly and fluidly, bringing up his knee and smashing Rolf savagely in the groin. As the punk gasped, the Russian drove the edge of his hand into his windpipe.

Kurt was caught by surprise; before he could gather his wits, he received a kick to the side of his kneecap, knocking him off balance. His leg was paralyzed. Only the handrail, which he grabbed for, prevented him from falling on the moaning Rolf. Worse was to come. The old man seized Kurt by the scruff of his neck and drove his head three times against the steel handrail, making the car shake violently. Up and down the elevator shaft the hammering echoed.

Rolf got to his knees; he had dropped the knife, but that didn't matter. He was determined to tear the old man apart and was attempting to stand upright when a pistonlike elbow slammed into his face. Blood spurted from his nose, some into his eyes, blinding him. The Russian chopped down on the back of his neck with a double-fisted blow that caused Rolf's head to jerk violently forward, then snap backward. "It felt," he said later, "like a hundred-kilogram weight." He clearly heard the pop as several vertebrae snapped and sank to the floor of the car, wide-eyed, froth at the corners of his mouth. The coup de grace was a well-aimed kick to the Adam's apple. Down Rolf went, blood filling his mouth.

Drakov took stock. He was unmarked. His pulse rate had increased slightly, but otherwise he was unaffected. It pleased him to discover he had lost none of his skills in hand-to-hand combat.

From Rolf came choking sounds; his face was turning blue. With a sigh, Drakov bent over the writhing body and, careful not to get blood on his coat, reached in and pulled the tongue clear of the back of the throat. There was a brief spurt of blood and then great heaving sounds from the air-starved lungs. Drakov rolled the body on its face so blood would not block the air passage again.

There wasn't a sound from the other youth. Drakov took a look at him, peeling back the eyelid. "Unconscious but alive," he murmured, starting the elevator again and sending it to the top floor.

It stopped three times but only on the twenty-sixth floor was anyone waiting. He kept the door from opening more than a foot, and passed himself off as an inspector. "It will be out of order for one hour. Please wait until then," he said.

Obediently the woman returned to her apartment; when he heard her door shut, Drakov took his foot from the door track, allowing it to open and then close.

Rolf's legs suddenly began to thrash. Drakov rolled his body over and saw the eyes ballooning in their sockets; the face was blue. He seized the body around the waist and pulled on it. Blood flowed from Rolf's mouth. "Internal bleeding," muttered Drakov to himself.

In the end, he took the risk of leaving Rolf. A mugging, especially of punks, was unimportant; but murder, even of the dregs of society, would mean a full investigation that might inconvenience him.

He propped Kurt in the elevator doorway in a sitting position directly facing the electric eye of the door sensor. The elevator was now immobilized. Across Kurt's knees, facedown, he positioned the other tough. He was pleased to see the trickle of blood form along Rolf's chin and cheek. He put the knife in Kurt's hand; Rolf's knife in Kurt's possession might cast doubt on the boys' account of what happened.

Then he wiped his fingerprints from all the possible contact points even though they were not on file anywhere in the world, walked briskly down nineteen flights of stairs, and knocked on the door of number 1206.

3

Frau Thummel was not as Drakov had imagined her. On the telephone or in person her voice was cultivated, not a country accent. But she turned out to be a big, strapping woman with the rough, reddened skin of a peasant used to outside labor. Her hair was gray, and she wore bifocals. Although the apartment was warm, Frau Thummel wore a knitted sweater with a skier on the front. At the collar of her blouse, just visible, was a cameo brooch.

She ushered Drakov to a comfortable chair before an electric fire, and he appraised the apartment, quickly eliciting from her the information that there were two rooms and a bathroom. While admiring the view, he discovered, as he'd expected, no outside fire escape.

There was little of value in the apartment, though the carpets and draperies hinted at a good standard of living. An elaborately carved cuckoo clock caught his eye.

"I brought that from Switzerland many years ago," said Frau Thummel, following his gaze. "Before Papa lost his business and I married my late husband and went to live in Berneck."

"You are Swiss?"

"I was."

"Ah."

"You have some questions about Ingrid, Herr Doktor. Perhaps I should see . . ."

"Of course." Drakov reached into his jacket and pulled out a business card.

"Doktor Berthold Leibermann, Social Services," she read before returning the card.

"Your niece ran away how long ago, Frau Thummel? Did you say two years?"

"Two years ago. I reported it on her birthday."

Drakov nodded encouragingly. "Of course, but these matters must be followed up. No strand must be left dangling. We want to find your niece, naturally."

"Naturally."

Drakov caught the note of ambivalence. Doubtless the girl had led the older woman a merry dance before leaving for good. And what could Frau Thummel do? It wasn't even her child.

"Would you like some coffee, Herr Doktor?"

"Thank you, yes." He hoped giving her something to do would calm her. "Why did Ingrid run away?"

Frau Thummel had retreated behind the counter and was measuring coffee with a large spoon. "She had a problem adjusting here. The buildings were incomplete, every junkpile was going to become a playground—someday." She paused. Drakov heard a grinding sound, then the air was filled with the smell of freshly ground coffee. "From the window you can see the Wall. Ingrid and the other children played there, but soon workers shooed them away. Then the fields were quickly taken up by buildings. There were a few fields to the south. I walked there with her once." She savored the memory. "The state had purchased them from the farmers, so the fields were overgrown with corn, poppies, cornflower, and tall grass, but in a short time they, too, were cleared off."

The coffee came on a blue tray with a Chinese willow pattern on it. There were two cups and saucers with matching designs, stylized sunflowers being cut by reapers. On a plate were small vanilla wafer cookies. Drakov refused cream and sugar but thanked her for one of the wafers.

"So Social Services is at last waking up to Ingrid's problem," said the aunt, bitterness apparent. "After two years."

Drakov sipped his coffee. "The new director in Bonn is concerned about the problem of runaways. Ingrid was unhappy here?"

Experienced as he was in reading the faint indicators of people's true feelings, Drakov caught the woman's uneasy vibrations. He must find out what she was hiding. He hoped the damn girl hadn't gotten herself pregnant or, worse still, had a baby; that would complicate things terribly.

"Why don't you tell me about it?"

She was startled and sipped at the coffee as if to focus her thoughts. Drakov waited.

"Ingrid didn't just run away." She began weeping. She put the cup on its saucer, and there was a brief rattling noise. "She . . . Oh, Herr Doktor, what can I do?"

"A man?" asked Drakov smoothly.

"No, no. Drugs. Ingrid had become an addict." She broke down completely, ugly sobs forced from her.

Drakov remained still, his mind racing. He hadn't bargained on anything like this. The damn girl might be anywhere; she could even be dead, her body rotting in some canal.

"Frau Thummel," he began, placing his cup and saucer on the tray. "Do not despair. My organization can track her down."

She looked at him, hope in the beaten eyes. At that moment, had Drakov claimed to be Martin Luther, she would have believed him.

"There was a Center House," she told him. "The authorities realized the kids had nowhere to go. They did try, you see."

"And?" He got to his feet and stood at the window, looking out.

"The faster crowd began smoking pot, marijuana, you know. Ingrid wouldn't have done it if they hadn't pushed her." She stood up, went to the kitchen, and he heard her blowing her nose. Then she came back. "A boy called Peter attracted her. He showed her how to inject herself. I couldn't do anything." Raising her voice, she spoke angrily. "The authorities did nothing. I could see her getting thinner and thinner; she was haggard. None of her clothes fit after a while."

Drakov made encouraging sounds, but he wasn't listening fully. The problem of finding Ingrid was horribly complicated now. It was one thing to track down someone who wouldn't be expecting him, quite another to trace a junkie who was afraid of everything, especially strangers.

"And do you know, Herr Doktor, well, of course you do, there's no drug treatment center for children in *all* Berlin?" She found a handkerchief in her purse and dabbed at her eyes. Finding Drakov an easy listener, she rapidly unburdened herself.

"Drogeninfo and Narkonon wouldn't even look at her unless she paid in advance; I live on a state pension and don't have that kind of money. You don't know, Herr Doktor, what I suffered." She joined him by the window. "The girl was willful and disobedient. I think . . ."

"Did she go anywhere special in Berlin?"

Silence.

"Well?" Drakov's eyes were boring into her.

"There was a place, I believe it was a sort of club."

"Its name?"

"It sounded French, but it wasn't real French. Le Kinki or something. She sent me a card with a picture of the club on it and told me not to worry and not to try to find her. She and this boy Rudi—"

"Rudi?"

"Rudi Fleischer . . . was a friend of hers for a time. I did go to Berlin. He tried to help her. He was a pleasant young man, a librarian, I think, with a nice apartment. He took us to his favorite spot, the English Garden. Rudi tried to—" She stifled a sob. Drakov waited until she had recovered. Spreading her hands in a gesture expressing the futility of it all, she asked, "Why do they do it, *mein Herr?*"

He shook his head. "Do you have a recent picture I might borrow? The file photograph was old."

"Of course. I'll get one."

She left the room, returning almost immediately with a four-by-six color snapshot. Drakov took it, still standing by the window. Below, in the distance, a tractor was plowing a furrow across a small field on the far side of the Wall. The gray line of the Wall enclosed Gropiusstadt on three sides. Beyond, the East Germans and their Russian allies were pumping drugs into the Western world as fast as they could. Drugs were cheap and effective weapons in the eternal struggle.

"Why do they do it?" Frau Thummel repeated helplessly.

Drakov remained silent, continuing to stare out the window.

9 Business As Usual

Moscow, late April; the snows melting fast and a greasy rain falling as KGB chief Viktor M. Chebrikov, dressed in a fur hat and imported raincoat, stepped briskly across Red Square. Behind him were two burly bodyguards and creeping around the edge of the square was the ZIL limousine that had brought him from his palatial apartment on Kutuzovsky Prospekt.

Chebrikov's appearance reflected his peasant heritage, though his face was now puffy, and the black heavy-rimmed dark glasses had dug grooves into his skin above the ears. His mouth, turned down at the edges, gave him a permanently disapproving look. Beneath the sable fur hat, his remaining hair collected along the sides of his head, almost colorless, giving the impression that the KGB leader was bald.

April was dreary; workers, mainly female, were shoveling the dirty snow and ice from the gutters into piles, and trucks with crablike pincers called "Stalin claws" loaded them on trucks for dumping in the river. The blue streetlamps still gave out some illumination though the half-light of dawn was spreading from the east. A cold wind whistled across the square, making the banners praising the Communist Revolution crack all around him. Soon it would be May Day; after that the brief period of pleasant weather might begin. To Chebrikov, who pretended to some aesthetic taste, it was as if Moscow's ermine fur had been stripped off and a dirty rag left in its place. The few Muscovites who hurried past still wore their furry cocoons.

Chebrikov had continued Andropov's policy of treating the KGB, the sword and shield of the state, as a part of the military. The grumblings had almost all died away on that score; those that had never worn a uniform now owned the three they needed—day-to-day, ceremonial, and dress. But to consolidate his power, Chebrikov canceled his predecessor's six-day schedule and reverted to the five-day week.

Viktor M. Chebrikov was something of a hypochondriac; he complained regularly of insomnia, dyspepsia, and hemorrhoids. To his surprise, he'd found a doctor who more or less agreed that he was not as healthy as he could be. When the KGB leader talked fearfully of strokes and heart attacks, his doctor agreed no one was safe. Chebrikov immediately cut down from three packs a day to one. He also discussed his health a great deal less.

He held the rank of general. The gold star and blue shoulder boards were concealed by his raincoat, or the few people who were permitted to pass close to him would certainly have given him a much wider berth.

The *Komitet Gosudarstvennoy Bezopasnosti* held the unenviable position of being the most feared and hated organization in the world. Its function, beyond that of keeping the entrenched minority at the top safe at nights, was nothing less than the conversion of the entire world to Communism. Begun as the Cheka in December 1917 and continuing under a variety of names, the organization had succeeded in establishing a way of life loosely based on economic theories that were hopelessly inadequate even for their own times. Thanks to the KGB, a large part of Eastern Europe lurched from one crisis to another, obeying the *Legal Statutes of the Organs of the USSR KGB,* which laid down the rule: The KGB fulfills the Party directives and laws, decrees, and instructions of the Central Committee.

Only blind obedience mattered; any deviation or originality was rigorously put down. Viktor M. Chebrikov, like Andropov and Fedorchuk before him, was a hardliner, an ex-army general, and a dedicated Communist with the selective memory so essential for rising in the Russian hierarchy.

At sixty-three, Chebrikov expected to draw his pension and live in graceful retirement in his *dacha* outside Moscow, continuing his privileged life in ignorance of the dreary life of the average Russian. It had been an unpleasant surprise when he began to lose his hair and put on weight. His original doctor assured him it was a simple matter of a shift in metabolic rate. Neither of them felt able to discuss openly Chebrikov's fear that he was a target for discontented subordinates, but at that point the second day off was suddenly restored to KGB employees.

Viktor Chebrikov engaged in a regimen of exercise that included walking the last mile or so to his office and spending an hour a day on an imported rowing machine. He also changed doctors. The KGB leader was determined to die in his bed of old age surrounded by grieving relatives, as Yuri Andropov had.

Glancing at the lighted clock face in the Spasskaya Tower, he quickened his pace without making it too obvious. It wouldn't do for the baby-sitters to think he was anxious about anything.

It was not yet eight o'clock, but already a line was forming to view the remarkably well preserved body of Lenin in its granite and porphyry mausoleum. It still astounded Chebrikov to learn that the body was changed every ten years as the ashes crumbled to dust. Nothing had surprised him more than this. Only a dozen people in the whole country knew it.

Passing under one of the giant "No Smoking" signs, he walked briskly across the square into 25 October Street. Chebrikov had a great deal on his mind. It could not be said that things were going well for his organization. The army spent four billion rubles on propaganda and covert action, and there was increasingly less to show for it. If the country couldn't even pacify Afghanistan, what hope was there for advances in Europe?

The headquarters of the KGB were located in a complex of unmarked buildings two long blocks from the Kremlin. The main building, number 2 Dzerzhinsky Square, was a stone structure that before the Revolution had belonged to the All-Russian Insurance Company. For some incongruous reason the first floor of the building was gray, while the remaining facade was a grimy yellow. Next to it, seeming to lean against Number 2, was the nine-story extension built by German POWs after World War II. The old section of the building enclosed a courtyard, on one side of which was the notorious Lubyanka Prison. There hundreds of Soviet men and women had been tortured and then, finally, dragged to execution—including at least four chiefs of the sword and shield of the state. The KGB had a well-deserved reputation for eating its own.

Groups of people had already gathered outside the windows of GUM, the state department store, as he passed. Most were middle-aged, dour, and built to stand the rigors of Moscow's long, punishing winters.

As Chebrikov strode briskly toward the square opening up just beyond the end of 25 October Street, he planned the day's activities. A disturbing cable had reached his office late the night before. Something was up in London. The cable was in the special code; only a computer could unravel it. The computer, of course, was down. The computer was always down. The whiz kids from Tech Section no sooner had it up and running when down it went.

Chebrikov, thinking of the cable, forced his face to relax. At no time must he seem to be in less than full control. As he reached Dzerzhinsky Square, he saw the huge statue of the founder of the Cheka, Feliks Dzerzhinsky, a Polish aristocrat who had undertaken Lenin's "wet affairs" for him. Ironically, a large white and red Intourist bus was just circling the monument. Andropov had decided to romanticize the organization by spreading the idea through his creature, Anton Drakov, of late unlamented memory, that the KGB was merely the Russian version of the CIA. A television series about one of its operatives had become immensely popular; there were no location shots in Lubyanka Prison or from the Gulag.

Chebrikov's bodyguards, well aware of their leader's routine, had stopped traffic into the square, and Chebrikov entered Number 2 by one of the pedestrian entrances. Above him was the chimney of the Lubyanka and next to it the boxlike concrete enclosure on the roof. The walls rose twenty feet so that prisoners could hear Moscow but see only the chimney and the guard in the seventh-floor tower. The chimney sprayed out soot whenever it was used; strict instructions forbade its use at eight o'clock when Chebrikov arrived. Bodies were cremated only at night. When the backlog became excessive, victims were carted off to Lefortovo and Butyrskaya.

Only Chebrikov, his deputies, and their immediate subordinates were allowed to enter KGB headquarters through the original building, at the entrance to which there was a large bas-relief of Karl Marx. Even Chebrikov had to stop, remove his glasses, and submit to a retinal scan. Next he placed his ring finger in a black box and waited while the diamond was analyzed and identified. Only then did the doors of the elevator open and admit him.

His office was on the third floor; the secretary rose as he entered, an ugly woman devoted wholly to Party causes. She took his coat and hat. A large aluminum teapot boiled in the corner.

Chebrikov wore a neat khaki tunic and dark blue cavalry trousers with two thin red stripes. On the breast of the tunic were three rows of medal ribbons. Above them hung a Hero of the Soviet Union. The gold braid on his cap was imported from England.

"There is a document being decoded, Comrade Director. It will be down in thirty minutes."

Trying to conceal his impatience, Chebrikov entered his inner sanctum, a large room paneled in mahogany and decorated with Crimean tapestries and thick pile carpets. There was a chandelier and a large ornate brass floor lamp. Several large, framed pictures hung from a picture rail high above; Andropov was given almost equal prominence with Iron Feliks.

No sooner had he seated himself than the secretary brought in tea in a tall glass. In Russia there was always water for tea. A man could travel across the country and not find hot water for shaving, but there was always some for tea.

From a ring, Chebrikov carefully selected a small gold key and unlocked his in-tray. The pickings were slim, culled from the best local residents could glean, then forwarded in diplomatic bags. The Americans were still rattling sabers about Beirut terrorists, but they were doing nothing. Everyone in Europe was being irritated by social unrest of one kind or another.

When the clock on the mantelpiece struck the half-hour, another cup of tea arrived in its silver holder.

"I shall need you for dictation at ten, Marrietta Iosifovna," he said in his soft, low voice. "Where is the decoded message from last night?"

"It will be here in fifteen minutes, Comrade Director."

"See that it is," he said, an edge to his voice.

She withdrew.

In his desk was the latest edition of the Soviet satirical journal *Krokodil.* The contents always displeased him, and this issue offended him more than usual. One passage contained a statement that every citizen would receive a television and a jet plane in the next five-year plan.

"Why the jet plane?" queried the dupe.

"So that when it is announced on television that there are eggs in Vladivostok, everyone can fly there and buy them."

There was a knock on the door. "Come in," he called, and his secretary hurried toward him, holding the translated signal. He took it, not wanting to appear too eager.

Before she had closed the door, he was devouring its contents. What he saw made him pale. He sat at his desk for a good minute until he felt calm. Only then did he reach for the intercom on his desk.

"Ask Comrade Director Popovich to come to my office immediately."

Marrietta Iosifovna relayed his instructions, her excitement building. Something was up, she was sure of it. The Party was on the brink of another great victory. And just before May Day, too. It was all too wonderful.

10 Tech Section

After his trip to Israel, Joshua Davies' duties reached a nadir. His weekly visit to Soo Ling was the only interruption of a perfectly tedious time. Preoccupation with day-to-day office work made him grouchy. He was twitted once or twice by his colleagues and called Keeper of the Queen's Moles, which did little for his mood.

There were no accidental deaths of agents. All was tranquil. That worried him a great deal.

An astonishing feature of Service life, at least as far as Davies was concerned, was the utter dullness of Directors' meetings. Incredible though it seemed, the meetings of the DIC were fraught with passion and excitement by comparison. The more cynical might have deduced that the Directors met simply to ensure a goodly attendance at DIC meetings.

Monday morning found Davies in a surly mood. On the Sunday before, the preacher had been an imported one who insisted on singing "Eternal Father Strong to Save," one of the organist's pet hates in the Methodist hymnal. In addition, the only good singers in the choir had left their spouses and gone off for a weekend at Brighton, so Dol had no help with the hymn singing. The only recourse had been to play a good deal louder than usual in hope of drowning out the congregation.

Now he had just spent two hours arguing about who had proprietary rights to material called Narrative from a source code-named George. The issue shouldn't have taken up more than ten minutes since the files were thin, notoriously unreliable, and their contents highly suspect—a mixture of low-level intelligence flotsam that smelled. On several occasions Davies had questioned the value of Narrative and George's *bona fides.*

"Well, Joshua," said Jimmy Reynolds of F Branch, "you must see there's a principle involved here."

"Damned if I see it," growled Davies, wreathed, as usual, in cigar smoke.

"There are six branches of MI 5," pointed out Cubby McGlenn, "A through F. Everyone has his own little bailiwick, Josie-boy. Can't have everyone mucking in each other's manors, old chap."

The Director ignored McGlenn, who, despite a speech pattern taught only in lesser public schools, was a miner's son from Manchester with pronounced High Church tendencies.

"As I see it," Davies announced in a tone he employed when lunch was fast becoming a concern, "we have an asset, code name George; some dubious material, file name Narrative; and a struggle over proprietary rights."

"Right," said Cubby, "in a nutshell."

"Well, draw straws for it," he said, getting to his feet and throwing his agenda into the shredder. By the time the little worms of paper finished falling into the basket, he was pounding down Curzon Street heading for a cab.

He could not select just any restaurant, not in his present state. Something very different was needed; it was a time to be adventurous. With this in mind he directed the cabdriver to Greek Street, where, delicious irony, stood London's best Hungarian restaurant, the Gay Hussar. He was known there, having dined at the restaurant after some of his meetings nearby with Soo Ling. Besides, Soho was one of the liveliest places in London.

Victor, head chef and owner, was on hand to greet Joshua Davies personally; he had been welcoming the intelligentsia since 1939, and he conducted his guest to a quiet corner with an excellent view of Greek Street. He thought the fat man enjoyed the view; actually Davies liked to check the street every so often; it paid to be careful.

Victor's features were Slavic, decided Davies without really knowing what that meant. Was there gypsy blood in him? Being both Slav and gypsy would account for his arrival in 1939, he decided. Victor never seemed to age; like Davies, he had all his hair, but his was still jet black. It would have destroyed some of Davies' equanimity to learn that Victor was, in fact, from Barrow-in-Furness and only an honorary Magyar because he had studied cooking in Budapest.

The menu needed careful study. Victor served enormous portions; looking around him Davies saw diners tucking into huge plates of roast goose, red cabbage, dumplings, and the special cranberry sauce laced with slivovitz. Lamb in any form was barred; it was a reminder of the hated Turks.

In the end, he selected the *Fasirt Tokfozelekkel*, minced veal with shredded marrow in a sweet dill sauce. The fish soup he tended himself in a little black caldron swinging over a candle flame.

When he concluded, ninety minutes later, with one of Victor's summer puddings made from sponge cake instead of bread and accompanied by a fruity glass or two of Bulls' Blood, he felt ready for anything. Rounding off the meal, as they do in Budapest, with a glass of Tokay, he reluctantly produced his Barclay's bank card and found another cab.

It took a good three-quarters of an hour before he reached Queenhithe Dock, home of the Tech Section. After the driver had gone, Davies entered a large warehouse that had once held fruit. Litter and junk, carefully renewed each Thursday, was piled along the walls and in heaps around the floor. Some light came from bulbs with flat shades suspended on long wires. A couple of potbellied stoves with long galvanized iron chimneys gave out heat in the winter. They were not lit, and Davies felt the chill in his bones. Hurriedly crossing the damp floor to a metal door with "NO ENTRY" painted on it in large red letters, he banged loudly with the palm of his hand. A buzz sounded as the latch was disengaged; Security had identified him via one of the three cameras trained on him.

He descended a short flight of stairs to a second door, where the same ritual was repeated. Tech Section handled all the equipment needs of the services. They manufacutred all the tools necessary for spying on or eliminating the enemy. Under the direction of the talented if sometimes loquacious Harry Clarke, known to those who had a need to know as "T," the engineers could fashion almost anything. They manufactured and serviced bugs and pagers; they built the device to make speech out of vibrations on windowpanes. In a disused subway tunnel, there was a large armory where any kind of weapon from a Nationalist Chinese Generalissimo to a homemade Belfast Saturday night special could be found. They supplied cameras, enlarged microdots, and tested paper to find the most edible kind. In the poisons lab, in conjunction with the government germ researchers at Porton Down, Tech Section experimented with the most efficient and inefficient ways to kill people.

T did not look like a deranged killer. Almost sixty, he was thin, with a spiky little gray mustache and a worried expression. Davies had never seen him without his corduroy jacket and baggy pants, partially covered with an acid-stained lab coat.

It was T himself who ushered Davies into his office, a small room permeated with the smell of oil and solder in battle with Property Services Agency floor polish. While Davies liked T and had a profound respect for his achievements, he dreaded the man's occasional bouts of verbal diarrhea. Once, despite strenuous opposition, he had regaled Davies for twenty minutes on the virtues of a nipple transmitter for female agents that could be swallowed in a crisis.

Davies engulfed T's thin outstretched hand. "Good to see you, T."

"Delighted, delighted," enthused T, his head bobbing. He wore, as usual, a little porkpie hat. "Quite an honor, I'm sure. Coffee?"

"Ah. Yes."

"Thought so. Had it on the minute I saw your face in the monitor there." While T hummed, the coffee was ground, settled, percolated, then lovingly poured into two large china mugs. Davies hunted through the little shelves that covered one wall until he found several packets of sugar.

"It's been an exciting day so far," burbled T. "One of our agents was almost nabbed in Mongolia. They had her fingerprints on a letter, but she had a good fallback plan."

"Really," said Davies.

"They said she posted the letter, so they analyzed the saliva on the flap for blood group."

"And?"

"She beat it. We give them a few milliliters of someone else's saliva when they go out now."

"Did she have a phony nipple?"

T turned, hesitated, then laughed. "I see, sir. A joke. I get it. You're referring to my nipple transmitter; Badger thought it was funny, too." He looked a little hurt, and Davies felt a twinge of guilt. "I don't see why people think it's funny," he added lamely. "It works very well."

"I'm sure it does," said Davies soothingly. "It's simply that when it's most needed to transmit, it's most likely to be discovered. But I didn't come here about the nipple," he said firmly.

"You're going in the field?" asked T.

"No fear," replied Davies. "You don't see me blending in with the scenery, do you?"

"How is Badger these days? I had the time of my life with him in Berlin. There we were, swinging over the Wall on a catenary curve, Vopos everywhere—"

"Badger's fine. He's running a private inquiry agency with the Russian."

"Colonel Novetsky?"

"The same. But, T"—he put down his coffee mug on a pile of blueprints—"after Badger left he sent me some disturbing information. I'm here to learn about those bomb pieces you got after the explosion at the Ship and Whale."

"They're next door, sir." T led the way into an unfurnished room. On a long table covered by a white paper tablecloth lay several fragments of metal and a white piece of rubber.

"I wondered why we were sent these," murmured T, putting down his coffee and taking a slim metal tube from his lab coat pocket. Pulling firmly, he extended it to an eighteen-inch pointer.

"It looks like a typical IRA pipe bomb," he said, indicating two large sections of pipe that had been twisted and melted into fantastic shapes. "They used at least two seven-and-a-half-inch sections of pipe."

"Diameter?"

"The usual, six and a half inches. This piece"—he touched it gently with the pointer—"is the priming pipe. It was welded onto a top plate, threaded, and a pipe terminating nut was screwed onto it."

"Yes, yes, T, everyone knows that. And the detonator is fitted into the nuts and connected to a timer and battery."

T looked anxious. "No timer, sir. It was set off by remote control."

"All right then. Did you trace the explosive?"

"We didn't know what the explosive was at first," said T, fiddling with his pointer. "There was shipyard confetti but—"

"Confetti?"

"Pieces of metal they pack in with the explosive. Works like an antipersonnel bomb. The IRA calls it shipyard confetti, sir."

"A sense of humor is a wonderful thing," said Davies humorlessly.

"I ruled out instant napalm—they make that from petroleum and soap flakes mixed with oil. But it leaves a quite distinct smell, so I knew—"

"T, this is beginning to sound like a lecture," Davies warned. "So you think the IRA blew up this pub, is that it?"

"They haven't done as much explosive work as they used to," T began cautiously.

"Of course not," cut in Davies. "It loses support and it's risky. Blew one of their own up this time, didn't they?"

T did not want to disagree with his superior, but he was visibly distressed. The Director caught his expression. "Well?"

T looked embarrassed. "You see, sir, I've made a special study of bombs." Clearing his throat apologetically he added, "Sort of a hobby with me, if you get my meaning."

"What's the white stuff?"

"Part of a Durex, sir."

"A what?"

"A condom, sir." T looked embarrassed. "Detonators are often carried in them—though they must have taken some getting in Eire."

"Get on with it, T."

"Well, everyone thinks he can make a bomb these days. Every recruit thinks he's a pro. Too late some of them 'score an own goal' as the Provos put it. They're careless. They steal commercial explosives that have begun to sweat; they smoke while around TNT." When Davies didn't interrupt, he gained confidence. "The Weathermen were smoking in Greenwich Village in 1970 when they blew up. People smoke so automatically they don't notice."

"You don't think this is IRA, is that what you're telling me? You don't think it's an own goal?"

"It's too pat, sir, if you ask me. This section of pipe has a manufacturer's ID on it. We read it with a special tool I invented. It comes from the same batch the IRA used in Dover a month ago."

"Well then?"

"And the explosive was a combination of nitrogen fertilizer and fuel oil."

"Not commercial explosive?"

T shook his head. "No. The chemical companies insert certain compounds or colored threads into their stuff so it can be identified."

"So they used garden chemicals that couldn't

be traced. We all know that, T." Davies couldn't fathom what T was being so damned cagey about. He, too, wanted to believe it wasn't an IRA job, yet everything pointed to the IRA. "So speculate, T."

The spiky mustache twitched; T scratched his head. "The explosive mixture made from fertilizer is very inert; it needs a powerful priming charge of one or two sticks. . . ."

"Come on, T. You've got something."

The engineer moved to the end of the table. On a white doily was a tiny piece of red-and-white thread less than a quarter of an inch long. Davies bent to examine it.

"That thread is used by the French company that makes Nitromite."

"Nitromite?"

"Yes, sir. The IRA got a huge batch from Colonel Qaddafi a year ago. It's more powerful than Frangex, which they usually use."

Davies straightened up slowly. "So it *was* IRA?"

T shook his head. "It was the lack of the timer that worried me, sir." He spoke quietly but with confidence. "The average terrorist doesn't go in for remote control; that's more a government approach. When the Israelis killed what's-his-name in retaliation for the Munich Massacre, they used remote control to be sure they got him. You see, a time bomb might have gone off when he wasn't there. Important targets often change locations without notice and at odd hours. Think what could have happened that time when we were moving the PM."

Davies grunted.

"Did you learn anything about the body that was found in this explosion?" asked T.

"Minor crook from Belfast. Could be a plant."

"He *might* be IRA, sir. Undercover."

"Yes, and so might your aunt, T, but I don't quite think so. No, someone waited for Hawk to go to that pub and detonated a charge when he was inside. No clock mechanism, no egg timer, because the person had to be sure he was in there."

"Speculation, sir."

Davies looked once more at the bomb parts laid out neatly in front of him, and said severely, "We've been sold a bill of goods. One of our agents has been blown apart with two hundred pounds of dried shit, and half a dozen people died along with him. Keep your mouth shut on this one, T. If anyone asks, it's an IRA bomb. Right?"

"Right."

"Anyone comes after me, that's the tale you tell them. Then bell me and give me the person's name."

T nodded, looking anxious.

"Now," added Davies, "I'm going scalp-hunting. Fight fire with fire. Can you make me a georgi?"

"A georgi, sir?"

"Damn right. Can you make one?"

T nodded thoughtfully, reviewing the technical problems. "Yes, I can. I saw one after the Special Branch chaps got hold of it."

"Start making it, T." Then, without looking back, Joshua Davies marched from the room, leaving T with the familiar anxious look on his thin face.

11 Kuchino

Boris S. Popovich hurried from his office on the fifth floor in response to the imperial summons. In the presence of authority he was always nervous and tongue-tied. Today, luck being with him, he had just gotten his ceremonial uniform back from the cleaners and was trying it on. True, the double-breasted jacket still bulged around the waist, and his gray tie was throttling him. But the thick nonregulation leather belt held most of him in. On the breast of his blue tunic were three rows of medals and ribbons; the blue shoulder boards revealed his KGB status.

Looks were never more deceiving than in the case of Boris S. Popovich, who was the State Executioner, Director of SMERSH, the Russian acronym for "Death to Spies." Under his leadership a select group of men and women carried out state-sanctioned murder. His skill in *mokrie dela,* wet affairs, had gained him many grateful friends, and though he looked rather like a suckling pig, he was not a nonentity. He was ruthless.

Popovich was not the physical specimen he had been when he'd dealt personally in wet affairs. Now his pink face was razored close, an odd nick showing, and he smelled of an expensive Swiss cologne available to Party high-ups at the special store. The fresh shine, the increasing baldness, made him look like an amiable grandfather who, perhaps, cheated at chess. Assumptions like that were dangerous; the fear Popovich often felt himself found vent in terrorizing and murdering others.

He understood his primary function well enough. It was illustrated by the KGB coat of arms—a sword lying over a shield. The sword imposed the will of the Party oligarchy; the shield protected that oligarchy. Popovich saw nothing wrong with this. It baffled him that a large section of the population termed the KGB the "Office of Crude Bandits." He was jealous of Department V's reputation, regarding himself and his fellow practitioners as a hospital regards its top surgeons. The Party Chairman's emphasis on immobilizing Western countries through internal chaos struck him as pussyfooting and ineffectual. The truth was he didn't understand anything remotely subtle, let alone intellectual. Popovich thought in terms of necks crushed in dark alleys, sudden disappearances, bodies put where they'd never be found.

He wasn't very bright but possessed a low cunning. When his masters talked of excessive emigration, he put the screws to Jews. If there were murmurs about food shortages, he shot a few black marketeers. Nobody really liked him, but many were in his debt. When it was discovered that Andropov's mother was Jewish, it was

Popovich who had hastened the Chairman's death.

Standing nervously before the throne a few minutes after the summons came, Popovich waited for the head of the KGB to speak. Chebrikov waved his hand, indicating an elegant eighteenth-century chair upholstered in red crushed velvet. It was theoretically on loan from the Kremlin Museum. Popovich sat.

"Let us smoke," came the edict. Chebrikov used a holder on doctor's orders. There was a silver cigarette case on his desk full of Moskva-Volgas; he did not offer one, and Popovich was too obtuse to notice the slight. In any case he preferred a Prima and used an American Zippo to light one.

Then came the moment Popovich dreaded. Chebrikov's eyes, shrouded by their dark lenses, would seek a spot on the ceiling and he would begin long, tedious disquisitions on various topics, none of which the Director knew anything about. His only defense, learned from the late Anton Drakov, was to nod knowingly.

Popovich sat on the edge of the chair trying to look thoughtful. He took the opportunity of slipping a finger under the knot of his tie and letting the air circulate. The index finger of his right hand was yellowed from nicotine. He struggled to suppress a cough. His greatest recent disappointment was the discovery that changing offices had not gotten rid of this chronic rattle. Convinced it was the steam radiators that tormented his cilia, and not smoking, he had eagerly seized the opportunity to move into Drakov's office with its coal fire.

After three minutes of intense concentration on the ceiling, Chebrikov spoke. "The Jewish problem is still concerning the Politburo."

"Yes, Comrade General."

"Russians do not breed enough. There are swarthy Georgians and Turks, yellow hordes of Kazaks, Mongols, and Tartars. Uncounted millions of ungrateful Central Asians. There are the Transcaucasians, and the Balts. *They* breed."

Popovich stole a quick glance at Chebrikov; his head was still back. No response was expected from Popovich. Silence reigned for half a minute.

"Krokodil."

Popovich jumped. *"Krokodil?"* he echoed.

"Do you read it?"

"No, Comrade General."

"It is widely touted as a safety valve; I do not believe in safety valves." The eyes slowly descended behind their black shields until the stare was fixed on Popovich.

The Director squirmed uneasily under the stare.

Chebrikov spoke again. "They are the dangerous utterings of dissidents. They think, these *Krokodil* people, they can do what they like." Leaning across his desk, he flipped open a copy of the magazine and said, "Look at that."

Popovich hastened to the desk and, clutching the magazine, retreated back to his chair. He studied the magazine. There was a series of cartoons; a delegation of Soviet workers was in America. The captions read: "This," said John to Ivan, "is my little house. Here is my sitting room for guests." The next cartoon showed a huge nursery. "This is the nursery." Popovich looked up.

"Go on. Read the rest of it."

"Here is my dining room. This is my bedroom, where I occasionally meet my mistress. This is my wife's bedroom, where she may greet her lover. And now, how do you live in Russia, Ivan?"

"I have all this," Ivan replies, "and without partitions."

"Well?" The baleful black stare focused on him.

Popovich nodded.

"I don't want this magazine sold for a few weeks. That should be enough."

"Yes, Comrade General." Popovich stood up, smoothing his uniform.

"I haven't finished."

Popovich sat down hurriedly, crossing and uncrossing his legs.

"Do you know where the biggest collection of illegal books is in all Russia?"

Some instinct of self-preservation told Popovich to keep his head still.

"The Lubyanka Library. I have just found that once every ten days the prisoners in Lubyanka can request books—many of which have been banned for decades! These books were seized for evidence and somehow became part of the biggest collection of filth in Russia. There are books by Zamyatin, Pilnyak, P. Romaov, and that traitor Solzhenitsyn."

"I will burn the library today, Comrade General," Popovich said.

"Do not be too extreme, Boris Sergeevich. Just get a list of disapproved authors and burn their trash." Chebrikov rubbed the side of his nose vigorously with his index finger. "Burn them."

Popovich replied, "Yes, Comrade General," and made a note in a slim book he kept in his inside pocket. He was very pleased to have been addressed by his name.

"Soviet citizens have the right to complain and criticize," Chebrikov added heavily. "Chairman Gorbachev has stressed that a thousand times. It is a right guaranteed by Article Forty-nine of the Constitution."

Popovich echoed, "Article Forty-nine, yes."

The head of the KGB settled back in his chair and surveyed his office. There was a dark square on a wall where a painting had once hung. It had been Stalin's picture, vast and glowering. "Anything could happen," Chebrikov continued. "A sudden explosion of blood in the brain and you're dead, or worse. I have an uncle who's a mere vegetable. Just sits and drools. *My God,"* he suddenly roared, slamming his hand on the desk. "When I think of that and then hear these antisocial bastards attacking this country it positively *makes my blood boil.* I mean, we could go mad tomorrow, a sudden protein deficiency, too much oxygen to the brain. Those renegades will get no support from the Soviet people."

"I'll have some of them drafted into the army," promised Popovich, alarmed by the outburst. "There is also space at the Serbsky Institute. I'll take a few at random."

"*Pour encourager les autres,*" said Chebrikov.

Popovich nodded.

His master was relieved to find such blind obedience; if Popovich had any intellectual pretensions or, God forbid, political ambitions, the man would be a force beyond controlling. A veritable unthinking juggernaut!

The eyes refixed themselves on the ceiling. "We need an assassin. Someone who can be trusted. I still shudder when I think of that bastard Khokhlov."

Popovich was sweating. Only by a miracle had he been out of Moscow when that disaster was set in motion.

"A defector who gave away two good men, then went on to lecture all over the West about our technical weaponry. It's beyond belief," Chebrikov finished in a whisper.

"There is a defector, Comrade General?"

"Worse. A British agent, origin unknown, who must be eliminated. There is more, but you do not need to know it."

Popovich replied, "I will find an assassin."

"There must be no mistakes, Boris Sergeevich. I should warn you, there is talk of reorganizing your department."

"My department—"

"You were friendly with Drakov, weren't you?"

"He was an associate, Comrade General, *not a friend.* I didn't know him well."

The Kremlin phone on Chebrikov's desk rang shrilly; after the third ring, he picked it up and listened. Popovich was sweating more. "Reorganize" didn't mean reassigning his secretary and moving his file drawers into another office. It was a euphemism for . . . well, as long as this mission succeeded, everything would be fine again. And he had exactly the man for the job.

Chebrikov replaced the Kremlin phone in its cradle. "It seems our British friends are after the same target. And despite the fact that we owe them a favor for eliminating Drakov, we must get to this target before they do."

"I have just the man. His name—"

Chebrikov raised his hand. "I don't want to know anything." There was the briefest pause. "The state has no room for enemies, my dear Boris Sergeevich," he continued. "They take up too much time, and there is much to be done. And in a country of two hundred million what are a few thousand troublemakers, eh?"

Popovich suddenly found the black lenses staring straight at him. He nodded quickly.

"Exactly. The problem, as the Nazis learned, is to suit the man to the job. If they had performed well, the world would be a lot freer of kikes, gypsies, and other subhumans. Do you know the gypsies are the only people in the Soviet Union who won't *work?*" He paused. Then to Popovich's astonishment, he took off his glasses. The eyes behind were a watery blue. Massaging the bridge of his nose, Chebrikov continued. "Whoever is being employed by the British must be sanctioned. Even if he is SIS, he must be burned."

"And our source, in England. Is he safe?"

Chebrikov looked at Popovich sharply, then replaced the dark glasses. "He is, for a time. Then you will be asked to take care of him, too."

Popovich was stunned. There was no mistaking the meaning. "But, Comrade General—"

"You see, the British are getting close. Someone must be sacrificed. It protects all our other agents, for one thing, if we get rid of our central man. We had to burn Fuchs to preserve Philby. Of course, that did irreparable damage to their atomic information exchange agreement, too, but . . ." He took a key ring from his jacket pocket and selected a small silver key. With it he unlocked his desk and took out a plain brown envelope. "Give this to your man." Flipping it over, he showed the seal. "This must not be opened in anyone's presence, not even yours."

Popovich, much to his own surprise, found himself protesting. "But, Comrade General, our asset in England . . . I mean . . . we have a reputation for saving our people."

Chebrikov leaned across his vast desk, smiling. "Your loyalty is well known, Boris Sergeevich, but this is a matter of policy. When the agent in Britain is sanctioned, all leaks will be blamed on him. Normally we would simply arrest some foreign agent and trade for him, but this time he must go, so as to allow us to reposition other agents. It will take time, but we have plenty of that. Every year"—he smiled, having taken upon himself the role of a kindly teacher explaining the mysteries to a not-very-bright student—"every year, another plum falls."

Popovich nodded. "Another plum, yes."

"As for our agents and their hopes that we will look after them, well, what do they really matter? We're all they have anyway. If they don't believe in us, what can they believe in?

That's why peasants are forever mouthing religious mumbo jumbo. The fools claim they have to believe in heaven because the alternative is too awful to contemplate. Imbeciles."

"And we . . . we are . . ." began Popovich, sweating and groping desperately.

"Heaven," said Viktor Chebrikov with a broad encouraging smile. "Think of us as a sort of heaven."

He stood up suddenly; Popovich jumped up as well.

Chebrikov lifted his hand as if it contained a glass. *"Na Zdarovye,"* he proclaimed.

"Na Zdarovye," repeated Popovich, overwhelmed by it all. *"Na Zdarovye."*

Popovich returned to his office at a fast trot; people walking along the corridors parted before him like the Red Sea. He didn't notice. His secretary rose to her feet as he swept through the outer office.

"Find Kroptkov," was all he said before gaining the sanctuary of his private office.

Placing his hat on the ornate bronze coatrack, he sat heavily in the leather armchair and allowed himself a sigh. He reached across the desk for the ivory cigarette box with an inlaid mother-of-pearl lid. It had once held Anton Drakov's cheap cardboard *papirosa* cigarettes. Now it held a mixture of Prima and gold-tipped Troika. Popovich lit a Prima with the elegant ivory desk lighter, then depressed a key on his intercom. "Tea," he snapped.

All he could do was wait now. He looked around. Everything he saw had belonged to the traitor Drakov, and before him Propov. Now both were dead. It was an ill omen. Feeling the cold, he crossed the room and poked the coal fire. The andirons were English and very elegant. Popovich liked beautiful things. In his work he amassed a great number of elegant bits and pieces. Drakov had had no interest in such things, and one whole bookshelf was bare. A set of leather-bound books had filled it once, but what the ex-Director had done with them no one knew or cared.

Though he would sooner have died than admit it, Popovich had possessed a sneaking regard for Drakov. The man was immensely capable; he understood computers. He was a genius. The computers alone made him suspect. The rest of the KGB high-ups avoided them absolutely, leaving them to the pointy-headed geniuses in Tech Section. Though Popovich didn't understand what Drakov had done—much less how he'd done it—it was rumored that he had encoded all the data amassed on possible dissidents, Jews, and targets for disinformation, and had done it in such a way that it would take twenty-five years to make any sense of the stuff. The very next office contained the two Minsk 34 computers that had caused the trouble. Nobody could get them to work, so they stood there, useless except as reminders of their master's passing.

"Come in," he growled, in response to a knock on the door. His secretary scurried in with a glass of black tea with a lemon slice secured to the rim.

"Fruit jelly stirred in?"

"Yes, Comrade Director."

"What about Kroptkov?"

"The call is out."

He waved a hand in dismissal and she retreated, leaving the glass on his desk within reach. No one was safe, he thought, sipping gloomily. "Anton Mikhailovich was a Hero of the Soviet Union, too," he reminded himself.

The intercom buzzed.

"Well?"

"Comrade Kroptkov is at Kuchino."

"Send for a car and driver immediately," he ordered. In five minutes, he was on his way, settled comfortably back against the cushioned seats of his chauffeured car.

"Kuchino," he told the driver as the automobile was checked through the great iron gates of number 2, Dzerzhinsky Square. The man knew the address but had no idea what went on at the large country *dacha* just outside Moscow. Popovich ruled at Kuchino; it was his fiefdom, a finishing school for agents. Here were taught rifle and pistol shooting beyond basic agent instruction. A particularly crippling form of unarmed combat was mastered; the nonperson Drakov had learned it a decade before with the concentration and scrupulousness he applied to all his tasks.

Traffic parted before them; an official limousine counted for something. The window glass was tinted; he could see out, but no one could see in. People were hurrying along the sidewalks as the car headed for the river. On the street corner as they passed Manezh Square he saw a sure sign of warmer weather—brightly painted little wooden kiosks selling cigarettes, theater tickets, and Moscow's perennial favorite in winter or summer, ice cream. Ahead were the old-fashioned red-brick turrets of the Historical Museum and on their left the length of the Kremlin wall, broken almost in the center by the Kutafya Tower.

Popovich was proud of himself for the work done at Kuchino. There were classes in the use of poisons and drugs that dissipated in the body within minutes. Even under detailed pathological examination, they gave the impression of natural causes. Agents practiced vehicle sabotage so that a fatal crash could be staged and made to look like an accident. Kuchino was for specialists only; Popovich was proud of that, too. At Kuchino, the best from all the world came together to rehearse their art, but none could match the Russians.

They passed the huge wedding cake of Moscow University, haunt of foreign degenerates. Fat rich boys playing at being revolutionaries to spite their parents. They took a few classes, then took up drinking and other antisocialist hooliganism. Popovich shook his head in disgust. He remembered Carlos. That was another time Anton Mikhailovich had been right. Carlos was a spoiled brat. The Revolution should have remained a strictly Russian affair.

The limo turned off the road fifteen minutes later. There was a tall wire gate; the driver showed his pass and a guard peered into the car. Another guard manned a fixed position, training his PKS machine gun on the car.

They were waved through, and moved up a long sweeping driveway leading to a guard-house. From there visitors walked the last hundred yards to the huge nineteenth-century *dacha* with its five acres all enclosed by a stone wall. Not surprisingly, the English-speaking trainees called it "the Great Wall of 'Chino."

A guard checked Popovich's credentials even though the pink face and blue veins were familiar. Inside the door was another guard at a desk, an AK assault rifle within easy reach.

With a nod of approval, Popovich noted that the safety was opposite the Cyrillic letters AB on the receiver. The rifle was on automatic. Pressure on the trigger would cause all thirty 7.62-mm rounds to fire in less than three seconds. It was the kind of precaution that pleased the Director of Department V.

There was an inflexible rule that no one, not even Popovich himself, could carry anything metal into the building. All weapons were issued from the armory on the first floor. Handing over his keys and heavy Stechkin machine pistol, the Director stepped around the desk and passed through the metal detector. A large white German shepherd panted softly and looked at Popovich, as his master did, with an unwavering stare. Both were ready to kill.

Popovich ascended, unaccompanied, to the second floor. Kroptkov, the assassin, sat in his room. Through the steel bars there was a view of the firing range and, beyond, the large *dacha* where the swallows were trained. The ceiling was high and peaked; fine oak beams connected one side of the A-frame to the other some ten feet above the floor. Despite the bars, it was a luxurious apartment.

Popovich sat opposite Kroptkov. The assassin was blond, six feet one, handsome in a way the cruel thin mouth helped rather than hindered; He had the good looks of a Nordic athlete and was allowed a manicure and haircut once a week, and all his clothes were imported from England and Italy. The assassin never smoked and never drank. Thirty-six years old, he had lived a hundred times that; he spoke four languages fluently; he never raised his voice. Really dangerous men never did.

Kroptkov was an expert and a specialist; he killed silently and effectively, using the silenced automatic, the garrote wire, the knife or stiletto. The sudden, silent demise of an enemy of the state was his lifework. Kroptkov liked knifework to be especially neat—the presence of blood was a silent critic, he told his trainees. If the entry wound was jagged, he failed a student. Most of the time trainees practiced on dead pigs; the skin had a feel similar to that of human skin. Occasionally the KGB supplied live targets. Kroptkov enjoyed these best because they were unpredictable—a true test for his students. The victim was released and stalked. The best students killed in daytime; night was for beginners.

Naturally, men working under pressure needed diversions. Often they were sadists, though once in a while there was a masochist. Whatever the agents wanted they got; these were the elite of Department V. Gambling, drinking, even certain drugs were permitted. Women, of course, were in demand, and the Gulag was full of them. Kroptkov himself never had a woman before he set out, however. He liked to find one while hunting; it added an extra dimension to the kill.

The man lay on his bed in uniform trousers and shirt, gazing at the ceiling. The pose reminded Popovich of Viktor Chebrikov and irritated him. Nevertheless he did not rebuke the assassin. Men like Kroptkov were rare, very rare. Mere killers were two a ruble, and you got what you paid for. Popovich took the envelope from his inside pocket, placing it in Kroptkov's hand. The assassin turned it over and looked at the seal.

"You are to open this only after I leave," said the Director. "The seal is unbroken, as you see."

Kroptkov looked at Popovich with the dangerous calm and hungry strength of the true fanatic.

"Of course," was his entire response.

The Director left him still stretched out on his bed. Popovich was not one for philosphical considerations, but he wondered how it was that a man whose good looks and intelligence could gain him anything would become a professional killer. Kroptkov was remarkably attractive to women and a quick thinker. He delivered the goods every time.

Kroptkov waited until Popovich had left the building. He saw the limousine pull away. Then, stripping, he slipped on a terry-cloth robe and his slippers. Locking the envelope in his safe unread, he made his way to the private sauna and steam room at the end of the corridor. While he sat in the steam room, naked, muscles rippling with each movement, he cleared his mind of all but the pleasures of his body. The room was filled with swirling steam and the smell of camphor; it cleared the nasal passages, but Kroptkov had never had so much as a cold. He lay back without flinching as the hot vapor collected on the ceiling, beaded up into drops, and fell onto his chest and face. When he had remained in the steam for fifteen minutes, he sat up and shook his head. Drops of water fell from his thick blond hair. He next took an ice-cold shower.

When the KGB looked for agents, they sought the unstable but controllable type. Such people were very rare. It would be safer to follow the Western practice of selecting the kind of killer who suffered nightmares from the killings he ordered or carried out. The Western maxim apparently was, get men trained to kill who possess an aversion to killing. But such men were useful for only a short time; and it cost millions to train one assassin. The KGB could not afford to waste money the way the CIA could.

Kroptkov returned to his room, opened the safe, and took out his instructions. With all speed, he was to trace an Ingrid Thummel and bring her back, unharmed, to Moscow. A British agent, details unknown, not of British origin, was also following her. He was to be eliminated. There was no photograph of the agent or of Ingrid Thummel. A plane would be ready for Kroptkov in twelve hours.

Kroptkov did not wonder why the girl had to be captured. He never concerned himself with questions like that. The assassin did what he was told; that was perhaps his greatest attraction. Burning the instructions, Kroptkov closed the shutters and locked the door.

Next he went to his wardrobe and took out a small block and tackle that he attached to one of the wooden cross beams. He looped a length of rope through the pulleys. Removing his robe, he put it away with almost feminine precision and care. From his dressing table he took a stick of greasepaint and wrote obscenities on all the exposed parts of his body he could reach. He admired the effect in a full-length mirror. The Cyrillic letters in reverse image pleased him, and he tried to read them aloud, backward. The strange sounds amused him.

Taking a small towel, he wrapped it around his neck and then fashioned a noose from one end of the rope. Carefully pulling on the other end, he took up the slack until the pressure on his neck caused the pulse in his neck to throb. Kroptkov was ready.

In seconds he massaged himself to erection. Then he took a short length of rope and, using his teeth, knotted the rope so his hands were loosely tied. It was essential that he seem helpless.

The hands were free enough to grasp the rope. Pulling on it steadily, he increased the pressure until it was hard to breathe. His Adam's apple jerked spasmodically. Soon Kroptkov was poised between life and death.

For two minutes he hung there, achieving the most sublime sexual experience, obtaining orgasm by risking death. Kroptkov was practicing autoerotic asphyxia, hanging himself in a ritual largely unknown to the general public.

Suddenly he groaned. His face, turning blue, contorted with pleasure. The great wave of sexual release, intensified by the self-induced hypoxia, was, in its turn, overwhelmed by a second, more powerful wave, and a third. The semen shot from him, hot and plentiful.

Almost beyond saving now, Kroptkov struggled with the bonds on his hands and reached above him to pull on the rope. The pressure slackened. He collapsed to the floor, gasping for air. Kroptkov would sleep where he lay. He had had enormous pleasure. Shortly he would kill for the state, and that, too, gave him enormous pleasure. He had the best of all worlds; he owed everything to the KGB and served them with all he had.

12 The Abbey

The man, code-named Ivan, crossed Russell Square on foot; it was 12:31 on a bright Saturday afternoon. The carefully manicured grass was neatly divided by geometrically shaped tulip beds of red, white, and yellow. Whores who frequented the park for quickies against the tall ash trees would have to step carefully when the flowers were in bloom, he decided.

When he had satisfied himself that he wasn't being followed, Ivan slipped into the Russell Hotel, feeling a surge of adrenaline. He was afraid, of course. Only a fool would underestimate his present danger. Joshua Davies was getting too close; the others were fools or bureaucrats, usually both. The fat man was rat poison. It was Davies or him now.

An additional problem Ivan faced was that innocent men didn't look for tails and didn't shake them. That could be done only once. One time the suspicious might accept the excuse, "I thought the opposition was following me." But it wouldn't fly twice. So, if there were someone dogging him, it would have to appear the tail's fault when he came up dry.

He crossed the vast entrance hall with its monumental staircase, memorials to the Victorian love of ostentation, and turned down a long corridor with steam pipes suspended above him, head high, walking as if he had every right to be there. No one challenged him. He heard voices behind an office door and a radio playing. Seconds later, he was at a service entrance. If anyone quizzed him, he would insist he had taken a shortcut.

The door led to concrete steps, and a small parking lot filled with cars jammed in at all angles. The only clear space was in front of two overflowing trash dumpsters where a hand-lettered sign stated "Don't even think of parking here."

Within two minutes of slipping out of the back of the Russell Hotel, Ivan was in an elevator descending rapidly to the platform of Russell Square underground station. A train was about to pull out. At South Kensington, he changed to the Circle Line, getting out at St. James' Park. Glancing at his slim gold wristwatch, he saw he had less than ten minutes before his rendezvous. A brisk walk down Tothill Street brought him to the West Entrance of Westminster Abbey.

Above him, as he mounted the steps, were the two great towers designed by Nicholas Hawksmoor. Truth to tell, he thought, they were little more than mock-Gothic and not really in keeping with the incredible, almost brutal strength of the rest of the medieval building. Ivan prided himself on his aesthetic sense.

Sidney Ricketts was already there, looking at

the display in the bookshop. Possibly he thought he would be less conspicuous browsing through books than standing on the steps of the abbey. Wonderful; the man was learning to think—though it wouldn't do for him to think *too* much.

They didn't greet each other or shake hands. Ricketts replaced the large illustrated book he had been glancing through and followed Ivan to the nave.

The fact of their serving the same masters in Moscow did not spark any affection between them. Ricketts, a Cockney, shared all the prejudices of his class against toffs. Disliking anyone of the officer class, he also despised upper-class accents. To Ricketts, Ivan sounded like one of those toffee-nosed bastards who still ran England to suit themselves. Still, Ivan had shown enough courage under fire in the SAS to earn Ricketts' grudging respect; he didn't want his friendship.

Ivan used Ricketts because he was good, and he never let the man get under his skin. Ricketts' opinions meant nothing to Ivan; the Cockney sensed this, and it made matters worse.

"You're late," said Ricketts in a low voice as they stood looking at the huge east-west axis of the abbey. A considerable distance in front of them were the choir stalls. They could hear the singing above the ceaseless to-ing and fro-ing of visitors.

The Tomb of the Unknown Warrior lay at their feet, its flame burning brightly. Ivan drew back the sleeve of his raincoat and examined his watch. "Right on the dot, I think."

"I was waiting a good ten minutes."

A couple shepherding five noisy children moved past the two men toward the memorial to Sir Winston Churchill just inside the great west door. Ivan heard one of the boys ask if he was buried underneath. The mother thought he was.

They took a few steps, Ricketts impatient to know what was on; they had met like this only twice before in ten years. But Ivan took his time getting to the point. For one thing, he wanted to see if anyone was following Ricketts.

The Cockney had been thrown out of SAS because he was a loner and a canteen cowboy. Fighting in bars was not what the SAS was looking for. Good fighting units sometimes had a reputation for being rough and ill-disciplined—the Australians were a good example—but the SAS couldn't risk men like Ricketts. Now Ricketts pretty much behaved himself. He knew not to ask questions. He could kill a dozen ways without fuss or mess, the SAS had seen to that, and he was a maestro with plastique.

Glancing at Ricketts, Ivan realized he'd never seen the man smile. Ricketts had brown hair parted on the right and a thick mustache that covered a skillfully repaired harelip. He had a habit of smoothing down the mustache as if to hide the thin white scar. He had the neck of an American football player, almost as wide as his head. His face was long and oval with brown tufts of eyebrow over large, widely spaced green eyes. His eyes didn't have the wild look Ivan had seen in many operatives. Killing relaxed Ricketts.

A time will come, thought Ivan suddenly, when Ricketts will try to kill me.

"I don't know what your bitch is," Ricketts said suddenly, out of the blue. "The whole bloody world's your oyster."

"And unless you come from the slums, you can't have any idealism, is that it, Sidney?"

Ricketts' face clouded. He knew he'd be bested in an argument with Ivan.

"The future belongs to dancehall cowboys who get cashiered for D and D? Is that right?"

Ricketts was not astute enough to realize he had gotten to Ivan. He merely growled, "I beat the clock, didn't I?"

"Beat the clock" was SAS jargon for surviving; those who did not had their names memorialized on the wooden clock tower at the headquarters of 22 Regiment in Hereford.

"Aha! Perhaps a sign, an omen?" Ivan said. "We are just passing the grave of Thomas Tompion, the father of English watchmaking."

Ricketts had had enough. "Look, what's this all about? I don't like it, see? You know who I am, and I know nothing about you. 'Call me Ishmael,' you said. What the hell kind of bloody name is that?"

"Keep your voice down." Ivan sat in one of the chairs. "And sit here." He indicated the chair next to him. He glanced around to be sure no one was within earshot.

Ricketts joined him with ill grace.

"You'll be told what you need to know. I contact you; therefore I need to know who you are. That's the way it works."

"So get on with it then."

Ivan had picked up a hymnal and was thumbing through it. "I would not have sent the emergency signal unless it was important." The choir sang a loud passage, and he bent nearer to Ricketts. "You'll have to do a job and be very quick about it, too."

"Moscow Center won't like it," replied Ricketts, "not so soon after that pub job."

"They won't be told until it's over. Maybe not then, either."

Ricketts got to his feet. "Count me out."

Ivan sighed and stood up. "There isn't time to contact Moscow Center. It's got to be as soon as possible; the target is narrowing down suspects. He's fat but he's no fool. Once he gets me in his sights, I've got to be absolutely sure not to do anything suspicious. If he burns me, he'll track you down."

"Not if you keep your mouth shut."

Ivan put the hymnal down and walked slowly down the nave. A boy's soprano voice soared into the air. "He will find you. Once he has me, Davies will unravel the puzzle."

"That's his name?"

"Yes. Watch two-seventy-five Lower Marsh Street. His office faces the street, third floor. When the light goes on, that's him. No one's allowed to clean it. How will you do it?"

"You don't need to know that," Ricketts said spitefully. "But Center doesn't let locals decide policy."

Ivan seized Ricketts' arm and squeezed. "It's our necks we're talking about. If they snuff us, they're hurting, but we're dead!"

Ricketts broke Ivan's grip with his free hand.

"Not scared, are you?" he said in a mocking voice. "Still showing self-discipline, independence of mind, and a sense of humor, are we?"

The soprano's voice filled the air around them. It was incredibly clear; Ivan was reminded of the noise icicles made when a wind blew through them. It was a brittle, fragile beauty. "Get rid of the fat man, that's all."

Nothing more was said until they had passed the choir and crossed the south transept.

"Start tonight. He sometimes works late on Saturdays. I'll have an alibi for the next few evenings."

Ricketts nodded. "He doesn't have a woman, does he? They're more relaxed then."

Ivan gave a dry laugh. "A woman? He weighs twenty stone. She'd be crushed to death." Standing under the wall painting of the Incredulity of St. Thomas, Ivan added, "It's got to look like an accident or those IRA bastards."

A black nun dressed in flowing blue robes joined them for an instant, then moved into Poets' Corner; Ivan was forced to keep his voice down. "This is the last job for a while."

"Center said that?"

Ivan waited until the nun moved away. Examining the medallion of Ben Jonson above the door to the crypt, he said quietly, "When you do for the fat man, at least two people will be able to figure out that he was getting too close to something." The nun, entered the crypt.

"They have nigger nuns now?" Ricketts was genuinely shocked.

"Never mind. You deal with Davies. When

it's done, lie low somewhere. Find a whore to keep you amused and out of sight."

Ricketts nodded and turned away without any farewell. For the first time, he took a good look at their surroundings. Everywhere he looked was a dull brass or stone marker. "They won't be able to bury him in here, will they? Not with all these blokes here already."

Ivan shook his head and walked quickly to the side door by the Chapter House.

"Fuck you," said Ricketts to the retreating figure. Out of the corner of his eye, he caught sight of the black nun staring at him, mouth open. "And fuck you too, Sister."

13 The Second Shoe

Joshua Davies was feeling reckless, so he lunched at his club. The chef was a notorious alcoholic, but when he was on the wagon his meals were atrocious. Today he was three sheets to the wind and the meal surpassed all superlatives.

One attraction of the club, of which Davies was a charter member, was its strict policy of keeping out government types whenever possible. Fifty members paid five hundred guineas each to belong. There were, needless to add, no women members and no members of the High Church; Catholics and Jews were admitted without restriction as long as they held no official position as clergy.

The leather armchairs, the silver cutlery, the sprightly waiters were a marked contrast to all other London clubs, which were feeling the effects of England's slow, graceful economic collapse. For one thing, there was no rent to pay on the elegant building in Grosvenor Square: Joshua Davies owned it. It was infinitely superior to the club Rossiter had once invited him to where, amidst split leather armchairs and tarnished knives and forks, one was served by waiters who remembered the Great War better than they remembered one's order of steak-and-kidney pie. Rossiter had hinted he might like to join Davies' club; the fat man was successfully evasive.

Later, Davies sat in his office in Lower Marsh Street wishing he were doing something besides keeping up with his paperwork. He was a meticulous worker; his accounts always balanced, and his handwriting was precise. It had astonished the auditors for years to find his operation made a small profit from its cover activities. During the previous fiscal year, Davies, Greene & Co. had made two hundred thousand pounds by selling machine parts abroad. A third of it was pure profit, and no one knew what to do with it.

Davies' attention wavered. In the folder on top of his in-tray lay Badger's list. Even Davies had his doubts—though they weren't really doubts so much as a desperate desire not to believe.

Ironically, the best hope was that Ivan, if there was an Ivan, had been given one task alone—killing British secret service personnel. If this were Ivan's only goal, then he might not be permitted to undertake any activity that would compromise his actions. God, what a situation! Hoping an assassin was content *only* to kill.

He had sent Dol home; perhaps Davies unconsciously nursed the hope of seeing Soo Ling. It wasn't the usual time, but . . .

A loud buzz from the phone on his desk startled him. Someone was outside the office. "Yes?" he spoke into his intercom.

"Rossiter."

Puzzled, Davies reached under his desk, pressed a button, and released the door lock. Two minutes later, Rossiter was at his office door. The Director rose from his chair and peered through the spy-hole. It was Rossiter all right—military bearing, Guards tie, and an umbrella over his shoulder to symbolize his reserve officer status.

If the opposition shot everyone with a Guards tie who carried an umbrella the way Rossiter did, there'd be damn few of us left, thought Davies. He frowned.

They went through the usual courtesies and Davies went back to his seat. As colleagues, they kept up a veneer of friendliness, but apart from a couple of evenings out at a topless bar well over a decade ago, they hadn't seen much of each other.

"Drink?" asked Davies.

"No. No, thanks." Rossiter paused, then said, "I imagine that ashtray thing cost quite a bit."

"Nothing is expensive if you can afford it," said Davies.

"Ah yes. Quite."

Silence reigned for a while. Rossiter didn't want to take the chair opposite Davies, and lit upon it very lightly, poised for flight. He was restless, as if he wanted to go somewhere, but wasn't sure where. He gazed at some of the photographs of Davies, in waders, hauling fish from streams and lakes. A glass case on the desk containing a large fish with needlelike teeth held his attention.

"Is that a pike, Joshua?"

"Sort of; it's muskellunge. Caught it in Kentucky a couple of years back." He smiled, looking like a contented Buddha. "Took two hours to land him."

Rossiter stared at the mantelpiece, and said, "I've always wondered why you have a bust of Hitler on—"

"It's not Hitler; it's John Wesley."

"Ah."

Nothing else was said for a good three minutes. Davies contented himself with offering Rossiter his rosewood humidor, and when it was silently refused, selected a fine Monte Christo for himself. Rossiter took out his slim cigarette case and slid out a Dunhill, glancing at his own long, thin fingers.

The Director lifted his glasses, pinched the bridge of his nose, then reached into his pocket to produce a large white linen handkerchief. Polishing his lenses, he waited.

Suddenly Rossiter blurted, "It's about Badger's idea that there's a mole in our midst."

"You thought it was baloney."

Rossiter gave a nervous dry cough, then noticed for the first time that he still had his umbrella in his hands. Laying it on the floor, he said, "I didn't see how someone could have infiltrated us so successfully. But I'm willing to admit there might be some merit in the idea." He drew a breath. "After all, the reason we were so long getting to Philby was because some of us couldn't imagine a *bona fide* betraying his country."

"What's your point?"

Rossiter twisted a little away from him, facing the door. "I want to know if Badger suggested any names. He didn't like me."

"And you—"

"He might have given my name."

"Because he doesn't like you?"

"Well . . . I know you're still poking around, Joshua. It would suit Badger to leave the service with the impression there's something rotten about it, and you could play the role of the avenging angel."

Davies studied Rossiter's face. "You don't have anything to fear, if you're innocent."

Rossiter got to his feet. "Look what happened to Hollis. They attacked him with innuendo and circumstantial evidence. Now half the country thinks he's guilty."

Walking over to the mantelpiece, he picked up a piece of stone labeled "Wuthering Heights," studied it, and put it back. "You don't have to dig too deep to find a little pink in all of us. Dammit man, Cambridge was pink before the war, and apart from the 'hearties' all of us suffered from juvenile enthusiasms. I mean, Britain was losing an empire and not finding a role."

"And how does this relate to Badger?"

"Well, he's not one of us. He regards the public school-Cambridge axis as dangerous. He'd like to bring us to our knees."

Davies got up, moved around the desk, and sat on the edge of it, hands clasped across his belly. " 'Play up! Play up! and play the game,' eh? Well, Badger went to Charterhouse. How much more public-school can you get?"

"But he also went to Manchester University

and studied God knows what. Sciences. That doesn't teach you how to command men."

"I took sciences myself," Davies said. "Chemistry, physics, and algebra. At Oxford."

"Yes. But you were a scholarship boy." Rossiter seemed to think that solved everything. It was true, Tristram Davies hadn't made his pile until Joshua left Christ Church and Dol was in her second year at Girton.

"So given Badger's prejudice and upbringing, don't you see, he may well target one of us."

Davies wasn't sure whether he himself was included in that "us." Probably not.

He got up and went back to his swivel chair, slumped back down in it, and looked at the hapless Rossiter.

Rossiter said, "It's like the damn Phony War. Everyone is waiting for the other shoe to fall. They know you won't give up, Joshua."

Davies leaned back in his seat, eliciting a squeak of protest from the tortured spring. "I didn't know I was so powerful," he replied.

Rossiter went back to his own chair. He lowered his voice. "I expect you know a lot about me, Joshua. You're too perceptive to fool. I'm married; I go to strip joints on the q.t. There's a place that serves a lunch with topless waitresses." He paused, then added lamely, "There's no harm in it, but you've had watchers out, I'm sure. It's in your damn files."

"I don't judge morals; I deal with traitors."

"I know, I know." Rossiter made little deprecating gestures with his hands. "I trust you, Joshua. We all do," he trailed off, then added, "Er . . . could I have a drink?"

"Surely." Davies crossed his office and opened the cabinet; the light inside bounced off the mirrored surfaces. "Whiskey and soda?"

Rossiter nodded and Davies poured two stiff doubles, squirting in a touch of soda. Rossiter took the heavy glass and sipped. "I suppose you heard about Carnation?"

The Director turned, all attention. "What about him? The Islington job?"

"It wasn't anything sinister after all. Carnation owed his bookie a thousand quid. The damn fool couldn't, or wouldn't, pay, so two men were sent to lean on him. They overdid it."

The Director's face reddened. "They damn well did."

"So there's no mole there. We got their confessions via the Yard."

Davies' tongue clicked against his palate. This was a setback; at the very least it cast doubt on Badger's list. Possibly even killed the whole damn idea. He wished Rossiter would get the hell out and let him look at the autopsy reports again.

The next ten minutes were spent in painful small talk, and both men were relieved when Rossiter left.

Davies' cigar had gone out; he relit it, then went to a large framed photograph of him being awarded the East Anglia Salt Water Fisherman's Trophy for 1984. Tilting it to one side revealed a wall safe. The combination was John Wesley's birthday. From inside he took a manila folder, locking the safe and carefully aligning the photograph.

Rossiter was a suspect; Davies made no prejudgments. True, he hardly seemed the type, but the best enemy agents never seemed like agents. That way they survived. Whoever it was, the mole had staying power.

The folder contained autopsy reports which Davies had been collecting quietly. Only that morning, one had been brought from Manchester by a special friend of Davies'. The subject was an agent, code name Nigel. There was a bonus; a private autopsy had been done before the coroner got to it. Therefore the study was more precise. Enclosed was a special notice signed by Sir Gerald Tavistock, ordering that no details be released to the family or the public. The suppression order was standard. It didn't prove anything.

"Suicide by drugs and alcohol, specifically whiskey," the report concluded. Victim had choked to death on his own vomit. Davies skipped around until he found what he was looking for. Several loose hairs from the victim's head were found on his clothes, and there were minor lacerations of the scalp. Davies growled. No conclusions had been drawn from this detail, nor was there any mention in the official autopsy of a discoloration around the nose.

Lord, he didn't know. But the loose hairs might have come from a struggle to hold the man down. The discoloration around the nose might be the result of pinching the nose so the mouth had to open to allow the victim to breathe. The killer might have poured whiskey and pills down the open gullet. If it had been a one-man job, the killer was no skinny runt.

Davies closed the folder. He was pretty sure the mole didn't do the sanctions himself; that would be suicidal. On the other hand, it was unlikely the killer would employ someone at random to help fake a suicide. And Badger was wrong about Carnation.

Davies had memorized Badger's list; ten years, thirty SIS and MI5 agents dead. And for every agent killed, there was the question of his support troops. It wasn't simply a case of sending out a replacement. The loss of Lucretia had put the Argentine intelligence people out of business for eighteen months just when the Falklands mess was warming up. Even now they hadn't produced any real intelligence of note. It took a long time to establish a network from scratch.

A thought struck him. Supposing some of the agents weren't dead at all? Some bodies had been blown to bits and nothing found; two had been burned beyond recognition. The real agents might be locked up in Lubyanka Prison, spilling their guts!

Worse! If agents could be killed or captured, they could also be fed the wrong information. Right now, a dozen high-placed assets might be thinking they were risking their necks while they were actually funneling out disinformation.

The bitter truth was, if Badger was right, that the whole intelligence apparatus of Britain wasn't worth a fart in hell.

But the picture wasn't all bad; life, after all, was not a Thomas Hardy novel. Some luck was good luck. The discovery of Drakov had been a totally unexpected piece of good fortune. While the ex-KGB man was relentlessly busy, others would be watching him as best they could. Eventually someone might stick his neck out.

The muskellunge caught his eye. It had taken two hours to land the brute. It couldn't just be reeled in; a skilled fisherman allowed his catch some room to run, then, little by little, he took up the slack.

Davies speculated on whether the mole had bitten. The girl was too big a bait to pass up, so the mole would have to act. No time to consult his masters in Moscow, either. In fact—and Davies was counting on this—the man was probably too sure of himself to buck this to the KGB. That organization made DIC seem like a racehorse; the mole would fear that, by the time the KGB acted, all would be lost. He wouldn't chance it.

Davies was too restless to sit there any longer. He got up and moved to the window. Dear God. Ten of his best men were on Badger's list, and the list didn't even include Hawk.

14 Geli

Anton Drakov sat in a little *backerei* eating breakfast at the only table. He had a cup of coffee, which was excellent, and a fresh bread roll just out of the oven. He wore a blue shirt, its collar folded down over the top of a dark brown sweater. The previous night he'd spent at his lodging consulting a secondhand *Baedeker's City Guide to Berlin.* After that he had turned on the black-and-white television in his room; there seemed to be two channels, but only one came in clearly and even then it was necessary to point the rabbit-ear antenna in a very low V to pick up a clear image. At one point, there had been seven solid minutes of commercials ending with a fifteen-second spot for a brand of Sekt; a collage of bouncing bottles on a field of shifting grays danced to a breezy tune.

On the other channel, which faded and then reasserted itself through a snowstorm of static, the station appeared to be run by an army of cheerful gnomes with huge extended bellies. One of them had a large curly pipe. He reminded Drakov of Joshua Davies. The gnomes sang a jingle together, the station logo rising behind them like the sun. The Russian wondered if he would ever understand the West. Russian television was continually exhorting its viewers to gird themselves for the final battle. In dozens of the languages spoken in the Soviet Union, the same theme was broadcast. "Prepare for the Imminent Victory of Socialism." In Berlin, the citizens were watching gnomes! Shaking his head in disbelief, he had switched the set off. The cheery dwarfs shrank to a large bright dot in the center of the screen, then faded from sight.

Drakov left the little bakery and walked along the street, already filling with Turkish guest workers. He was lucky enough to find a cab; it was drizzling, and the roads were greasy. Drakov had not risen to the top by blundering into alien territory. Nothing would be more idiotic than appearing that night at the club Le Kinki without having first taken the pulse of the neighborhood. The guidebook implied that the area was sometimes called "region of shame." Western decadence was something Drakov exploited whenever possible, but his own first-hand experience of it was limited.

The driver let him out near the Kudamm. Drakov gave him a generous tip, and contrary to tradition, the man thanked him.

The Russian surveyed the seamy side of West Berlin. After ten minutes, he realized how far out of his element he was. Prostitutes were hanging around even at nine in the morning. Several of them eyed him with the calculating look of their breed. Judging from the area, Drakov knew they had to be the cheapest whores in Berlin.

He studied display windows in some of the seedier shops. It didn't take a genius to figure out that "Doll for Sale—Fifty Marks" had nothing to do with china toys. "Lady owner-driver offers French sports car adventure among pink upholstery" challenged Drakov's imagination.

Some of the displays were in news agents' shops. There would be a display of magazines, and if Drakov showed any interest, the owner would hint broadly that he had better things "in the back." No one suspected Drakov of being anything other than what he appeared to be; men in their sixties were the main source of income.

Having nothing better to do, Drakov entered one of the dilapidated storefronts. The owner led him through a door in the back of the shop into a shed filled with pornographic magazines in a dozen languages. There was one in Russian. Looking at it, Drakov remembered that the KGB financed the magazine because it produced a useful subscriber list. He recalled ridiculing the idea on the grounds that no one would subscribe to such a magazine; within six months, four thousand subscribers—a quarter of them women—had sent in a year's subscription fee to an address in Latvia. Several names proved valuable.

The man left Drakov to probe the recesses of the inner sanctum. There was a small viewing room; inside there was just room to sit and feed coins into an insatiable machine that projected color films onto a screen. Drakov watched a segment in which a hideously old blonde stripped off her underclothes until she wore nothing but a G-string with a tiny Iron Cross, First Class, on it.

He left the bookstore and its disappointed owner without buying anything.

There were more exotic places. Passing a dingy doorway with a hand-painted sign that read "Massage Parlor," he was called to by a man speaking with a heavy accent. The man thrust a piece of paper in his hand. It announced, in misspelled German, that there would be no "rip-offs" or extra charges.

"And what do I get for my fifty marks?" inquired Drakov.

The man leered; he would have put his arm around the Russian's shoulders and led him inside except some sixth sense warned him to keep his distance.

"You get a rubdown from one of our girls—all teenagers."

That meant the average age would be forty-five.

"Or you can paint their bodies, or get tickled with feathers . . ."

There was more puzzlement than anticipation in the Russian's face, so the barker took a chance. "We have snuff films, or boys, if—"

Drakov crumpled up his paper and stuffed it into the man's pocket. The man waited until Drakov was a safe distance away, then shouted curses at him.

When Drakov paused for lunch, he chose a small cafe and sat by the window. From there, over a lunch that consisted entirely of sausage and starch, he had a view of the front doors of Le Kinki.

The waiter noticed him watching the scene.

"Curb crawlers," he said disgustedly. "And BPs."

"BPs?"

The man wiped the edge of Drakov's plate where yellow gravy had congealed. "Baby prostitutes," he explained.

The Russian toyed with his meal while observing the choreographed activities just down the block. Streetwalkers adhered to a complex set of rules. The real hard professional whores worked Potsdammer Strasse. On this street, the tarts were much younger. They waited until a car pulled up to the curb; then, with forced nonchalance, they strolled over and made deals. This, he realized, was very dangerous; when the woman got into the car she was at the driver's mercy. The older professionals took men with them into sleazy hotels; in that case, it was the client who took the risks.

With ambivalent feelings, Drakov noticed the BPs chose older men, particularly men in his age bracket. The most popular BPs were those without any trace of adult sexuality. One girl with no breasts at all and a rear end like a boy's never waited more than a minute between engagements. In the time Drakov took to finish his meal she was picked up and returned to the curb three times.

Drakov smoked a cigarette while he drank a glass of Sekt. The waiter had an American brand, Lucky Strike, and Drakov bought a pack knowing they would be so full of additives the taste would be bland. It was. Nevertheless, along with the Sekt, it took away the taste of the food. Drakov resolved never again to order the daily special and instantly was surprised by himself. He hadn't bothered about the taste of food for at least thirty years. Why now? Was it because he was getting old?

The street life fascinated him. He was, of course, familiar with the brothel business. The CIA, SIS, and KGB all monitored such activities carefully. The KGB had a whole division keeping watch on call girl agencies, massage parlors, nightclubs, and brothels. They'd gotten to quite a few people through that kind of blackmail. Unfortunately, permissiveness was rampant, which made blackmail more difficult.

Using up the rest of the day until Le Kinki opened proved to be quite a task. His temptation was to start trying to track down someone who knew Ingrid Thummel. That would be a grave error; the fewer people aware of his task the better. In Drakov's business, patience was the hallmark of success. It wasn't exciting work; it was slow and painstaking.

In the end he allowed a painted creature to lure him into a bar; at least it was out of the rain. She was a spindly creature with badly dyed, ragged blond hair and she wore an equally disheveled black dress. She smiled at him all the time, whispering all sorts of promises in a hoarse voice and smoked incessantly. She told him her name was Cleo. Whenever her glass was empty the barman took her glass and Drakov's, replacing them with full glasses of what was billed as vodka and orange juice.

Cleo promised, drank, and scratched incessantly. Once, out of the corner of his eye, he caught a glimpse of a great hulking creature lurking in the gloom. If anyone was foolish enough to complain the drinks had no vodka in them, which they didn't, or to abuse Cleo, the bouncer would put in a muscular appearance.

Finally, one hundred marks poorer and full of vitamin C, Drakov left the scratching Cleo. He felt he had the rhythm of the area, and he'd had enough.

He then astonished himself by going to the zoo. The last time he remembered visiting a zoo was forty years ago with his youngest son, Peter. There had been no contact between Drakov and his family for ten years. It was better that way. They would not have been made to suffer for his crimes. And now, of course, they thought he was dead.

After the zoo, Drakov saw a film, something else he hadn't done in years; it was a silly thing about a secret agent working for the British. The spy bedded all the women he met, and the Russian agents were so slow-witted they couldn't catch him. Drakov smiled in all the wrong places. The KGB high-ups drove around in luxury cars with twenty-year-old secretaries who were also their mistresses. The SIS man carried clever gadgets strapped to his wrist, and the devices saved his life several times. Surprisingly, the hero harbored no ill feeling toward the Russians. Drakov wondered how even the film's makers could believe any of it.

By ten o'clock he was seated in a booth at Le Kinki with a real vodka and orange juice in front of him. The place was a shock. The noise was so great, it hit him like a solid wall. Every piece of furniture, every single item, was of stainless steel. The one exception was the huge revolving central strobe light that made the dancers seem to move in slow motion and which changed color every five seconds.

The standard dress was tight T-shirts for both sexes and even tighter jeans. A great deal of black leather was also in evidence. Through the dense fog of cigarette smoke, he caught a glimpse of a blond girl dancing frenziedly in a steel cage suspended from the ceiling.

Realizing that he might attract attention, the Russian had purchased a fresh set of clothes and dumped his others in a canal. He now wore a silk shirt, blazer, slacks, and a scarf. As soon as he entered the building, he realized no one would notice if he entered in full Nazi regalia.

The smoke was occasionally whirled round by ventilators, permitting him to see around the room. The sound was controlled by a man wearing a black leather suit and a wolf's head. Every so often the man would let out a loud howl that was picked up and echoed by the dancers. He spoke into the microphone in a strange, singsong way, making it very hard to understand him. There was even more than the usual quota of German profanity.

The focal point of the room was a long steel bar. Whenever the music stopped, the dancers rushed up the three steps and drank. When the music started again, the human tidal wave swept back down to the floor.

Drakov was squashed into a tiny steel cubicle, and it was some time before anyone noticed him.

"My name is Geli," a garishly made-up waitress shouted at him at last. "Another drink?"

The Russian ordered a cognac. When the girl returned he asked her to join him. She refused until a twenty-mark note appeared on the table.

Geli delved into her pocket and took out a pack of American cigarettes called, oddly, Eve. They were excessively long and thin. The woman inhaled deeply and then fixed her gaze on Drakov. "Want a feel? Hand job?"

Drakov produced the photograph of Ingrid he had borrowed from Frau Thummel. "Do you know her?" he asked.

Geli studied the photo and Drakov studied her. She wasn't very tall, no more than five feet; her hair was long and straw colored.

"Ingrid." Geli said the name without prodding or hesitation. "Used to come in here with a fellow called Rudi Fleischer. Bit queer, he was."

Drakov was about to ask another question when the music began again, accompanied by loud wolf howls around the room.

"Where does she live?" he shouted at Geli.

Geli shook her blond hair, her face blue in the spotlight. "Don't know," she said, her features turning green.

"Can we talk outside?"

"No. Got to hustle drinks. The owner's a real *Scheisskopf.*"

A fifty-mark note appeared on the table, and three minutes later they were in the alley behind the discotheque.

"Where's your car?" she asked. "Or do you

want a blow job?" She shivered in the rain. "Or do you want to do it standing up over there?"

Drakov said, "I want information about Ingrid."

"I told you. I don't know any more. We can do it over there. I've done it here plenty."

The Russian felt a growing desire to throttle her. Everywhere he went lately, women were offering him their bodies.

"Look," she said suddenly, "I don't normally do this, but I have a room. Because you're special, I'll take you up there."

"How much?" said Drakov in exasperation.

"A hundred"—she scratched her leg, bringing the hem of her black miniskirt almost to her waist—"and fifty." She paused. "Satisfaction guaranteed."

Drakov took out his wallet and put two hundred marks in the top of Geli's blouse. "Now listen to me."

"Aren't we—?"

"Listen."

Geli shrugged. "Your money."

"I want to find Ingrid. I am her uncle and I want to take her back to Bavaria with me, away from this awful city. Can you find her?"

Geli decided she'd struck a gold mine. "It'll cost some money."

"How much?"

"Wait here."

Five minutes later she was back. "I've scored some H," she told him. "Keep half, you'll find it's better than cash. No junkie can refuse it. Now give me two hundred more."

Drakov handed her two hundreds. The

woman was more businesslike and sensible than he had thought. "Find the girl," he said, "and you'll get a thousand."

Geli's heavily made-up face registered astonishment. "She must be really good at something new," she said.

"I'm her long-lost uncle."

Geli grinned at that and Drakov noticed she had slightly buck teeth. Apart from the miniskirt and makeup, she might have been a blowsy housewife making a little extra money by turning tricks.

"Rudi," she said suddenly, "lives in an apartment on Detmann Strasse, number two-twenty-seven D, off Clay Allee. He liked Ingrid. They did cold turkey together."

The German phrase was unknown to Drakov. "That's some kind of sexual, er . . . ?"

Geli laughed, a low throaty sound. "Tried to break the drug habit. He did, she didn't. That was that."

"Can you find her?"

"Don't know," she sighed. "Junkies disappear. I don't know. Come to my place tomorrow night at ten o'clock. I'll know something by then." She told him where to find her, then asked, "You sure you don't want to come up now? Won't take a minute."

"Some other time," said Drakov. "I'll take a . . . a . . ."

"Rain check?"

"Exactly," he agreed. "A rain check."

15 Central Registry

Dressed in his huge, flapping raincoat, the Director of Department D surged along the sidewalk under the gray facade of the Admiralty Building and entered a small guarded door near Admiralty Arch. He passed through the cloakroom, surrendering his raincoat en route, and setting off the metal detector because he'd forgotten to put his keys in the tray.

This vast subterranean world housed the files MI5 had been acquiring since the days of the first "troubles" in Ireland. The cards had been almost destroyed in the war; microfilm copies at Blenheim Palace were often so overexposed as to be worthless. In fact, the system had been largely useless for years. One Director of Registry insisted on filing all the Smiths under "Schmidt," and relevant inquiries for years were able to elicit no more than a "nothing known against" or "no likely trace"—which could mean everything or nothing.

Badger's constant urging had gotten results; the materials were being updated from their Hollerith punch cards to a true data base. The results were extraordinary. In seconds, computers searched, compared, and printed out the results of inquiries that would have taken days by hand. It was most impressive, and had been undertaken in the teeth of the most concerted opposition Davies had ever seen at Five.

There was a strict no-smoking policy in the computer room, so Davies took out an empty pipe, clenched it between his teeth, and marched along the corridors following a yellow line that became red at a critical juncture. Stacked along the walls were old filing drawers. This part of the building had long since been condemned by the fire marshal. Davies had to duck as the steam, electricity, and phone cable pipes hung low from broken ceiling stanchions.

Once he left the old building, his surroundings changed from government green and chocolate brown to white. Some sections were even a restful light blue or green. The area was guarded by a sergeant on loan from the Welsh Guards. By his side, also at attention, sat a large German shepherd.

"Morning, Taffy; morning, Adolph."

Taffy's clipped military mustache moved minutely, but his mouth never looked open.

"Morning, sir. Nice day outside?"

Davies opened his briefcase and Adolph sniffed the contents. For the Director, this was the ultimate in irony. The sergeant couldn't inspect anyone's briefcase; he didn't have the security clearance. With the increase in bombings, there was always the faint chance that someone would attempt to smuggle explosives into the computer area. In what Davies thought was a reductio ad absurdum, he had suggested using a dog, thus getting by *both* problems, clearance and safety. To his astonishment, the idea had been taken up with alacrity. Monty Abrahams had pointed out that the dog could also check for drugs. As Davies sat back, mouth gaping open in astonishment, the DIC unanimously approved his facetious motion.

"Well, it isn't raining," he said to Taffy.

"Not raining in here either, sir," replied the guard.

This was Taffy's one and only joke; his father had used the same joke, referring to the coal mine where he had labored for thirty years.

"Right," agreed the Director, sliding his ID back into his wallet. He signed in, took a fresh white coat from a nearby peg, and allowed the sergeant to pin a security badge on his lapel. Davies made no attempt to button the coat; it would have been futile. The badge had a red background indicating Davies had access to everything except the computer room itself.

A series of small locked cubicles were ranged around the computer room, which lay behind one-way glass. Everything was ultramodern, not so much by choice as through necessity. The temperature was strictly monitored, the air continuously filtered. Each cubicle had a cipherbox with ten keys. Inserting a giant fist, Davies dialed 6, 4, 2, 7, 1. The door opened.

Placing his briefcase on the floor beside him, the Director tested the swivel chair. It rotated nicely and traveled smoothly from left to right. The monitor also swiveled comfortably.

A console with a telephone gave him access to

the computer. He dialed 6 and said, "I'm going to need you. Looks like a three-cupper." Bending to his right with considerable puffing, he took out the manila folder with Badger's list in it. He logged in to the computer, typing in his password, "Butcher."

In the far room the IBM hummed almost imperceptibly as the flying laser head began to read the disk.

Each time Davies typed in a code name the computer checked his clearance, flashed "RED 3" for ten seconds, and asked for a second password. Then the code name was translated to the agent's work name. The file could then be summoned. The work name and code name were known only to the computer and those few who had a need to know. Also, the files and code names were quite separate; without access to the computer, there was no way to discover which agent had what particular code name.

A metal arm traveled along a stainless-steel rod in the tape storage room where shelves of gray plastic housed thousands of tapes. Within five minutes Davies had over fifteen requests for tape mounts in the queue.

Idly he ran the mount queue. Fifteen requests unscrolled; he ran the queue again and stopped the printing. The first command was only partly decipherable. Not for the first time, he wondered if the operations personnel were being deliberately obscure, or whether there was a twisted logic to what he read.

Volume Status Type Write Req Job

NSCR 67 Waiting Tape WL 11826 3
Volume-set: MTA—JMZKXX
Label-type* No, Track 9, Density, 1600 BPI

It was pretty automatic now; the tapes would be mounted and the appropriate file copied into his area. He still would not know any agent's work name. Only the data under a code name would be supplied.

There was a tap on the door; Davies rolled back on his chair and opened it. A tall, thin girl with bright red hair bent down and kissed him on the cheek. It was a feat, for she had a large mug of coffee in each hand.

"How's my boy?" she said cheerfully. "I hope you're not going to drink this fuckin' coffee in a terminal room."

Davies grinned. Big Red swore like a sailor and ignored all the rules. Because she was a computer whiz and could type at a hundred-fifty words a minute, no sensible person was inclined to remind her of them. She was already lighting a cigarette. Davies still sucked on his empty pipe; a lifelong Methodist, he suffered if he sinned. Some deep urging in him insisted he obey the rules because he was a person in authority.

"Jesus. What a day we've had," said Big Red, leaning back against the table and flailing ineffectually at her cigarette smoke. "For the last three hours, every goddam message I got said there was a parity error on the tape. Then the bleedin' monitor went wonky. What's up?"

Davies drank his coffee. Red always put in an extra spoonful of sugar; it helped.

"Want to run some comparisons; it'll take all day."

"Well, you said it would be a three-cupper."

Davies grinned; the way Big Red was puffing away, he might as well have used Doctor Watson's words and called it a three-pipe problem.

"I'll get a chair." She waited while Davies pressed the button to unlatch the door, then went out, leaving her cigarette balanced on the edge of the table. Davies watched, fascinated, as the ash suddenly detached itself and fell to the floor.

A bang on the door told him the programmer was back.

"Christ, I'm glad to be out of general circulation; that silly cow Nadine went and got herself preggers." She grinned, picked up her cigarette, and tried to rub the fallen ash into the brightly polished linoleum tiles. "Wait till the bitch supervisor finds out."

"Mrs. Gleeson?"

"The shit will hit the fan! It's the third girl this year. They must do it every chance they get. They don't have time to take precautions or summat?"

A message appeared telling the Director that information from three tapes was in his area. Davies typed a nine-digit number, and a brief message encased in asterisks confirmed his RED-3 clearance.

"There's only Dollie Pratt and me left," Big Red went on. "We went into Positive Vetting together. PV's the shittiest hole in Five."

Davies tapped his keyboard. "It makes women of girls and boys of men, so they say."

"Bloody true."

Davies looked at her out of the corner of his eye. She wasn't bad looking, he thought. Like most of those who stayed around, she wore glasses. Unquestionably she smoked too much. Big Red was contemptuous of makeup, so the freckles in her face were never smoothed out, but given time the woman could make her mark. It didn't help that she wore a baggy sweater and jeans under her white coat. But if she were better looking and more man hungry, she would long ago have quit CR and become a housewife.

Another message informed him that fifteen files of data were available for interrogation.

"You remember Badger?" asked Davies.

"Of course. About the only senior man who knew his arse from first base."

"What?"

"Arse from first base. It's a Yank expression. Dollie dated one. They say 'ass,' though. You know, ass, like a donkey."

Davies shook his head. "Good job they're on our side," he said. "Well, Badger gave me a list of names; he thought there was something fishy about their deaths." He pressed the keyboard. Thirty names appeared on the screen in two neat columns.

Big Red lifted her glasses and squinted at the screen. "So what can we do?"

Davies sat back in his chair. Fumbling in his jacket pocket, he took out his pince-nez.

"There's got to be something about them, some way to link them into a pattern."

"Put them up with dates of birth and death."

Davies stroked several keys; the names and dates appeared on the screen.

"I don't see any pattern there," grunted Big Red. "Why not remove dates of birth?"

After that the two of them tried everything. At first it was fun; manipulating the data gave Davies a certain satisfaction. Then it got tense because it wasn't going anywhere. They argued with each other and had to take a break.

Davies ordered up a printed dump of all the files. The main printer took twenty minutes to print out all they had, and when they examined it, they had everything and nothing.

Big Red left at two and went to the basement gymnasium, where she punched a large inflatable rubber doll that looked suspiciously like the head of the Computer Ops. Then she tied a scarf around his neck to simulate Davies' bow tie and pummeled the thing for fifteen minutes. Finally she retrieved her supper from her locker. Only in this respect did she disappoint Joshua Davies; the meal consisted of raw vegetables, unflavored yogurt, and goat's milk. She was dining alone when the Director summoned her.

Davies had a sandwich in the cafeteria, which put him in a foul mood. It was supposed to be a turkey club, but he claimed there was no turkey in it. The waitress, who had no idea of his rank, told him smartly that it had no club in it either.

One explosion later, Joshua Davies returned to the terminal room. Bundling all the green printouts into one huge pile, he returned to his cubicle. Big Red was just coming along the passageway talking with a blonde pushing a basketful of tapes. She grinned at him. "Round one over, then?"

"Damn right," agreed Davies. "Let's be having you."

In the computer terminal room, they both sat forward in their chairs, heads almost touching, and scoured the printouts.

"I've got to tell you more," Davies muttered, "otherwise you can't help."

"Okay." Big Red knew he was breaking the rules. She appreciated the compliment.

"Badger was convinced there is someone killing our agents and covering his tracks. Sometimes it's an accident. Other times it looks like a natural death. According to Badger, who hasn't any proof, our agents are dying too soon, too often, and too easily."

Red sniffed. "Badger knew his computers. I figured he was up to something when data was sent to a remote."

"The thing is," continued Davies, "this isn't like the usual op. You won't find any servicing of this mole; he's too subtle for that. He lives within his means. When he leaves, there will be a few million rubles stashed away somewhere. If he needs money, a cut-out will handle it for him. For damn sure he won't do the actual sanctioning either. He's not a trigger man."

Big Red sat back and felt in the pocket of her jacket. She produced a cigarette pack and lit up a thin filter tip.

"How about the trigger man?"

"Well, he won't be found unless he makes a slip. But even if he does, you can be sure nothing will make him tell who he's working for."

Davies picked up his pipe and clamped his teeth around the stem. "So all we've got is a list of our people who died when, perhaps, they shouldn't have. There could be more, but these fitted the profiles Badger drew up."

Davies found the simplicity of the plan its most brilliant aspect. An agent, any one of the names unscrolling in front of him, was given an assignment. It was discussed at DIC, and a week later, a month later, the man was dead. It wasn't every agent, and it wasn't every operation, but agents died.

Sometimes, when the man's guard was down, perhaps when he was sitting in a pub as Hawk had been, waiting to receive the congratulations of his superior, it was suddenly and violently all over.

"God!" Davies cried, slamming his hand in fury on the desk. The print on the monitor jiggled, broke up briefly, and reformed.

"Steady on, big boy," Big Red said softly. "That's government property."

"I'm going to nail this bastard if it takes a lifetime," growled the Director. "Now let's see what the common denominator is. There has to be a relationship between these names. Find the link"—he stared at the screen—"and we've got him. So let's get our asses in gear."

They worked until seven o'clock. Davies tried every analysis, concordance, cross reference, and reformatting he could devise to find the common strand in the twisted skein. Two thousand pages of green computer printouts were ceremoniously fed into the shredder at one minute before seven and converted into long worms. Nothing had worked.

They went down to the cafeteria together; Davies took a cigarette from Big Red's pack and put it in his mouth. It felt like a short drinking straw. It tasted like one, too. Big Red seemed to enjoy hers.

"You're on overtime now, I suppose," he said, looking closely at all the little windows in the food dispenser. A square centimeter of trifle in a large plastic container caught his eye. Neither of them had any change. The pound changer had been useless since the paper note went out of circulation.

"Not bloody likely," retorted Red later as if the intervening three minutes had not taken place. "I'm a senior programmer now—on straight salary. I've risen to the top."

Davies stared at her. Suddenly he let out a roar, picked up the astonished woman, and clapped her to him in a bear hug. "Damn right," he shouted. "You've risen to the top."

A couple in the far corner looked up in astonishment. Davies ran out of the cafeteria, Big Red in hot pursuit. As Davies pounded up the three stairs to the computer room, the new guard shouted cheerfully, "You get him, lass! There's enough and more. And put those bloody cigs out."

The Director, breathing heavily, was manipulating his data. "You see, there is a pattern," he said excitedly. "Here is everyone by date of death, first at the top, Hawk at the bottom. Now. Look at the ranks of them."

Big Red studied the list. "There's no pattern. Hell, this one was next to last, and he's way below the previous one."

Davies began to summon the names one by one, deleting some and leaving others. When he'd finished he assigned the list to the printer. The names were swiftly formed by the ink jet, and Davies said, "Now look."

When Big Red looked at the list, she saw at once the enormity of what had been happening for over ten years. She began to feel horribly sick, and Davies, sure at last, felt none of the elation men feel upon discovering the truth.

2

Six hundred miles away, the only completely innocent man in all the storm was not in the best of moods. After work as assistant research librarian in the large library on the west edge of the Hansa District, Rudi Fleischer had hurried to the Tea House in the English Garden. It had finally stopped raining, though the dark clouds refused to disperse.

The tea garden was set amid formally landscaped gardens. A dozen large white swans, a gift from the Queen of England, floated on the lake.

The previous evening, Rudi was taking an aperitif when he received unmistakable vibrations from a young man wearing a high-necked sweater and navy-blue blazer with gold buttons. The exquisite youth signaled nine with his fingers; seconds later, an older man with gray hair and a thick mustache returned from the counter to the blond man's table carrying two glasses of Sekt. When the two men left, Rudi felt more joy and anticipation than he'd felt in a long time. Rudi had quarreled with his long-time partner over the vexing matter of who should pay for their excessive long-distance telephone bill. A silly situation, Rudi admitted to himself, but since he was the only one working, he'd refused to pay for five calls to Klaus' mother in Lower Saxony, especially because Klaus was telling her about how badly Rudi treated him. Rudi was glad his own mother was safely in the East, though it did mean that ghastly weekly subway journey to Ullsteinstrasse.

There was, then, a great deal of eagerness in Rudi's step as he hurried up the steps to the Tea House. He didn't cast a look at the tiny bushes all cut into symmetrical shapes or the diamond and triangular flowerbeds of English daisies. The only beauty on Rudi's mind was the tight globes he had seen when the young man sauntered off with his older protector.

He ordered a glass of Sekt, wondering whether to risk his new tight pants on a wet chair on the promenade. Deciding to do so, he sat in splendid isolation at a tiny table with an umbrella proclaiming "Drink Braunschweig Mumme." Rudi had tried it once; Braunschweig was a dark, bittersweet beer made without hops. He'd decided it would do better as motor oil, though not for his new car, of which he was inordinately fond. An imported Honda Accord LX, it was precisely the vehicle for Klaus and him to be seen in. The Honda had a rich red interior and all kinds of gadgets from a cassette player to an electric antenna that had to be lowered each night for fear toughs would break it off.

The blond wouldn't speak to him at first, of course; there was always the mating ritual. First came the display of plumage. Even though it was often a giveaway, Rudi always dressed well. Everything he put on matched. Even when heavy jewelry was in, Rudi refused to wear it. Instead he put on a narrow S gold chain around his neck; it became the fashion. He still wore business-dress ties and button-down shirts, though no one else in his crowd did. On him they looked right.

Rudi was thirty years old, of medium height, and, while not a queen, moved rather too lightly on his feet. His gestures were a shade limp, and his voice a trifle plummy.

These characteristics were mitigated by a thick hairy chest and good muscle tone. Rudi worked out at his gym regularly. Everything about him was tasteful and neat. His beard was trimmed very short and his jet-black hair cut close. Beyond Rudi's control was a gently receding hairline. There was nothing to be done about the hairs left in the shower every day. A friend of his had told him seriously that orgasm hastened death. Rudi, an experienced research librarian, knew this medieval view was rubbish.

Recently Rudi had noticed, despite strenuous sessions at the gym, that a slight inner tube of fat was growing amidships. Klaus had praised his love handles, but Rudi knew a sign when he saw one. He wasn't getting any younger.

On his way to the Tea House, he'd stopped off at a subway station and used the facilities to check out his appearance and apply a subtle feminine essence he liked. It had a French name that meant "Forget Me Not." The scent stirred him.

Rudi always wore female underwear; it was briefer and more comfortable. His shirt was silk in a severe geometric pattern of tiny white and blue triangles. His pants were tight, form-fitting knits. He wore a fawn lightweight raincoat imported from Italy, its buckle knotted rather than fastened. All his jewelry was gold.

Just as the waiter came out to ask if Rudi wanted another Sekt, the blond and his lover approached. Rudi wasn't listening to the waiter. He saw the young man leave the older one, who walked on. The waiter looked at the blond, then looked down at Rudi.

"Police," he whispered, taking Rudi's empty glass and leaving.

In the silence, the librarian broke out in a cold sweat; another two minutes, and he would have lost everything. His life flashed before his eyes, the disgrace of it all. The library director would hear of it and call him in. Rudi's boss was the straightest man in Berlin, in Germany—West or East. Rudi would be asked to resign.

Oh, he could fight it. West Germany was still a democracy. But everyone would learn his secret—his widowed mother in East Berlin; all his aunts and uncles, living in blissful ignorance in Düsseldorf.

A memory of Oscar Wilde's fate passed before him, and then a vision of the look in Aunt Greta's eyes. He would be publicly humiliated. The prosecutor would demand in a loud voice, "What is the love that dares not speak its name?" Oscar Wilde was in jail for less than two years; it destroyed him.

The blond approached, jiggling a bit as he moved. He spoke with a lisp. The librarian despised him from the time of his first word, for, truth to tell, Rudi himself was inclined to stammer under pressure. "Ith thith plathe taken?" asked the youth, gazing at Rudi provocatively and reaching for the little white wrought-iron chair across from Rudi.

With a courage he did not know he possessed, Rudi replied without any trace of a stutter, "No, it isn't." As the young man sat down, Rudi rose to his feet and added, "And neither is this." With that he marched down the central avenue, quite surprising the second undercover policeman, who was only just beginning to read the evening paper, expecting he was in for a long wait.

Once he was safely in his Honda, surrounded by automatic door locks and window controls, Rudi got the shakes. For a second he rested his forehead on the steering wheel. There was sweat on it when he raised his head. The adrenaline was still pumping, but now he was having only the normal psychological reactions, breathing faster, anger replacing terror. He'd come within a few seconds of losing everything—including this beautiful automobile.

It was five full minutes before he could trust himself to drive. As a consequence, he was not paying too much attention when he parked his car and took the elevator to his twelfth-floor apartment with its magnificent view of the Grunewald.

He nodded politely to the only other occupant of the elevator, a man in his sixties who returned his nod and said pleasantly, "*Guden nacht.*"

Rudi couldn't place the accent, but then, in Germany, who knew where anyone was from?

The man got off with Rudi, smiled, and waited for Rudi to open his apartment door.

"Something I can do for you?" Rudi asked, irritated. He'd had one narrow escape, and now there was some old creep following him.

"No."

Rudi was stumped; he couldn't very well open the door with the man just standing there. "Well, what do you want then?"

"I'm here to see you, Rudi," said Drakov. "You owe me a favor."

"I've never seen you before in my life," Rudi said indignantly. "I'll have to ask you to stop pestering me."

The old man chuckled; Rudi found no comfort in it. "There's the matter of the twenty marks, Rudi."

"What twenty marks? I know nothing about any twenty marks."

"I advanced it to you by giving it to the waiter

at the Tea House. I didn't want you in jail, Rudi."

Rudi flung open his door and hurried inside, waiting for the man to follow, then slammed it shut and fastened the chain.

A dachshund with a peculiar rolling gait came over to stand by Rudi. He looked up at the men, panting.

"My dog, Pumml," said Rudi.

"It may stay unless it barks. Why does it move so peculiarly?"

"Dachshunds often have spinal problems," Rudi said. "There is tremendous pressure on the spine because they are so long in proportion to—"

"Feed it, if that's what it wants."

Rudi placed a can of dog food in his electric can opener, feeling acutely embarrassed. The stranger was giving orders as if *he* owned the apartment. Already he'd taken off his coat and hung it in the closet, and was drawing back the striped yellow-and-crimson curtains. He looked out from the small balcony where Rudi and Klaus used to sit on warm summer evenings, looking toward the Grunewald.

Rudi put Pumml's food down on a plate.

"We are—"

Rudi jumped; the man had come in without making a sound. "We are on the twelfth floor, Rudi. That's about a hundred and twenty feet. If you do as I say, you may *not* commit suicide tonight."

"Su-su-suicide!"

"Exactly. I am a man of few words. I get what I want. You may call me Herr Kreugar."

The stranger was smaller that Rudi and

thirty to thirty-five years older, but Rudi Fleischer never doubted for a moment that he must do as he was told.

Drakov looked around the flat; it was what he'd expected. There was even a baby grand piano. The wallpaper reminded him of rooms in the Kremlin Museum stuffed with what that nauseating Ivan Ivanovich Teplyakov called Louis Quinze. There was a dining table on very thin legs, set for one. The china looked fragile, and the pattern was a very finely drawn rose and trellis. There was a generally oriental motif to the interior decoration; a thick rug with a dragon woven into it lay under the black-lacquered heavy dining table, and there was a fine painting with Chinese figures. The bookcase was built into the wall, filled with stereo equipment and a VCR. Below was a large color television. The books were expensive, richly illustrated volumes on a wide variety of subjects. Drakov spent several minutes looking at some.

Finally replacing a thick book entitled *Moscow and Red Square,* Drakov said quietly, "If you have fed that silly little creature, then perhaps you can turn your attention to a little supper for two. What have you to offer?"

Rudi was an excellent cook, and so the Russian was astonished when the librarian said, "I was going to have warm duck livers on a bed of chicory salad, a *pot-au-feu* with a creamy gratin of potatoes. For dessert an *ile flottante.* The wine, a Beaujolais Primeur."

"Fix it," the Russian managed.

While the librarian bustled in the kitchen, Drakov fumigated the apartment with his fountain pen. He didn't expect to find any listening devices and didn't. Pumml followed him awkwardly, watching through huge brown eyes.

"It's a long walk for this dog when he has to go outside," Drakov said conversationally.

"He can't do it at all on his own," said Rudi, "because of an injury. I have to catheterize him."

Drakov looked at Pumml. The dachshund looked back at him, afraid to come any closer. Whenever the Russian moved, the dog followed, twisting its neck to keep him in sight. Drakov inspected the rest of the apartment. There was only one bedroom, with a platform bed covered by satin sheets. A large color television faced the bed. Indirect lighting illuminated the room and also focused on a painting of a huge Japanese mounting a geisha. It looked genuine.

There was a broad silver frame around the picture, and Drakov used it to check behind him. Rudi had not followed him; he was relieved. This was not the time for the librarian, full of Dutch courage and making use of the thick cream-colored carpets, to sneak up behind him with a butcher knife. Rudi was needed alive, not dead.

The wardrobe was full of clothes, all of them cleaned and pressed. There was no smell of mothballs. A lingerie chest contained silk underwear and several battery-operated devices Drakov had seen demonstrated by female KGB operatives. One was a mechanical penis. He tossed it back in the drawer without making any judgments. Queers were useful: the Russian didn't care who did what to whom. Emotions were unpredictable and sometimes uncontrollable. Emotions were dangerous; Drakov tried never to have any.

On the spindly bedstand by the bed were a phone and alarm clock. An address book contained several names in code. It was a simple cipher based on the letters in Rudi's name. Drakov could read them almost at sight. Phone numbers were rendered as prices of things and were even simpler to deduce. If the librarian's lover could not figure out the coded phone number from 3.76 marks plus 96 pfennigs plus 42 pfennigs, he had to be a congenital idiot.

In the space where the mattress met the springs, he found several glossies of naked men, muscles oiled and prominent. He picked up the television remote control and pressed the on button. A few seconds demonstrated the programs were no better in color than in black and white. A learned discussion was taking place on East-West reunification, a German fantasy without hope of realization.

When he finally found Rudi's gun he was more amused than anything else. It was just what he might have expected, a Walther Model 9 pocket pistol from the ninth series, the last before the famous PPs came out. It was one of the neatest self-loading pistols ever made, perfect for concealing in a pocket or a lady's handbag because its overall length was four inches. Slipping it into his pocket, he went back to the living room.

The librarian had everything ready minutes later. Drakov took his seat; Rudi didn't know whether he was supposed to serve the stranger and eat in the kitchen or join him at the table.

An alternative, increasingly attractive, was to sneak up silently behind him on the thick carpet and kill him with the butcher knife. The man wouldn't expect that. Trouble was, Rudi didn't think he could do it. He wasn't a violent person, and the blood would never come out of the carpet.

The unwelcome guest didn't look like the violent type either, but Rudi had once brought home a divine creature from Wannsee, and the brute had tied him to the bed and whipped him with a belt studded with nail heads. That had been Rudi's last one-night stand.

The stranger was looking curiously at the various dishes before him. Rudi found the perfect compromise: leaving on his apron, he served Drakov first, then sat down to eat his own meal. He was both server and guest.

Drakov didn't bother much with food; he believed, though there was less and less proof lately, that a person had to eat to acquire energy. Consequently, he ate. Rudi's food was pleasing as well as filling. The man had talent, and Drakov always respected talent. He complimented his unwilling host and did not talk business until Rudi had brought in coffee and a cheese tray.

"Doubtless," said Drakov, heavy on the irony, "you are wondering what I want from you." Rudi caught the wintry smile; the apartment felt suddenly chilled.

"I don't think you have anything to worry about," the Russian continued, "unless you become foolish." He sipped his coffee and fixed

Rudi with a stare across the top of his cup. "If you do, I shall kill you. Painfully."

Rudi tried to suppress an involuntary shudder. If the stranger noticed, he gave no sign.

"Let us assume, therefore, that you cooperate. When I leave, you will be five thousand marks richer, possibly more. I have a lot of money that will not be of any use to me where I am going."

Rudi hoped he was going to hell, but was wise enough to nod appreciatively.

"I'm looking for Ingrid Thummel."

So that was it! The threatening individual was only a private detective, for God's sake. Rudi went limp with relief. "And you want me to find her."

Drakov nodded. "I want you to help me find her."

"For five thousand marks."

"For your life. The money is a bonus."

The relief ebbed away. "And if I refuse?"

"The thought never occurred to me."

Rudi Fleischer submitted; he would serve this new master and hope to come out of it alive. First things first. He was in over his head.

"Can I smoke?"

Drakov nodded and Rudi took a pack of Marlboros from the kitchen table drawer. On the sideboard was a lighter. It lit up all by itself.

"Show me that."

"It's a Colibri touch lighter," said Rudi. "You put your finger in this gap, and the lighter ignites on top."

Drakov tried it several times. It was utterly

beyond belief. The West was locked in a seesaw battle for control of the planet and brilliant minds were devising a lighter that ignited when a circuit was broken. He supposed Popovich had appropriated his own elegant desk lighter. "Give me a cigarette, too." Rudi quickly complied. "So how will we find Ingrid?" Drakov asked, slipping the lighter into his pocket. His host said nothing.

Rudi said, "We'll go to the Zoo Station first."

"I was there today."

"You would stick out like a sore thumb. I mean . . ." He sighed miserably.

Drakov expelled smoke slowly.

"I . . . I . . . I mean . . ." Rudi began again.

"I know what you mean, and you are right. Never be afraid to tell me the truth."

Rudi breathed more freely. "If we go together, p-p-people will assume that we . . ." He looked sheepishly at Drakov.

The stranger's eyes were like tiny coals of fire. "People will think I am a homosexual?"

"Th-that's not quite—"

"It doesn't matter," the stranger broke in, "what people think. Why the Zoo Station?"

"The girls get money by prostitution. The drug pushers give them stuff at first. Then, when they're hooked, they have to sell themselves to get more money. Boys have it tougher." Rudi stopped.

"Go on," said Drakov.

"I met Ingrid at the Free University; there was a clinic and counseling center. It's closed now. There isn't any cure once you're an addict unless . . . unless you can do cold turkey."

"You mean stay off the drug for a few days?"

This time Rudi gave a hollow laugh. "You frighten me," he said boldly, "more than anyone I've ever met, but if I had a choice between you and CT, I'd take you every time."

"I'm flattered." Drakov offered a humorless chuckle.

"You should be," Rudi said harshly. "I wouldn't touch drugs if you gave me a year's free supply. After three shots you're emotionally dependent; after a few weeks you're a junkie and nothing can be done."

Rudi's unwelcome guest left the table and crossed to the fireplace, taking Rudi's favorite seat, an English mahogany-and-cane library chair with a green velvet cushion. "Go on, Rudi. You seem to know what you're talking about."

Rudi understood that the stranger had no fear of turning his back, and he was ashamed to admit that the intruder was right not to fear him.

"People doing cold turkey all think they've been tricked because they don't understand what they're being punished for." He threw up his arms in a gesture of helplessness. "I couldn't do anything for Ingrid." He saw the man looking around for an ashtray and hurried over with one. The visitor took it, examined it critically, and motioned with his cigarette for Rudi to sit opposite. "Yet you escaped."

"I found Klaus," Rudi replied without thinking. "I mean . . ."

Drakov said suddenly, "Can we find her?"

Rudi looked puzzled. "I suppose, but what for?"

"Something puzzles me," admitted the Russian. "You seem curiously unmoved by this girl's plight. You were friends?"

Rudi looked at Pumml; the little dog had staggered to the door. "There's nothing you can do for a junkie," Rudi informed him flatly, getting up and picking up Pumml. He took the dog into the bathroom. "If you shed one tear, it's a waste." Drakov sensed a note of hope in his next remark. "If you come by tomorrow we can set out early." The Russian remembered an old peasant story about a goat who promised the wolf he would get up early and go and steal apples. The wolf could never get up early enough to eat the goat.

There was a little yelp of protest from Pumml.

"I think the sofa is very comfortable," said Drakov. "You should have no trouble sleeping on it."

Rudi, still holding Pumml, looked around the door of the bathroom. Two pairs of eyes stared at the Russian. "Don't worry," Drakov said. "It will do my reputation far more harm than yours if I stay here. But," he added grimly, "sacrifices must be made."

3

Big Red was beginning to understand. "You see what's happened," Davies explained. "The mole was rising through the ranks. As he got more access to names, there was a comparable increase in the importance of his targets."

He stuck a huge finger against the screen. "So he couldn't resist the opportunity to bag the best game."

"But why did he kill the small fry later?"

"Because he had to obscure the pattern. First he kills a G-seven; he's probably a G-eight then. Next time it's a G-three. No correlation with his own rise means no trail to follow."

Big Red looked at the list. "With this new information we might find others he killed. Ones we don't know about. This is a big organization."

"It's worse. He could well have told the Russkies about a dozen ops and we'd never know. Last year we lost ten men, the Yanks seven, and they were all discussed in DIC!"

"DIC?"

"Damn right. Badger hinted at it because he didn't think there was any other group with the kind of information that's funneled through." The Director leaned back, stretching his arms and yawning. "Everything where there is any kind of liaison needed or any danger of an operation's cutting across someone's bows is discussed in DIC. Every goddam one!"

Big Red shook her head. "Jesus H. Fucking Christ!"

"Right. Now, you know what's next?"

"Comparison of employment records to see whose job profiles match the sanctions; it's just a sort." Already her fingers were stroking the keyboard.

Davies let her work uninterrupted. Badger was right; no operation and no agent were safe. With the death of Hawk, it was clear the mole had access to secrets on RED-3 level. He could get into all the computer records now. Anything he wanted to know was just a few keystrokes away. If he did, he could do more harm than the ones currently referred to grimly as England's Gang of Four—Burgess, Maclean, Philby, Blunt.

Big Red was frowning at the screen, occasionally tapping some instructions in. She wasn't standard government issue, thank God.

"Got it."

The terminal was blank. "It's sorting now," said Big Red. "Shouldn't take long."

"Off you go then."

"But I—"

"Out!"

She left with apparent ill grace, but it was only an act; she hadn't expected to see the results. She assumed it was a matter of security, but it was more. If she had the names, she would be at risk; if the assassin learned of Davies' progress, and he might, the tall, angular redhead would be dead.

The names came up soon after. There were no surprises. One was Davies' name. The remaining four were Alaister Strachan, Leonard Rogers, Sir Gerald Tavistock, and Wallace Rossiter. "Eeni, Meeni, Mini, Mo," he muttered.

When he'd deleted them and the sort program, he called Big Red back in. "It worked. If anyone asks, I was checking on some of my agents and their expense accounts." Then, plonking a wet kiss on her cheek, he was gone.

Joshua Davies' night had scarcely begun. Stopping briefly at the refreshment center to pop two hamburgers into the microwave, he made his way to the motor pool, got an old Zephyr Zodiac, and drove it to the large warehouse in Queenhithe Docks.

The lights came on automatically when he entered the long room filled with shelves and filing cabinets. He could feel the damp in the air. Before long the water vapor would steal up through thin layers of paper until all of it was reduced to pulp. These were the original documents. They'd been transferred to computer data base but had one advantage; they had not been weeded. There was always the chance the mole knew enough to remove incriminating evidence from the data tapes. Without the originals for comparison, there was no way to guarantee the accuracy of any computerized data. Of course, weeding-out could take place long before the files reached the computer center. Thousands of incriminating pages had been removed by Kim Philby to protect Burgess and Maclean. Dozens, maybe hundreds, were destroyed when the agreement was made to deal with Anthony Blunt. If, as seemed likely, Roger Hollis was found to be an agent, more would burn—if only to cover up the miserable inadequacy of the vettors.

Terrierlike, Davies was seeking a tunnel that would lead to his mole. He moved box after box. He dug and he dug.

When the guard looked in on him, he saw nothing more than the fat Director wandering from one pile of mildewed paper to another, muttering to himself. At midnight, the watchman left, receiving only a grunt in response to his cheery "Good night."

Davies became hungry; he grew tired; he wanted a cigar but couldn't find one. Finally the Director sat on an upturned tea chest of expense accounts, took out his pipe, and filled the bowl from a pouch of Borkum Riff, Ultralight, he couldn't remember buying. He used the matchbox to draw the flame. The rich smell of tobacco overcame the rotting smell of damp paper.

He went back to it, reading until his head began to throb and his eyes watered. And then he found it. Suddenly. The evidence that would damn Ivan, the little detail that carried a death warrant.

One of the four suspects had a secretary who had worked for him for eight years. She'd resigned suddenly. He held the letter in his hand.

"Bloody strange," said Davies to the stacks of papers around him.

He found the telephone logs. In three neat rows were the black folders containing phone logs stretching back for a decade.

There was no table to work at, but by lugging a few boxes to one place, he was able to make a long table of sorts.

The mole had forgotten, or never knew, that all phone calls were logged from MI5 or SIS numbers and recorded twice, once in the phone log books and once in the summaries. The summaries were destroyed annually, so there were none for the years in question. But the original logs were religiously carted off into storage. Opening the first book, Davies began a methodical examination of its contents until, all at once, he had it—the proof.

As always, the discovery came quietly. There wasn't any dramatic revelation, just the steady accumulation of evidence. The phone logs over a two-year period showed calls to the home of the secretary. Then they ceased, abruptly.

And in Davies' hands was the letter of resignation, short, curt, and somehow sad. What a strange last line: "I cannot serve my country as faithfully as I had hoped."

They had been lovers; then they quarreled. Nothing strange about that. It happened. But she resigned and gave as her reason her inability to serve her country faithfully. Jobs were not that plentiful, but she left the service. Why not ask for a transfer? It was common practice in cases like that. Neither was then married, and the elaborate pretense that the two were involved in official duties at her flat was nothing unusual. An emergency occurred; the duty officer rang the number; no one had to assume anything.

But then suddenly she was gone, sans farewells, sans explanations, sans anything.

Part Three

The Walk

Rough wind, that moanest loud
Grief too sad for song;
Wild wind, when sullen cloud
Kneels all the night long;
Sad storm, whose tears are vain,
Bare woods, whose branches strain,
Deep caves and dreary main,—
Wail for the world's wrong!

Percy Bysshe Shelley, *A Dirge*

16 Frenzy

It was just past eleven o'clock when Geli Bauer left the apartment of her friend Mitzi, who lived in a back street off Potsdammer. Geli decided to walk home; it was only four blocks, and the rain had stopped. It was a fine night.

All the stores on Potsdammer had their windows brightly illuminated, and the summer fashions attracted her attention. Normally Geli had little time for evening window shopping, but this was the one night of the week when Le Kinki closed its doors. She was tiring of the place anyway. More and more, it seemed, Le Kinki was becoming a mere discotheque! Even the grubby DOMs, the dirty old men who hovered nervously in the distant booths, seemed to have been scared away. The leather and blue jeans crowd was taking over.

Geli and Mitzi had drunk four beers each, cooked and shot up a half of a half apiece, stopped scratching, upbraided the male sex, and got into giggling fits while watching a learned and very solemn discussion on television about Botswana—a place neither girl had heard of. When the news came on, Geli left, still a little unsteady on her feet. Mitzi wanted to call a cab, but that was silly for only four blocks. Geli did make a halfhearted attempt to catch the Number 24 bus, but she was unsteady on her stiletto heels and fell into a fit of laughing. The bus turned on to Lutzow before she could straighten herself out.

The short blonde in a miniskirt peering at the displays in stores turned a few male heads. Several men approached her, and Geli told one of the more persistent to fuck himself. He retreated to his two friends, calling her every foul name he could think of; Geli ignored him, and his friends took considerable raucous delight in his discomfiture.

Only later, when the bright lights of Potsdammer were behind her and she was making her way up Pohl Street, the church well behind her, did Geli become aware she was being followed. It didn't alarm her; it wasn't the first time; it wouldn't be the last.

Sometimes they were shy; there were businessmen who owned huge factories, whose word was law to thousands, but who froze in Geli's presence. Then she had to go through a sort of guessing game, a series of questions, such as, "Do you want to . . . ?" Finally they nodded.

Geli turned to let him know she had seen him. Then she paused to look in a store window, hoping to see his reflection. In the one brief glance at him, she had sized him up. He looked clean, and, God knew, that was a plus. Also, he was over six feet tall. That meant little when it came to judging sexual equipment, but anything—anything—was better than the little Herr Direktors with bald heads and potbellies that cut off her breathing. At the end of the encounter, whatever weird or disgusting activities had taken place, these men always insisted on doing it once "the right way."

Geli moved on and he matched his pace to hers. She saw in a window reflection that a dark, well-cut raincoat with its collar turned up hid most of his face. He had a thick head of hair, though, and he was white, definitely. Not a wog. Like all German prostitutes, Geli despised Turks. They used women without even the pretense of romantic interest. That was all right, but when it was over, they suddenly had language problems. Clients had to pay first, but there were cases where the money had been taken back forcefully. A guest worker learned quickly that street women would not call the police.

A lighted window in a boutique caught her eye, and she stopped to look. He did not stop but continued past at the same pace. To anyone else it was a normal scene taking place a thousand times all over the city. A woman, short and blond, looking in a store window; a man, tall and well dressed, passing by.

It was Geli's particular mating ritual; as the man passed, she muttered, as if thinking of the dress in the window, "If you like what you see, two hundred marks is nothing."

The man stopped, as if considering. The truth was, he was fighting a wave of resentment. He had always hated women, even during his childhood. Kroptkov had been the only boy among four children, his widowed mother bringing them all up on a meager pension. She and his sisters ordered him around. They always got their own way. A woman would enslave a man if given the chance. Their weapon was between their legs, and the bitches all knew it.

Kroptkov paused, pretending he had missed her meaning. "Excuse me," he said in good German, feigning surprise. "Did you say something?"

No, he wasn't a wog, but he did have an accent.

"Two hundred," she repeated, making her voice as seductive as she could.

The whore moved on slowly, casting back occasional glances, heading toward a dark side street piled with refuse from the restaurants and stores. Suddenly she stopped and motioned to him.

When he reached her, she took his hand and placed it on her left breast. The man expertly unfastened the top two buttons of her silk blouse and slid his hand under the fabric until he could feel the nipple inside. It was raised and taut. Her hands were already massaging his member through his trousers. He drew back suddenly, and the woman seemed to understand.

"You want to go somewhere safe?" she whispered into his ear. Kroptkov nodded. The breast was firm and rounded; he wanted to feast his eyes on her. His mother's breasts, even after four children, had been perfect. All the uncles who had visited her loved to feel his mother's breasts. He had watched through a spy-hole. They kissed and did other things.

Taking his hand, Geli led him like an obedient child to her apartment above Le Kinki. On the way he said nothing at all.

She had two rooms above the club and a small kitchen curtained off from the living room. The apartment was dimly lit, and when Geli threw their coats on the armchair and lit a large candle, the smell of bayberry filled the air.

"Do you want a drink?" she asked from habit. Many of her clients needed the stimulation. Some drank so much they fell into a stupor and were easily convinced when she woke them an hour later that they had had the most beautiful time.

He shook his head, so Geli led the way to the bed and pushed on it with her fists. It shook. "Waterbed," she said proudly.

Kroptkov took off his jacket and sat on the edge of the mattress. At first the bed's movement took a little getting used to. The bitch sat and took off her watch and gold bracelet and placed them carefully on the small dressing table. She was watching him in the mirror. He remained silent. There was something cruel about his mouth. Kicking off her shoes, Geli walked over to him and sat down beside him, looking at that mouth.

He looked at her bare feet and removed his own shoes. "Now your shirt," said Geli, reaching out and undoing the top button.

Kroptkov's hand seized her arm and held it. "You strip," he said, letting the arm go. Geli's arm clearly showed the impression of his hand, and she massaged the redness. "No rough stuff," she said. "Or else."

The man smiled sardonically. "Or else?"

He was right, of course; she was on her own.

Kroptkov studied her through half-closed eyes; he missed nothing. The girl had his attention, but he was alert to possibilities as well. There was no way a "husband" might suddenly burst through the door and confront them. That had happened to Kroptkov once, and he had relished the opportunity of killing them both.

She wore black stockings on a garter belt and black silk panties. Whores, he believed, were now the only women who didn't wear pantyhose. He caught a glimpse of a triangle of dark springy pubic hair before she brushed past him into the bed.

Geli was surprised by her own nervousness; there was something so terribly unnerving about the way the man stared. Still, in her business you met all types, so it was surprising to be caught off balance by this voyeur.

But he wasn't just a voyeur; she'd had a dozen of those, and they were the most harmless of all, pathetically grateful if she would play with herself and fake an orgasm for them. None of them ever caused her a moment's anxiety.

"I have been looking for you," he said suddenly. "I spoke to a thing called Manne."

Geli sat up in the bed, chilled, holding the black silk sheet up to her chest. "That bastard! I hope you killed him."

The man started. He eyed her closely. Satisfied she knew nothing, he continued. "He told me where to find you."

"I'll bet he did; he's always creeping around hoping for . . . a handout."

The man laughed. "You're a fool. You're an

addict; I got the whole story from Manne." He reached over and tore the sheet from Geli's body. Then he flipped her over on her stomach and bent her legs back, immobilizing her. Carefully he inspected the region between her toes. He found the needle marks. "Soon you will abandon all restraint and start pumping the stuff into your arm."

Standing up, he let her regain her composure. She was sobbing more with frustration than anything else. This man knew too much. Rip-off Manne was a giant who waited in women's toilets until a junkie took one of the stalls. Just at the moment she was ready to pump paradise into her veins, he would leap over the partition and seize the heroin. The one time it happened to her had scared her so badly she hadn't shot up for a week. The huge man was afraid of nothing. He hadn't a spot left anywhere on his body where he could shoot; his body was literally rotting away, inch by inch. He banged the needle into his carotid artery where the effect was almost instantaneous. Bleeding like a stuck pig, he wandered away mumbling, "Many thanks." The creep was always following hookers around town looking for a chance to score from them.

"He says you know a girl called Ingrid."

She said nothing.

"I would like to contact her."

"She's not on the game."

"That's not the point."

He began to undress; the action made Geli courageous. "Why not ask your friend Rip-off Manne?" she asked.

The man smiled cruelly and Geli froze again. This man was dangerous, very dangerous. Her best hope was to humor him; otherwise he might give her a beating she would never forget. She must play along, keep him pacified, do everything he asked and hope sexual release would tranquilize him. If she escaped this encounter with her face undamaged, she would find herself a lover and let him set her up in an apartment and never leave it.

Geli began undressing him with skilled fingers . . . unbuttoning his shirt, kissing the short black hair of his chest. Her fingers were lighter than snowflakes. The Russian scarcely sensed the soft moving away of garments, the silent slide of the zipper.

Then it struck him suddenly, violently. Why hadn't he seen it before?

The bitch was *using* him! All women would use men if they could. That was the natural order of things, wasn't it? His mother had gotten all those men to promise her anything. Sometimes she made them grovel before her; standing naked, she made them kiss her in the strangest places. As he grew older, Kroptkov learned that those men, his "uncles," paid his mother for the pleasure. She used them, and he resolved to serve no woman. They would do *his* bidding; they would satisfy his needs.

Geli moved above him, astride him, and he felt the velvet softness enclosing him. Reaching up, he pulled her face to his. Like most whores, Geli regarded kissing as a private matter; she fought him. Then, thinking better of it, she allowed him to crush her lips against his. Biting fiercely, he drew blood.

When at last he released her, she forced her arm against his chest and pushed herself upright. "You animal." She felt the warm taste of blood in her mouth. "You fucking animal. I said no rough stuff."

The man laughed, enjoying the irony of a woman sitting above him, astride him, being dominated from the inferior position. Holding his hands on her thighs, he began to thrust up into her, causing her body to rise and fall in a rhythm that suited him.

Faster and faster they moved, Geli forced to lean forward over the man's face, using her hands to keep her balance. She felt his mouth capture one of the nipples and imprison it. The other breast swung forward and backward, making a slapping sound, echoing the liquid sound of their mating.

Despite her fear, despite her hatred for the man, Geli felt an orgasm building. Warm juices flowed from her body, her breasts felt full and electric. The hardness inside her was expanding, and instinctively she tightened her muscles.

A sound rose from deep in Kroptkov's throat, a fierce groan. It was low at first, but as his rhythm quickened so did the frequency of the moans. Then they became loud exhalations. Releasing the nipple, he reared back his head and let out a loud howl of release. He wrenched free of her, simultaneously striking out with his fist, knocking Geli to the floor. The bedsheet and blanket went with her, rolling over and enveloping her.

For several minutes, Kroptkov lay unmoving, naked, utterly drained. He was satisfied; he had used the woman.

The bitch groaned. He went over to her, dragged her to a small coffee table, and slammed her head against it. Blood pulsed from her forehead. It pleased him. He flung her naked, face up, onto the bed. He tore the black sheet into four strips and tied her to the bedposts, then stuffed part of a pillowcase into her mouth, and went into the kitchen, where he found a large wooden spoon.

Prowling around the apartment, Kroptkov discovered six stashes of marijuana and a syringe and some white powder secreted behind a hot air duct.

Geli whimpered, her jaw sending out agonizing jolts every few seconds. Her head was too heavy to lift; opening her eyes required the full concentration of all faculties. When the lids rose, there was a shower of brilliant multicolored lights. Hurriedly she closed them. The next time she opened them more slowly, gazing fearfully around the room. What Geli saw caused her eyes to open wide despite the pain. She was spread-eagled on the bed, and between her legs, its purpose all too obvious, lay a large wooden spoon.

The man was completely naked, his organ shriveled and partly hidden by thick light brown hair.

"I have only one question."

Geli nodded; her eyes told him she would tell

him anything. Removing the gag, Kroptkov watched with detached interest as the woman licked bone-dry lips.

"Where is Ingrid Thummel?"

"Oh God, I don't know. Jesus!"

The exclamation was forced from her as she felt the wide end of the spoon caressing her pubic hairs. It nudged at the entrance.

"Where?"

"All I know is she was caught in a police sweep a few days ago." Speaking was horribly painful, and her words were slurred.

"And?" he urged.

"She would have been taken to Friedrichstrasse Police Station." Terror was overtaking her. The assassin felt good. He was using her, and now he had a lead.

"Does she have any friends?"

"I don't know. Ahh!"

"Someone who might know her whereabouts?"

"There was one person. Rudi. Rudi Fleischer."

"Where can I find this Rudi Fleischer?"

"Detmann Strasse. I don't know the number, I swear. Oh God!"

Almost all the spoon was inside her. He replaced the gag. She could writhe all she wanted to now. She didn't know any more. He had no further use for her. He had *used her up.*

With great interest, Kroptkov watched a figure step out of his body and approach the girl. Geli had never screamed before, not like that. All that was left in her of the will to live screamed, and it was all in vain. The gag silenced her. The form covered her mouth with one hand, but still she screamed, the effort forcing blood from her forehead. The figure was excited by her frenzy. She bit its hand and it laughed.

Kroptkov remained a detached observer; the figure took a fruit knife from the dining table and approached the girl, who began screaming in vain again. The thing struck the girl with the knife, deep into her chest. Blood spurted everywhere. Kroptkov shook his head. An amateur, whoever he was; there shouldn't be any blood. He was glad to be naked. Now the creature was kneeling between the girl's legs and stabbing her breasts. There was less blood; but then the knife had little chance of hitting a vital organ. Finally the knife penetrated the water mattress and a flood of water poured over the body and bed frame.

How long the apparition continued its deadly work, Kroptkov didn't know. He remained fascinated by it all—the whore, the blood, the passion of it all. With surprise he found he was erect. The solution was obvious: the girl could still be used. With a feral snarl, his hands set about their familiar task.

"You can pull in over there," commanded Drakov. "Down the alley out of sight."

Rudi Fleischer did as he was told, even though he knew the dangers of leaving the new Honda in such a sleazy neighborhood. He had been commanded—it wasn't too strong a word—and he obeyed. He'd been told to wear something dark, so now he was sweating in his navy-blue winter coat. He had been forced to call in sick, this being his night on the reference desk. There were the beginnings of a migraine headache. And all of it was the doing of the little old man sitting beside him.

Drakov got out and waited impatiently while Rudi made sure all the Honda's doors were locked.

"Come on," said Drakov, in his imperious tone. "A lady is waiting." Seizing Rudi's arm, he hurried him along the alley. Too late Rudi realized he had left the Honda's antenna extended, but he knew better than to ask Drakov if he could go back.

They had to behave like people in a television thriller, keeping out of the streetlight wherever possible and approaching the woman's apartment from every direction except the simplest one. Rudi realized it was a weeknight, and the usual crowds would not be around. He might not be seen by anyone he knew. He hoped fervently not to be. After all, he could hardly say the man was his father from Stuttgart. Everyone knew his father was dead. Worst of all, if he met any of his innermost circle, they would assume he had a new lover. God. The thought began to torment him. What if the divine Peter saw them? For months Rudi had fantasized . . .

A hand dragged him roughly to the outdoor stairs leading to the back of Geli's apartment.

"Concentrate, Rudi," the man hissed in his ear. "Something is very wrong."

Rudi listened; he thought he heard water dripping. His unwelcome companion began a silent climb up the stairs. The wooden steps turned at right angles, so both of them could soon see the last six steps and the back door of the apartment. It was half-open. They approached in single file.

Rudi would have gone right in, but Drakov grabbed him. "That open door is a little too attractive."

"Well, we *are* expected."

"Just so, just so."

Drakov crouched near the back door; he seemed to be straining to hear. Rudi listened. From inside the apartment he thought he heard water dripping. And was there a kind of buzzing sound?

"What is it?" he whispered, crouching by Drakov's side.

The Russian didn't answer.

"What is it?" Rudi insisted. "That buzzing."

"Flies. Many flies. You'd better wait here." But not for the world would the librarian be left alone outside the apartment. He followed Drakov.

Inside, Rudi found himself in a small kitchen; he could just make out the outline of Drakov creeping into the room beyond. There was a sickly sweet smell that clawed at him. The buzzing was louder.

To Drakov, the smell of death was hardly new. At the moment of death, sphincter muscles relaxed; the failure of the bowels and the resulting stench were familiar. A hundred times he had witnessed the execution of prisoners, and almost all of them had known how their bodies would betray them. If given a choice between being shot or hanged, they all preferred to be shot. All refused a final meal.

Turning on the light, Drakov gave an involuntary cry. Even he was shocked by what lay before him.

"Stay where you are, Rudi," he called. "This is not for you."

Still, Rudi overcame his timidity and looked in. Then he ran back to the kitchen and threw up.

Everything had been destroyed. Nothing remained except a single bulb hanging from the ceiling. Everything else had been torn apart in a frenzy of destruction. There was water all over the floor and carpet. A table, all its legs missing, lay at his feet. The upholstery on every piece of the cheap furniture had been slashed from end to end; torn shreds of material hung from smashed wooden framing. The draperies had been torn from the window, slashed, then piled on the floor in endless lengths, none wider than an inch. Three twisted picture frames hung crazily from the walls, their pictures slashed from corner to corner. A stereo, its electronic guts hanging out, lay inside the fireplace. A hundred stereo records had been smashed, one by one, and their covers ripped apart.

On the floor, by the sofa, lay what had attracted the flies and sent Rudi stumbling to the kitchen sink. The thing was white, white like the belly of a fish, but punctuated by a hundred red mouths from which flowed tiny rivulets of blood. The face was beaten beyond recognition, and between the thighs was an oozing crimson mass.

"You should have listened to me," said Drakov, as Rudi sat in the kitchen, pale, the taste of vomit clinging to him.

"Who did that to her?"

Drakov went to the sink, filled a glass with water, and handed it to Rudi. "This is not an ordinary murder; this is the work of someone exceptionally talented in his work. A very dangerous man."

Pausing, he mused, "I knew such a one some time ago."

"Who are you?" Rudi cried hoarsely.

"No one." Another pause. "Can you be trusted to stay here while I examine the body?"

"But shouldn't we call the police immediately?"

"And tell them what?" Drakov asked. "How do we explain our presence? And it doesn't matter to her whether the police come now or next week."

Rudi nodded.

Drakov went back to the other room, frankly puzzled. Only once in his life had he seen anything like this. Popovich had a dangerous psychopath on his leash, an assassin whose work was very similar. His official executions were models of refined and delicate surgery, but there was often a report of a bizarre murder in the same vicinity at about the same time.

Examining the body while impatiently brushing the flies away, Drakov picked up Geli's hand. The fingernails had been uprooted. Her face and head were a single pulpy mass. There were at least a hundred stab wounds. Blood settled after the heart stopped pumping, so he could see that most stab wounds had been made after the woman died. It was the work of a deranged man. There were bruises on the surface of the skin at the point of entry; the knife had been forced into the body so savagely its handle had bruised the body. He turned her over. When he did, he thought the half-severed neck might tear, leaving the head facing the ceiling.

Across Geli's buttocks were a series of perfectly carved knife notches, three on the left side, three on the right.

Kroptkov! Straightening up slowly, Drakov saw that his problems were multiplying fast. The KGB was now involved; presumably they did not know Drakov was alive, but their interest boded ill.

In the distance, he heard a police siren. Quickly closing the window, he left the remains of Geli Bauer. She would become irrefutable proof to the smug bourgeoisie around her of the wages of sin. They would sleep better because of this.

Drakov hustled the still-shaking Rudi down the stairs. Kroptkov had drawn first blood.

17 Ivor Place

Joshua Davies left his taxi driver a larger tip than strict justice required. The driver was a Sikh who had seen him standing at the curb in the rain and actually stopped.

Davies crossed the sidewalk and opened the small wrought-iron gate. The houses on Ivor Place were the typical three-story postwar reconstructions. Neat enough but nothing grand. There were four steps up to the front door. On both sides were basements. Often the landlord would live there, allowing three floors to be let. They were private with their own narrow flight of stone steps leading to a tiny flagged courtyard, known as an area.

There was no bell, just a small brass knocker whose sharp *rat-a-tat* sounded crisply in the evening air.

Ethel Scott had changed little in the five years since she resigned from the service. There was some gray in her chestnut hair, and the once-trim waistline showed the start of middle-age spread. Still, at forty-five, Ethel Scott was an attractive woman.

"Mr. Davies," she said, a pronounced nervousness in her voice. "What a surprise."

"It's official," he told her, following her along a narrow passageway to the sitting room.

"I guessed as much," she replied over her shoulder. "I've been expecting someone for a long time."

They sat in chairs opposite each other, Ethel Scott in the rocker, Davies on the couch. He kept his coat on; a small coal fire burned in the grate, but it gave off more smoke than heat. Once again the Director found himself longing for the warmth of distant lands. England was dreary; he was feeling old, tired. The issues never got any simpler.

"A cup of tea, Mr. Davies?"

"Er. No, thanks."

The room was comfortably furnished in the slightly stuffy style of English middle-class women. There were the usual photographs on the mantelpiece, but Ethel Scott had not become a Miss Haversham, surrounded by souvenirs of a shattering disappointment.

Looking through an arch, he could see a kitchenette with a small refrigerator. On top, a Siamese cat was eating dry food from a paper plate. To Davies' left was a shelf filled with books; he scanned the titles: every one was a novel by a famous author—English, French, Russian. He remembered that Ethel Scott spoke several languages.

She followed his gaze. "I earn my living translating books. Some of the publishers pay quite well—quite well for translations, I mean."

"We can spend the evening sparring," said Davies, "or I can come straight to the point."

"Please do." She was crisp and self-assured.

Moving forward in his chair, he said, "About five years ago you resigned the service. Why?"

There was a fleeting look of uncertainty, but within a second she had composed herself. "I needed a change. The work made me nervous. There was never any letup."

"And that was the only reason?"

"Isn't that a sensible reason, Mr. Davies?"

From his inside pocket, Davies produced a leather-bound notebook and looked inside it. "Your letter of resignation said 'personal reasons.' "

"When you say 'personal reasons,' there's no exit interview."

"No awkward questions, you mean?"

"I didn't say that." She sounded just a little uneasy. "Mr. Davies, do you have any authority to—?"

"Make us some tea."

She rose, a little too eagerly, and walked into the kitchen. Though he could not see her, he heard the rattle of crockery. The cat was eyeing its mistress from its seat on top of the refrigerator.

"No one is perfect," Davies said, loud enough for her to hear. "We play elaborate games to maintain fictions."

"Fictions? What do you mean?"

The Director waited until she returned with their tea. The cat followed her in, brushing up against Davies' leg. He scratched its forehead, and the brightest blue eyes gazed up at him.

"She's called Tuptim," Ethel Scott said. "From *The King and I,* you know."

Davies nodded. "It was no secret to those who

needed to know that a relationship existed between you and a senior—"

"Well!" she bristled. "Did that present a threat to national security?"

Davies shifted his weight, thinking of Soo Ling. "Not in itself."

"You can't blackmail unmarried people because they have . . . a relationship."

"You loved this man?"

"Obviously."

"I checked the phone logs in storage; on several occasions he was at a number registered in your name."

Her lips tightened. "I admitted the affair; so what?"

"It must have been . . . difficult."

She poured the tea, and he noticed with admiration that her hand was steady.

"One thing you learn in our game," she said, "is that everything is a compromise. It was a fair compromise."

"You didn't discuss marriage?"

"None of your damned business."

Davies nodded. "You're right, but you broke with him, and I think I know why. But I want you to tell me why."

"Personal."

"Not any longer. You work for eight years with a man; you share his bed"—he looked up quickly—"and then you resign."

"For personal reasons."

"Those reasons are now of national significance. What did he do?"

"You'll never hear it from me."

Davies sat back, suddenly very tired. "You

were a deeply honest and patriotic woman. Your work record showed hours of unclaimed overtime."

"So?"

"If your love affair fell apart, you wouldn't quit the service. *Au contraire*, you would throw yourself into it even more vigorously. Something happened. You couldn't bear to report it, so you walked away. And because you walked away, perhaps thirty people have been killed."

She went white. "You can't prove anything. I didn't do anything wrong."

"You did. You compounded an act of treason. Because of you, men and women have been tortured and killed."

The following silence was broken by occasional snapping sounds from the fireplace. The woman stared at Davies. She began tapping her fingers nervously on the little coffee table between them. They both knew she was about to bring up something she dreaded.

"He altered a file; I saw him do it. Then he altered the computer index."

"So the record was untraceable."

"Don't play stupid, Mr. Davies. Without the key code, the record would be lost unless someone dumped the whole bloody tape. If it was ever found, he could claim it was a mistake. Then to protect KGB agents he issued a 'hands off' so no other intelligence service would stick its oar in."

Davies got to his feet, fury barely suppressed. "Who got the 'hands off' at the other end?"

"Who else? The Yanks of course." She looked up at him.

"They were on to someone," he said, "and he told them we were running that person. Then he misfiled our copy of the order."

She nodded. "At first I thought he was mistaken, then he cut loose another report. In the computer he added several archival notations—'checked without result,' 'subject not traceable,' and finally 'subject believed dead.' "

Davies grasped her wrist roughly. "Who told you?"

She wrenched her arm away, knocking the teapot off the table. Neither of them gave it a glance. "I can read an audit trace. I checked every morning after the first incident; the next time he was careless, the audit trace showed changes in a protected file. That day I came in very early, and at night, after he left, I checked again. The audit trial had been cleansed."

"And you didn't tell anyone?" Davies shouted. "Do you know what you've done? You've helped compromise Five and SIS for over ten years. *Why* in God's name didn't you report this?"

Ethel Scott looked at him for a long time before trusting herself to speak. "You poor fat bastard," she said softly. "You'll never understand, will you? I *loved* him—do you think I could *kill* him?"

Davies looked away, bent down with a grunt, and picked up the teapot.

"I suppose you'll kill him now?"

Davies sighed. "It's never that easy. We play a deadly game, and we're trained not to care what happens to people on both sides. When someone cares too much it distorts his . . . or her . . . reason. People begin to break down under pressure. You broke, Ethel."

She got to her feet; even so, he towered over her. "And you're above love, are you, Mr. High-and-Mighty Joshua Davies? Well, one day, if a miracle occurs, someone may show you what love is. Go back to Curzon Street and look for spies."

Davies stood, hands in pockets, as she faced him defiantly. She hadn't finished with him.

"You know what's happened to you? Your mind has become separated from your body. Your head lives in a world of codes and dossiers and theory. Someday, one of those paper figures is going to become flesh and blood. *Then* we'll see. Now get out and leave me."

She turned to go back into the kitchen. Davies reached under his coat and jacket and took out a tiny Hi-Standard Victor with a 5½-inch barrel. It was almost hidden by his great hand. A silencer wasn't necessary, for the .22 was one of the quietest automatics on the market.

She fell to the floor almost silently, yet Tuptim let out a high-pitched cry of alarm and slipped under the sofa. The Director picked up Ethel Scott and placed her body in the rocking chair. "You forgot the question of your own guilt," he said sadly, brushing hair from her face.

The cat ventured out and went after the tiny brass cartridge that had fallen to the carpet, batting it back and forth between her paws. Davies reached down and picked up first the shell, then the Siamese. Holding both, he walked to the back door and unlocked it.

Then he left by the front door, still carrying the Siamese. He walked half a mile to Park Road, where he hailed a taxi. His butcher boys would tidy up.

18 Holding Pen

The morning after Geli Bauer's death, Rudi Fleischer woke with a headache and an upset stomach and a moment of sheer panic; there was no feeling in his left arm. Then he felt light twinges of pins and needles run up the arm. His arm had gone to sleep because he was lying on it; the sofa wasn't wide enough for him to sleep comfortably.

As he sat there nursing his arm, the bathroom door opened. Out stepped Drakov, fully dressed and freshly shaved. His suit was protected by Rudi's favorite bathrobe, the one he'd bought in Thailand with the temples of Angkor Wat on the back.

"Good morning, Rudi," Drakov said. "I trust you slept well."

It wasn't a question, and Rudi remained on the sofa. He would not answer. He would not say, "Good morning." He wanted to kill his uninvited guest. He would do it himself; he would . . .

"I've never worn silk pajamas before," Drakov was saying. "As for sleeping in a bed with silk sheets—that is the height of bourgeois decadence."

"When will you leave me alone?" Rudi asked, on the brink of tears.

"Not until my business is concluded," replied Drakov. "We lost the thread last night, my dear Rudi. Call in sick, then turn your attention to breakfast. We'll be meeting a lot of unsavory characters today."

Rudi pulled on a cheap terry-cloth robe he'd never bothered to throw away, and picked up the phone. He cordially hated the head reference librarian. She was a bitch. The job should have been his, but with the recent stress on equalization, he'd been passed over. There'd been a vote, of course, but the women all voted for the female candidate, and some of the men did, too. Rudi got a poison pen letter from someone assuring him no queer would get the job. This frightened him a great deal.

When she came to the phone, Rudi told her he was still feeling ill. It might have been prudent to say he wouldn't be in until Monday, but please God, the hated Herr Kreugar would be gone before then.

Drakov, of course, had heard every word; Rudi's confiscated pistol was in the pocket of his borrowed robe, but he knew he wouldn't need it. After the call, Rudi returned to the kitchen.

"I'm fixing Jamaican Blue Mountain coffee," he said.

Drakov grunted, deep in Rudi's morning paper.

"It's the best coffee in the world," added the librarian. "Two hundred marks a can."

Drakov didn't respond. Rudi inspected his refrigerator. The cantaloupe, which he had been saving for a more welcome encounter, was sliced in half, and the seeds and pulp ground up in the waste disposal. Pumml watched every move from his wicker basket.

Because the librarian didn't know what cereal the stranger liked, and since nothing would make him ask, he took down a variety pack so the man could choose his own.

The coffee was ready just as he finished squeezing two Jaffa grapefruits. His guest had not offered to help, and it was safe to bet he wouldn't.

Drakov looked up as Rudi arranged the food on the table. "I have to tend to Pumml now," the librarian stated with as much defiance as he dared.

The Russian looked at him shrewdly, having caught the edge of determination in Rudi's tone.

"You mean feed it? Does it get soft-boiled eggs and marmalade?" Drakov lit a cigarette, poured himself a cup of coffee, and sipped. "Excellent," he pronounced. "Rudi, you outdo yourself."

"Pumml has to have his enema."

Drakov looked at Rudi in amazement. "An enema?" Shaking his head, he said, "I'm glad you fixed breakfast first."

When Rudi returned, there wasn't much breakfast left. It didn't matter; he only drank his juice and ate a little melon. The last croissant was cold, and all the orange marmalade had been eaten. There was some ash from Herr Kreugar's cigarette on the tablecloth, which Rudi carefully swept up with an envelope and put into the little wastebasket. While he was drinking the last half cup of Blue Mountain, Rudi felt the stranger's eyes on him.

"So you're a librarian," he said.

Rudi nodded glumly. Then, in a flash of wit, added, "When I'm permitted to work, that is."

Drakov's eyes narrowed; Rudi felt himself turning pale. He could actually *feel* the color draining from his face. "Just a joke," he said miserably.

"I lack a sense of humor, my friend." Rudi said nothing. "Get dressed," Drakov ordered.

Closing the bathroom door tightly and locking it, Rudi turned on the shower and filled the air with heavy steam. The mirror and window were clouded, and droplets of water ran down the white bathroom tiles. He felt safer hidden in a fog of his own making. Herr Kreugar had found his cocoa butter soap and used his imported Nexus shampoo. Still, when Rudi emerged from the tub, his skin had been treated with a preparation guaranteed to restore the natural oils and emollients, and his hair had been shampooed and conditioned with a botanically fortified polymeric acid-balanced pH3 keratin enhancer. He put a brave face on things with a loosely knotted cravat, his white vicuna sweater, and tight pants. Feeling melancholy, he slipped the ring Klaus had bought for him on his little finger. It was all the little prick had given him; everything else had been charged on Rudi's credit cards.

"Tomorrow I think I would like a large, sweet pineapple," Drakov said, eyeing him up and down. "You look wonderful. Now get your little car."

The Berliners were, as usual, either hurrying to and fro or deliberately forcing themselves to relax with coffee and croissants at the busy sidewalk cafes. It was a bright, warm day. Several young men of Rudi's acquaintance were parading in front of the Alexander at the intersection with Bleibtreustrasse. He prayed they wouldn't acknowledge him. A fat woman of incredible proportions was leading a tiny dog no bigger than a rat along the center median.

A light sweat covered Rudi's face. It was hot and stuffy in the car, and for the first time, he had an opportunity to try the air conditioner. It worked beautifully. Encouraged, Rudi switched on the radio; classical music came from four speakers, but the sound was muffled. Drakov looked at him inquiringly.

"I forgot to extend the antenna," Rudi mumbled, feeling foolish. He pushed the button, there was a whirring sound, and the music came in very clearly.

"This car seems too complicated for you, Rudi," said his passenger.

The librarian stared stonily ahead; Drakov chuckled. They rode in silence for ten minutes.

"Park somewhere near the Zoo Station," Drakov ordered. "On the street."

"Can't we take it into a parking structure?" pleaded Rudi. "It's so much safer."

"You are too fond of this little car; if it is damaged I will pay. And if we succeed, I shall have no need of my large amount of German money and you shall have it. I have already explained this. Buy a computer for your research or write a novel. Now park!"

The two men got out; despite Herr Kreugar's claim to wealth, he allowed Rudi to feed the parking meter.

There followed one of the weariest days of Rudi's life. Because of the warm weather, the prostitutes were out in force. Drakov himself was astonished by what he saw. Three times, girls no older than thirteen offered to perform sex with him. If they knew of Ingrid Thummel, they refused to say.

Rudi became increasingly nervous. "If I'm recognized," he pleaded, "I'll lose everything. Suppose someone sees me here? I'll be fired. I'll lose everything!"

Herr Kreugar wasn't concerned. "We have a job to do, Rudi. These are your countrymen. Find out about the girl and I will show my gratitude. If you fail me, the loss of your job will be a minor detail."

The note of profound menace in the stranger's voice made Rudi throw caution to the winds. He questioned, cajoled, bribed, and pleased even Drakov by his diligence. But they learned nothing about Ingrid Thummel.

"She just isn't here," Rudi said as they sat in a cafe. "Addicts disappear for days on end. She could even be dead."

"Let us hope not, Rudi . . . for your sake."

Rudi hurried to the men's room and splashed cold water on his face.

When he returned, he found his companion deep in conversation with the waiter. Sitting down, Rudi tried a little bratwurst with a thin slice of pumpernickel. It tasted good.

"The waiter is an observant fellow," Drakov

told him. "He is also an addict and open to being bribed. Despite your heroic efforts, my dear young friend, you move in the wrong circles. Get the car; we are going to Bulowbogen."

"That's one of the worst parts of the city," exclaimed Rudi, genuinely frightened now.

Herr Kreugar paid no attention. Throwing a handful of bills on the table, he said, "Don't worry, Rudi, I'll protect you. And"—he turned to look at Rudi over his shoulder—"God will look after your little red car."

The man had a small plastic bag. From it he took a syringe, a spoon, and a lemon.

"I started like all of us. No shooting. Just an occasional snort." Carefully he poured the white powder from its purple foil paper into the spoon. "It has a sharp bitter taste. Your limbs become heavy and, at the same time, quite light. You feel tired, yet it's a fantastic feeling."

From his pocket he took a small bottle of water, added a few drops to the white powder, and squeezed in a little lemon juice. "The H is never quite pure, *meine Herren,*" he muttered apologetically. "That is not your fault. And it dissolves easier this way."

Taking a lighter from his pocket, he used the flame to heat the spoon. "We all say we were lured into being junkies, but it's a lie. We get on it because we want to."

From his tattered jacket pocket he drew a small tobacco tin. Inside was a needle wrapped in plastic. Inserting the needle in the syringe, he continued, "I was happy with snorting, but of course I finally tried the needle."

During the entire operation, his hands, which were constantly twitching when they met him, remained steady. "I was going to be a joy popper. I was going to keep the needle out of the vein." He shook his head in disbelief. "I was going to do what no one else has done—make heroin *my* slave."

The liquid was filling the syringe. Waiting until the spoon was sucked completely dry, he added, "Then it went into the vein, and not all the king's horses and all the king's men could put Wilhelm together again."

Clenching his fist, he crooked his arm and searched for a vein. At last he found one and slid the needle in. The heroin was commingled with his blood in the syringe. Then slowly, as the pressure on the plunger increased, the bright red liquid disappeared. Wilhelm's words no longer made sense. His pupils, caught in the light, became tiny.

For Rudi it was horribly familiar. This was the nod. The nod was preferable to sleep; it was the culmination of the shot, representing the narcotization and stimulation the addict craves.

"How long will this last?" whispered Drakov.

"Maybe fifteen minutes," replied Rudi. "It's a Sisyphean task."

"What?"

"The nod becomes harder and harder to achieve."

Drakov studied Rudi, then the addict.

For twenty minutes the addict sat where he was, his head nodding occasionally. Then, as if there had been no pause, he spoke. "They tried Nalline; I'd rather be a junkie. I needed four grams a day—seven hundred marks. And I got it, too, ripping off the chickenhawks."

"You knew Ingrid Thummel?" asked Drakov.

"Ingrid?" He sounded disoriented. "Oh, Ingrid."

He chuckled grimly. "I warned her, but they never listen. She had seen it done a hundred times, but she got the jitters anyhow."

For a long time he said nothing. Rudi was transfixed with horror; the gaunt creature in front of them was only seventeen years old. "Well . . . I was high, and her nervousness affected me. Three times I jammed that needle into her arm before I drew any blood. Then I shot up a whole quarter."

"Where is she now?"

"She's no good for anything now; you can get a BP to do anything you want for twenty marks." He was anxious to help. "Clean, too, some of them."

"Ingrid."

"I don't know. She lived with someone at Reichenberger Strasse, thirty-six. Facing the Landwehr Canal. I took the stuff there." Then he added, "I wasn't always like this."

As they left, Drakov threw down two tin foil packages; the addict scrambled across the floor on all fours to seize them. "Live long and prosper," he called to them in a hoarse, strained voice.

They picked their way across the refuse-laden street to Rudi's car. The Russian muttered, "There's no limit to human weakness."

"It's a Communist plot," said Rudi confidently.

Drakov stopped short and Rudi almost bumped into him. "Explain that," Drakov said.

The librarian felt on safe ground; he was, after all, a reference specialist. "The Europeans almost wiped out the North American Indians with alcohol by accident. In Europe, the Russians funnel heroin through Bulgaria and almost give it away to dealers." He felt a flush of pride in his professional knowledge.

"And what do you think of Russians, Rudi?" asked his companion in a silky voice.

"They're all right, I suppose," replied Rudi. "The Russian people, I mean, not the KGB and that type. I wouldn't want to get too close to one of them. They're *fiends!*"

"Admirable sentiments," said Drakov approvingly. "I feel exactly the same way."

19 The Spanish Patriot

What Alfred Nelson thought when he was hailed by a large man carrying a Siamese cat will never be known. Alf had seen stranger sights; driving a cab was not for the squeamish, as he often told his passengers. Davies and his traveling companion were deposited in front of the Spanish Patriot in record time, and without conversation.

There was no guard on the premises of Davies' office because Davies, Greene & Co. was a *bona fide* business, and the stealing of anything would only have enhanced the cover.

An elevator suitable for three people, or Davies alone, was available, but Davies decided to climb the stairs. A long staircase led to the third floor, and Davies used the handrail as he climbed the wooden steps, holding the cat in the other arm. At the top, neatly stenciled in white on the small opaque glass window of the door was "Eros Film Studio." The blue-movie component of Davies, Greene, & Co. did a thriving business.

When the Director turned his key, a green light above the door went on. He used his key card to unlock the security lock. Inside the office, Davies took a small carton of milk from the small refrigerator and, pouring some into a blue saucer, put it on the wicker chair. Tuptim leaped into the seat and began lapping the milk with its long pink tongue.

While his computer was warming up, Davies cast his eye over his pile of mail, which was secured by a large paperweight. It was a rock he had purchased in Jerusalem from an Arab who assured him it was the very one Christ had offered the villagers who wanted to stone the woman taken in adultery. The rock cost two Israeli pounds. It was a fine complement to the bust of John Wesley.

Now he sat in his swivel chair, got his bulk comfortably distributed, and summoned up form T46D1. It was a simple screen, and all he had to do was to fill in the details; it was the free text under "Comments" that involved the most labor. There was nothing difficult about filling in the name of the deceased, the time of death, or its cause. Ethel Scott's death was reduced to a few words and numbers. All these data and Davies' comments would be encoded by the software and stored. In 99 percent of the cases, no reference would ever be made to it. Indeed, if he were to change one digit in its reference location, it might never be found. To prevent such a course of action, the computer made its own audit trace and immediately signaled when a change of this kind was made. But Ivan had altered audit trails; *that* required great skill.

Davies hated filling out reports; the adrenaline was always gone an hour after the event, and the impersonal facts seemed all the more cruel and cold-blooded when they were being recorded on the computer.

Tuptim finished her milk and sat in Raison's favorite haunt, a hollow in the piles of newspapers heaped in front of the window. Those at the bottom were yellow with age; Davies couldn't remember which year he'd started collecting them. Guiltily he thought it might have been when they started including the "nudie pic."

A whiskey became imperative; he went to his bar and poured a very stiff one, no soda and no ice. He toasted the memory of John Haig.

He padded over to the window. Tuptim looked up at him a little apprehensively, but the Director's thoughts were on the Spanish Patriot, directly opposite. It was just closing; all over London, five thousand pubs were disgorging their customers. Most drinkers would get home all right, a few wouldn't. Ancient, bizarre rules made the British pub an institution. There was nowhere else to buy that ridiculous concoction Pimm's Cup Number 1. If pubs had any failing at all, Davies decided, it was that they could never make a really dry martini.

A little of the whiskey spilled; with his forefinger he made patterns in the amber liquid. He'd decided: no trade for Ivan. If there were any squawks, let them come when it was too late to do anything about it.

Below, the street cleaners arrived, a squad of four men, all black, moving down the street and hurling everything into the back of the garbage truck. Once they'd passed, cars filled up the empty parking spaces. The original planners of the city, and every one of their successors, had refused to acknowledge the existence of any form of transportation since the sedan chair, so the streets of London had become dormitories for cars of all sizes and shapes. One was pulling in under Davies' window. A man got out, and just at that moment a striking redhead with hair falling to her shoulders left the Spanish Patriot and crossed the street in the company of a girlfriend. It was not quite summer, but, Davies noted with approval, miniskirts were already making an appearance. The driver got into a conversation on the sidewalk with the woman while her friend stood by impatiently. Davies saw their faces quite clearly in the headlights of a passing blue Ford Escort. The girl seemed interested in what the man had to say, but her friend pulled her away. The man shouted after them, and the girlfriend turned and made an obscene gesture. The driver walked across the road to Launcelot Street and disappeared.

Davies returned to his report, but he couldn't concentrate. When at last it was done, he sighed, logged off, and pushed the computer away on its cart.

The only other things in his in-tray were the daily translations from the Communist press. The Russian ones were done by Freddy Gilbert. Davies had to admit they were good. The Chinese translations, especially from the *Red Flag,* were worse than the subtitles in a Japanese science fiction film—though the translator assured everyone they were accurate.

Also in the in-tray was a copy of James Joyce's *Finnegan's Wake.* The bookmark was on page 130, where it had been for over a month.

The Director was hungry. An overwhelming desire to dine at Carrier's swept through him. Even Davies' favorite salad, fresh Moroccan orange, would suffice. Any of the Bordeaux wines would be enough to cheer him up. Robert Carrier's little restaurant in Islington had done something Davies would have deemed impossible—taught him to enjoy *nouvelle cuisine.* A glance at his digital clock told him the worst. It was almost midnight; the supper menu started at eleven-thirty. He was too late for the savory trio of baby lamb chops with *beurre vert,* the sauté of lamb with *flageolets,* or the calf's liver with black currants.

Davies was aware of another discomfort, but he couldn't put his finger on it. Something wasn't right. He sat back, closed his eyes, and tried to concentrate. It was late and he was tired; his huge hand removed his pince-nez and pawed at his eye sockets. Something was unsettling him. What was it? Operating on a sense so fine and remote it couldn't be called instinct, he reviewed the events of the last hour.

There wouldn't be any problem about Ethel Scott; that was simple justice. A doctor would certify a heart attack, an autopsy report would follow. All insurance and social services would do whatever they had to. No one would know the extent of the woman's treachery. Davies understood love, knew the devastating effects of rejection, but that was not any kind of excuse. Because of Ethel Scott, the whole of Britain's intelligence apparatus had been compromised, and God knew how many killed, how many tortured.

His reports were done, and he could go home, back to Cockfosters and his wine cellar. Reaching for the phone, he began dialing for a taxi, but before reaching the fourth digit, he banged the receiver down. Then he paced the room, ending up at the window. Everything looked peaceful, but something nagged at him and wouldn't let up. Tuptim had gone to sleep on the stack of newspapers; her rhythmic purring was loud and steady.

Crossing the office, he poured himself a double whiskey and added soda. He'd never acquired the American habit of drinking everything with ice. Once in California he'd seen someone surreptitiously drop a chunk of ice into a glass of white wine.

Why did he feel the bodies of invisible insects crawling up the back of his neck? Going back to the window and keeping out of sight, he carefully surveyed the street yet again. A double-decker bus rumbled by, and then Davies found himself staring at the car in front of his building.

The driver hadn't locked the car. That was what was bothering him. The man had left it unlocked, talked with the redhead, then walked away. It might have been a simple oversight. Was he getting paranoid? Had he reached the point where he was frightened of shadows?

Davies peered down; the car was an old Humber, two-toned, white on blue, and he shuddered at the lack of taste. It was old, a 1966 or 1965, definitely pre-OPEC, larger than today's matchboxes on wheels.

Shooing Tuptim from her perch, Davies

scrambled onto the windowsill with one knee, squinting until he could just make out the first letter of the license plate. It was a *G*.

He hurried to his desk, picked up the receiver, and dialed. There was no answer. Quickly he dialed another number. This time a voice said, "Yes?"

"License plate check."

"Yes?"

"What year did *G* plates begin?"

"Wait."

Tuptim wandered over and looked up at him.

Davies held the phone under his many chins and scooped up the cat.

"1969 . . ."

Davies was already running, the cat clutched to his chest. The phone fell to the floor; the voice said, "Hello? Hello?"

There was no time for the elevator; Joshua Davies wrenched open his door and ran for the stairs, plunging down them. Midway he stumbled, and with a loud cry of fear and indignation, Tuptim flew from his hands, falling feet first on a packing case. Grabbing at the handrail and missing, Davies tumbled down the last three steps, landing on his side.

It all fitted together. It was an old IRA trick. Because automobiles kept the same license plate, they could be traced. When a car was junked, its plates were sent into the local vehicle registry. A 1967 Humber had been taken from some junk heap and stolen plates put on it. The *G* plates had been issued well over two years after the car's manufacture.

Casting one despairing look around for Tupim, he raced through the front door. He was ifty yards from the building when he heard the ang. It was more of a dull *crump* than a loud xplosion. Instinct took over. He flung himself ull length on the ground just as a blast ripped he jacket from his back. Covering the back of is head with his arms, he remained motionless s masonry and glass fragments flew through he air. Above and around him he heard the tin-ling of broken glass. Strangely, through his nind ran the familiar scripture: " . . . as sound-ng brass or the tinkling cymbal." Then it was uddenly very hot and impossible to breathe. omething very large and heavy fell near him nd broke into fragments. He felt the impact ut heard nothing, for the sonic pressure on his ardrums blocked out sound.

Seconds later his head was ringing. He was lso wet; he was lying in front of a tiny bou-ique, and the heat had set off the sprinkler. ounds followed quickly, one after another: nore breaking glass, fire and burglar alarms, olice sirens.

Davies was attempting to stand up when aid rrived. His trousers were ripped to shreds and is shoes were gone. When the first policeman eached him, Davies had found one shoe and vas looking for the other. Of Tuptim there was o sign.

When her brother arrived home two hours ater, Dol screamed. His head was bandaged.

"Oh, Josie!" she cried in horror. "What hap-ened?"

"Our office fell on me."

Dol threw her arms around him and clung t him. "You might have been killed."

"That was the idea. It's out in the open now Dol. The son of a bitch will be mine soon."

His sister sobbed as she helped him stretc out on his king-sized bed. "Don't fret, Dol," h said, wiping her tears away with a giant thumb "I can still tango."

Dolores Davies burst into tears all over agair and nothing her brother could say would com fort her.

20 Pumml

ɩudi was so shaken by the encounter with the ɩoomed junkie that he could scarcely drive ɩhem home. After he narrowly missed another ɩar, Drakov ordered him to stop the Honda, and ɩe took the wheel himself. The librarian turned ɩale, but he understood where thoughts of rebel-ɩion would lead him.

Drakov had a great deal of sorting out to do. ɩn extra element had been added to the equa-ɩion. Kroptkov, the most dangerous man in ɩussia, was evidently also looking for Ingrid. ɩhe State Assassin would have to be elimi-ɩated. But how? This wasn't the kind of man ɩho might be trapped by someone flattening ɩimself against the wall and jumping out unex-ɩectedly. It would be impossible to overcome ɩroptkov in any conventional manner.

This creature was the best there was. Drakov ɩnew this. He was not, however, Anton Mik-ɩailovich Drakov. If there were a weakness, and ɩhere always was, Drakov would find it.

"For you, it will soon be over," said the Rus-ɩian to Rudi, who was huddled miserably in the ɩassenger seat. "You will be able to return to the reference desk with renewed vigor and e larged experience after this adventure."

They parked the Honda and entered Rudi building. The elevator passed Rudi's floor, an Drakov explained, "We do not get off at our ow floor. Nothing is as unpleasant as opening an e evator door and looking into the muzzle of Stechkin APS. We go one floor above and wal down. Just in case."

Rudi waited until Drakov had checked th hall and signaled to him. He took his ke out of his pocket, but Drakov reached out an prevented him from opening the door.

"We are playing for much higher stakes now Rudi. Every door may conceal somethin deadly."

Drakov studied the apartment door; it ap peared firmly locked. Rudi gave a little gasp c apprehension when Drakov's Beretta automati suddenly appeared in his hand. The Russian di not believe in the so-called sixth sense, but lon experience had taught him to be extremely wary and there was nothing worse than approaching closed door across an open hallway.

Drakov checked the doors of the other thre apartments sharing the hall. All were firml closed. Not that that meant much—they coul be opened in a flash, and he and the cringin Rudi cut down in a hail of bullets. Nevertheless he decided to risk it. He crossed the hall, goin down on one knee in front of Rudi's door. For th nth time the librarian wished with all his hear Herr Kreugar would leave his life forever.

"You will observe, Rudi, this hair I place across the door and the post."

"The jamb."

"Thank you, Rudi."

Rudi got down on one knee. "It's still there," he said. "No one's been here."

He would have risen to his feet, but Drakov seized his collar and hissed, "Not so fast, my librarian friend. If we can see this hair, anyone else who knows what to look for could do the same."

Releasing Rudi, Drakov took his pen from an inside pocket. "Observe. You will see the hair is an inch above the top of this pen."

Rudi nodded.

"When we left it was exactly level. Someone has been here and has carefully replaced the hair."

Drakov got to his feet.

"Well, he's gone then," the librarian said, also rising. "You can't replace a hair from the inside."

Drakov didn't miss the pride in Rudi's voice. "Very good, Rudi. Unless, of course, there were two of them."

The German's confidence disappeared.

Drakov looked calm enough, but he was thinking furiously. Certainly a professional was involved; the replacing of the hair proved that. Kroptkov always worked alone. So the visit was in the nature of a warning, was that it? Drakov's caution had spoiled the surprise.

"It is safe to enter, Rudi. The assassin still needs us to point the way for him. However, when I first visited you, that little dog made a sort of . . . of snuffling sound."

The librarian put his ear to the pine door.

"Pumml," he whispered through the door. "Pumml." There was no snuffling noise.

"We may go in," said Drakov. "I already knew someone had paid us a visit. You see, the hair trick was meant to be obvious. Before we left, I carefully placed a piece of cigarette paper between the door and the edge of the door sill." He stooped and picked up a tiny shred of white paper several feet from the door. "You see, we *have* had a visitor."

Drakov carefully pushed open the door with his hand, while he and Rudi remained flattened against the wall out of the direct line of fire. Then, swift as lightning, Drakov slipped silently into the apartment, keeping his body low.

For an eternity, the trembling librarian remained flattened against the outside wall. Finally Herr Kreugar returned and said in a strangely tired voice, "You may come in, Rudi. Our visitor has left."

As the librarian entered, a cry of deepest anguish was forced from him. Everything he owned had been destroyed; there wasn't an item of furniture, a piece of material, or a single ornament left. The two table lamps on their Chinese vases had been pounded to tiny pieces and each shade meticulously cut into bits no bigger than a pfennig.

Drakov was not astonished at the orgy of destruction. Experience had shown what Kroptkov was capable of. Turning to say something to Rudi, he found himself alone; the librarian was vomiting in the bathroom.

The bedroom was, if possible, worse. Every drawer was smashed, contents ripped to shreds.

The bed was tilted; only one leg remained attached. The slats supporting the springs were all broken in two, and the springs themselves were poking out of slashed fabric. The quilt had been torn into long strips and these knotted into fantastic shapes. The television had been disemboweled and its many components flung around the room.

Rudi was still in the bathroom when Drakov got there. The pipes in the bathroom had been ripped from the walls, but the water was turned off. Kroptkov didn't want someone coming upstairs to complain of water leaking through his ceiling. He'd intended Drakov to witness his handiwork without prior warning.

The kitchen was not a separate room, so Drakov could see into it from the living room. All cupboards above the sink and refrigerator hung open crazily. The fridge was pulled out from the wall; its door was open. All doors had been wrenched open and subjected to savage abuse.

Except . . . the microwave oven.

That appliance was unharmed. Its door was closed, and the digital clock still operated, its red numbers recording the passing seconds. Stepping across the kitchen floor, his feet crunching on broken cutlery, Drakov approached it.

"What are you doing?" Rudi called to him in a quavering voice.

"Go back to the bathroom," Drakov ordered coldly.

Rudi went.

There was no way to see into the oven, for the front was covered with wire mesh. Drakov pushed down on the handle and the latch released with a *snick*. He opened the door only a little way. Inside was a mass of bloody flesh and fur. He had found Pumml.

They sat in a cafe. Rudi had needed considerable persuasion to leave his building. The destruction of his apartment had moved him from fearful to downright truculent. It wasn't the same thing as courage, but it was tricky to deal with nevertheless. Drakov let him pass through the stages unhindered. He knew when to push and when to let nature take its course.

"This place has atmosphere, Rudi," said Drakov. "I didn't catch the name."

"Die Zentrifuge," muttered Rudi.

"Die Zentrifuge!" The Russian looked around. On the wall were a hundred paintings in the Western decadent mode. None was even faintly realistic. Abstraction, Drakov believed it was called.

"It used to be a potato cellar," volunteered Rudi, horrified to see a flaming queen he knew smiling at him from a corner of the room.

"A friend of yours?" inquired Drakov.

"No," said Rudi shortly.

Drakov smiled; there was no warmth in it. He had decided not to tell Rudi of Pumml's fate but instead insisted that the dog had run out of the door and been taken in by a neighbor. Rudi wanted to inquire immediately, but the Russian told him there wasn't time. The librarian looked around at his apartment in abject misery, nodded, and obeyed. Drakov knew the warning signs; Rudi no longer cared whether he ived or died. He had reached the limit of his endurance. If he lost all of his truculence, he'd be obedient enough, but so passive as to be useless.

Rudi was well known, but he failed to acknowledge any greetings. His companion was the object of many appraising stares. Most held pity in them. Surely Rudi wasn't going with the little bald man? God, he must be in his seventies.

Drakov found it increasingly uncomfortable to be the focus of so much attention. He was overcome with an absurd desire to announce that he was not a homosexual. Neither Rudi nor Drakov ate anything. The Russian studied Rudi's map of the city taken from the glove compartment of the Honda, while the librarian stared vacantly into the middle distance.

As luck would have it, Drakov was quite familiar with the area where they were to search next. The Landwehr Canal flowed into the Spree just beyond the Schlesische tower. It would face the Wall across the canal. It all fit. No one in the West wanted to live in a building facing a ten-foot concrete wall surmounted by barbed wire. The place was surely a slum, so many years after the Wall had gone up. It would be ideal for addicts because they would be near the canal and the Spree. Drug deliveries could be made by boat; there was less chance of surprise, and plenty of opportunity to get rid of the evidence in case of police raids.

Night life was picking up its pace as Rudi, directed by Drakov, drove across the city. The Russian preferred the side streets to the Kudamm, which was always brightly lit at night. Police patrols were less in evidence, too. Though Drakov's papers were in order, Rudi was unpredictable.

Once clear of the blocks surrounding the Kudamm, the Honda and its occupants entered a no man's land. Crime festered in the back streets of Berlin, and Drakov eased out his weapon and put it in his coat pocket. Then he closed his eyes and appeared to be napping. He was not; he was allowing his subconscious to mull over his problems while resting his conscious mind. After such a session, he awoke refreshed. His body was no more immune to fatigue than anyone else's, but by controlling his mind, Drakov could exert a willpower that overrode physical strains. If the mind failed nothing could prevent the body's collapse; the mind was the key to everything.

He did not bother to look over his shoulder to see if they were being followed. It was certain they would be. Any thought of giving Kroptkov the slip was idiotic; Kroptkov was the best.

The neighborhood became rapidly more seedy. There were bars with neon signs offering drinks at prices that hadn't been valid since the signs were manufactured a decade before. Outside every one of them were groups of women. These were the professional whores, hard; a pimp and his seaman's knife would never be far away. These women were probably not addicts; junkies died young.

The canal was a turgid black mass of unmoving water. Boats lay still at their moorings. Some were hulks; some simply sank into the canal as their planks rotted away.

Rudi was getting agitated; twice men lurched out of the shadows and bumped into the Honda. A stream of poisonous invective followed.

"Stop here," ordered Drakov, at the end of a narrow street. "Now drive north until you feel comfortable, then wait. I shall join you later." It was not necessary to warn Rudi of the consequences of betrayal.

The Russian made his way parallel to the canal. On the far side was the Wall, a dingy gray concrete ribbon following the far bank. He could see that the sunken boats were all on the far side of the canal; they had been left there the day the Wall went up. Their owners claimed the insurance; the boats stayed.

Derelicts were lying in doorways; some stirred hopefully as he passed. Those clutching bottles turned away, fearing he would want to share their liquor. A tall woman with broad shoulders spoke to him in a curiously deep voice. He realized she was a transvestite, Germany's peculiarly national form of ultimate revolt.

The apartment building Wilhelm had directed him to was one of the grand postwar stone structures built to house the 90 percent of Berlin that was homeless. The exteriors were imposing, but the workmanship was shoddy. Inside, nothing was right. Most of the buildings could have been rebuilt for what it cost to fix them over the years.

A wrought-iron gate swung open at his touch. Not bothering with the elevator, for he knew it wouldn't work, Drakov moved up the stairs. At each floor there was a door leading into a hall four apartments faced it.

He knocked on the first door; when he thought the person inside was eyeing him through the spy-hole, he held up two purple foil packets. The door opened to the full extent of its chain and a face framed with matted hair and several days' growth of beard presented itself. Drakov silently handed over one of the foil packets. The door closed. A minute later it re-opened; the hand holding the door had white powder on its finger.

"Good stuff," said the man hoarsely, "but it isn't Christmas."

Drakov held up the other foil packet. "I'm looking for a girl called Ingrid."

"What for?" The tone was suspicious.

"She's special," said Drakov, trying to sound nervous and embarrassed. "Special."

The face smiled. "Give us the stuff, pervert."

Drakov didn't move.

"She's on the third floor of nineteen, next door." He reached out and seized the foil package. "Pervert."

The next building was identical except that its windows had all been boarded up with plywood. There was no sign of Kroptkov yet, but Drakov knew he wouldn't be far away. His hand closed on the butt of his Beretta.

In the near darkness, a barge went by, a line of clothes suspended by a rope from bow to smokestack.

Number 19 smelled awful. There was the familiar odor of cabbage, urine, and cheap disinfectant. Guest workers might have lived there at some time; that would account for the disinfectant. In the walls he heard the scampering of many tiny feet. Underfoot, the linoleum was cracked and curled.

By the time Drakov reached the second-floor landing, he was in darkness. He had a penlight, but it did little more than project a narrow beam ahead of him. He began his ascent to the third floor, the light shining ahead of him, his hand holding on to the wall for guidance. Halfway to the final landing his foot hit something heavy but yielding. Instantly he dropped to his knees, turning off the light. The Beretta was in his left hand. All was silence around him. In the distance, someone was shouting in a high female voice.

He turned on the flashlight. A man's body lay sprawled across the stairs. By the thin beam, Drakov saw a large gash in the forehead. It was five centimeters long, and the blood had congealed. Probably the man had fallen, knocking himself out, split his head on the edge of the concrete steps, and died of loss of blood. Since the corpse was stiff and the eyes cloudy, he estimated the body had lain there for at least three days.

Drakov searched the body; he found a plastic disposable syringe, a box of matches junkies used to resharpen blunt needles, and a cork with a needle in it. The body was beginning to decay; in a day or so, people walking by would be able to smell it.

The door to an apartment on the third floor was wide open. Before he stepped over the threshold, he stopped and listened. There were no sounds either in the apartment or on the stairs.

He stepped swiftly and silently into the darkened room. The stench hit him hard. Waiting until he was certain there were no sounds besides a leaking faucet, Drakov took out Rudi's lighter, broke the circuit, and adjusted the flame without looking at it; he didn't want dazzling floaters in front of his eyes for the next hour.

There was a light switch; when he pushed it, a single bulb in an otherwise empty brass chandelier above him went on. There was nothing left of the room. Garbage had been left where it fell, carpeting stripped away. Holding his automatic, Drakov made his way across the room, trying to place his feet on the cracks between the floorboards so as to stifle creaks.

A filthy blue army blanket shrouded the room beyond; Drakov stood next to it, listening. The sound of dripping water was louder, but he heard nothing else, not even the low breathing of a woman asleep.

Then all at once he realized the significance of the body in the hall, and with a cry of anger and frustration, he swept the blanket aside.

He was in a bedroom. A single sixty-watt bulb burned sullenly in a large cracked blue lamp. By its dim light, Drakov saw the girl.

Death had seized her days before. Looking at her wasted face, yellow with jaundice, he realized he had not prepared himself for this. All his careful planning had come to nothing. Too many of his hopes had rested in the pathetic wasted creature before him.

This dead sixteen-year-old girl had beaten Anton Drakov, deprived him of any hope of a welcome in Britain. Davies would not need him now. Worse, Drakov would be out of the game of foxes. The cleverest man in Europe had been beaten by a pitiful runaway teenage girl. That was bad enough; worse would follow. There was no question of going to Davies cap in hand. Without a bargaining chip, that deal was off.

And still there was Kroptkov. Outside. Soon the malignant spider would come looking for his fly.

Quickly, Drakov made preparations. A smell of gas began filling the room.

21 The Georgi

Ricketts left his flat in Culford Gardens at ten o'clock and drifted down to King's Road. He'd had a flat in the Gardens for five years. Before being thrown out of SAS, it had been handy because it was near the Duke of York's HQ, a sprawling mass of stone that served as the London base of Strategic Air Services.

Usually he walked down to Sloane Square, where there was always a decent pickup either in the square itself under the plane trees or in front of the Royal Court Theatre, near the fountain. This time he turned right and went west. The weather was warm and that brought the tarts out. They couldn't whine to their nigger pimps that it was too cold to go outside. They'd be fucking like rabbits tonight.

The King's Road on a sunny weekend was the magnet for locals and tourists alike. There was plenty of chance of meeting something decent strolling in front of the boutiques and specialty stores. The farther away he went from the square, the lower the prices got. He preferred whores to ordinary horny bitches looking for a good time. The girls on the game couldn't squawk to anyone except a pimp, and Ricketts

.ad dealt with a score of them. It was an added hrill.

Across the road, in front of the Duke of 'ork's, the punks were gathering on their fa- orite perches, the windowsills of the HQ.

A furtive creature slid out of a side street, ap- roached him, and began his routine. "Mister, I aven't eaten for—"

Ricketts seized the young man's hand, wisting and forcing the youth to the kneeling osition. Then Ricketts put the boot in, and the nan collapsed to the ground and lay there ;asping for breath. He would have kicked him a ew more times, but a few strollers were looking n, so he quickened his pace. Slipping across the oad by threading his way between the bright ed double-deckers and the taxis, he breathed asier. He had been told to stay out of any un- necessary entanglements; a thing like that ould bring unwelcome attention. Still, punks nd panhandlers made his blood boil; colored piky hair and gold rings through their noses, hey were arseholes. They should be castrated r, better still, drafted into the army. They'd earn some fuckin' discipline then.

It struck him that the King's Road was be- coming more and more fairy. Boutiques were pringing up everywhere, Fiorucci, the Jean Machine. Everywhere he looked there were queers nancing around in tight pants with eather accoutrements. Last week one had ap- proached him in Limehouse; Ricketts went with nim to a narrow street and broke two of his fin- gers. He could still hear the pops—and the screams of agony. Jesus, everywhere he looked there were queers. Wellington Square was fu of them. Dumb bastards glaring at him; he gav them the finger, but they didn't go for hin They knew who he was. Forty-five years ag they'd have been Nazis except they lacked th discipline for it. Instead of beating up Jews, thi bunch took to Pavki bashing whenever the could find an Indian or Pakistani. Ricketts ha no great quarrel with this, however. Years i the SAS had confirmed his belief in the whit man's superiority over niggers and wogs. An Arab would steal the fillings from your teeth i you turned your back on him. They had th right attitude on women, though, he had t hand them that. You fucked them any way yo liked, and after a few weeks you chucked ther out and started on something fresh. Wogs coul handle cunts all right.

He was outside Henry J. Bean's, a so-calle American-style beer parlor. Going in, he walke through to the back garden. A sign claimed th parlor was built on the site of an inn frequente by Charles II; probably got the clap here, though Ricketts.

He cast a look around the garden with it little tables and colored lights and realized h was the only single person there with the excep tion of a fat woman who'd followed him in Christ, no one would touch her. She squinte through thick glasses and had no eyebrows.

Ordering a beer, he inspected the drinkers. I was disappointing not to find a single woman o a couple of working girls. It was a matter c waiting; all waiters and barmen were in cahoot with call girls. They took 10 percent of the ac tion, and everyone was happy. Presumably the same system worked at an American beer parlor.

The fat woman dug around in her handbag, then seemed to despair of service. Up she got, a galleon in full sail, and left. Fat bitch. The thought of laying that tub of lard make him puke.

It didn't worry him to be alone. He'd always been a loner; even in the army he'd kept to himself. Without his great strength and superb marksmanship, he would never have made it into the SAS, because teamwork was everything to them.

The waiter was looking down at him. "Watney's Dark," he told the man. Ricketts disliked the pissy taste of American beer. Most of all he hated those television commercials. Some ex-jock with a fat gut tried to be charming and got a million quid for doing nothing.

When the beer came it was in one of the liter glasses. The good old pint was a thing of the past. The beer was ice cold, so the taste was all but lost.

A brunette came into the garden and took the table next to his. Eyeing her over the top of his glass, he wondered if she was a professional. Ricketts preferred blondes and had lost his virginity at the age of fifteen to one in a hayloft. Damn, the very thought of it gave him a hard-on. He could still remember her name, Suzette Gormly. None of the hundreds after her had made any impression on him. Most were whores, and if they told you a name, it was probably phony.

Suzette wasn't perfect; she had small tits an smoked like a chimney. The smell of burnt to bacco clung to her, but she had mad eyes an loved to screw.

Her father caught them at it one afternoo when he came home from work early. Both c them stark naked, and Suzette, who was a rea moaner, the type he liked, bellowing like a bul Smiling at the recollection, he took a long drin of his beer. Neither of them knew a damn thin about protection. It was a wonder he hadn' knocked her up and a dozen more.

When he was eighteen his parents kicked hin out. Since he'd left school illegally at fourteen he couldn't get anything but casual unskille laboring jobs. That didn't worry him, but hi parents wanted him off their hands. "It's up t you, Sidney," said his father. "You can't sponge off us forever."

That left the army.

"Another?" asked the waiter. Ricketts shook his head. "Tastes like iced piss," he said, bu without any rancor.

Until he'd been recruited by Ivan, life wa rough. To be kicked out of SAS for continua drunken fighting in bars was no recommenda tion for Civvy Street. His pension was next to nothing, yet his unemployment was adjuste downward accordingly. It seemed a godsen when he was given the chance to rig up some little accidents for several thousand each time The bastards probably deserved to die.

Looking at the brunette again, he summe her up. He didn't want a high-priced hooker. N one but a foreigner or a raving lunatic went af ter nightclub hostesses. The bitches sometimes charged a tenner just to talk to a man. While they talked, they drank water and the client drank watered-down whiskey. The bar bill alone would take the backbone out of a stiff prick. He'd seen the old empty-glass routine worked a hundred times on Lancashire businessmen and a few stupid but rich wog kids. A champagne bottle was opened and a couple of glasses poured. After that the hovering waiter whisks away the glass "empty" and tops it up with an "empty" glass from another sucker. Small drinking clubs were best; girls new to the game would do a lot for a tenner because they still liked fucking. Finally they would get like the rest of the sisterhood—hard as precast concrete.

The brunette was drinking hard stuff. She looked clean. A couple of young things tottered by on high heels, miniskirts up to their crotches and short leather jackets. They giggled incessantly, jabbering about finding the loo. Experience told him they were jailbait. As they disappeared, he saw they were already developing the strange ducklike walk of Englishwomen.

The brunette spoke. "You like that? Or do you prefer a woman?"

Ricketts didn't answer. She was testing him; the laws of England did not actually make prostitution a crime, but it was a crime to solicit.

She stretched out her legs; they were long and, as far as Ricketts could tell through her jeans, shapely. The tits were clearly outlined under her T-shirt. Already he could feel the nipples against the hair on his chest. Jesus, she was a good piece, long, dark hair parted in the middle and falling around her shoulders. The way she was manipulating her cigarette between thin fingers with bright red nail polish . . . it was as clear a come-on as any he'd seen. He stood up; she took his arm. "Name's Frances," she said.

She had a flat in Labrooke Grove, so they took a cab. He wanted to paw her in the taxi, and she took his hand, placing it inside her blouse. He would have gone further; he liked the idea of doing her in the taxi, making her yell, getting the driver's respect. He would have done it, too, except she cradled his head and whispered promises of what she'd do once they were alone in her room. She massaged him through his pants.

Ricketts carefully checked out the house and its approaches before he let himself relax. He wasn't afraid of the old bunco game; if any enraged husband came through the bedroom door, Ricketts would take great pleasure in smashing his face in. No, it was his business with Ivan that made him wary.

The bedroom was pleasantly furnished and there were clean sheets on the bed. Frances, opened the dresser drawer. Ricketts' hand closed on her wrist and she gasped in pain.

"Let's take a little look," he said, rummaging around. It was clean. The girl took out a black negligee, the uniform of the amateur. He was surprised.

They undressed, throwing clothes carelessly

on the single chair. Frances allowed him a quick fondling of her breasts, then laughed, running out of the room, leaving him a fleeting vision of firm, tight buttocks. She slipped into the bathroom, taking the black negligee with her.

"There's some photos in the top drawer," she said. "I've got to make a visit."

The photos were porn of the kind selling for several pounds each. Some were Polaroids, and he wondered if any were of Frances. There was no way to tell, since all were gynecological shots. "Any of you?" he asked, hearing the toilet flush.

"You'll find out," she called to him. "But I've got to go to work tomorrow. Special order. Wind the alarm and set it for eight, will you?"

Ricketts threw the pictures on the dresser, sat down on the side of bed, and turned the key on the back of the alarm clock.

Immediately there was a short, burning pain. Examining the back of the clock, he saw a small projection welded to the winder. While he was staring at it, he heard the front door slam.

And because there wasn't anything he could do about it, he lay back on the bed and laughed and laughed.

Ivan would be next. The bastards knew; they had lured him to this flat and given him a georgi. A poison named for the unfortunate Bulgarian, Georgi Markov, who had been poisoned by a tiny pellet jabbed into his thigh by a man's umbrella. The poison was racin, a highly toxic substance derived from the seeds of the castor oil plant. It was too rich. Ricketts had been the man with the umbrella.

Soon he stopped laughing; the racin, twice as strong as cobra venom, was racing through his system. The pinprick enlarged to an unbearable pain. He put back his head and howled in agony. Both lungs were like steel mesh, solid and unyielding. He was drowning in pain. From head to toes, he was being crushed in a vise, which was his own body. His eyes stood out from their sockets. The room became a blur, then nothing. From every pore in his tormented body, sweat drenched him. Any movement caused the most exquisite pain. His temperature quickly climbed to 105 degrees. After that he lost consciousness and then, his life.

When the butcher boys' van pulled up in front of the house, Sidney Ricketts was staring lifelessly at the ceiling.

22 Standoff

In the shadow, Kroptkov, the assassin, waited; he had all the time in the world. From his position in a doorway he could see the apartment. The tiny flickering light that strayed occasionally through the ill-fitting plywood sealing the windows allowed him to follow Drakov's progress through the darkened rooms. The pleasant ruminations that often intruded on Kroptkov's consciousness at other times—frightened women's faces, himself kneeling over naked bodies—were banished. He was fully alert, his hunter's instinct finely tuned. Tonight he would find the girl, kill her, then deal with the British agent as painfully as possible. True, he'd been told to bring the girl back, but they must know that was impossible. Much easier to kill her and the agent, then disappear home to Russia and a grateful Popovich.

A couple came along the street beside the canal; he shrank back. They were both drunk and fell into fits of laughter as the man relieved himself in the dank, still water. They moved on, unaware that they had passed within a few yards of Kroptkov.

Surprise overtook the assassin as a steady,

weak light shone in the apartment. That was unexpected. He had assumed the agent and the girl would come out of the building, making his task simple. The light puzzled him. Possibly the agent was helping the girl prepare for her journey, possibly he was telling her what he knew. Whatever it was, he must be aware he was being followed. The light was almost a challenge. It said, "I know you're out there. Come in and get me."

Noiselessly he slid across the street, hugging the shadows; a minute later he was inside the apartment building, standing at the foot of the stairs. Three floors above, light spilled out onto the darkened landing.

Kroptkov had a premonition of danger. The apartment was a bomb waiting to go off; someone had measured a fuse, cut it, and was waiting to light it. Yet frontal attack was the only possible way. There was no way he could climb up the front of the building and gain entry by the wrought-iron balcony. He had considered it, but the windows were all covered with plywood. They couldn't be pried open without everyone in the street hearing, and inside the apartment it would echo like a drum roll. There was no rear exit, he had checked that. The metal fire escapes had all been carted off for scrap years before. No. He would have to climb those stairs if he expected to enter the apartment.

He took a Sauer Model 39 pistol from its holster. It was his policy to use a weapon from the country he was in. Weapons were international, it was true, but there was no need to start any unnecessary line of questioning.

The Model 38 was extremely valuable in situations like the one he found himself in. Gently pulling on the slide, he cocked the weapon. The sound was distinct and brittle. Looking up anxiously at the landing above, he checked for movement. There wasn't any. Mentally he cursed himself for not cocking the weapon when he was outside the building. It was a mistake and a stupidly unnecessary one.

In the darkness he could feel the loaded chamber indicator projecting from the rear of the slide. A round had been chambered; he pressed down on the cocking lever, safely lowering the hammer so the cartridge could be carried in the firing chamber in complete safety. Even experts might trip and fall in dark places. It wasn't injury to themselves that counted. It was the alarm that was inevitably sounded. Should anything happen suddenly, the Sauer could be fired by pulling straight through on the trigger, which would trip the hammer to fire the cartridge. Alternatively, pressure on the cocking lever would recock the hammer if he waited to take more deliberate aim.

A silencer was necessary. Like all excellent marksmen, he hated them; silencers were like lead shoes on a racehorse. They suppressed the sound of the discharge but they also reduced muzzle velocity until it was below the speed of sound. The bullet didn't penetrate the sound barrier with its characteristic crack. But the automatic had to have a specially modified barrel with tiny holes allowing the gas to escape into a diffuser. Bullets traveled at only a thousand feet per second. Worse still, the balance of the weapon was all wrong, and it was bulky.

Groping his way in almost total darkness, his weapon at the ready, Kroptkov made his way up to the first landing. The concrete wall was cold and damp. He felt a light switch but didn't dare try it, for if the bulb were anywhere near him, he would present an easy helpless target, standing in the light. Creeping up to the first landing, he paused to control his breathing. Then he resumed climbing.

He paused again to listen for sounds; outside he heard a car door slam and an engine turn over three times before catching. But ahead, where the patch of light spilled through the partially open door, he sensed no movement and heard no sound. Kroptkov swallowed; his lips were dry, but his pulse was steady. If his heart beat a little faster than usual, it was from excitement, not fear.

The British agent had been inside the house for almost an hour. He would certainly know the danger he was in, and he would not underestimate his adversary. But *what was he doing?*

The assassin sensed the presence of something lying directly ahead of him; his superb training and natural instinct alerted him. He stopped, knelt, and felt the body. It was cold; rigor mortis had set in. It was not his adversary's body. He eased past, keeping himself low against the wall, eyes fixed on the door above. He caressed the Sauer against his cheek; the feel of the metal against his skin was comforting.

Still he heard nothing; the normal sounds,

furnaces or gas fires, televisions, people fighting, all were missing. If the agent was in the third-floor apartment, why was there no sound? Floorboards always creaked.

From the canal came the sound of a hooter; then the barge chugged by. He followed the noise for several minutes until it disappeared into the Spree. While there was noise outside he could do nothing; all his senses must be riveted on the apartment above.

An awful thought crossed his mind and quickly he descended to the second-floor landing and tried the apartment door. All his attention had been focused on the apartment above; what if his adversary were lying in wait behind him? He might have fallen for one of the oldest tricks in the book.

The door did not open. Feeling around the frame, he encountered several large nails; the door had been nailed shut. Quickly, silently, he checked the other two doors. All had nails in them.

Kroptkov pressed on the cocking lever of the Sauer. The hammer was recocked. The bullets, despite their lowered velocity, would not merely kill the British agent, they would disintegrate him. All were soft-nosed, designed to tear an adversary apart. The sound of the lever startled Kroptkov. He froze, pressing his body against the concrete wall. He waited, listened, then continued his journey.

Midway up, he went into a low crouch; there would be little target for someone above to aim for. Now the balance tipped in his favor. From his low angle, Kroptkov could see anyone outlined against the light inside the room, while he himself would be only a dark smudge in the blackness. The British agent had delayed too long. Now it was too late.

Kroptkov heard him at last. Someone was breathing; straining all his senses, he could just hear the regular breathing and, occasionally, a movement.

The last four steps scarcely felt his passing; he brushed by like a breeze and stood beside the door. He touched it, and it began to swing open slowly. He was to the right of it, and as it swung open, he could see into the room.

The only furniture was an old leather armchair and an ancient rickety table. On the table was a lamp, its shade gone. A forty-watt bulb glowed feebly. In the chair sat a small man in his sixties, his elbows resting on the arms, his fingers laced together.

"So we meet at last," the man said, speaking Russian.

Kroptkov raised the Model 38. The man in the chair merely smiled.

2

The Sauer was aimed directly at Drakov's stomach. The first shot wouldn't kill, but the bullet would take out enough bones, flesh, and viscera to immobilize. The coup de grace could follow immediately or, if Kroptkov felt like it, some time later.

"I see you have the silenced Model 38," said Drakov in a voice so quiet it betrayed nothing of the emotion racing through him. He was taking a terrible risk with a creature little more than a killing machine. If Kroptkov had any mercy in him he would be aiming for the head. When a man aimed for the guts, he was preparing to enjoy himself.

Kroptkov was standing very still, just inside the door, his back to the wall so he could see the stairs outside as well as Drakov. Finally he closed the door with his free hand and locked it.

"Who are you?"

"Anton Mikhailovich Drakov."

The Sauer wavered briefly.

"You know my name." Drakov inclined his head ever so slightly. "I'm flattered."

"You're dead."

Drakov stood. "An exaggeration. As you can see I am in excellent health."

"Where's the girl?"

"In the bedroom. I'm afraid we have both been wasting our time. It seems she took an overdose, and the boy out there was going for help when he fell. They've both been dead two or three days."

With a slight movement of the Sauer, Kroptkov indicated that Drakov should turn around. Running his fingers over him, he found nothing more significant than a cigarette lighter.

Kroptkov stepped back from Drakov and looked quickly around the apartment. It had ten-foot ceilings and expensive-looking wallpaper. Nothing else remained, for its series of occupants had stripped the place long ago of anything that could be sold. Empty fish cans had been tossed on the floor, cigarette butts floating in the oil. Paper cups, each with a little water and more cigarette ends, dotted the room. The carpet had long since been taken up. No doubt it was in some guest worker's front room. On the wooden boards, stains of all kinds mingled in a patchwork of muted colors. Some were human blood; most addicts cleaned their spikes by filling the pump with water and shooting the pink residue onto the floor.

There was a strong odor of gas.

"Where's the gas smell coming from?"

"There was a burner left on on the gas cooker, but I turned it off."

Kroptkov nodded. He knew junkies would boil water in an attempt to sterilize needles. But the nearness of the drug made them frantic and they didn't wait for the water to boil. Instead they shot up and forgot about the boiling saucepan of water until they came out of it hours later. The girl and the man on the stairs hadn't come out of it.

"Bedroom," he grunted, and Drakov led the way.

There was just an old army blanket serving as a curtain. Kroptkov understood; doors made noises and addicts found noise unbearable.

The bedroom was large and nearly empty. Someone had taped to the wall a large poster with the hand of a skeleton holding a syringe. Its original words had been blocked out, and over the top of them was written, "Party time."

Beyond lay the bathroom, its mosaic tile walls and floor evidence of pre-Wall elegance.

Now the toilet was blocked; water dripped over the rim. The sink hung crazily from one bolt, its waste pipe going nowhere. In the bathtub lay several crushed beer cans, and dozens of cigarette ends floated in the rusty, scummy water, as well as some swollen sanitary napkins.

Still pointing the Model 38 at Drakov's back, just to the right of his spine, Kroptkov knelt and looked under the bed. A large, white, stinking chamberpot and a brassiere covered with dust mice were all he found.

Only then did he turn his attention to the body of Ingrid Thummel. She was dressed in panties and a man's shirt. He had thought she would look older; her face was yellow and emaciated, but unmistakably young. Lank brown hair hung next to her long, hollow-cheeked face. Incredibly, she had bothered to put on makeup. Her eyes were constricted, characteristic of heroin addicts.

The rest of her body was badly wasted: her arms were no more than matchsticks and her legs were pallid, shapeless flesh.

"Turn her over," Kroptkov said, and Drakov did as he was ordered, sliding his arms under the body. As he turned her, a syringe and an opened purple foil package were revealed. Kroptkov motioned Drakov away and picked up the syringe. The spike had broken off; he found the tip in a vein in the girl's leg. He suspected a hot shot. The few grains of powder left in the packet were not white or brown; the greenish speckles told him it was the ultimate shot—M powder. The effect was a tremendous jolt to the heart. The strain had killed the girl; the boy, running for help, tripped and died from his fall. It was neat. They wouldn't be happy in Moscow for the girl was dead. But with Drakov's death they would at least be relieved, possibly even grateful.

Drakov must be dealt with correctly.

Kroptkov inspected the kitchen next, keeping his weapon trained on the older man. The kitchen was a filthy, stinking room and the smell of gas was powerful. He was glad to drop back the curtain, cross the living room, and return with Drakov to the bedroom. He told the little old man to sit in the only chair.

"I suppose you're going to shoot me now," Drakov said in a dry, old man's voice.

Kroptkov nodded. He'd heard so much about Drakov; the reality was disappointing. Even the first mention of Drakov's name had made his chest tighten. The little bald creature was so . . . ineffectual.

"Just aim the Sauer, pull the trigger, and no more Drakov."

Kroptkov nodded. "Unless I decide to prolong it."

Drakov looked increasingly frightened. In his right hand was the lighter, and he was nervously playing with it. Kroptkov wondered if he should make Drakov beg for his life, make him go down on his knees and grovel.

"I could be merciful," he said slowly.

"Merciful?" Drakov's voice cracked.

"Hit a vital spot. Or I could smash a bone. Have you ever seen anyone shot in the spine?"

When Drakov didn't answer, Kroptkov felt

excited. He had the famous Drakov at his mercy.

"If you kill me," Drakov spoke, "you will be a hero in certain quarters. And I'm sure money holds no appeal for you."

Kroptkov snarled. "You fool. Money is nothing to me."

"Exactly, exactly," agreed Drakov soothingly. "I said to myself, what is it Vasily Romanovich Kroptkov values?"

The assassin found himself listening. The weary eyes of the old man seemed, somehow, compelling.

"And then I thought to myself," Drakov continued, settling back in the chair, "I thought to myself, while Vasily Romanovich is climbing the stairs, what can I do?"

"Run for your life?"

"Naturally, I thought of escape. At my age"—he made a deprecating gesture—"every day is precious."

"So?"

"I thought, if I go downstairs, I will be shot. If I hide behind the door and wait, Vasily Romanovich will know what I am up to. He is a master in these matters. In books"—he stressed the word contemptuously—"the hero escapes after a dramatic chase and shoot-out. In real life, even Drakov must lose when he's opposed by the State Assassin."

Kroptkov nodded. "You're pretty smart."

"Thank you," said Drakov gratefully. "You've made my point. I am smart. And you, Kroptkov, are not."

The assassin was irritated by the unexpected

change in Drakov's behavior, but he controlled himself. "Then why am I holding this gun, and why are you about to die?"

Drakov was no longer lounging in his chair. He was sitting upright, his eyes boring into Kroptkov's skull as if he meant to take control of his mind. Kroptkov wrenched his eyes from the hypnotic stare.

"For me, Vasily Romanovich, intellectual contests are all that matters. Things of the flesh do not concern me. The great chess players seldom make mistakes, but if they are defeated, it is because the opponent has found a chink in their psychological armor."

Again Kroptkov found his eyes held by Drakov's.

"The thing that Kroptkov values most is his life. That is why, once a month, he hangs himself in ropes to achieve a sexual orgasm. To the brink of death he goes, and then pulls back."

"You know about that?" Kroptkov's astonishment was comical.

"I know all about you."

The assassin sought to regain his self-possession. "Talk all you want," he said triumphantly, "but I have this." He pointed the Sauer at Drakov's head.

"And I," replied Drakov, "have this." Opening his palm, he showed the cigarette lighter.

Kroptkov felt absurdly relieved; the desire to laugh at the old man's stupidity was almost overpowering. Was he senile? Unless . . . unless . . . the lighter was a weapon of some sort. Had it been modified to fire a poison dart? He shrugged off his fear. Any movement by Drakov and Kroptkov would kill him long before there was any danger to himself.

"It's just an ordinary lighter."

Drakov sighed elaborately. "My friend Rudi would hate to hear that. It's very expensive, at least I think it is. To ignite it, you merely break a contact between these two points." He showed Kroptkov. "Then a spark ignites the butane gas and—"

"Gas!"

Kroptkov whirled around. The smell of gas was much worse, wasn't it?

Drakov stood up and the assassin turned to him. "Do not be foolish, old man. The slightest move and I shall remove your head."

Drakov eyed him shrewdly. "In the end, one is always defeated by stupidity—in this case, your own. If you shoot me, this lighter will certainly ignite. I have set it for the longest flame possible. This apartment, and several more, will go up in a new holocaust."

"You'll be killed too." Kroptkov's voice faltered for a moment.

"Yes, but I will die *either* way," Drakov pointed out reasonably. "You have a chance to live."

"A chance?"

"I will spare you, if you give me the gun."

Kroptkov looked at him incredulously. "What do you think I am? And you turned the gas off, anyway."

"I *told* you I turned it off, but . . . surely you noticed it has been getting worse?"

The assassin realized the smell of gas was far more powerful than when he'd entered the apartment. Frantically, he tried to think. What kind of gas was it? Would it explode? Could he reach the door before it did? Could he turn it off?

Kroptkov was in the grip of an emotion he had never known; it was fear. How could this little man be so detached while discussing his own death? He didn't seem afraid to die—yet Kroptkov knew he must be. The assassin certainly was.

Beads of sweat formed on Kroptkov's brow. He had the weapon, after all, and Drakov had nothing.

"Use the cocking lever to lower the hammer."

"I can't. I . . ."

"Vasily Romanovich, lower the hammer."

Kroptkov was wavering. While urging him to lower the hammer, Drakov had halved the distance between them. He was now three feet from Kroptkov. He could ignite the lighter anytime.

"Lower the hammer. Then there will be less danger of an accidental firing," said Drakov softly, taking another half-pace.

The automatic came up quickly, pointed directly at his face. At this distance it was supremely dangerous because so many unpredictable factors were involved. Timing, above all, would decide the outcome.

"The gas is very volatile," Drakov added gently. "It could explode on its own. There are always bare flames . . ."

Now, if he chose, he could reach out and grasp Kroptkov's weapon. That in itself would guarantee nothing. If the man fought he would throw Drakov off as a dog shakes off water, or the Sauer would go off.

Kroptkov felt the air heavy with gas, closing
n on him. If it exploded . . . if . . . In his mind
e saw himself, a ball of fire rushing helplessly
round the apartment as the flames consumed
is flesh. Once he had seen a man burned by na-
alm; for weeks the man pleaded for death. And
hen he was finally released from the hospital,
eople turned their heads. A day later, the man
illed himself.

So when Kroptkov, the assassin, looked into
)rakov's eyes, he saw not the hazel-tinted
enses, and not the gaze of an old man. He saw
he eyes of a man who could not lose.

The quiet voice held absolute authority.
Give me the gun, Vasily Romanovich."

Perhaps it was the voice, perhaps it was the
yes, perhaps it was no more than the familiar
se of his name, but Kroptkov lowered the
auer. Anton Drakov reached forward and took
t from his limp hand.

The old man was standing beside him, his
and on the automatic. Kroptkov felt Drakov's
reathing on the side of his face. It was a relief
o let the old man take the weapon from him.
here was now no danger of burning.

Too late, he saw the flash of the needle in Dra-
ov's hand. Too late he pulled back from the brief
tinging pain as the needle slid into his vein.

When the flash came, he had to hold his head.
tremendous cramp seized the region of his
eart. The arm with the needle in it was in-
tantly paralyzed. A sledgehammer blow struck
is head and his skin tingled as if pricked by a
nillion sharp needles.

Then nothing.

3

When the assassin regained consciousness, hi feet were tied, one to each leg of the bed, an his hands were fastened together and secured t the dresser, which had been dragged across th room. The bonds were fashioned from the bec sheets. He was naked and ashamed.

Drakov sat on the foot of the bed, looking a his prisoner.

"Is your head clear or shall I throw som water over you?"

Kroptkov nodded.

"Good. My mission has been completed, but have a question or two. I will get the answer one way or another. There is, of course, n chance of your escaping alive. You have see me."

His hand went into his pocket; to Kroptkov' horror he pulled out the packet of cigarettes h had taken from the unconscious Kroptkov.

"The gas!" he screamed. "The gas!" His voic sounded far away and puny.

Drakov nodded. "The gas, yes. You were no chosen for your wits, Vasily Romanovich, or yo would not have fallen for that old trick. I turne the gas on for a while, then off. Once you plan the idea"—he paused—"in a weak mind, tha there is gas escaping, it is extraordinarily eas to suggest the situation is worsening. It wa not."

Passing his hand through the lighter, he watched the flame shoot out. Adjusting it, Drakov added, "You see, I didn't lie about this fancy lighter." He drew a lungful of smoke and continued. "So the only question is, Are you willing to tell me who sent you here or not?"

Kroptkov was silent.

"Do I have to hurt you to demonstrate how serious I am?"

To Kroptkov it appeared all his senses had been heightened. His body had no feelings in its limbs. Floating, that was it: he was borne up by some thick liquid. Only in his arm, where the needle had found the vein, was there a slight sting.

"The natural effect of heroin is to take away pain," continued Drakov, "but I have some knowledge of such matters, and I would like to get out of here as quickly as I can."

Kroptkov looked at him. "No!" he said defiantly.

Drakov shrugged and left the room. He was gone for a long time. Gradually the feeling crept back into Kroptkov's limbs. The drug left him on a rocky coastline. Intermittently the nerves in his legs and arms caused excruciating pain. Then he would be racked with cramps, making him try to double up. The bonds cut into his wrists and ankles. Sometimes he moaned.

Drakov returned at last and stood in the middle of the room, facing the spread-eagled Kroptkov. "Now. Who sent you after the girl?"

No answer.

"We have been here three hours," said Drakov. "I would like to be gone before morning."

"I searched you," Kroptkov said hoarsely.

"Of course you did. I knew you would, so I hi my Beretta and this syringe down the side the armchair. Who searches armchairs?"

The assassin strained at his bonds; Drako gave his wintry smile. "Naturally, I can g anyone to talk; the problem is time. A saltwat douche in the throat is ineffectual for a day c two. I cannot spare the time to grate your ski off even if I had a grater and some turpentine t rub in the wounds."

He sat on the end of the bed. "And I don't su pose I could beat it out of you as Ryumin love to do—once he had covered his Persian carp with an oilskin."

Drakov folded his arms. "All those method are barbaric. They date back to the tsars. But must know who set you on me."

He surveyed the assassin. "Who sent you? He was staring directly into Kroptkov's eye the assassin found he couldn't turn his fac away. The look in Drakov's eyes was like a ste bar joining the two of them. But Kroptko would not break. He said nothing.

Drakov shrugged. "Vasily Romanovich, yo disappoint me," he said, his voice low with me ace. "Surely you realize I will have my wa sooner or later. Who sent you? Answer only tha and you have earned yourself an easy death. He dropped his cigarette on the floor an ground it out. Then he stood between Krop kov's legs, the toe of his shoe resting on Krop kov's sex organs. Tentatively Drakov increase the pressure. The assassin struggled, his bod arching.

"Most torturers are either fanatical believer

deranged psychotics. They can be brain-ashed or motivated by giving them special rivileges. But they remain, like you, my dear asily Romanovich, the dregs of the human spe-es."

Looking down at the quivering Kroptkov, he dded more pressure. The strips holding the an's wrists bit deeply. "This was a favorite ethod of the interrogator Mironenko, who ourished in the Dzhida camps in 1944. It is ude but terribly effective." He increased the ressure.

The assassin's fingers were all extended rig-lly. His lips curled back, revealing the gums. A rrible smell arose as his bowels failed; a pool f urine spurted from the penis.

"I've heard it said," Drakov continued when roptkov lay still, "that if you remain immo-ile, and if I don't press down too firmly, you till have fifteen seconds in which to tell me ant I want."

The scream came after only ten seconds; ex-losive, born from Kroptkov's very soul. High-itched and loud, it would have been heard by ll the neighbors, but there were none. It might ave been heard by the police, but they didn't other with the canal region.

"Popoviiiich!" he screamed. "Popoviiich!" hen the scream became a sob and soon Kropt-ov, the State Assassin, lay silent.

Drakov knelt by him. "Did you say Popovich? e sure now." Kroptkov nodded. It was a relief tell the man what he wanted to know. Per-aps now he could die in peace.

"Who sent you? One more time."

"Popovich. Oh God, how many times?"

Kroptkov's eyes rolled up and his face we blank.

Before he left, Drakov turned on the g again. Eventually the building would fill wi explosive vapors; a naked light somewhe would ignite it, and all the evidence would gone. Hurrying down the street, he turned ov in his mind what he could do. The fat ma couldn't be trusted, and he didn't have Ingrid deliver, anyhow. He would go to England, ye But once there he would be extremely carefu At the first opportunity, Drakov would disa pear.

Rudi sat in the Honda, waiting for his maste Drakov wasn't surprised; he expected no les Waving at Rudi, he waited for the car to pic him up. When the car didn't move, Drakov a sumed the librarian had fallen asleep. H walked the street to the red car. Rudi wasn asleep. The deep jagged cut around his nec had stopped bleeding some time ago. His eye stared straight ahead. Kroptkov had kept thi final secret from him: Drakov admired that.

"Poor Rudi," said Drakov, closing the lid over the staring eyes. "I'm afraid we will not b having that pineapple together after all."

Anton Mikhailovich Drakov started walkin to the subway station at Gorlitzer. He was hal way there when the sky was lit by a burst brilliant orange light. The shattering sound the explosion was heard a mile away as ripped out a huge section of the front wall of th apartment building. At the epicenter of th blast nothing remained but a blackened hole, a a rotten tooth had been jerked from its socket. he facade slowly collapsed under its own eight and slid forward. The street was an :ean of glass and onto this base fell concrete, ·naments, wrought iron, plaster, and great 1uares of plywood, falling like giant leaves.

The shock wave stirred the turgid water of ıe canal, slapping it noisily against its banks. he rotten planking of a moored barge gave ay and the boat settled heavily in the muddy ater, its deck just above waterline.

There was only one fatality. When the emer- ency forces arrived, they found a woman, ressed in the shreds of her clothes, stumbling lindly through the ruins cradling in her arms ıe headless body of a child and screaming in urkish.

Before the first fire engine arrived, Anton Iikhailovich Drakov was boarding a subway ·ain. Within forty-eight hours, he would be in ngland.

23 Hell Fire Club

Alaister Strachan waited impatiently at th Red Bull in High Wycombe. It was almost nir o'clock at night. When Davies arrived, in black Rover, he said curtly, "It had better b worth it, Joshua. I had to catch the slow trai from Glasgow."

"Sorry," replied Davies as Strachan climbe into the backseat beside him, "but we must a make sacrifices. I was planning to dine a Keats. Aron Misan took my reservation him self."

Strachan rested his heavy-lidded gaze on hi companion's bulk. Without saying a word, h conveyed his distaste for Joshua Davies. Th rear of the car stank of cigar smoke. Th ashtray was full. Strachan slid it away, out o sight and smell.

"Must be something big then. Am I to be in formed as to what it is, or is it a secret?"

"I've just had a message from a very interes ing chap who just got back from abroad."

The driver sat ramrod stiff, watching the roa ahead. It was dark and they were taking second ary roads whenever possible. Interestingl enough, a second man sat up front beside th driver. Davies was packing two butcher boys. Something was up, thought Strachan, and Davies was being coy.

"It's a guessing game, Joshua, is it?" There was a soft, very Scottish sibilance to his speech. "It must be quite important if you've turned down an evening at Keats. The wine cellar isn't quite depleted, as I recall."

Davies cracked a smile, a great pink parting of the rolls of flesh, as if the memory were a joyous one.

"A few vintages survive," he agreed. "If you know what to order. Of course, I have to take it easy. Dol and I are defending our tango championship next month. We've held it two years running. Our mother was Argentine; she taught us."

Stratchan looked out the window. "We're off to West Wycombe, I see."

Davies had taken out his cigar case and was sizing up its contents. "Care for one?" he asked suddenly. "They're Jamaican."

"No, thanks."

The Director shook his head. "They take a little getting used to. Ever been there?"

"Jamaica?"

"No. The place on the estate."

"No." The gray gaze enveloped Davies. His eyes were hard under the heavy lids, inhuman.

"Dol and I are off to Jamaica this Christmas."

The Director was rummaging through his pockets. Strachan could stand it no longer, and from his own pocket he drew a slim gold lighter.

"Thanks," muttered Davies gratefully. Then they sat for a good ten minutes saying nothing.

The back of the car filled with smoke. Stracha wound his window down three inches. The rush ing of the wind past the car was loud enough t force Davies to raise his voice when he began t speak.

"You may recall my mentioning somethir about that girl in Berlin. Vice President Lette ville's daughter."

"Don't be smug, Joshua. Of course I remem ber. Is she in the bag?"

"She's dead."

There was a short silence.

"So. Your operation failed, then. Well, it's a I've always said, an intelligence service is lik an ugly woman. There's a terrible wait betwee orgasms. Our successes are like that, Joshua Very few and very far between. Still, it's a di appointment for all of us. Any lost chance to in gratiate ourselves with the Americans mus be—"

His companion cleared his throat. "This isn anything to do with the girl."

"You could have fooled me, Joshua."

"I did."

"Then what *is* it about?"

Davies settled back, took a long pull on his c gar, eyed it, lowered his window, and pitched out. It skidded along the road shedding spark then disappeared.

"You can close your window now; it's no fu shouting."

"Joshua, is there any point to this meeting or—"

"It all began with Badger. He was a smart la and not much given to playing by the rule:

Naturally he fell afoul of the old guard, Rossiter *et al.*, but he kept his wits. He didn't trust the organization. And when our agents had accidents, Badger didn't."

Gazing at the roof of the car, he added, "At first, I was a bit suspicious of his theory. What he discovered with some very fancy head work was a sinister series of connections all pointing to someone high up."

"And the Vice President's daughter gave you a name, did she?"

Davies sighed. "You're not making this any easier, Alaister. The daughter, and remember we only had Judas' word for her existence, was dead when he found her. She killed herself with a potent form of heroin according to Judas, who left me a polite letter but didn't stay for tea. Like you, Judas isn't much interested in the moral implications of things."

He slapped the arm of his coat savagely to remove some cigar ash.

Strachan appeared to be forcing himself to listen. "All very interesting, Joshua, but what does it mean?"

Davies answered, "It means that I know all about you."

"About me? What about me?"

"You've been systematically arranging deaths of our agents and disguising them as accidents."

Now Strachan knew why there were two butcher boys in the car. If he glanced back through the rear window, he would doubtless see another anonymous black limousine trailing them.

"And you can prove all this," he said casually.

"I don't have to prove it," Davies murmured

"Aye, I forgot. We're a law unto ourselves."

"Naturally, an investigation is under way the extent of the damage must be known. If I'm right, you've done more harm than anyone since Philby. It will take months to check through all the backstopping."

"Will we be bothering with such things as witnesses? Just asking."

"I found a witness, you bastard," Davies growled. "Ethel Scott. A woman who loved you enough not to turn you in."

Strachan looked genuinely shaken, not by Davies' fury but by the name. "Ethel Scott," he said almost to himself. "I swear, Joshua, I never knew. Tell her that, will you?"

"Tell her yourself," replied Davies. "If you meet."

Silence fell. After a while Davies said, "We've also dealt with Ricketts. Once we had you, he was easy. You were both ex-SAS, both in Aden. One of our people was supposedly killed in a mugging; the autopsy report said the knife went into the kidney. A favorite SAS trick."

Strachan arched a brow. "Ricketts never was very bright; he thinks everyone whose name appears in Westminster Abbey is actually buried there. What happened to him?"

Davies thought a moment. "No harm in telling you, I suppose. He was done in with a poisoned alarm clock."

Strachan searched Davies' face, wondering if the Director was being facetious. To Davies' asonishment, he laughed out loud. "He didn't beat the clock after all! That's rich. Man, don't you see the joke there?"

"No," said Davies. "We had him watched. Not you, of course, you're too smart."

Strachan was feeling for the door handle with the hand farthest from Davies. When he got a little pressure on the handle, there was no movement. Exerting all the strength he could muster without alerting his fellow passenger, he concluded the door was controlled from the driver's seat. In a way he was glad. There was no dignity in trying to jump out of a moving car. And how far could he get?

"The doors are locked," said Davies, "so don't bother getting any ideas."

Strachan gave him a lazy, insolent stare. "You must be joking. You don't have a thing on me, and when I get before the interrogators, I'll tell them it's a trumped-up fantasy." He drew himself up. "I'm not without friends in the organization."

Davies had both hands on his knees; he tapped them rhythmically.

"I gave you a barium meal."

"What?"

"A barium meal. Once Badger's list had been compared with the duties and access of senior DIC officers, it was simple enough to pare the suspects down to three or four. You all got the same barium meal. Then I followed its progress through DIC. Several of the more prominent members who refused to believe in moles were striking up conversations with me very soon after I dropped my little bombshell."

"Don't smirk, Joshua. Smirking doesn't look good on fat people."

"Within twenty-four hours," Davies went on, "an asset in Russia tells me the Russkies have let out their pet psychopath, Kroptkov. Someone tipped them off and not through channels. Someone had a direct line to the top. Next I was targeted. That never had official sanction. We never kill Directors. Gentleman's agreement."

"And you thought it was me; I'm deeply touched." Strachan attempted a little bow.

Davies continued. "Only members of DIC could know so much about our people. They have a need to know. And when you get down to it, who in DIC has the brains for this?"

"Another compliment."

"It's much easier to check on a suspect than to find him. Once I had proof it was you, the rest was easy."

The Rover entered the little village of West Wycombe. To the north lay the long low Chiltern Hills, the village nestled below them. A small but persistent stream, the Wye, ran along the east boundary. Some of the thatched-roof cottages lining the streets dated from the twelfth century.

They crossed the Wye by the little stone bridge and followed the slow incline toward West Wycombe Park. The park was two hundred acres dominated by a stately mansion on elevated ground in the midst of formal gardens.

"I suppose you've heard the one about the Irish laborer accused of rape?" asked Strachan.

Joshua Davies made no response, and he went on. "When they brought in the women to see a lineup, he steps forward and says, 'She's the one!' "

The Director grunted.

"So we're going to have a powwow now, are we? Who gives up whom for what? It will be interesting to see how much I'm worth," Strachan said.

The Rover slowed down; a set of massive iron gates was opened by a guard. In the distance was the great two-story mansion. The main façade of the ground floor consisted of a long colonnade of Doric pillars; above was a similar stretch of Corinthian pillars. In front of the house were magnificent stands of oak, beech, and ash, and beyond those was a large artificial lake in the shape of a swan. There was an exquisite Greek temple on the lake.

"You know, Joshua," said Strachan thoughtfully as their car and the one behind it stopped inside the gates, "my only real failure was not getting that damn Badger when he went to East Berlin. Life's full of ironies. I didn't get him, so he got me."

"No one gives a shit about irony," replied Davies. "We're here."

2

"You haven't asked me why I did it," said Stra chan as they waited inside the car for th butcher boys to unlock their doors.

"Does it matter whether I ask?"

"Not to me. I hate long explanations. Neve could stand Agatha Christie for that reason. Al that talk for the last sixty pages."

The doors swung open; Davies got out on on side, Strachan on the other. Davies led the way

"Aren't we going to the house?"

"No."

"My father was a Socialist, and when th crash came in 1931 he thought the millenniun had arrived. The poor bastard actually though Socialism would triumph. The next blood thing he knew, the Socialists were part of th ruling class. After that he thought only Mar could save Britain."

Davies grunted.

Strachan fell in beside him; the butcher boy kept a respectful distance, like mourners at a funeral. "This country's done for, Joshua, look around you. Soon it will be more pathetic than Spain and Ireland. The Americans use it as a missile launching pad, and some people think the U.S. will come to our rescue if there's trou ble. It's all lies, Joshua, lies."

"So you turned traitor."

That stung. "Is it treason," demanded Stra

ıan, "to follow the truth even if the country is o blind to see it? There are things more impor-nt than country. Do you condemn the Catho-cs in Elizabeth's time who supported Philip of pain because he was the Pope's agent?"

Suddenly it dawned on Joshua Davies that ıere was an element in Strachan's voice that ıust have been there before, probably always ad been, one that he'd missed. Vanity. The van-y of those who believe they are destined to play od. It was the old tired story. Men who believe ıey alone have the wisdom to see the right path.

They were walking toward a line of low hills, eeping to a gravel path. Davies stopped and oked around. On top of West Wycombe Hill as the Church of St. Lawrence, crowned by a iant golden ball.

Strachan cleared his throat. "You don't wake p one morning and say, 'The Russians are bet-r.' Doesn't work that way." He scuffed the ravel on the pathway. "It's gradual. You look t the mess around you, and you say, 'There's ot to be a better way.' "

"You know a better way then?"

"Damn, Joshua, of course I do. Those with rains and foresight have got to get in power so e can organize the mindless ants."

Davies produced another cigar; Strachan lit it r him. "You kill women, Joshua. I eliminate gents. We're not very different."

They left the gravel path and started across ıe huge lawns. There was dew on the grass and oon Davies felt the damp through his shoes. heir feet made swishing sounds and they left nprints behind them.

"You and your fascist friends use violence f one thing only," Davies said. "When you e counter any complexity, any subtlety, any co tradiction, you have only one response violence."

Strachan gave a dersive laugh. "Who kill Ethel Scott?"

"I shot Ethel Scott; you killed her."

"Can she tell the difference?" the Scotsma asked dryly. "You always play the game, Jos ua—and you always lose. You'll find I'm trad away tonight. All Five will get is some hal arsed asset, and I'll be away."

"On the slope of the hills over there," said D vies, pointing, "is the entrance to West Wycoml caves. They were carved out of the chalk by S Francis Dashwood in the eighteenth centur The secret rites of the Hell Fire Club were ca ried out there." He resumed his measure tread, pulling on his cigar, sending a lon stream of smoke into the night air.

"Sir Francis hired workmen to dig out a elaborate system of caves in the form of a sexu design." He coughed. Fellow had a one-trac mind. "The original road between Hig Wycombe and here was made from excavate limestone. We're going in."

They were climbing more steeply now, Davi surging on. "You'll never understand will you They lie *all the time*. The whole of Russia, th whole of Communism, exists merely to keep a fe men comfortably on top. I wouldn't have trade you anyway. What you've done must be paid for.

"They'll trade—for me."

"No. You're blown. All you could do is take u

space in Moscow and cost them money. They've washed their hands and sent the bowl away. Oh, a rumor will persist that you were traded, because that suits them *and* us."

"How 'us'?"

"We get to walk people we don't like, and they can't make capital of it."

It was dark. Davies couldn't see Strachan's face. He thought he heard a sharp intake of breath, perhaps a stifled exclamation, possibly the welling up of a cry of despair successfully overcome. Certainly the mole lurched slightly; it might have been a genuine slip on the limestone. Strachan regained his balance and walked on firmly. "So that's it," he said, voice steady. "The walk."

Joshua Davies had seen men, and a few women, face death. Some desired only to die with dignity; others had to be dragged out of their cells kicking and screaming. Davies never judged; there was no telling what a person might do when he realized the end of his life was minutes away. And Strachan had a greater burden to bear than most. He had given everything, and his people had not come to his rescue. Davies felt an involuntary shudder run up his spine.

"You must have known it would come to this," he said.

Their feet crunched on the limestone floor.

"Do you know, Joshua, I don't think I did."

"I believe you."

On the walls were carved devils' faces and sculptured gargoyles. The sheer amount of carving was extraordinary. The eighteenth century was an age of cheap labor, thought Davies, an of madmen.

"Getting rid of bodies is always a problem, said Davies. "There are policemen who insist o making inquiries even when we tell them not t In your case, because you're a rock climber, it wi be easier. Of course, we don't want to try an stage a *real* accident somewhere. Much too diff cult. Nothing is better for concealing bodies, a you well know, than so-called accidents. We ar nounce an accident and produce the body. No on can check; it's all over, including cremation."

A series of tangled passages slowed then down. Davies and one of the butcher boys kne the way, but it still took ten minutes before the were safely through them and in a long narro passageway leading to the banqueting room.

"This is the largest man-made chamber eve carved out of chalk," said Davies, leading the wa past the huge oak refectory table protected by canopy above. More carved figures, this time en twined in sexual passion, adorned the walls.

"Sir Francis seems to've had a one-trac mind," mused Strachan.

Davies was surprised to feel a growing admi ration for Alaister Strachan. He and the boy had brought several men to this place. Mos begged for their lives; yet the Scot was prepar ing himself with dignity. The man must b afraid; an hour ago, he had suspected nothing Now his bowels were churning, his nerves wer screaming, "Get away, fly for your life."

"At the end of the banqueting hall is anothe passageway leading to the triangle," said Da vies. "Either exit brings you to the same posi ion. Beyond is a narrow tunnel that ends bruptly. Below, sixty feet, is an underground iver. The 'monks' of the Hell Fire Club called it he River Styx, of course. A boat can be rowed ıp from the River Wye. It makes it easier to re-nove bodies."

"So I just walk along the passage until . . ."

"Yes. We can turn the lights off so you won't ee the pit. Or one of the boys can go with you, if ou like."

Strachan looked at Davies, then turned and ooked at the passage leading to the pit. "I don't old anything against you, Joshua. As my old ather used to say, 'When you're done shitting, ou're glad; when you're done screwing, you're ad; but when you're done, you're done!' Now nove your fat arse out of my life forever."

Davies left immediately; he wondered hether Strachan hesitated or lost his nerve. Ie rather thought not.

3

uring his long solitary ride home Davies sat reathed in smoke in the backseat. There was o feeling of triumph. Alaister Strachan had ied nobly. It took guts to step into oblivion. But r ten years that same man had been stealthily etting up the deaths of brave men and women, ome of them his own colleagues. To people like trachan, Communism became a religion, and ou didn't question faith, you just believed. The worst of it was that others would follow in h footsteps—equally dedicated, just as blind. Stil from what he knew of Strachan, it was imposs ble to think of the man as seeing himself in th role of the hero on a world stage. Too, any ide that Strachan had become a traitor because, a Scotsman, he hated the English, was absur

Davies shook his head. There was, no matte what anybody said, no comprehending motiv tions. The last war, as the old guard never tire of saying, was the last time issues were clear

Dolores didn't say anything until he wa seated at the table toying with rashers of bacc and four scrambled eggs.

In front of him stood a wooden gnome te inches high. Attached to the carving was a wi pince-nez. Even Davies had to admit it looke like him. It had been left on the front doorste two days before, along with Drakov's note. Th dwarf looked very German, down to its cur pipe, but underneath was stamped "Made Huddersfield by Fairies Ltd."

When he pushed his half-empty plate awa and went over to his sofa to hunt for Raison dish, Dol ventured a comment. "Everything se tled, is it?"

Davies poured milk into the cat's dish. Raiso hurried over and lapped up the milk vigorousl "It was Alaister Strachan."

"Alaister?" She sounded incredulous. "B . . . but we've had him here in this house! A all that time he was laughing at us."

"For what it's worth, he had a certain kind

ntegrity." He slumped down onto the sofa. "He ook the walk. He died game."

She left him to his thoughts and turned to her pple IIe. When the time seemed right, she ooked over at him and said, "I'm stuck. The overs are in the garden of the great house. I eed something with Jamaican trees in it."

Davies lay back on his sofa, great head back, gs crossed at the ankles. "Jamaican trees?"

"And lots of color, Josie."

Joshua Davies lurched to his feet and shuffled cross to his terminal in his huge house slip-ers. Switching on his machine, he paused, fin-ers above the keys, then began.

In the orchard, the banana trees had shed their purple flowers, and the green fronds caressed the single burden of yellow fruit. An ackee tree, its bright green leaves forming a backcloth, bore masses of fruit, three large black seeds set in yellow lobes. A poinciana, with a profusion of bright red flowers, dwarfed a tulip tree and bent low under the burden of its vivid blossoms. They walked hand in hand beneath a Golden Shower whose too brief blossoming had passed, leaving a fragile carpet as its memorial.

He sent it to his sister's machine. "Only ugh," he muttered.

Dolores examined it critically. "Oh, Josie," e said. "You're such a romantic."

"I know," he sighed. "I know."